KISSING EUGÉNIE VILLARET

"Down the alley," Will ordered, as he pulled her around the corner between the buildings, further into the dark than the others.

He pressed Mrs. Villaret against the wall of a building, shielding her from sight. It appeared fate was with him after all. He'd make sure the woman knew she was his. He brushed his lips across hers, trapping her against the wooden structure. Good Lord, she tasted of lemon and honeysuckle. He ran his tongue across the seam of her mouth, and she gasped, opening her lips enough for him to take advantage of her misstep and slide in, claiming her. Running his tongue over her teeth, he tasted before stroking her tongue with his. She was still for a few moments, then she moaned softly and reciprocated, mirroring his caresses, except that her hands gripped the sides of his coat rather than sliding up his shoulders and around his neck as most women would do.

God, she tasted better than the finest wine. Her lush body finally sank against his, and he cupped her bottom, holding her to him. With his other hand, he stroked the underside of one breast, brushing the tight bud of her nipple, and was rewarded with a sigh. It wouldn't be long before she'd be beneath him, naked, where he'd learn every inch of her . . .

Books by Ella Quinn

Published by Kensington Publishing Corp.

ELLA QUINN

ENTICING MISS EUGÉNIE VILLARET

THE MARRIAGE GAME

ZEBRA BOOKS
Kensington Publishing Corp.
www.kensingtonbooks.com

ZEBRA BOOKS are published by

Kensington Publishing Corp.
119 West 40th Street
New York, NY 10018

All Kensington titles, imprints, and distributed lines are available at special quantity discounts for bulk purchases for sales promotion, premiums, fund-raising, and educational or institutional use.

Special book excerpts or customized printings can also be created to fit specific needs. For details, write or phone the office of the Kensington Sales Manager: Kensington Publishing Corp., 119 West 40th Street, New York, NY 10018. Attn. Sales Department. Phone: 1-800-221-2647.

Zebra and the Z logo Reg. U.S. Pat. & TM Off.

First Printing: November 2023
ISBN-13: 978-1-4201-5596-9
ISBN-13: 978-1-60183-326-6 (eBook)

10 9 8 7 6 5 4 3 2 1

Printed in the United States of America

This book is dedicated to my husband, who will always be my original hero, and my darling granddaughter Josephine.

Acknowledgments

First I want to thank Mary Chen who came up with the title *Enticing Miss Eugénie Villaret*.

Every book takes a team, but this one took a village as the research was particularly challenging. It seems institutional knowledge, as well as most of the records on the islands only go back to around the mid-nineteenth century. Major thank yous to my good friend Katina Coulianous, who not only dug out all her old history books, but drove me all over parts of Charlotte Amalie I'd never been in before, and arranged for me to visit Crown House one of the oldest houses on St. Thomas. Thanks to Mr. and Mrs. de Jongh who allowed me to tour their home.

During my research, I discovered a legend of a pirate priest. However the references I found did not list the dates he was the vicar of St. Michael's in Tortola. Now, being a romance writer, I could not want my hero and heroine married by a pirate priest? But I had to know if he really existed during 1817. Thanks to Mrs. Chapmen the British Virgin Islands' historian who verified the existence of the pirate priest, and the actual date of St. George's and St. Michael's churches.

Thanks also goes to Jerry Smith and Abiola Jeffars, who directed me to the area in which St. Michael's was located and to Linda Leonard who finally drew me the map enabling me to find it. To Alison Stuart who sent me her photos and notes on Martinique. To the sailors at the St. Thomas Yacht Club who helped me map out sailing routes, distances, and traveling times.

My heartfelt thank you to the Regency Romance Critiquers and my beta readers for helping me whip the book into shape. To the members of the Beau Monde Chapter of

Romance Writers of America who are always available for advice and support.

As always to my wonderful agent, Elizabeth Pomada, and my editor at Kensington, John Scognamiglio, without whom this book would not be published, the talented staff at Kensington, and Jon Paul for the fabulous cover.

Chapter 1

July 1816, St. Thomas, Danish West Indies

Miss Eugénie Villaret de Joyeuse followed Gunna, an old black slave, down a narrow backstreet lined with long houses in Crown Prince's Quarter. Her maid, Marisole, stood watch as Eugénie and the woman entered the building.

"He be here, miss."

A baby, not older than one year, sat in the corner of the room playing with a rag doll. His only clothing was a clout, which, by the strong scent of urine, needed to be changed.

She and Gunna and the boy were the only occupants of the cramped, dark room. She crouched down next to the child. "What happened to his mother?"

"Sold."

Naturally; why did she even bother to ask? It was cruel to separate a mother and child, but there was no law against it here.

"When?"

"A few days ago." Gunna glanced at the child. "He be gone to a plantation soon."

Even worse. He'd likely die before he was grown. Eugénie placed the small bag she carried on the floor. "Help me change him. He can't go outside like this."

A few minutes later the baby's face and hands were clean, his linen was changed, and he wore a fresh gown.

She handed the woman two gold coins. "Thank you for calling me." Gunna tried to give the money back, but Eugénie shook her head. "Use it to help someone else. Our fight is not finished until everyone is free."

One tear made its way down the woman's withered cheek. "You go now, before the wrong person sees you."

Eugénie pulled a thin blanket around the babe's head, thankful her wide-brimmed hat would help hide his face as well as hers, and stepped out into the bright sunshine.

"That's her!" a male voice shouted.

She shoved the babe at Marisole. "Take him and run! I'll catch up."

Eugénie quickly drew out her dagger, concealing it in the gray of her skirts, and turned, crouching. A large man stood hidden in the shadow of a building, while a wiry boy, she guessed to be in his late teens, came at her. She waited until he reached out to grab her arm, then sliced the blade across his hands. Before he started to scream, she dashed down an alley between the long houses. Doors swung open, and several women stepped into the street behind her. That wouldn't help for long, but it would delay the pursuit.

Perspiration poured down her face as Eugénie pounded up the hill, using the step streets to cross over to Queen's Quarter. Ducking behind a large Flamboyant tree, she waited for several moments, listening for sounds of men running, but there was nothing and no one other than a few going about their business.

She took out a scrap of cloth and cleaned the blade before returning it to her leg sheath. Then Eugénie removed her bonnet and turned toward the breeze, drawing in great gulps of air as she fanned herself with the hat.

Several minutes later she caught up to her maid as Marisole descended another step street on the way to the house. "How is the babe?"

Marisole smiled. "Look for yourself. He is fine."

Wide green eyes stared up at Eugénie, and the child blew a bubble and smiled. "Come, *mon petit*. Not long now and you will have a family."

The front door of a well-kept house in Queen's Quarter opened as they approached.

Once in the short hall, she smiled. "Mrs. Rordan, thank you for agreeing to care for him. It will only be for a few days."

"As if I wouldn't." Mrs. Rordan grinned as she took the babe. "Captain Henriksen's already been in touch. There is a good family on Tortola who will adopt him." She handed Eugénie a bouquet of flowers. "For your mother, perhaps they'll help cheer her. You'd better get home, now."

"*Merci beaucoup*. She will love them." She kissed the little boy on the cheek. "Safe passage and a good life."

As Eugénie and her maid walked back to Wively House, Marisole said, "You were almost captured."

That was the closest she had ever been to getting caught. She drew her brows together. If they were after the child, why didn't the men follow? Did they know who she was? Yet, even with Papa gone, she had to continue. "Yes, but it is better not to question fate."

July 1816, England

William, Viscount Wively, caught a glimpse of sprigged muslin through a thinly leafed part of the tall hedge, behind which he'd taken refuge.

"Are you sure he came this way?" an excited female voice whispered.

Damn. He didn't like the sound of that. Will found himself in sympathy with the fox at a hunt.

"Quite sure," came the hushed response. "You must be careful, Cressida. If I reveal to you what Miss Stavely told me in the *strictest* confidence, you must vow *never* to repeat what I'm about to say. I swore I'd never breathe a word."

"Yes, yes," Miss Cressida Hawthorne replied urgently, "I promise."

He'd been dodging the Hawthorne chit for two days now, and unfortunately she wasn't the only one. The other woman sounded like the newly betrothed Miss Blakely.

"Well then"—Miss Blakely paused—"I really shouldn't. If it got out, she'd be ruined!"

"I already promised," Miss Hawthorne wheedled.

After a few moments, the other girl continued. "Miss Stavely said she followed Lord Wivenly to the library so that they'd be alone, and he'd have to marry her."

"What an excellent plan." Miss Hawthorne's tone fell somewhere between admiring and wishful.

"Well, it wasn't."

Even thinking about the incident with Miss Stavely made Will shudder. There were few worse fates than being married to her in particular. Fortunately, the lady was not as intelligent as she was crafty. The minute she'd turned the lock, she had announced he would have to marry her. However, she'd failed to take into account the French windows through which Will had made his escape.

"What do you mean it wasn't a good idea?" Miss Hawthorne asked.

"Have you heard a betrothal announcement?"

Their footsteps stopped. *Drat it all, there must be another way out of here.* He surveyed the privet hedge, which bordered three sides of this part of the garden. Across from him was a wooden rail fence about five feet high. Large rambling roses in pale pink and yellow sprawled along it, completing the enclosure. Whoever designed this spot had wanted privacy. Will's attention was once again captured by the voices.

."No," Miss Hawthorne said slowly, as if working out a puzzle. "So it didn't work."

"Do you know what Miss Stavely failed to take into account?"

When Miss Hawthorne didn't reply, Miss Blakely continued. "She didn't bother to ensure she had a witness at hand. Miss Stavely said Lord Wively looked her up and down like she was a beefsteak and told her he'd ruin her if she wished, but not to think he'd take her to wife."

Perhaps not his finest moment, though Will had wanted to scare the chit. Not that it had worked. She had practically launched herself at him.

"Oooh, how wicked." Miss Hawthorne giggled. "He's so handsome, and has such nice brown hair. I'd love to be compromised by him." She paused. "But only if he had to marry me, so you must make sure to bear witness."

Will had no intention of marrying Miss Hawthorne or any other fair English maiden. Harpies in disguise, all of them. More interested in being Viscountess Wively and the future Countess of Watford than in their duties as a wife. From what he knew of her, Miss Hawthorne would probably only allow him in her bed for the purpose of getting her with child. Surely he could do better. At least he hoped so.

When it came time for him to be leg-shackled, he'd be the one choosing. Yet even that would not be for at least another year or two. In the meantime, Will would be damned if he'd allow himself to be trapped into marriage. Thank God he'd already made plans to leave England for a while.

The sounds of the ladies' shod feet came closer.

Damnation. Will glanced around. The only escape was a large mulberry tree in full fruit. His valet, Tidwell, would have a fit about the stains, but needs must. As quickly and quietly as possible, he ascended the tree, careful not to let the slick leather soles of his boots slide off the branches.

"I am sure I saw him go this way," Miss Blakely said.

From his perch in the tree, Will had a view of the tops of

their ridiculous bonnets. Why women had to use all those ribbons and furbelows on their hats defied logic.

"As did I," Miss Hawthorne replied. "I wonder where he could have got to."

"Do not worry. I shall be vigilant. We will find a way to ensure you are Lady Wivenly."

The hell she will. Will scowled. Did a lady exist who would not be impressed with his title, and would allow him to do the hunting? Probably not.

"Oh, look," Miss Hawthorne exclaimed. "A mulberry tree. We must pick some. Perhaps the cook will make tarts, or I can have them with cream."

Will stifled a groan. Featherheaded females. Why had he ever allowed his mother to talk him into this house party on the eve of his departure for the West Indies?

Miss Blakely linked an arm in Miss Hawthorne's. "Perhaps it might be better to send a servant. You wouldn't want to ruin your gown."

"You are correct." As the two headed back to the formal garden, she added, "But let us find someone straight away. Lord Wivenly must be around somewhere."

Will tipped his hat. *Sorry, ladies, this fox is going Halloo and Away.*

He waited until they were half-way to the lake before climbing out of the tree. After regaining the house, he sneaked up a back staircase and strode to his bedchamber. "Tidwell!"

"I'm right here, my lord." The valet poked his head out from the dressing room. "No reason to shout. I'm getting your evening kit ready." He held up two waistcoats. "Would you prefer the green on cream or the gold?"

"I'd prefer to leave. Get everything packed. You've got an hour."

Tidwell bowed. "As you wish, my lord." His eyes narrowed as he took a sharper look at Will. "If I do not treat those stains, they'll never come out."

He glanced down. Not only mulberry juice, but leaf stains as well. "You'll just have to make do. It's not safe for me here."

"Another ruined suit." His valet sighed. "More problems with the ladies, I presume."

Taking pity on Tidwell, Will said, "Pack me a bag. You remain here until the toggery is cleaned. I'll take my curricle and meet you back at Watford Hall. Send the coachman a message as to when you'll be ready."

Tidwell immediately brightened. "Yes, my lord."

Changed into fresh clothing, Will donned his caped coat and hat, then found his host and made his excuses. By the time he stepped out into the stable yard, his carriage was ready and his groom, Griff, was holding the horses' heads.

Will climbed into his curricle. "Good job."

"Thought it might be gettin' a bit hot for you hereabouts, my lord."

"Right as usual. Let their heads go."

Griff jumped onto the back as Will maneuvered the carriage out of the yard and onto the gravel drive. He caught a glimpse of Miss Hawthorne. She smiled at him, but when he smiled then inclined his head and sprung the horses, her jaw dropped.

Another close escape.

Five days later, Dover, England

The docks bustled with activity as ships prepared to sail with the tide. Will had met his friend Gervais, Earl of Huntley, in London, and traveled down to the port city with him.

The early morning sky was about to lighten when they reached the packet setting sail for France, on which Huntley was booked.

"Godspeed in your travels," Will said.

Huntley clasped Will's hand. "Good luck to you sorting out the problem in St. Thomas. I'll see you in the spring."

"Only if I can't think of a good excuse to remain abroad." Will grimaced. "Before I left, my father made me promise I'd marry next year."

"My father said the same to me. We'll lend each other support." Huntley's grim countenance reminded Will of a man going to trial. "Perhaps you'll be lucky enough to fall in love."

Will almost choked. "You think that's lucky? I'd have to completely rearrange my life. No, thank you. I'll probably end up picking one of the ladies my mother parades before me. At least then I'll know what to expect."

And he wouldn't risk living under the cat's paw because of a woman.

"My lord, the ship's about to depart," Huntley's groom called from the packet.

"You'll do as you think best." Huntley slapped Will's back.

"You, as well." Will strode down the street to a Dutch fly-boat, one of the smaller sailing ships plying their trade ferrying passengers and goods to the many ports scattered up and down England's far western coast.

Griff sat on a piling at the head of the pier. " 'Bout time you got here. Tidwell's got the cabins all arranged, and the captain's just waitin' on you."

"Let's get on board then. I can't miss the tide, or we'll be late for our rendezvous with Mr. Grayson." Will drew in a deep breath, savoring the air's briny scent. At one and thirty, Will hadn't had his blood rush with the excitement of a new challenge for years. "Is there anything else you'd like to tell me?"

A large smile cracked Griff's weathered face. "Mr. Tidwell turned a nice shade of green when he got on the ship." He scratched his head as if he was giving the occurrence some thought. "Don't suppose he'll like the trip overmuch."

"Unless *you*"—Will paused, letting the word sink in— "wish to learn how to take care of my kit, you'd better hope Tidwell doesn't become too ill."

Griff, who'd been with Will since he'd sat his first pony, had carried on a good-natured feud with Tidwell since the valet had joined their household over eleven years ago. Will softened his voice. "Come now, I can't go about looking like a shag-bag, and I daren't go without you. Who'd have my back when I get into trouble?"

"Well, ye're in the right of it there." Griff nodded. "That peacock sure ain't goin' to haul you out o' some of the fixes you get yerself into. Why I recollect when—"

"Ho, Lord Wivenly, is that you?" A short, middle-aged man with salt-and-pepper hair strode toward him. "I'm Captain Jones."

"Yes, sir. Are we ready to cast off?"

The captain directed an eye toward the water. "Just waiting for you, my lord."

Shortly after noon the following day, the boat docked at Plymouth's bustling port. Will descended to the pier wondering how, in all the hubbub, he'd find Andrew Grayson, an old friend of his who'd agreed to accompany Will, only to spy Andrew leaning up against a piling near the midsection of the ship.

"Handsomely done, Captain." Andrew straightened and inclined his head to Jones. "You've arrived in good time. We've a change in our travel plans. Lord Wivenly will need his baggage transferred to the *Sarah Anne* as soon as may be."

"Aha," the captain called out in a satisfied tone, "so Captain Black's going back again." Jones grinned. "I win my wager. I'll have it done straight away, Mr. Grayson."

Will furrowed his brow. "How do you know Jones?"

Andrew cast a glance at the sky as if searching for patience. "My maternal grandfather's in shipping, remember? I've spent time learning the business, as it will be mine."

That was one of the main reasons Will had asked Andrew to accompany him to St. Thomas. As they walked in the direction of the main dock area, he said, "I didn't know you planned on actually running the business. I thought you only wanted to be knowledgeable. Didn't some aunt leave you a snug little property with an independence?"

"Yes"—Andrew nodded—"but my grandfather's bound by the settlement agreements to leave the shipping line to me as the second son, and I like knowing how to control what I'm going to own." He glanced back at Will with a raised brow. "Don't tell me you're worried I'll smell of the shop? Shipping is as respectable as banking, and look at Lady Jersey. She spends a good amount of time at the bank her father left her."

They reached another pier, where Andrew hailed a tall man with broad shoulders who'd clearly been at sea for a while. "That's Captain Black. His ship is one of the fastest you'll find, even with cargo."

"Mr. Grayson." The captain grinned. "I see you've found his lordship, and in good time."

"His gear will be here directly," Andrew said. "Captain Jones is seeing to it."

Captain Black turned his attention to Will. "Welcome aboard the *Sarah Anne*, my lord. I'll have you in St. Thomas in no time at all."

An hour later, Will stood near the bow of the ship, looking out over the water and trying to decide how to approach the problem his father had asked him to look into in St. Thomas. Though it would delay his exploration of the other islands, he knew that the Earl of Watford's protective arms encircled all of their family, no matter where they were located, and Will felt the same way. Anyone in the Wively family was his to care for.

Andrew joined him. "Have you decided how you will approach the problem yet?"

Will wished he had; the whole thing was deuced strange. He shook his head. "My original intent was to pay my respects to my great-uncle Nathan's widow"—funny that Nathan was only a few years older than Will—"then meet with the manager, Mr. Howden. Yet after her last letter to my father, telling him the business was failing, right on the heels of a report from Howden showing it was as prosperous as ever, I don't know what to think, or whom to trust."

Andrew leaned against the rail. "Someone is being economical with the truth."

An understatement if Will had ever heard one. "The question is, who? I can't think of a reason my aunt would be dishonest. Her distress was clear from her letter. However, Howden has an impeccable reputation."

Andrew frowned. "Could there be another actor?"

Now *that* was something Will hadn't considered. "It's possible. I'll take great joy in making sure whoever is causing the problems will pay for their transgressions."

He'd make sure of it.

Chapter 2

Early September 1816, St. Thomas, Danish West Indies

Eugénie entered the large drawing room where her maman could usually be found. She sat at an old desk against one wall. "Maman?"

A soft breeze from the windows fluttered the sheets of paper her *maman* held in one hand. The other was fisted and pressed against her lips.

"Is it more bad news?" A few months ago, her step-father, Nathan Wively, the only papa she had ever known, had been on board one of his ships returning from England. Not a day from St. Thomas, they had been attacked by pirates who had murdered Papa and the crew. Ever since then, the import-export business the family owned had begun to fail. The problems were due to the lost goods, or so Mr. Howden told her mother.

Eugénie didn't believe him. Papa always had insurance. If only she had proof the manager was being dishonest, she'd be able to assist her family. Papa would expect it of her. She dug her nails into her palms. "Maman, if you will allow me to look at the books, I know I can help."

"You remember the last time you asked to see the accounts?" Maman stuffed the documents in the desk drawer. "Mr. Howden threatened to leave." Tears filled her eyes. "How would I replace him? I know nothing of commerce."

It was on the tip of Eugénie's tongue to say they couldn't do worse, but that would only further upset her mother, and it might not be true. She'd learned to run a household, not a company. Since her younger brother, Benet, would inherit the business, Papa had seen no point in teaching her. "Have you heard from the Earl of Watford?"

Maman's lips formed a thin line as she shook her head. "Your father always said I could rely on his nephew. I'm sure we shall receive an answer soon."

Yet would the letters they'd sent by fast schooners arrive in time? Could the earl act before they were ruined? Eugénie pushed away the thought that despite what Papa had always believed, the earl did not truly care about his uncle's family living in the West Indies.

"Perhaps"—she searched for something, anything to help make her mother feel better—"you could ask Baron von Bretton for help, or Mr. Whitecliff."

Maman shot to her feet. *"Eugénie!"* She took a breath. "I appreciate you trying to be of assistance, but it is for me to deal with."

Ever since Papa had died, Maman had become a shadow of herself, and was in no condition to act. Her brown eyes, which had always been alight with laughter, were now haunted. In just a few short months, small lines had begun to bracket her mouth. Something had to be done, and soon, before they hadn't any money at all.

"I am one and twenty. I have a brain and can add columns." Why was her mother being so stubborn? "Please allow me to—"

"No. You cannot make a good marriage if you are involved in business." Maman locked the drawer to her desk.
"Your papa would not 'ave approved."

Maman hadn't pronounced the words in her usual clipped
British fashion. The fact that her French accent had become
more pronounced was sufficient evidence of the strain she
was under. Since marrying Nathaniel Wivenly when Eugénie was six, and joining the English society in Jamaica,
then in Saint Thomas, Maman had cultivated the English
ways, including their way of speaking.

"*Oui*, Maman." Well, Papa was no longer here. Eugénie
wanted to stamp her feet in frustration, or throw something,
or break down in tears. She wanted to mourn as well, yet
how could she when someone had to take care of the family?
Why was it that men, even perfect ones like Papa, always
seemed to manage to get themselves killed at the worst possible times?

"If need be," Maman said in a weary voice, "we will
travel to England. I am sure Papa's family would not turn us
away."

The Earl of Watford had done nothing to help so far.
Eugénie gritted her teeth. *"Naturellement."*

"English, Eugénie," her mother reminded her, "English."

"Yes, Maman." Eugénie stifled a sigh. There was no
point in continuing a discussion that only upset her mother.
"I must go into town later for some new ribbon. Is there anything you need?"

Maman gave a weary smile. "I shall be grateful if you
will bring me some pressed paper. I must write the invitations for your sister's birthday party."

Another reason to discover what was going on: Her
brother and sisters' futures were at risk. Jeanne, the youngest
sister, would be six next week. The others were not much
older. Even though they were in mourning, Jeanne would
have friends over for cakes and lemonade. Eugénie nodded
and turned to the door.

"Don't forget your bonnet." Her mother frowned. "You are becoming much too brown, and remember to take your maid with you."

Eugénie ran back to her mother and embraced her. She wouldn't tease Maman any more, but proper or not, she would find a way to help her family. Papa always said she was the cleverest one in the family. Surely she could think of something. Eugénie could not leave their well-being to the vagaries of fate, the ocean, and an earl who lived thousands of miles away.

Will braced his feet on the ship's deck and held the telescope to his eye. A large group of buildings stood at the water's edge. "That's it then, the free port of Charlotte Amalie?"

"Indeed." Captain Black grinned. "It will soon be one of the largest ports in the West Indies, if not the entire Caribbean."

"What are those spaces on the hills?"

Black looked where Will pointed. "Stairs used as streets. They are called step streets. They make going up and down the hills easier. I've heard some European cities have them, as well."

Anything to make hills easier would be welcome. Drat, he hated hills. He'd been ecstatic when his family had moved to Hertfordshire, where it was nice and flat.

Wharves lined the shoreline, each with its own warehouse, followed by taller buildings that spread up the three hills behind the city. Palm trees punctuated the landscape in an orderly manner, and a large fort jutted out into the harbor. The numerous ships at anchor added to the picturesque view, but what really struck Will was the color of the water. Ranging from darker blue to turquoise closer to shore, it took his breath away. He'd never seen anything as beautiful, and right now he'd like to dive overboard. The sun wasn't even directly overhead and already the day promised to be hot. How the devil did gentlemen dress in suits here? Or perhaps the question should be why Englishmen must behave as if even the tropics were no warmer than the home counties.

He passed the glass back to the captain and rubbed a hand over his short beard. Tidwell had been threatening to take the razor to Will's face, but with the movement of the ship, his valet had resigned himself to merely trimming his beard. Once on land, he'd have a good shave, though whether his coats would still fit him was uncertain. His normally lean frame had filled out as he'd handled the ship's lines and sails. Will smiled to himself. Learning to sail had been every bit as fun as his friend Marcus had told him it would be, though remembering some of the terms had been a bit more problematic. Now he needed to turn his attention to the problem of the Wively family of St. Thomas.

During the passage, Will had tried to surreptitiously draw information about the island and its inhabitants from Captain Black. One night the man had laughed and said, "Just tell me what it is you need to know, my lord, and I'll be happy to give you any information I have. You don't need to worry I'll be indiscreet. I take pride in my prudence."

Will had reluctantly realized that he needed the captain's assistance and told him about the apparent problems with his late great-uncle's business. "It appears prosperous on paper, yet the widow is claiming poverty."

Captain Black rubbed his chin, then took a drink of wine. "Mr. Howden, the manager, is a well-thought-of man of business, but he's ambitious, and I can't see him wanting to work for a woman." Black paused for a moment. "On the other hand, I've met your aunt on a few occasions. She must be devastated by Nathan's death. She relied on him for everything. It would be pretty easy to pull the wool over her eyes." A call came from somewhere in the ship and the captain cocked an ear before continuing. "If only she were older, Miss Eugénie—that's Mrs. Wively's daughter from her first marriage—could help." The captain chuckled. "Now there's a firecracker for you."

"How old is Miss Eugénie?" Will couldn't remember if he'd heard of her or not. Could the daughter be the problem? Will wasn't naïve enough to think women weren't capable of doing anything they set their minds to. Still, why would she try to beggar her mother? He tossed off the rest of his wine. None of this made sense.

"Maybe about twenty now." The captain frowned. "Last time I saw her was a couple of years ago. She was still coltish then. Skinny little thing, all arms and legs. Brown as a nut because she kept losing her hat. Nathan spoiled her to death."

Lovely. In addition to everything else, he'd have to deal with a willful, probably bran-faced brat.

"You know, my lord," the captain said thoughtfully, "St. Thomas is a small island, and your family is well-known. If you use the name Wivenly, you'll not be able to hide your interests."

Will grinned. He knew just the one he'd use. "That's Mr. Munford, Captain. A mere factotum for the earl. I'll have to rely on my servants to give me any consequence at all."

"You haven't been Munford since Oxford." Andrew barked a laugh. "After that girl tried to trick you into marriage, I thought you'd sworn off it."

"That was years ago. No one in St. Thomas will recognize the name." Will refilled his glass. "Besides, it won't be for long." At least he hoped it wouldn't. He'd discharge his duty as quickly as possible then get on to the real purpose of his journey, having fun and avoiding marriage-minded ladies and their mamas.

By early afternoon, they'd docked. Captain Black found a carter for Will's trunks and sent a message to the Queen Hotel concerning rooms.

An hour later, Will clasped the older man's hand. "I hope I see you before you're on your way again."

"I'll make a point of it." Black gave Will a sly wink. "*Sir*. You'll find a tailor on Main Street, what the Danes call Dronningens Gade, as well as most everything else you'll need."

"Is there a printer there as well?" Even if he only used his assumed identity for a short time, calling cards would be necessary.

"Yes"—the captain nodded—"just down from the tailor. Gentlemen, enjoy your stay. It was a pleasure having you on board. Perhaps we'll make the return trip in the spring."

Will tipped his hat. "Thank you, Captain, for all your help."

Captain Black indicated a woman garbed in a colorful skirt leaning against the door of a building. "A word to the wise. St. Thomas has a reputation for being the healthy island, but that doesn't apply to the brothels."

"Good of you to warn us." After over four weeks at sea, Will was definitely in need of female companionship, but his tastes ran more to widows than members of the impure. He'd never had any trouble finding willing women, even when he'd used the name Munford.

Andrew's valet, Blyton, stood with Tidwell making sure the carter collected all their baggage. Most of Will's coats would need to be replaced. The one he was wearing was so tight across the shoulders any sudden movement might rip the seams. It was also looser around his middle.

They walked up a side alley to the main street, then turned east and continued for several blocks until they came to a large building set in a garden, with a sign announcing it to be the Queen. Will studied the three-storied structure. Massive windows surrounded the ground and first floors, their louvered shutters closed on one side against the afternoon heat. Under a hipped roof, dormer windows lined the second floor. It must be hot up there. He wondered if that was where his servants would be expected to sleep.

"Here ye be, sir," the carter said. "The best inn in Charlotte Amalie."

Andrew and Will were soon ensconced in a large suite with two bedchambers, dressing rooms, and a parlor, which he and Andrew would share. Smaller rooms for their personal servants were on the same floor. All the windows had a view over the harbor, giving them a good breeze.

After settling in, their small coterie met in the parlor.

"Griff," Will said, "you'll need to arrange for a carriage."

"You're on foot, my lord." The groom grinned. "This here town's like Bath. From what that carter said, they got no horses on this side of the island."

"The devil you say." That was an unwelcome surprise. Will glanced at the hills surrounding him. If he would be on foot during his stay, before too long he might need to make a visit to a cobbler as well, or find a flatter island.

Griff wiped his shirtsleeve over his forehead and eyes. "I hope we get used to this heat soon."

"It may lessen," Andrew said. "According to the hotel's porter, we are already in their storm season and the weather will cool."

"I'd give a lot to stand in some rain right now." Griff took out his handkerchief and mopped his face.

"My lord." Tidwell stepped gingerly into the room, as if the floor might move on him. It would probably take a while for all of them to regain their land legs. Even Will still felt the roll of the ship.

He groaned. "I'll never get away with being Mr. Munford if all of you keep *my lord*ing me."

"Sorry, my . . ." Tidwell at least looked abashed. "*Mr. Munford*, sir, I have directions to a tailor and the printer. I suggest you take care of both those errands as soon as possible."

How was it Tidwell managed to appear cool even in this heat? "First I want a bath and a shave. This beard itches."

The valet gave a slight bow. "The bath is on its way." He glanced at Andrew. "For Mr. Grayson as well."

Andrew closed his eyes as if anticipating bliss. "Thank you, Tidwell. You've answered my prayers. Blyton, make sure the razor is sharp. Mr. Munford isn't the only one who needs a shave."

"Andrew," Will asked, "when do you want to visit Wively Imports?"

"While you are running errands, I'll make Mr. Howden's acquaintance on the pretense of buying the business."

"I'll be interested to hear his response." Will wouldn't be satisfied until *he* straightened out whatever mess he found his uncle's company in, if indeed there was a problem at all. "Once we know the lay of the land, I'll switch back into myself and meet the widow."

"Marisole," Eugénie called to her maid, "are you ready yet?"

"I would be if you were. I'm getting your bonnet, miss. I know you did not."

Eugénie twisted her lips into a rueful smile as her maid stepped out of the dressing room. "I do not suppose we could forget it."

"Non." Marisole pulled a face. "Even Dorat mentioned it to me."

"We certainly do not want Maman's dresser involved. Very well, give it to me." Eugénie took the broad-brimmed hat from her maid, placed it on her head, and tied the wide black ribbon off to the side of her chin. "There, are you happy?"

Marisole looked critically at Eugénie. "Now you're ready. Dorat is correct, you know. You are almost dark enough to be a mulattress, and that gray gown does you no favors."

"That cannot be helped. I am in mourning." Eugénie glanced into the mirror and had to acknowledge her maid was right. Between her tan and the dull gown, she appeared older than her one-and-twenty years. Black might have been a better hue, but her mother insisted she go into half mourning. She pulled on her silk knit gloves and took the parasol from her maid.

"Dorat says that you are no longer in mourning and should wear colors again."

Eugénie ignored her maid. Her *beau-papa* was the only father she'd ever known, and if she wanted to continue to mourn him, she would. Papa would understand.

Half-way down the step street to town, a gloved hand grabbed her arm.

Her friend Cicely Whitecliff took a breath. "Stop. I waved, but you walked right past. What are you in such a brown study about, and where are you off to in such a hurry?"

"Sorry." Eugénie gave a rueful smile. "I was just thinking." An inkling of an idea crept into her mind. She couldn't put Marisole's position at risk by asking her to help, but Cicely would be perfect. She knew everything there was about the shipping business. "I'm going to buy some ribbon. Would you like to come with me?"

"Yes, that is my destination as well." She linked arms with Eugénie. "The ships will soon cease arriving for a couple of months. I don't wish to take the risk of running out."

Which meant that any other lady needing pale blues, pinks, or white would be out of luck until November. "I'm glad we don't wear the same colors. I'd never find what I need."

When they got to Kongens Gade they turned right. Eugénie needed to put her plan in place soon. She lowered her voice. "I need to speak to you alone."

"I take it you don't want Marisole to overhear?"

"Exactly. What she does not know cannot hurt her."

"Well, then"—Cicely glanced back at the maid—"come

to my chambers on our way back home. Marisole can chat with my maid, and you and I shall have a comfortable coze."

"Thank you." Eugénie squeezed her friend's arm. "I don't know what I'd do without you."

Cicely smiled. "You need never find out."

A weight slid from Eugénie's shoulders. At least she wasn't in this alone anymore.

Several minutes later they entered the haberdasher's shop. As she had suspected, the stock was already low. She'd just finished paying for her purchase, when Cicely gasped.

"I've never seen *him* before!"

"Who?" Eugénie stepped over to one of the front store windows.

"The tall man with the broad shoulders and the most lovely wavy blond hair." Cicely's tone was all breathless anticipation. "He looks like a gentleman, as well."

Eugénie stared at the man on the other side of the street. "I do not recognize him either."

Cicely's blue eyes had widened slightly, and her breath came a little faster. Eugénie raised her eyes to the ceiling and shook her head. Her friend was the biggest flirt she knew. Fortunately, all the gentlemen they knew here realized it was all done in innocence. A gentleman from elsewhere might not. "I thought you said you were not going to look at another man until you went to England for your Season."

Her friend's mouth opened and closed. "I *couldn't* have said any such thing." Cicely glanced back out the window. "And even if I had, it wouldn't apply to *him*."

Eugénie took her friend by the elbow. "Come, I need to buy paper for Maman."

"Perhaps I can manage to bump into him," Cicely said hopefully.

"More likely," Eugénie responded in her most acerbic tone, "you'll trip over your feet staring at him, or run into someone you don't want to. How can you even think of men at a time like this? When my family is in so much difficulty?"

"Just because you are not . . . Oh, look." Her friend came to a stop. "He's going into your family's warehouse."

Eugénie jerked to a halt as well. So he was. What business had he there? Could that stranger be part of the reason the company was in trouble, or that Mr. Howden was lying? Her heart thumped painfully against her ribs as she fought down the fear that the business was indeed in difficulties. She took a breath and gave herself a shake. Even more reason to enlist Cicely's help in discovering what was going on, and immediately.

As Will left the printer's, he saw Andrew head down an alley between two warehouses. Hopefully his friend would be successful. Will made his way to Mr. White's tailor shop. He was just about to enter the premises when a young woman, who appeared to be towing her friend down the street, ran into him. He put out a steadying hand and gazed down into the warmest brown eyes he'd ever seen. Curls the color of roasted coffee beans escaped from beneath her wide-brimmed hat, and for some reason, he couldn't let go of her. A whole different kind of heat, unrelated to the climate, rose within him. God, she was beautiful. Her rosy lips pursed briefly before the ends curled up a bit. He'd never been so immediately struck by a woman in his life. Will took her hand, bowing over it as he felt along her fourth finger of her left hand. There was no indication of a ring under her gloves. He sent up a brief prayer. *Please let her be a widow.*

"Excuse me, ma'am." He smiled. If she was a *miss*, she'd correct him. "I must not have been watching where I was going."

Her eyes widened as she stared boldly back at him.

When her lips parted slightly, it was all he could do not to kiss her. Feel their softness against his. Explore her mouth and the rest of her body.

"No," she responded slightly breathlessly. "I believe it was my fault."

A giggle caused her to glance away. The lady's companion, the perfect picture of an English maiden—golden-haired, dressed in a froth of muslin and lace—giggled again, reminding him why he'd left home. He turned his attention back to the dark-haired woman, willing her to gaze into his eyes again, but the moment was lost.

She blushed and glanced at his hand, still holding hers. "My friend and I must be going."

Unfortunately, he could no longer see her face, but her sultry, accented voice caused every muscle in his body to tighten. Who the devil was she, and when could he see her again?

"Sir." Her tone grew colder. "I must insist you release me."

Will was surprised at how hard it was to remove his hand. One by one, he peeled his fingers from her. "Yes, of course. Just making sure you were steady on your feet." God. That sounded weak even to him. The plain fact was that he didn't want to let go of her at all. Something about her made him want to pull her to him and ensure the woman knew she belonged to him.

It suddenly occurred to Will she was dismissing him. He couldn't remember the last time that had happened. Or the last time he'd acted a complete fool over a woman. When she raised one well-shaped brow, he hid a smile and bowed again. "I'll just be on my way."

The woman inclined her head and continued down the street. Will watched her for a bit before entering the tailor's shop. He had to discover who she was. The bell rang as he opened the door.

"Good day to you, sir," a man said, in what Will thought might be a thick Danish accent.

Will glanced toward the darker interior of the shop, waiting for his eyes to adjust from the bright sun.

A stocky young fellow with light blond hair came from around the counter. "May I help you?"

Or at least that's what Will thought he said.

"Yes." The woman's scent, one he'd never smelled before, lingered in the air, tantalizing him. He had to find her again. "I'm in need of new suits."

The clerk smiled. *"Hoop om indruk Juffrouw Villaret?"*

That sounded something like a form of German. Drat, the man was deuced hard to understand, though Villaret sounded French, which would explain her accent. Will knew German, and the title sounded like Frau. Which would mean she'd been married. "Is that her name, *Frau* Villaret?"

The man grinned.

This was exactly the turn of events Will wanted. His voice was calmer than he felt as he anticipated the chase. "Well then, suits."

The clerk motioned Will to the back of the shop, and said something that sounded almost like "quite an armful." Even if Will couldn't understand all the words, the clerk's tone was insolent. He had the sudden urge to plant the young man a facer for referring to her in that manner. *Damn.* He couldn't even ask about her now.

"I've told you before, Mr. Linden"—a thin, bespectacled, older man who spoke the King's English entered from a side room—"keep your mind on your work and not on the ladies." The man addressed Will. "I'm Mr. Smith, the owner."

"Munford. I've recently arrived from England."

"We are glad for your custom, sir. If you'll follow me, we'll get you measured."

A half hour or so later, the bell on the door rang. Will looked over to see Andrew enter and give a short nod. That must mean his meeting with Howden had gone well. Good, perhaps this endeavor would go smoothly, giving Will the opportunity to discover more about the delectable Mrs. Villaret.

Smith stepped back and made another notation in his notepad. "If you'll come back around in the morning, Mr. Munford, I'll have a coat for you to try on."

"Thank you. Do you know of an inn or tavern nearby, where I might get cold water to drink?"

"The Happy Iguana is down the street. Turn right when you go out the door. It's got a bar downstairs and a dining room on the first floor. If you get tired of water, the rum is excellent, as is the brandy."

"Thank you again, Mr. Smith." Will slid a glance at Andrew before walking out the door. They could talk at the tavern. "I'll see you in the morning."

As Will stepped onto the pavement, he searched the street, but, of course, there was no sign of Mrs. Villaret. Surely there must be a way to find her. All he had to do was figure out how.

Chapter 3

An hour later, Eugénie and her friend entered the large parlor on the lower level of Whitecliff House. Cicely's apartment consisted of one large room, flanked on one side by her bedchamber and dressing room, and on the other by a small parlor with her piano and books.

Cicely called for coconut water. After her maid left, she motioned to a settee positioned against the back wall. "No one can hear us from here. Now, tell me what is wrong."

With her flaxen curls and wide cornflower-blue eyes, Cicely gave every indication of being a silly widgeon, yet she had the sharpest mind of anyone Eugénie knew.

She chewed her lower lip. "I need to look at the business's books, without Mr. Howden catching me."

"Because?" Cicely asked, drawing the word out.

"He's been telling Maman that it is losing money."

Cicely heaved a loud sigh and made a "come on" motion with her hand. Eugénie told her about her previous attempt to view the ledgers and Mr. Howden's threat to quit.

"Hmm." Cicely pursed her lips in thought. "I know my

father hasn't heard your family's company is in poor condition."

"Mr. Howden said he was keeping it a secret." Eugénie untied her hat and flung it down next to her. "It's bad enough that Papa is . . . gone." She fought the tears threatening to fall. "That is dreadful, but now Maman worries all the time about money as well. Nothing cheers her."

"And you can't talk her round?"

"Not on this." Eugénie pressed her lips together. It hadn't been for lack of trying either. "She is too frightened."

"Well, then"—Cicely drew out a long pin, then plucked her bonnet from her head—"we shall pick an evening and go to the offices. It will probably be better if I invite you to spend the night with me. That way we'll only have to worry about sneaking back into this house, and that is easily done." She frowned. "We won't have much time."

"Yes. That is an excellent idea. It would be just my luck that one of my sisters would awaken if I attempted to steal back into my house." As her friend was an only child, she had the floor beneath the main one to herself. No one would notice them leaving or returning. "Do you know what to look for?"

"Of course." Cicely grinned. "My papa has been showing me what I need to run the company. After all, I do not have a brother to take it over. Of course, his fondest wish is that I will marry a gentleman in shipping. Just don't tell anyone. Mama says it will scare potential suitors away."

The tension threatening to make Eugénie's head ache eased. Perhaps now she would be able to protect her family. "I'm so glad I decided to confide in you. I knew I'd have a hard time doing it myself."

"You're not alone." Cicely hugged Eugénie. "I'll do everything in my power to help you. We shall involve my papa if need be. Now tell me, what do you think of the blond gentleman we saw earlier?"

"I do not think anything of him, but I do wonder what he wants with Mr. Howden." Eugénie couldn't help but scowl. Something felt very wrong.

Cicely closed her eyes as if she were in pain.

If Eugénie didn't say something, her friend would go on about him until she did. Cicely could talk about men all day. Eugénie capitulated. "Oh, very well. I suppose he was handsome." She paused for a moment before adding, "If you like that sort."

"Then it's a good thing I do." Cicely laughed. "I shall ask Papa to invite him to dinner. He won't be hard to find. It's a small island and he's new."

"Cicely Elizabeth Whitecliff!" Eugénie couldn't believe how brazen her friend could be. "You know *nothing* about him!"

A crafty look appeared on her friend's face. "No, but if I show an interest, Papa will discover all that is necessary." She widened her eyes. "Just think how much money I'll save him if I don't require a London Season."

Cicely would, of course, be a success. Yet from what Eugénie had heard about the English, her own coloring was too dark for her to be considered a beauty in London. Why would she want to go to a place where she would be pitied for her brown hair and eyes? And now she might not even have Cicely to keep her company. Eugénie slumped back on the sofa. "I'm afraid I'll have no choice about a London Season. Maman is talking about all of us going to England."

"Oh no!" Cicely jumped up in a very unladylike manner. "I'd never see you again."

The thought of not being with her very dearest friend caused Eugénie's throat to close painfully. "You could visit."

Yet even to her, Cicely visiting didn't sound likely.

"Not if you are treated as a poor relation to the earl."

Cicely plopped back down on the settee. "I'm quite sure poor relations aren't allowed visitors."

"You are probably correct." Sooner rather than later, they needed to inspect the books. At least then she'd know the truth. Though if Howden was lying, she didn't know how she'd broach the subject to Maman, or what to do about it. Eugénie would just have to leave that for later. "Let's go to the warehouse tomorrow evening. There is nothing else going on."

Cicely nodded. "I'll ask Mama to send a note to your mother."

"*Bon.* Then all will be well." Once Eugénie discovered exactly how Wively Imports fared, perhaps she would write to the earl herself.

"And I," Cicely said, grinning, "shall be able to concentrate on the gentleman I saw today."

Eugénie might not be interested in the fair-haired gentleman, but the other one she'd run into this afternoon had enthralled her senses. She could still feel the heat of his hand on her arm, and the look he'd given her, as if he could see her soul. His lips were shaped as if a sculptor had chiseled them from marble. There was nothing soft about the rest of his face either. His nose had a slight bump, as if it had been broken at one time, and that saved him from looking too pretty. His hair, what she could see of it, was brown with gold streaks. His eyes were sapphire. They reminded her of the color of the deep blue water between the islands.

However, this was no time to be thinking of men.

One saw many sailors and other travelers, but it was odd to have two such comely new gentlemen in town at the same time. Especially one interested in her father's business. She hoped for Cicely's sake her concerns were groundless.

Will sat at a corner table on the ground floor of the Happy Iguana, away from the windows but where a slight breeze could still be had. He would have liked to sit right in front of the large openings, but didn't want what he and Andrew had to say overheard.

Even in here, the range of skin colors seemed infinite. It was so different from England, where pale complexions abounded. A couple of well-dressed men entered the bar. Without the red-and-white cockades on their hats, Will would have thought they were white. But they were free men, and obviously well-to-do. Still, the Danes refused to grant them rights equal to white men of their same status, even those born free. Thank God the English had ended the slave trade.

A young serving girl with skin the color of tea lightened by milk brought cold water and coffee. He turned down cream and sugar. After hearing from the captain about the plight of the cane plantation slaves, he'd do what he could to avoid using it. When he returned home, he'd make sure to use only sugar made from beets. Taking a sip, he put the hot coffee back down to cool.

Thoughts of Mrs.—that had to have been what the clodpole of a clerk had said in German—Villaret stole into his mind. He gave himself an inner shake. This was no time for self-doubt. She was exactly what he'd wanted, and it wouldn't do to look a gift horse in the mouth. Whoever she was, the woman hadn't been at all shy when she'd met him eye to eye. A companion, perhaps, to the flighty young lady? She'd been dressed too well to be a maid, yet the gray of her gown did nothing to complement her. At first he'd thought her skin had been browned by the sun—but now, after seeing the different hues—was it the sun? Perhaps she was a light-skinned mulattress, and that was the reason the clerk called her "an armful" instead of being more respectful.

He was almost certain she hadn't worn a wedding ring. She'd probably had to sell it to make ends meet. Whoever Mrs. Villaret was, he planned to know her intimately. At last a woman who wasn't chasing him, and if he must work a bit for it, his conquest would be all the sweeter. A delightful task he'd attend to as soon as his business was complete.

"Will."

He jerked his head up as Andrew slid into the seat across the table from him.

"What's got you so distracted?" Andrew signaled the bar maid. "I had to repeat myself twice before you heard me."

Lush, chestnut-brown hair and bold eyes the color of fine brandy, with a figure made for love. "Nothing." Will took a sip of his coffee, now lukewarm. When the servant came over, he ordered two grogs. Once the drinks arrived, he asked, "What did you discover?"

"I met with Howden and told him I represented a gentleman who wished to invest in or possibly buy a company here." Andrew took a sip of the rum. "It took me quite a while, but I allowed him to think my principal had a large shipping and import business. After a good deal of talking, he told me, quite confidentially"—Andrew rolled his eyes—"that the company is for sale but the owner wishes to keep it quiet—and it's in shipshape and Bristol fashion." A sparkle appeared in his eyes. "Which, for the uninitiated, means doing extremely well."

"You're quite the wit." Will tried and failed to scowl. "I know what the phrase means. Go on."

"Someone else is interested in buying the company."

Will put down the glass he'd raised to his lips. He didn't think he was going to like what came next. "And?"

"That was the end of his confidences." Andrew took a long pull on his drink.

"No one has approached my father about buying Wively Imports, and he couldn't make a decision without my aunt's approval in any event." The only scenario Will could imagine was straight out of the romance books his sisters read: The dastardly villain convinces the poor widow to sell, thereby enriching himself. All it would lack was the young daughter whom the scoundrel wanted to marry. "You're not going to tell me that this Howden fellow has lied to my uncle's wife?"

"I don't know." Andrew shrugged. "It certainly seems far-fetched. Still, stranger things have happened."

This was preposterous. Will tossed back the rest of his drink. "How dare he think he can do this to a member of my family! Not to mention the additional grief he's caused my uncle's widow."

"There was something else." Andrew paused for a few moments. "I was unable to see his books. He said he'd have to get permission from the owner."

"We need to move quickly in the event he attempts to hide anything." Will caught the barmaid's attention and ordered two more drinks. "It's time to become myself again."

"If you do that, you'll scare him off." As Andrew stared out the window across the room, his lips tilted up. "There must be a second set of books to show the widow, in the off chance she asks. As Mr. Howden didn't wish to show me the accounts, care to do a midnight run to the offices of Wively Imports?"

Will's lips curved up as well. He hadn't had a real lark in ages. "Break in, you mean?"

Andrew's gaze sparked with mischief. "Indeed."

They couldn't get in any real trouble. After all, Will's father was a trustee, and he had documents authorizing him to act on his father's behalf. "When?"

His friend lifted his glass. "Tomorrow night. We'll need to send someone round to keep watch and discover what time the office opens and closes, and if there is a guard."

"I'll send Griff. He needs an occupation." Will lifted his tumbler in a toast. "To a mission swiftly resolved."

                              * * *

The next evening, shortly before midnight, Eugénie and Cicely helped each other don dark gowns.

"Why did you have to wear *that*?" Cicely turned up her nose. "It didn't become you when it was new. I still don't know why you bought it. It's not at all like any of your others."

"It *is* the only gown that would not be missed if something happened to it." Eugénie swung her cloak over her shoulders. Her friend was right. With the high, tucked bodice of twill, one would have to have a much longer neck than she did to wear it comfortably. The dark color, more closely resembling the vegetable's dull shade rather than the usual lovely purplish red normally associated with aubergine, made her look ill. Even after she'd picked off the bright yellow trim, the gown was still hideous.

She'd only accepted it because she felt sorry for the seamstress. "My maid was to have cut it up for rags, but I told her I'd already done it. I knew it would come in handy one day."

Cicely's lips formed a *moue*. "If anyone saw you in that, who knows what they would think."

"The whole point is *not* to be seen." Eugénie pressed Cicely's cloak into her hands. "Please, may we go?"

When they reached the gate letting out onto the step street, Cicely's footman, Josh, awaited them. He had to be in love with her to take such a risk. If they were caught, he would be let go. However, Cicely always could twist men around her fingers.

The three of them took care in descending the step street, moving as silently as possible. Whether it was due to the water surrounding the island or something else, sound traveled quickly here. After reaching Dronningens Gade, Eugénie, Cicely, and Josh hugged the sides of the buildings, keeping to the shadows. Soon they reached the long rectangular warehouses that stretched to the waterfront. Each building was separated from its neighbor by a narrow alley. Fire hazards, Papa had called them. He was the first to build his warehouse of brick and add a second floor. Finally, they reached the one where the door to Wively Imports was located.

"How did you get the key?" Cicely whispered.

"I took the chance that Maman had forgotten to take it out of Papa's desk. Now hush. We cannot risk anyone hearing us."

She turned in to the pitch-black alley where the entrance was located. Even the stars couldn't penetrate the dark here. Eugénie ran her fingers along the stucco-finished wall until she came to the raised edge of a doorway. "Josh, unshutter the lantern just a bit. I need to see the lock."

A narrow beam of light twisted and turned until it stopped on the door. Eugénie carefully pulled the ring of keys from her cloak pocket, trying to keep them from clinking, and began trying the ones most likely to fit. The only sound was her breathing and the roar of her heart pounding in her ears. Her hands were suddenly damp as the sound of the lock clicking back seemed much louder than it probably was.

The door swung open on well-oiled hinges. "Come, quickly."

Cicely swept past, followed by Josh. Eugénie closed the door.

Her friend took the lantern from the footman. "Josh, you stay here." The lantern swung around the room. "Where is it?"

"Upstairs."

A few moments later they entered a plainly furnished outer office lined with shelves. Eugénie was thankful all the window shutters were tightly closed, and no light would seep through. "Now, where to begin?"

"Let's start with the bank ledger dated right after your father died." Cicely pulled off her gloves in a businesslike manner. "That should tell us when things started going wrong."

Row upon row of thick record books filled the shelves. Eugénie had not realized how many there were. Would they be able to find what they needed in the short time they had? "Do you know what they look like?"

"Give me the light," Cicely replied. "I'll know when I see them."

Eugénie handed over the lantern and watched, impressed by the way Cicely rapidly reviewed the books until she found what she wanted.

"This is it." She carried two of the ledgers over to the desk, taking a seat behind it. "Let's see what it tells me."

Not knowing what else to do, Eugénie brought a small wooden chair over to sit next to her friend. An hour later, after reviewing the past six months' worth of ledgers, she rubbed her eyes. "None of this makes sense. The company is doing even better than before. Why would—"

"Well, well," came a deep voice from the door. "What have we here?"

Eugénie's heart dropped to her toes, then immediately jumped into her throat. It was the man she'd run into yesterday. While she struggled to speak, Cicely turned her big blue eyes on the man's companion. Was she actually going to flirt at a time like this? Eugénie opened her mouth to speak but nothing came out.

"I fear, sirs"—Cicely rose from her chair as smoothly as if she were at a ball—"you have us at a disadvantage."

Good Lord, she was going to get them killed. Eugénie rose so that she stood next to Cicely, and smoothed her hand down her skirts, ready to pull out her dagger if necessary. She might die, but not without a fight.

The dark-haired man bowed. "Mr. William Munford, at your service. This," he said, indicating his companion, "is Mr. Andrew Grayson."

Mr. Grayson bowed as well.

They waited, probably for her and Cicely to provide their names, but even Cicely wouldn't go that far. When the two gentlemen came into the light, Eugénie identified the second man as the gentleman her friend had been mooning over yesterday.

Yet compared to Mr. Munford, Mr. Grayson was easily dismissed. In the darkened room, Mr. Munford was even more handsome than he'd been on the street, and the way he studied her made him appear more dangerous. The light from the lantern caught hints of gold in his brown hair, making them shine like Spanish coins.

She cleared the lump in her throat. "What are you doing here, and where is Josh?"

Mr. Munford raised a brow, and his mouth tightened into a thin line. "I assume by *Josh*, you mean the lad snoring downstairs by the door?"

She narrowed her eyes at Cicely, who shrugged as if it didn't matter that their guard couldn't stay awake and they were being accosted by two strange men.

"As to what we are doing here," Mr. Munford continued, "I was called in to discover the status of the company."

Eugénie took a deep breath. Could it be that help *had* arrived? "By whom?"

He speared her with an intent stare. "By Watford, of course. As head of the family, he is concerned about the welfare of Mrs. Wivenly and the children."

"The Earl of Watford?"

"Naturally, who else?"

Her brief feeling of relief gave over to trepidation. She stifled the urge to groan. This only got worse. What if he went to her home? If Maman found out about her midnight

trip—a shiver ran down her spine—it would be catastrophic.
And Mr. Munford! He would discover her identity, and for
some reason, aside from the probability he'd betray her to
Maman, Eugénie knew that would be very bad indeed. She
had to avoid any further meetings with him. Perhaps she and
Cicely should leave the books to the men. That was assuming they would let her and Cicely go. How had they gotten
into this mess, and what were they going to do about it?

Chapter 4

"The Earl of Watford!" Mrs. Villaret's eyes had widened, and her breathing had quickened.

Until then, she had been holding up quite well. Yet for some reason Will's disclosing that he represented the earl seemed to frighten her. But why? And what the devil was she doing here in the middle of the night, alone save for another female and a sleeping escort?

Her trepidation did not last more than a few moments. He was unable to keep his eyes off her as she straightened her shoulders and raised her chin as if preparing to do battle. He had to admire the fact that even though he'd caught her in someone else's office and without protection, she was apparently not going to back down.

Andrew sidled up to the desk, placed a hand on the ledger, and turned it toward him. "Do you even know what you're looking at?"

"Naturally, she does," Mrs. Villaret replied forcefully.

She reminded Will of nothing less than a tigress protecting her cub.

The blonde huffed. "Of course I do."

"All right then." Andrew smiled. She smiled back. "What did you find?"

Mrs. Villaret drew her full bottom lip between small white teeth as she watched the scene playing out between Andrew and the other woman. The flame from the lantern highlighted her dark hair, revealing streaks of deep red. He wished he could tell how long it was, but her hair was pulled back from her forehead and done up in braids pinned around her head. He had an overwhelming desire to take them down and run his fingers through her long tresses. The bodice of her gown rose and fell more rapidly than was normal. Which again begged the question: Was it the fear of being in the room with two unknown men, or of what Andrew would discover when he inspected the books?

Mrs. Villaret gave an imperceptible shake of her head. "Not what we expected to learn."

"All the finances appear to be in order." The blonde twisted her lips ruefully.

Andrew raised a brow. "And that's a problem?"

The blonde raised a brow of her own. "Yes. It means someone is lying to Mrs. Wively about the company's finances."

"In your opinion." Andrew's tone was as dry as dust.

"To our certain knowledge." Mrs. Villaret's chin rose, yet her voice remained low. "It is a small community. I am acquainted with the family."

"Yes." The blonde nodded. "We are here to help Mrs. Wively and her family."

Will took three steps forward, bringing himself only inches from Mrs. Villaret. He didn't touch her. His size and proximity would be intimidation enough. He'd discover what the devil was going on with the two women if it was the last thing he did. "Who asked you to intervene?"

"Mrs. Wively is very timid when it comes to commerce." A defiant spark came into Mrs. Villaret's eyes, and her jaw firmed. "Someone had to help her."

Damn if he didn't admire her strength. Most women would have cowered or fled. "Show me."

She remained standing as the Englishwoman resumed her seat and slid the ledger back in front of her. "Look at this."

Andrew leaned over her shoulder, peering down at the accounts. After a moment, he sat in the chair Mrs. Villaret had abandoned.

While the other woman and Andrew delved deeper into the books, Will decided to further his acquaintance with Mrs. Villaret. He may as well start his pursuit of her immediately. "How do you know the Wively family?"

She flicked a glance toward her friend, then back to him. "As I told you, it is a small community."

He stepped forward and she retreated, attempting to put distance between them, but that wasn't what Will wanted. The chase was on. He followed until her back hit the wall, and her eyes widened with the shock of realizing she had nowhere to go. "Who asked you to investigate?"

Beneath her dark purple gown, her breasts heaved with what he hoped was lust and not fear. Damn, he wanted her, and when she was his, she wouldn't wear out-of-date clothing that would be better off in a rag bin. The contrast between the other female, who was obviously a lady of means, and Mrs. Villaret was striking. She was clearly much less affluent. Another problem he could remedy. All he needed to do was overcome any hesitation she might have in becoming his mistress.

"There is something missing," Andrew said, interrupting Will's ruminations.

"Yes," Mrs. Villaret's companion agreed. "What would the manager have shown Mrs. Wively if she'd asked for proof of the company's decline?"

Mrs. Villaret adroitly slipped away from him. "I'll search the other room."

Will took a step toward her and the door. "I'll help you."

"Non!" She bit off the word, glaring at him for a moment, warning him away. "It will be quicker if I do it myself. I know the office."

Had she been his uncle's mistress? Before he could follow, Andrew called him over.

"Search the shelves for books that look like these. They should be exact duplicates, except the numbers in the columns will be lower."

Will glanced quickly at the door to the other room. Every part of him screamed out to follow her. To have her alone with him. To know why she didn't want him in the office with her. Hell and damnation. He'd have to wait.

Eugénie fled to her father's office, closed the door, leaned back against the solid wood panels, and waited for her heart to slow. *Mon Dieu.* Occasionally other men had looked at her like Mr. Munford did, but she'd never before truly understood what the look meant. Nor had she been even remotely tempted to respond, and Papa had always been there to warn them away. Eugénie didn't know very much about what went on between a man and a woman, but she knew enough to understand Mr. Munford was dangerous.

She could still feel the heat from his large body as he'd hovered over her. He both attracted and terrified her. What was it about him that made her heart thud in her chest and her lips want to meet his?

Even if he was interested in marriage, nothing could come of it. She'd never be allowed to make a misalliance by marrying one whose breeding was inferior to hers. After all, he was only an agent, and she was the granddaughter of a count and a viscount. Yet something about him gave her the impression marriage was not his intent, and that was far worse.

Maman, and even Marisole, had told Eugénie that her coloring was too dark, and perhaps it was time she paid more attention to her garments, or she'd not look as a lady should. Mayhap she had been allowed too much freedom from what Papa had called "the strictures of Polite Society." Was that what fascinated Mr. Munford? It mattered not. Eugénie had to stay away from him for her own peace of mind, as well as the preservation of her virtue. She gave herself a shake. She would give her reaction to him and how to combat it more thought later. Now she needed to see what could be found in the office.

Using her hands as guides, she felt her way around Papa's desk to the drawer where he kept the tinderbox. Giving thanks it was still there, she extracted a wood splint and lit it, in turn igniting the oil lamp. Hunting through the unlocked drawers, she found nothing. She took the keys out, fitting the smaller ones to the one locked cabinet located under the windows behind the desk. Finally, it slid open. A journal stood next to a half-filled bottle of brandy. She withdrew the diary, took it to the desk, and opened it to the first page.

> *Eighth of May 1816—The Widow Wively bade me keep the company going. She is still in sad shape after the death of her husband. I fear there will be no chance of advancement for me here. I shall attempt to convince her to sell.*

Maman had become so distraught at Mr. Howden's suggestion she sell the company that she'd taken to her bed for over a week. Eugénie skipped ahead a couple of weeks to when the first of the bad news came.

> *Twentieth of May 1816—Mr. S, a merchant of some means, approached me concerning purchasing Wively Imports. When I explained Widow Wively would refuse to sell, he suggested I inform her the company was failing. He also said that he was expanding his*

*concerns and was in need of an intelligent man of
business, intimating the position was mine if I could
assist him in buying the company.*

Eugénie's hands trembled in rage. How could Mr. Howden even consider such a thing? Papa had always treated
him well, and the family needed him. Flipping to August,
she found the first entry.

*First of August 1816—Met with Mr. S today. He is
extremely anxious to make his offer to Widow Wively.
I explained that nothing can be done until she is out of
mourning. He expressed concern that Mr. Wively's
family might involve themselves well before then.
However, on this point I was able to reassure him. No
one in the family appeared to care. In fact, when the
son went to England, only Mr. Wively's widowed
mother was willing to take the boy in before he begins
his term at Eton.*

Eugénie frowned. That was not precisely true. Grandmamma wanted Eugénie's brother, Benet, to spend the summer with her before he started his first term at school, but
the earl had offered as well. More importantly, Howden must
think her family was alone in the world. Apparently he did
not know the Earl of Watford was a trustee. Her mother had
asked that the reports on the business be sent to him. How
was it possible Howden had not made the connection? Her
pulse raced with anger. How dare he attempt to take advantage of Maman? *Fripouille!*

She closed the diary. After placing everything else back
where it belonged, she extinguished the light, then opened
one of the windows and its shutter for a moment to allow the
smell of burning oil to lessen.

The moon hung in the night sky, surrounded by thousands of stars casting a path over the water, where ships'

lights bobbed, adding to the illumination. One day she would most likely be forced to leave. Would the next place she lived be as lovely?

"It's captivating," a deep voice said softly.

Eugénie's hand flew to her chest as her heart jumped into her throat. "Mr. Munford, you should not sneak up on a person."

His breath fluttered over the back of her neck. "I'm sorry. I didn't mean to frighten you."

Scare her half to death, more like, and now her body wanted to lean back against him. She held herself rigid. It would not do to let him know how he affected her. "I was not afraid, merely startled."

"You've been in here for a long time." His voice was low, almost mesmerizing, as if it called to her, wanting to capture her somehow.

One of his fingers traced the line of her shoulder, lighting fires along her skin that she didn't know how to extinguish—or whether she wanted to.

What was he doing to her? This was madness. Eugénie struggled to think of anything to say. "I found Mr. Howden's diary."

"Diary?" He dropped his hand, leaving her somehow bereft. "Is it interesting?"

She turned to face him. *"Oui."*

Mr. Munford's presence was almost too much to bear. It made her want to do *things* she didn't even understand. Skirting around the man, Eugénie grabbed the book and strode quickly to the other room.

When she reached the desk, Cicely and Mr. Grayson were still poring over ledgers. "I found Mr. Howden's personal journal. It explains in great detail what he is doing."

Mr. Grayson took the diary, flipped to the last date and sucked in a breath.

"What is it?" Drat, why hadn't she thought to read that one herself?

His lips formed a thin line. "Not something even close friends of the family should be apprised of."

It took all her control, really she was amazed at how much she had, not to declare herself and snatch the journal from his hands. "Will you take it?"

"No." He shook his head. "Howden posts entries too often. I shall make notes and hope that we'll be able to access it the next time we need to."

Mr. Grayson's calm good sense acted as a balm on Eugénie's nerves. She might not trust his friend, but she knew Mr. Grayson would do her no harm.

Right now the most important thing was to remove herself from Mr. Munford's presence. "It is late. My friend and I must go home."

"We'll escort you." Mr. Munford's voice was soft and hard at the same time. He was definitely a man who was not accustomed to being gainsaid.

Her nemesis came to stand beside her, bringing with him all that male energy that she so unwillingly responded to. She calculated the chances of avoiding him. They were not good. "As you wish."

Cicely stood, causing Mr. Grayson to shoot to his feet. "I'm tired as well. Poor Josh, we'll have to wake him."

"He'll get up fast enough," Mr. Grayson growled, "with my boot in his behind."

"Oh, you would not be so unkind!" Cicely's eyes twinkled with mirth. "He's just a boy."

"He is a lad"—his frown deepened—"old enough to know better than fail in his duty to protect you."

Eugénie's jaw almost dropped. Cicely had done it again. Mr. Grayson was as much a captive to her charm as every other man. Except, however, Mr. Munford, who, for some reason Eugénie didn't understand, had attached himself to her. Suddenly his smile was too broad and showed too many white teeth to bode well for poor Josh.

"I definitely think," Mr. Munford said with a cheerfulness Eugénie didn't trust, "the young man could use a lesson in not falling asleep on the job."

Mon Dieu. Save her from protective males. "You will not hurt him. He was very brave to accompany us."

"The lad may have been brave, my dear"—Mr. Munford moved behind her as he spoke—"but how safe would you have been if it had been two scoundrels that came upon an open door?"

Her whole back tingled with his nearness. She couldn't stand this much longer. His hand hovered for a moment at the nape of her neck. Then he touched her curls. Sparks flew through her as his caress followed down her spine to the top of her derrière. What would the man have done if they were alone? Already he touched her as if she was his. *Seigneur*, she had to escape him.

Eugénie tried to step away from Munford, but he held her in place by gripping her waist. "I must replace the journal." She wrenched herself from him and grabbed Cicely's hand. "Come with me, please."

Cicely glanced up in surprise. "Yes, of course."

Eugénie pulled her into her papa's office and closed the door. "I cannot be alone with him. The man is a *loup*."

"A what?" Cicely asked, as Eugénie made her way to the cupboard by feel and replaced the journal.

"A . . . a, oh, I cannot think of the word. It is in 'Le Petit Chaperon Rouge,' a story my Maman told me. He is in lamb's clothing."

"A wolf?" Cicely asked doubtfully.

"Oui, oui, exactement." Eugénie was so glad her friend understood. "He will devour me." She drew a shuddering breath. "And I fear I will allow it."

Cicely caught Eugénie in a hug. "No, you will not. I'll protect you."

"If only you could." Perhaps after tonight she would never see him again. If he came to her home, she'd lock herself in her chambers. In fact, she would not leave her apartment until he left St. Thomas and returned to England. Surely the earl would want him back quickly.

Will watched as the two women entered the other office. "Did she tell you her name?"

"No." Andrew grinned. "She's much more intelligent than you'd think."

That was hard to believe. "Is she, indeed?" Will picked up a stack of ledgers. "Be careful or you'll find yourself caught in the parson's mousetrap."

His friend had a lopsided grin on his face. "The right woman is all that is needed to make the institution not only bearable, but enjoyable."

"You must be jesting." Love complicated everything. It turned a perfectly normal man into a fool. At least it had for all Will's friends and his father.

The back of his neck prickled with awareness as Mrs. Villaret reentered the main office. At least the current object of his desire was not a woman he could ever consider marrying. She would no doubt come around quickly when she discovered he was a viscount. Until then, he'd enjoy the hunt.

After the women returned, Will studied the room until he was convinced nothing was out of order. When the four of them reached the outside door, he nudged the still sleeping servant with his foot. The boy turned over and mumbled something.

"Josh," the English lady said in a harsh whisper. "Get up."

The last bit was reinforced with a nudge of her foot to his ribs.

"Miss—" His eyes widened, and he glanced wildly around until the woman laid a hand on his arm.

"It turned out to be all right," she said in a firm tone, cutting the lad off before he could reveal her name, "but it could just as well not have."

Will almost felt sorry for Josh as the young man hung his head. Still, his failure to keep guard could have ended badly.

"Now go out and make sure there is no one around."

"Yes, miss."

As they filed through the door, Andrew held his arm out for the blond lady. Will was about to do the same for Mrs. Villaret when she drew out a large set of keys, then locked the door behind them.

He put out his hand. "I'll take those."

"What do you need them for?" she asked in a defensive tone laced with suspicion.

"To go back inside again. You *do* want to help the Wivenlys, do you not?"

It was almost impossible to see her face, but her motions were hesitant.

"I'll figure out a way to return them when I've sorted this mess out."

Reluctantly, she handed them over. "See that you do. They might be missed."

Before she had a chance to walk off on her own, he tucked her hand around his arm and they followed the others to the main street. A little over half-way to where his hotel was situated, Josh motioned for them to stop. Up ahead, a small group of drunken ruffians stumbled down the street singing songs, but if they saw the women, it could turn ugly.

"Down the alley," Will ordered as he pulled her around the corner between the buildings, further into the dark than the others.

He pressed Mrs. Villaret against the wall of a building, shielding her from sight. It appeared fate was with him after all. He'd make sure the woman knew she was his. He brushed his lips across hers, trapping her against the wooden structure. Good Lord, she tasted of lemon and honeysuckle. He ran his tongue across the seam of her mouth, and she gasped, opening her lips enough for him to take advantage of her misstep and slide in, claiming her. Running his tongue over her teeth, he tasted before stroking her tongue with his. She was still for a few moments, then she moaned softly and reciprocated, mirroring his caresses, except that her hands gripped the sides of his coat rather than sliding up his shoulders and around his neck as most women would do.

God, she tasted better than the finest wine. Her lush body finally sank against his, and he cupped her bottom, holding her to him. With his other hand, he stroked the underside of one breast, brushing the tight bud of her nipple, and was rewarded with a sigh. It wouldn't be long before she'd be beneath him, naked, where he'd learn every inch of her.

All too soon the men had passed, and Will lifted his head, reluctantly breaking the kiss. He would have gladly remained there for much longer. If he could have seen her expression, he knew her eyes would be glazed with desire. "Come, it's safe now."

She touched the tips of her fingers to her lips and nodded slightly.

Obviously, it had either been a long while since she'd been properly kissed, or her husband had been a lout, unconcerned with her pleasure. If that was the case, Will would take great delight in teaching her the joys of the flesh. He might even take her back to England with him. He twined his arm with Mrs. Villaret's as they caught up with Andrew and his lady.

When his little group reached one of Charlotte Amalie's many stair streets, the Ninety-Nine Steps, Mrs. Villaret held her hand out. It trembled a little. "G-Good night. We can go safely from here."

That's what she thought. Will wasn't letting her out of his sight until he had to. "We are perfectly happy to accompany you the rest of the way."

One slender shoulder lifted in an eloquent French shrug. "As you wish."

As silently as possible, they climbed. The smallest noise seemed louder the higher they went.

Suddenly the blonde stopped and her footman opened a door built into a wall.

Mrs. Villaret tugged her hand from his grip. "Now you

must leave. Please be quiet going back down. No one can know you were here."

"Very well." Will lifted her fingers to his lips and lowered his voice to a seductive whisper. "Sleep well."

If he only had a few more moments alone with her, he'd ensure she'd dream of him.

She turned from him and fled through the door, following Josh and the blonde. After it closed and the lock snicked into place, he and Andrew made their way back down the stairs.

They refrained from speaking until they had almost reached the hotel.

"This," Will said, "has been an interesting evening. Not that I'm complaining, but I don't understand why the scoundrel kept a diary."

"Some men are obsessive about keeping a record of everything they do. He wouldn't be the first man who'd been caught due to his compulsion."

At least the journal made it easier for Will to deal with Howden. "What did you find in the diary?"

"A merchant by the name of Edgar Shipley is behind the conspiracy to make Mrs. Wively think the business is broke. He also has hopes of marrying her daughter."

So that was Mr. S. Will's fist clenched. "Does he indeed?"

"You can easily see how he might believe it would work," Andrew said thoughtfully. "A wealthy man offers security to a family by marrying a daughter. It occurs often enough."

"Not in my family." The man was an encroaching mushroom as well as being a scoundrel. "I suppose I shall have to stop such a misalliance from occurring." His next thought made him grin. "I shall be a hero, just like in one of those novels my mother likes to read."

Andrew rolled his eyes. "Only in your own mind." His tone turned solemn. "You're right, though. If he was in any way an eligible parti he'd not be forced to resort to such a scheme." They reached the front steps of their hotel. "You appear to be very interested in the dark-haired lady."

"Mrs. Villaret. She's the widow I told you about."

Andrew glanced at him skeptically. "Are you quite sure? She seemed rather . . . green, I suppose, to be a widow."

No, Will was sure his friend was mistaken. "What do you mean by that?"

"Not only did she look too young, it is also the way she reacted to you." Andrew shook his head. "It just feels wrong."

"Maybe she wasn't married long." That would explain her lack of experience, but there was no need to guess about her status. No ring, poorly garbed, and after all, Andrew hadn't touched her. She hadn't responded to Will like an innocent. Though, naturally, he didn't make a habit of kissing young unmarried women. Had he ever kissed one? It didn't matter; he was not about to change his ways now. It was clear to him that Mrs. Villaret was as interested in him as he was in her.

"What language did you say the clerk spoke?"

"Stubble it. I know enough German to understand *frau*." Will gave himself a shake. Andrew could not be right.

A sleepy porter opened the door to the hotel.

"Have it your way. When it comes to females, you always do." Andrew made his way toward their apartment. "But you'd better be careful, or *you'll* find yourself caught in the parson's mousetrap."

No chance of that happening. Will had been stalked by the best of the matchmaking mamas and their devious daughters.

"By the way," Andrew continued, "Howden has a meeting with Shipley at the Green Parrot tomorrow at one o'clock. You should be there."

What Will really wanted to do was find out where his widow lived. "What are you going to be doing?"

"I shall dig about in Shipley's business interests." Andrew yawned. "Any information I can find is bound to be helpful."

"Very well." It was only luncheon after all. Will would have the rest of the day to look for Mrs. Villaret. He'd need to be discreet. His groin tightened in anticipation. It must be all the weeks at sea. He couldn't remember ever wanting a woman as badly as he wanted her. He'd better bed her soon.

Chapter 5

Once inside the Whitecliffs' garden, Eugénie and Cicely made their way to her rooms.

Eugénie's lips still felt swollen from Mr. Munford's kisses. She didn't understand why she was so drawn to the man, and it terrified her to think what might happen if she spent any time with him. He was a devil, and he didn't even bother to hide it.

"This was such an exciting night." Cicely bubbled with exhilaration as she took out two glasses and poured chilled white wine into them, handing one to Eugénie. "To think I actually met the man I was looking for." Cicely untied her cloak. "What took you and Mr. Munford so long to catch up?"

Eugénie touched her lips for the second time that evening, and wondered if her friend would be able to see a difference. "He kissed me."

Her cloak half off, Cicely froze. *"He did what?"*

"He kissed me," Eugénie repeated, almost unable to believe it herself. Actually, he'd done much more than that. Her whole body had been alive with sensations she'd never had before. She sank onto a small wooden chair in front of the breakfast table, taking a sip of wine to steady her nerves. "I don't know how it happened."

Cicely finished removing her cloak. "Well, it can't happen again. If word gets out you'll be ruined. Even if he is well born, which we are not at all sure of, he certainly did not behave as a gentleman should." She paused, rubbing her forehead. "I should never have left you alone with him."

"No one has ever tried to kiss me before." Unable to remain sitting, Eugénie rose and placed her wrap on the sofa. "I mean, some men have given me looks, but they would never have acted upon them."

"Eugénie." Cicely took Eugénie's hands. "Your father was always there to scare them away."

She drew her brows together much as her mother did when she was concerned, and suddenly she didn't want to hear what her friend would say.

"Look at me." Cicely waited until Eugénie did as she asked. "You cannot be with him alone again. He doesn't know you and how innocent you are. My goodness, he doesn't even know your name."

"*Oui, oui*, I know." Eugénie gave herself an inner shake. She'd never even imagined a kiss could be so wonderful. Still, her friend was correct. She could not allow him to do what he had done tonight. "The good thing is that I'll probably not meet him again."

"You will." Cicely closed her eyes for a moment, and gave an imperceptible shake of her head. "Don't forget I asked Papa to check into his friend. At least I now know his name is Mr. Grayson. That will make it easier for Papa. I shall ask Mama to plan a dinner and small soirée suitable for your mother to attend. I've no doubt Mr. Munford will accompany his friend, and even if he doesn't, he will want to at least present himself to your mother."

This was the worst news possible! Drat Cicely's single-mindedness. Eugénie would have to find some way out of this. Mr. Munford could never discover who she was. "I thought I'd remain in my rooms if he calls. As to the party"— she rubbed her temples—"I'll tell Maman I have a sick headache and remain home."

They stepped into Cicely's bedchamber and she started unlacing Eugenie's gown. "That won't work. You never have a headache."

"At this rate I shall have an enormous one."

"I'll just have to remain next to you." Cicely started on Eugénie's stays. "Don't worry. I won't give him an opportunity to take any more liberties."

"Do you not think that once he knows who I am, he will leave me alone?"

"I think it may be worse. He could see you as a way to increase his status in life. In any event, we cannot take the chance. Some men like to ruin women."

Eugénie glanced over her shoulder. "How would you know anything like that?"

Cicely smiled smugly. "Papa told me. Which is the reason I am always careful when I flirt."

"I should have slapped him or stabbed him with my dagger, anything to prevent him from touching me." Of course, to do that Eugénie would have had to have been in her right mind, which she obviously had not been. How could she have allowed him to caress her as he did? Her face burned with shame.

"You cannot blame yourself. It would have been difficult to do anything to stop him," Cicely said as she finished unlacing Eugénie's stays and Eugénie started on Cicely's gown. "Remember that bunch of drunken oafs was passing by. To have drawn their notice would have been worse."

That was a valid point. In point of fact, she had been trapped, and Munford took advantage of the situation. How had he got the idea that Eugénie would enjoy being kissed? Had she given him a signal she didn't know about? Oh, why hadn't she paid more attention when Mrs. Whitecliff had explained all of those kinds of things? "I still do not understand how it happened. Or why."

"You are very beautiful. What man wouldn't want to kiss you?" Cicely paused. "Was it wonderful?"

"That's the worse part." A small sigh escaped Eugénie as she remembered the feel of his firm lips on hers. "Once he started, I didn't *want* him to stop."

"Oh dear, if only he were the right gentleman for you. Come to think of it, if he *was* a gentleman he'd marry you after taking such advantage." Cicely sighed as well. "I do so hope Mr. Grayson wants to kiss me." She paused, wrinkling her forehead. "Though not until he's declared himself."

Eugénie finished unlacing her friend's stays. "You barely know him. Are you sure you wish to marry him?"

"Absolutely. He is just what I've been looking for." Cicely smiled saucily and donned her nightgown. "He said I had an insightful mind. Papa always says I should marry someone who likes my mind. That way he won't become bored with me."

"Why then do you spend so much time with your appearance?"

"Mama said I need to attract the right type of gentleman." She gave Eugénie a considering look. "Perhaps that was the problem this evening. You've allowed yourself to become so brown, you could be taken for someone of mixed blood. Our cook has a cream you can use to lighten your skin again, and *that gown*"— she kicked the offending garment—"shall be burned tomorrow."

Eugénie donned her nightgown and climbed into the bed. It was a bitter truth to swallow, but her mother had been right. She needed to look and act like a lady, or she'd come to a bad end. Particularly when she liked being kissed so much. If only Mr. Munford were a gentleman, and one who wanted to wed. Why couldn't she have met the man she wished to marry, as her friend had? Someone who would help her look after her family and keep them safe from predators such as Mr. Howden.

She lay awake for a long time after Cicely's soft breathing took on a regular pattern, reliving Mr. Munford's caresses. The way he'd cupped her breast, the warm slide of his tongue against hers. The way his hand held her derrière. A warm throbbing began between her legs. What did it all mean? Eugénie turned her pillow and punched it.

Maudit! How was she supposed to stay away from him when all she wanted was to kiss him again?

Nathan Wivenly lay in the large bed, staring up at the high, beamed ceiling of his elegant prison. He didn't even know how long he'd been there. For weeks after his capture, he'd been delirious from the bash his head had taken from one of the ship's booms. He still didn't know where he was being held, who had him, or why. Only that they were French and the leader was upset at Nathan's injuries and subsequent condition.

If his captors applied to Watford, Nathan supposed he'd be worth something in ransom. Yet whoever held him might deduce that his nephew would have the British navy after the pirates when it came time to collect.

Best thing he could do for everyone was to find a way to escape. He studied the room for the hundredth time since he'd woken. The only open windows large enough to crawl out lined the top of the outside wall, a good twelve feet up. All the shutters of the lower ones were fastened shut from the outside. He'd briefly considered trying to kick them out, but that would bring the whole house down on him, even if he had the strength to break the thick wooden planks. Though he'd been regaining his health, he was still not back to normal.

The door had a regular lock, but he was no longer in pos-

session of his dagger, or any other implement, to pick the
damned thing open. All he could do was to continue to act as
if he had not recovered. If his captors believed Nathan was
still weaker than he was, he might be able to overpower one
of the servants.

The door opened and a small, pretty, light-skinned mulattress, who'd never come before, entered the chamber followed by the largest Negro male he'd ever seen. Now was
the time to start getting answers. "Who is your *patron*?"

"You are Nathan Wivenly from St. Thomas?" the woman
asked in perfect English.

He narrowed his eyes. "That's right."

She smiled up at the man. "He will help."

What the hell was she talking about? "In case it's missed
your notice," he said in his driest tone, "I'm being held pris-
oner, thus any aid I might be disposed to give you is ren
dered moot."

A grin split the man's face. "We will help you too."

What the devil was going on? Though if it meant getting
out of here and back to his family, Nathan would agree to almost anything.

Will rose early the next morning. Lascivious dreams of
Mrs. Villaret had interrupted his sleep. Her large brandy-
colored eyes alight with passion, his fingers spearing her
long rich mahogany hair, spreading it out around her. He'd
awoken to find his pillow beneath him, just as he'd dreamt
she was. *Damn.* He punched the pillow, then pushed it away.
The sooner he finished this family business the better.

He splashed his face with water and brushed his teeth before pulling on his shirt and pantaloons, then entered the
parlor. Covered dishes sat on the sideboard with small cards
labeling the offerings. How Tidwell knew when Will would
awaken never ceased to surprise him.

Once he'd devoured a plate of eggs and ham, he decided

to try the sautéed fruit, which resembled a banana they'd had on one of the other islands. He took a bite expecting it to be sweet, yet it was not. Still, the flavor was good. He read the card. Plantain. He'd add it to his list of new foods.

Will poured a second cup of tea and sent for his groom. As he stared out over the harbor, his thoughts returned to Mrs. Villaret.

Several moments later, Griff entered. "Ye sent for me, my lord?"

The groom looked as if he'd been up for hours already and sitting on hot cockles for something to do. "Yes, I need you to find a Mr. Edgar Shipley, merchant, and discover what you can about his personal habits."

"He the gent that's causin' problems for the Wivenlys here?"

"The very same." Will took a sip of tea. "Do you have sufficient funds?"

Griff patted his pocket. "Got plenty left from yesterday. Good thing this place ain't too big."

"See if you can discover if he keeps regular habits and where he lives." Tidwell had already ascertained the man was not staying at the Queen.

"You leave it to me." The groom tapped the side of his nose. "I'll be back as soon as I can."

Andrew entered the parlor as Griff left. "The merchant?"

"Yes." Will nodded. "My groom saw a man who might be Shipley enter and leave Wivenly Imports yesterday. Griff couldn't follow him at the time, but made inquiries about where a man might stay on a semipermanent basis. If anyone can locate the blackguard, he will."

When a fresh pot of tea arrived, Andrew poured a cup. "I shall do a bit of investigating myself, but in the business quarters."

Will swallowed his tea and frowned. "How are you going to do that? I thought you didn't know anyone here."

"Ah"—Andrew gave a sly smile—"I had the forethought to bring letters of introduction from my grandfather."

"You're a good friend, Andrew." Will's gaze was pulled to the water in the harbor as he took a bite of the buttered Dum bread stuffed with cheese.

"I am, and you can be sure I shall not allow you to forget it." Andrew glanced at the table and sideboard. "Any chance of getting toast?"

"Only if you want it cold or soggy. I've been told the kitchen is too far away. Try this." Will pushed the plate of bread toward his friend. "It's not bad."

He went back to wondering when he'd be able to search for Mrs. Villaret.

Andrew inspected the dishes set on the sideboard. "I'm sure it's fine, but I'm going to eat something more than bread."

"I'll join you." Suddenly hungry again, Will rose. "Starving myself won't help anyone."

Andrew pulled out his quizzing glass. "I don't know where you put it. The way you eat you should be as fat as Prinny."

"Healthy appetites run in the family." Will slapped his flat stomach. "Even my sisters have them."

"Harrumph."

He helped himself to another piece of Dum bread. Fortunately luncheon wasn't too many hours away.

After breakfast, he visited the tailor, then walked around town hoping to see Mrs. Villaret again. Shortly after noon, in a new coat that fitted him, and armed with a description of Mr. Shipley, Will climbed the stairs of the tavern across the street from the warehouses and docks.

The Green Parrot was a whimsical name for the well-appointed restaurant and bar popular with the wealthy merchants. Blindingly white cloths graced each table. The roof's slight overhang helped to ensure the midday sun didn't broach the interior, yet even in the dim light, the flatware and crystal sparkled. Will was sure that in England it would be called the King's Arms or something like that.

He raised his quizzing glass as if to study the dining room, and his gaze hit the merchant, Mr. Edgar Shipley. He looked exactly as Will's groom said he would—fat, though a kinder person would have referred to Shipley as portly. The man was also balding, and his complexion was florid. Will stopped just long enough to see Shipley glance irritably at his pocket watch. Obviously a man who valued punctuality. Hopefully he placed an equal significance on regular habits.

"Sir, will you be dining with us today?"

Will looked toward the voice and then down. A short, rather rotund, dark-skinned man, dressed in a deep blue suit, waited for his response. "Yes, I've heard you have the best luncheon in town."

The man bowed. "That we do, sir. Dinner as well, but you'll be staying at the Queen, I imagine."

"Indeed." How the devil did the waiter manage to look so cool in this weather? Will's collar points were already wilting in the heat.

"My name is Connors. I'll have a waiter to you immediately." He surveyed the room and smiled. "I'll put you where you'll get a nice breeze. Our heat takes a bit of getting used to."

Will nodded gratefully. "Thank you, it does at that."

Not long after he'd ordered, a man who matched Howden's description joined Shipley. Although both Will's table and Shipley's were next to the windows overlooking the harbor, the two men kept their voices low, and Will was too far away to hear what was being said. Though Shipley appeared to be ringing a peel over Howden's head. Finally he stood and bowed, saying in a clear voice, "I'm going as fast as I can, sir. This type of thing takes time."

"I plan to visit the widow soon. Be sure I receive the answer I expect."

"I'll take care all is ready," Howden assured Shipley.

Will clenched his jaw until it ached. It was all he could do not to jump up and strangle the Wively Import's manager as he hustled out the door. Damn the man. Wasn't it hard enough on the family that their husband and father had died, without the added burden of poverty threatening them as well? Not to mention trying to marry off his great-uncle's step-daughter. Though not English, her family's lineage was excellent. Before Will left England, his mother was already talking about bringing her over for a Season. That's where he'd heard of her before. Had some deuced French double name; de Joyaux, or something like that. No matter. He'd discover it soon enough.

So much for going about incognito. It was time for him to reveal himself to Howden. No mere Mr. Munford would have the influence Viscount Wively did. At least he'd enjoy his luncheon and see a bit of the town as he searched again for Mrs. Villaret before heading back to the hotel and coordinating with Andrew.

Two hours later, Will had strolled up and down the main street three times. Much to his irritation, some of the shopkeepers had started to take notice and watched him carefully. A few people on the street asked if he needed directions. He almost told them who he was looking for, but that would raise too much interest concerning himself and his business and he'd already made them curious enough. Damn. He was at a standstill until Andrew tracked down the blonde, which Will was certain his friend would do.

Finally he gave up. As soon as he finished with Howden, he'd find Mrs. Villaret. It was almost four o'clock when he returned to the hotel and found Andrew in their parlor enjoying tea.

Will touched the pot and found it mercifully cool. Taking a seat, he poured a cup and drank it down. "What did you discover about Shipley?"

"I'm not sure he's what he appears to be. His family is from England, but he claims to be an American. He has significant dealings with the French. One nobleman in particular."

Will's Aunt Wively had been a Frenchwoman before marrying his uncle. She had no family to speak of, but her late first husband did. If only Will could remember who they were. "Name?"

Andrew pulled a face. "No one knew. He was referred to only as Monsieur le Vicomte."

"There are too many actors involved in this. I, for one, want it over. Let's go see Howden. At least we know where he is, and maybe we can get him to tell us the whole story." Will pushed himself away from the table and started for the door. "I forgot to tell you, Shipley's decided to make his offer of marriage in a few days."

Before Will could leave the room, Andrew held out a cream-colored card edged in dark blue.

"What's that?"

His friend's brow rose. "You haven't been gone from Polite Society that long. It's exactly what it looks like, an invitation. The Honorable Mr. Peregrine Whitecliff and his wife are requesting the pleasure of our company at a small dinner party and soirée the day after tomorrow." Andrew's eyes danced with unholy mirth. "Are you sure you wish to resume your identity just yet? There might be young ladies present. Mere Mr. Munford will not attract the amount of attention Viscount Wively almost certainly shall."

Will dropped into a large leather chair and ran a hand over his face. "You might be right. Perhaps we should pay the offices another visit this evening. I'll confront him after the party."

"We have all the information from the books we need." His friend played with the handle of his teacup. "Aside from that, I have other plans."

That was strange. "And that would be?"

Andrew stood. "A private dinner."

Who the devil could Andrew be dining with so soon after arriving? Of course. Will grinned. "The blonde."

A smile played on his friend's lips. "If all goes well, I might tell you. Until then, you'll have to wait."

Chapter 6

The Whitecliffs' butler, Henry, set a tea tray on the low table situated between two couches on the terrace outside Cicely's rooms.

Cicely handed a cup of tea to her mother. "Has Mr. Grayson responded yet?" Thankfully Papa had intervened when Mama had resisted sending the invitation to Mr. Grayson.

"Yes, Mr. Grayson will dine with us this evening." Mama took a sip, then set down the thin china cup. "Cicely, I do not know how you could be so interested in a gentleman you've only seen on the street."

"I thought you said you knew the moment you saw Papa he was the right man for you." She kept her tone as even as possible. If anyone could discover what she had done last night, it would be her mother. Then she really would be in a pickle.

"Well, yes, that's true." Mama hid her reaction by drinking more tea. "Yet my father knew Papa's family."

"Papa knows of Mr. Grayson's grandfather," Cicely said, pointing out the obvious.

"If," her mother countered, "it is the right Mr. Grayson."

She knew Mama's caution came from concern for her only child, but Cicely and Papa had each done their research. He had even discovered Mr. Grayson's name before she had. "The manager of the Queen said his name was Andrew Grayson, and his manner is that of a gentleman." Her mother opened her mouth to speak, but Cicely held up her hand. "Please allow me to finish. I looked in *Debrett's*. If he is who we think he is, then Mr. Grayson is not only the grandson of Mr. Joshua Belden of Belden Shipping, now B and G Shipping, the G standing for Grayson, but the second son of the Earl of Kelston, whose wife is the only child of Mr. Belden."

"That is all very well and good, my dear, but—"

"Please, Mama. If he *is* the *right* Andrew Grayson, and he likes me as much as I like him, please don't say we must wait."

Mama passed a hand over her eyes. "I think you are moving far too swiftly for a gentleman you haven't even met yet, but if you are correct I will not stand in your way."

Cicely hid her grin as triumph bubbled inside her.

Andrew. Now that she knew his first name, she could only think of him as such. He had told her last night his maternal grandfather was in shipping, and that he was the second son of an earl.

While they were conducting their research, Papa had made his little joke about not having to pay for a Season, but he was even happier that she might have found a good match. At least he trusted her judgment. Mama, on the other hand, would throw up one obstruction after another, just as she had when Cicely was to have traveled to London for her Season.

Last night when Andrew had hidden her from the intoxicated sailors, she could tell by the way his lips strayed close to hers that he wanted to kiss her but, being a gentleman, had not. Though he did say he'd find her and ask her father if he

could call on her. Cicely knew she was right about his identity and her feelings for him. Now if only he felt the same.

Andrew dressed with care for his engagement. Luckily,
the Whitecliffs kept what were called country hours, and he
was expected at five o'clock. He took up the carefully cut
sheet of foolscap that had been tucked in the envelope with
the request that he join the Whitecliff family for potluck.
The neat copperplate writing pleased his orderly soul as
much as the message did.

Dear Mr. Grayson,
Perhaps you will remember a lady with an insightful
mind.

The note was unsigned. He'd wondered how he was to
find her and was happy she'd found him first and had chosen
a solution that would be comfortable for them both. What
was even better was the letter of introduction Andrew had
from his grandfather to Mr. Whitecliff. That would give him
more than a little standing with his lady's family. Though
Andrew understood her caution, he had little doubt of his attraction to the lady.

After donning his hat, he picked up his cane. The porter
gave him directions up a nearby step street, the same one as
last night. Will may have spent his life running from the parson's mousetrap, but Andrew was only waiting for the right
woman.

Unlike last evening, he could see the bushes with colorful
flowers that lined the way, and stood as a buffer between the
walls punctuated by wooden doors. They must lead to the
other houses bordering the street. When he reached the top,
he turned left, and immediately entered a courtyard. Par-
tially hidden behind a gate, a set of stairs ran down alongside the house. He wondered where they went.

Unfamiliar spices emanated from a stone building at the end of the courtyard, opposite the house. In front of him was a long one-story building with doors and windows.

The darkest butler he'd ever seen opened the door.

"Mr. Grayson?" the man asked in an English accent.

"Yes." He handed the butler his hat and cane.

"Very good, sir, the family is waiting for you in the drawing room."

He straightened his shoulders and found he was a bit nervous. Not unexpected, considering he'd never courted a woman before.

"Don't let Mr. Whitecliff scare you off," the butler said confidingly. "Miss Whitecliff is his only child, and he's right protective of her. We all are."

It didn't surprise him at all that the servants knew what was afoot, and Andrew could recognize a warning when he heard one: Don't be afraid, but treat Miss Whitecliff respectfully. "Thank you."

The servant led him down a short corridor to a good-sized room resembling nothing more than an indoor terrace. Italian marble paved the floor. Across the room, openings that were similar to French windows yet without the glass, reached to the ceiling and allowed a cooling breeze from the harbor to drift around him. Decorative wrought-iron rails of fixed across the openings stood waist high to protect anyone from falling out.

The butler announced him and left.

A large-framed man with a wealth of white hair stood and greeted Andrew. "Mr. Grayson, I'm Mr. Whitecliff. I hope you don't think us presumptuous for inviting you sight unseen, but I'd heard you were newly arrived and looking at businesses to buy. I like to get to know newcomers."

This was very good. No mention at all of his daughter, though he knew she'd arranged the dinner. Andrew took the proffered hand and shook it. "Thank you, sir. I appreciated the invitation. Indeed, I have a letter of introduction from my grandfather, Mr. Joshua Belden. I look forward to meeting new people here and"—he met Miss Whitecliff's gaze and held it for a moment—"furthering my acquaintance with those few I've already had the pleasure of meeting."

Whitecliff nodded sagely. "Excellent. Though Mr. Belden and I have never met, we have corresponded on business matters. We will do our best to make you feel at home here, Mr. Grayson."

At least with his bona fides in place, Mr. Whitecliff accepted Andrew. He wondered how much the older man knew of his daughter's doings and decided she hadn't told him, or he would not be so welcoming.

"My dear"—Whitecliff turned to a handsome woman with silver-blond hair seated on a chaise next to one of the open windows—"allow me to introduce you to Mr. Grayson."

"Mr. Grayson, a pleasure, and this"—she motioned to the lady he'd met last night who stood against a narrow portion of wall separating the windows—"is our daughter, Miss Whitecliff."

She colored prettily before stepping forward and curtseying. "Mr. Grayson, I'm so glad you could come."

He took her small hand in his, brushing his lips against her knuckles. "Miss Whitecliff, the pleasure is entirely mine."

Her appearance was almost that of a china doll. Pale gold curls framed her heart-shaped face. Her eyes were the deep turquoise of the water. She was so perfectly lovely most men wouldn't think she had a brain in her head. Yet after last night, when they'd pored over the ledgers together, he knew how sharp a mind she had. Miss Whitecliff's beauty might fade, but an intelligent woman would never bore him. All that in addition to an even temperament. He'd never met another woman who enticed him as she did. Notwithstanding his and Will's unexpected appearance last evening, she had held her own. She was everything he'd ever wished for in a wife and more.

Mr. Whitecliff coughed and Andrew realized he was still holding Miss Whitecliff's hand. He couldn't resist giving it a slight squeeze before letting her fingers go.

When he straightened, Mr. Whitecliff had an indulgent smile on his face. "Mr. Grayson, have you had the opportunity to sample a rum shrub?"

"No, sir. I have not."

"Cicely, dear, will you call for Henry?"

Miss Whitecliff, Cicely, went to a braided rope hanging from the ceiling. A moment later the butler appeared.

Andrew was surprised when the ladies were served glasses of rum as well. He was even more shocked to find the glass chilled. "Have you ice here?"

"Yes. We use it sparingly, as you might imagine. It's brought down from upper New York State. We have a special building to house it in."

Andrew tasted the concoction of juices and rum. He recognized orange, but the rest of it was a mystery. The rum had a bit of a bite, though not nearly as much as the stuff they got in England. He wondered what the difference was. "It's very good."

"We shall have a toast." Mr. Whitecliff lifted his glass. "To new friends."

Andrew caught Cicely's gaze. "To new friends."

And, he hoped, much more.

"Well, Mr. Grayson," Mrs. Whitecliff began, "where are your people from?"

"As I mentioned to your husband, my maternal grandfather is Mr. Joshua Belden. That side of the family is from Bristol. My father, the Earl of Kelston, has his main estate near Bath . . ."

Bit by bit, Cicely's mother drew out his family history and divulged some of their own. It turned out Mr. Whitecliff, the third son of a viscount, had a good opinion of Andrew's grandfather, and Mrs. Whitecliff, a baron's daughter, had come out at the same time as one of Andrew's aunts.

Though money was, of course, never mentioned, Andrew dropped the necessary hints concerning his ability to not only provide for a wife but enable her to command the elegancies of life.

Throughout dinner and afterward as their party removed to the drawing room, he and Cicely exchanged glances and smiles. Yet never once was he allowed alone with her. A blessing and a curse. As much as he'd like to have her to himself, he didn't want to scare her. Unlike Wivenly, Andrew prided himself on his control.

He considered it a success that he'd been invited back for luncheon on the morrow. In true English style, the evening ended with tea, after which, under the watchful eye of the butler, Henry, Cicely was allowed to accompany him to the door.

He took Cicely's hand, bringing it to his lips and whispered, "I must speak with you."

Lord, how he wanted to hold her in his arms and kiss her.

"Tomorrow," she whispered back. "After luncheon, I shall suggest I be allowed to show you the gardens."

He turned her hand and placed a kiss on her palm, closing her fingers around it. "Think of me, as I shall of you."

She searched his face and smiled gently. "I will."

He turned to find the boy, Josh, waiting with a lantern and glanced back at Cicely.

"So you don't fall down the steps. They can be dangerous in the dark, and we have no street lights as I've been told England does."

Will was asleep by the time Andrew reached the hotel, for which he was grateful. His heart was much lighter than earlier, and he didn't want his almost giddy euphoria ruined. In fact, after seeing Cicely with her parents this evening, he was convinced her friend of the previous night must be an innocent. The Whitecliffs would never allow their daughter to associate with a lady who'd take lovers. If that was indeed the case, Andrew would have a serious discussion with Will.

Cicely might not have seen what Will had been doing with the Villaret girl, but Andrew had. This time his friend had gone too far.

The morning dawned bright and breezy. As Andrew consumed a substantial breakfast, several ships sailed out of the harbor, probably seeking safety in one of the hurricane holes he'd heard about last night or traveling to Central America or south to St. Lucia.

Midway through the meal, Will took a cup of coffee and joined him. "You're up early."

"I'd like to get a timely start. The Whitecliffs have invited me for luncheon."

"What are you doing spending so much time with them?"

Andrew tried to keep his tone light, but the words came out as if he was giving an order. "That, my friend, is none of your business for the moment."

Will paused in the act of raising his cup. "The blond lady?"

Damn him. "It. Is. None. Of. Your. Business." Andrew stood. "When do you want to leave for the warehouse?"

"Be a good fellow," Will said as he buttered a piece of Dum bread, "and ask your blonde for Mrs. Villaret's direction, will you?"

Andrew's fists clenched. "No, confound it all, I will not."

Will gazed at Andrew as if he'd lost his mind. "What the devil's wrong with you? Did you not have a good evening?"

There were times when Will could be the most maddening and oblivious person Andrew knew, and it was usually when the man was after a woman. His single-mindedness was reminiscent of a dog after a bitch in heat. "I'd like to see our business done."

Will raised the cup to his mouth. "Give me half an hour."

"I'll meet you in the lobby."

Will grinned. "I know it's the blonde."

"You're like a dog with a bone. Give it up. We have more important things to think about. Such as, whom you are going to replace Howden with when you sack him."

"You *do* know how to ruin a perfectly good morning."

As it was, Andrew was left kicking his heels until Will showed up almost an hour later at ten o'clock. Whatever happened, Andrew would not be made late for his engagement at the Whitecliffs'. "About time you decided to grace me with your presence."

"You needn't be so surly," Will answered, showing no remorse at all. "I had trouble with my cravat."

Neckcloth be damned. "It will be wilted in less than ten minutes. Let's go."

"You're probably right." Whatever had Andrew tied up in knots, Will hoped it would resolve itself soon. They strode rapidly down the street toward the main part of town. "I must stop by the bank and ensure Howden doesn't have access to the accounts."

His friend nodded tightly. "Good idea."

Fortunately, the bank manager was available and, although he expressed surprise when Will handed him his power of attorney, didn't delay them. When they reached Wively Imports, Will opened the door, causing a porter to step back sharply.

The man glanced at Andrew and greeted him. "Mr. Grayson, good to see you back. Is Mr. Howden expecting you?"

"No, however I did tell him I'd return."

The porter nodded. "Very well then. You know the way."

Will followed Andrew up the steep steps, reflecting on the last time he'd been here. Today there would be no Mrs. Villaret to feast his eyes upon. Andrew was right. They needed to finish their business so they could each get on with their private lives.

Leading the way, they walked past a clerk, bent over ledgers at the desk Andrew and the blonde had worked at, into the manager's office. In the daylight, it was clear this would have been Uncle Nathan's room, and for some reason, the mere existence of Mr. Howden sitting behind the large mahogany desk was an affront.

Will took out the keys he'd taken from Mrs. Villaret as Howden jumped to his feet. "Mr. Grayson, what is the meaning of this unexpected visit? I would gladly have made an appointment."

Andrew stepped aside and motioned to Will. "Lord Wively would like a few words with you, Mr. Howden."

The manager's lips moved, but no sound emerged.

When the clerk came to the door, Will closed it in his face, then strolled back to the desk and sat on it, allowing his leg to swing. He picked up the open journal.

Apparently recovered from his shock, Howden made a grab for it. "You can't take that. It's private."

"I know exactly what it is." Will pitched his voice in a low snarl. "What I don't know and intend to discover is how you thought you'd get away with your little scheme. *Sit*. It's time we had a bit of a talk."

Chapter 7

Will waited until Howden sank back into the chair before he continued. "My father, the Earl of Watford, was confused when he received conflicting reports concerning Wively Imports. One from you that the business was doing well, the other from my aunt telling him she had no money." Will pierced the manager with a glare.

No one harmed his family and got away with it.

"Therefore, Mr. Grayson and I visited this office the other evening. Would you care to hazard a guess at what we found?"

Howden's gaunt face paled as beads of sweat broke out on his forehead. "N-no, my lord."

"Then I shall tell you. We discovered two sets of books and *this*." Will held up the diary.

Howden flashed a glance at the door and started to rise. Andrew gripped the manager's shoulders from behind, forcing him back down.

How the hell did Howden think he'd be able to escape? Keeping his voice cold as ice, Will lifted his lip in a snarl. "I really cannot allow you to leave yet. You haven't told me why you did it."

For several moments the manager was silent. Finally, his voice full of venom, he spoke. "Without a recommendation from Mr. Wively, I was stuck here in this hell-hole. Shipley offered me a position in one of his companies if I helped him buy Wively Imports and marry Miss Villaret."

"Did you not consider"—Will pitched his voice so the manager could hear the menace in it—"that for honest work, for protecting the interests of our family, my father would have given you a recommendation?"

"No. Other than receiving reports, I didn't know he was involved." Howden stared at a space over Will's left shoulder. "I can make it up to you. After all, the company is doing well, and no real harm's been done."

Will's hands fisted, and he moved away from the desk to stop himself from reaching across and planting the man a facer. "Your services are no longer required here." He stepped to the door, calling to the clerk, "I need a length of rope and a constable."

The blackguard would go to jail for a long time if Will had anything to say about it. Too bad he couldn't put him on a prison transport.

"Will?" Andrew motioned him to his side. "If you have Howden arrested and tried, you will ruin the company's reputation."

Howden sat still for a moment, and Will prayed the manager would give him an excuse to do considerable damage to his person. "You're telling me I have to let the scoundrel go?"

"In a word, yes. There is nothing you can do without causing more harm to your aunt."

Howden glanced up at Will and sneered. "Do you know anything about running a company, *my lord*?"

His fists clenched, but Andrew moved to block any attempt Will might make to harm the manager.

"No, but Mr. Grayson here does." Will might not be able to put Howden in prison, but an even better idea came to him. "He'll also ensure you never work in *any* business again."

"How do you think he'd manage that?" Howden said, sure of his position, then suddenly the manager's face paled.

"B and G Shipping?" Howden's words came out as a squeak. "That Grayson?"

Andrew grinned wickedly. "The same. You are lucky Lord Wivenly has decided not to beat you senseless. I suggest you leave before he changes his mind."

"If it wasn't for the scandal it would cause"—Will's words came out as more of a growl than anything else—"I'd have the authorities take you away."

Howden looked from Andrew to Will. "There are some transactions I must complete before I leave."

Did the rogue really think he'd be able to stay? Will glanced at the ring of keys dangling from a fob on Howden's waistcoat. "Give me your keys." When the man didn't move, Will repeated himself. "Give them to me, or I shall do myself the pleasure of taking them from you."

Howden fumbled with the chain, then handed Will a ring of keys that matched the one he'd taken from Mrs. Villaret.

"You have until I count to thirty to leave the premises." In an attempt to keep his temper, Will bit the inside of his cheek until he tasted the metallic tang of blood. "If you return for any reason, I'll have you arrested for trespassing. That won't hurt anyone's reputation."

Amazingly, Howden must have finally realized he was dismissed without a reference. "But where shall I go?"

"To hell for all I care." Will's jaw clenched as the rage he'd been holding back threatened to break loose. "You're lucky I don't kill you now. Come to think of it, if I see you again I shall."

Howden bolted from the room. A moment later the sound of his heavy footsteps echoed up the staircase.

After taking a few deep breaths, Will nodded more to himself than anyone else. "I think that went well."

Andrew rubbed his forehead. "I hate to say it, but he did have a point. Who *is* going to take his place?"

Will's mind went blank. He hadn't actually thought past getting rid of Howden. "I thought you might, until I can find someone more permanent."

"I'll take it under consideration, but I'm not going to promise I'll do it." Andrew flicked open his pocket watch. "It's almost eleven o'clock. I have to visit the tailor before my luncheon engagement. Which, as I told you, I will not be late for." He clicked the cover shut, returning the watch to his waistcoat. "I suggest you have a conversation with your employees and get to know them. The clerk should be able to tell you at least a little about the company."

Will had turned to gaze out at the harbor, and when he glanced back around, Andrew was gone. *Damnation.* He'd been serious. Will walked to the door, then stepped into the outer office. "You out there."

The clerk's head jerked up. "Me, sir?"

"Do you see anyone else?"

"No, sir."

"Then I must be speaking to you, and it's *my lord*."

"What?" The young man stared at Will, his mouth gaping.

Will resisted the urge to find Andrew and demand his friend return. "I am Lord Wively. Therefore, I am addressed as *my lord*."

"Yes, sir." The young man scrambled out of his chair, almost running to Will. "I mean, my lord."

Progress. "How long have you worked here?"

The clerk's eyes widened. "Two years, my lord."

"Good." Now what was he to say? Will tried to remember the last time he'd interviewed a man for a position, and couldn't. Even his groom and valet had been hired on his behalf.

The clerk glanced nervously around. "When is Mr. Howden coming back?"

Will sat in the chair behind the desk. "Never, if he knows what's good for him."

"Oh." The young man fell silent.

"What's your name?"

"Smithwick, my lord."

"Excellent name, Smithwick. You don't happen to be related to the Sussex Smithwicks, do you?"

He frowned a bit before answering. "I might be, my lord."

This would never do. It wasn't a social call, after all. "It is not necessary to 'my lord' me all the time. Just stick it in every once in a while."

Smithwick nodded.

He was probably afraid to speak now. "Tell you what, get some of those ledgers and come in here. You'll need to explain the business to me."

"Me, sir?" Smithwick said uneasily.

Will raised his quizzing glass, glanced around the office, then back to his clerk. "For a moment I thought we'd been joined by someone else." My God, the man looked as if Will was going to flog him. "The thing is, I know about running an estate and farming. I know nothing about this type of business. Now, unless you have a roof that needs to be repaired, or need advice on how to increase a herd of cattle . . ." A hopeful thought occurred to him. "You don't, do you?"

The scared look turned into a dubious one. Perhaps Smithwick thought Will was mad. Which might not be far from the truth.

"No, my lord."

"As I thought." After all, how much more difficult could this be? "Bring the books."

At the end of an hour, Will was ready to jump out the window and had a suspicion his clerk would be happy to join him. He started searching through the desk drawers. "Is there any brandy in this place?"

"No, my lord, we have rum."

"That will work. Pour one for me and for yourself."

Smithwick returned with two half-full glasses, placing them on the table.

Will took one and raised it. "To farming."

He needed to find a new manager and fast. Perhaps he could discover a way to convince Andrew he wanted to help.

Cicely stood at the window of her mother's small parlor, which abutted her parents' bedchamber. A few minutes before the hour, Mr. Grayson came into her view on his way up the Ninety-Nine Steps. If only he'd look her way. As if he'd heard her thoughts, he glanced at her, smiled, and waved. Happiness surged through her, almost as if she'd been given the Christmas present she'd wanted most. She wiggled her fingers at him and waited until he was no longer in sight. She'd known from the first time they'd met there was a connection between them.

After he'd left last evening, Papa and Mama had spoken well of him and his family. Mama even admitted Cicely was correct as to who he was, but still wasn't convinced Mr. Grayson would make an offer or, should he do so, that Cicely should accept.

She turned from the window and after taking a breath and smoothing her skirts went into the drawing room, where their butler would bring Andrew. A few moments later, Mama joined her, but there was still no sign of him. After what seemed an hour, but could only have been half that, he finally entered the room with Papa.

"Mrs. Whitecliff, thank you for inviting me." Andrew

bowed to Mama before turning to Cicely. "Miss Whitecliff."
Mr. Grayson took her hand again and kissed it. "You are
lovelier each time I see you."

Her heart suddenly seemed to beat much faster, and it
was hard to catch her breath. This was probably the closest
she'd ever come to swooning. "Thank you. You are very
handsome."

He flushed under his tan, as though he wasn't used to
compliments. Or perhaps she wasn't supposed to have commented on his appearance. Her mind was in such a jumble
she couldn't remember. Oh dear, now what?

"Shall we repair to the dining room?" Mama said as she
rose, thus rescuing Cicely from her dilemma.

Andrew took her hand and placed it on his arm. His voice
was a faint whisper. "I'm glad to see you again."

"As I am you." Her fingers warmed as his touch lingered
just a moment too long. He was definitely the gentleman
she'd been waiting for. "What did Papa wish to discuss?"

Before Andrew could answer, Mama said, "Cicely, please
ring the bell."

She had no choice but to leave Andrew and step across
the room to the bell-pull. She had the distinct feeling her
mother had said that for the sole purpose of separating her
from Andrew. Had Papa warned Mr. Grayson away? Yet that
didn't make any sense. Perhaps Mama was just being difficult. Which was the reason Cicely had not been allowed to
travel to London last winter in preparation for her come out.

During luncheon, Cicely, Andrew, and her father discussed
shipping, with Mama interjecting the occasional astute comment. Finally, to Cicely's amazement, Papa suggested she
show Andrew the garden. She couldn't believe they were finally going to be allowed to be alone. Granted, it was broad
daylight, with all the servants within calling distance. Still,
she and Andrew would be allowed to speak freely, without
her mother's close scrutiny.

"Come this way." Cicely placed her hand on his arm and

led him through her mother's parlor to the stairs. She could have skipped with joy

Once outside, he glanced around. "I've never seen anything like this."

For the life of her she couldn't think what he meant. "Like what?"

"Your house. Are there no inside stairs?"

"No. The only ones are on the outside. I take it English houses aren't the same."

They descended to the next level, and he asked, "What is on this floor?"

Warmth rose up her neck into her cheeks. "My apartment. It is common for the parents to have the main floor and the children to live in the lower levels. The servants have rooms in the long houses." They continued down a few more steps, until they reached the garden level and the path leading to a large Flamboyant tree still full of bright red flowers. She sank onto the bench under the tree, and removed her wide-brimmed bonnet.

Now that they were alone, Cicely's stomach fluttered as if butterflies were having a party in it. Unable to meet his gaze, she stared out over the water. "Mr. Grayson"

"I would be honored if you would call me Andrew."

The fluttering moved to her heart, and she was suddenly breathless for the second time that day. "Andrew. It's a nice name."

"From my paternal grandfather. Miss Whitecliff?"

She turned and looked into his soft gray eyes. "Please call me Cicely."

He smiled gently and took her hands in his much larger ones. "It's a lovely name."

"Thank you."

He gazed at her for several moments. If he didn't say something soon she was going to expire on the spot. "I realize we've not known one another long . . . only a few days."

Surely he wouldn't suggest they wait before he declared

himself. What if it wasn't the same for him as it was for her? Cicely couldn't take this much longer. She had to know. Suddenly she blurted, "I feel a connection."

Andrew's countenance became serious. *Drat!* She'd been too impulsive.

"I do as well," he responded as if startled. "What I'd like to say—" A rueful grin appeared on his lips. "Pardon me. I'm not usually so inarticulate."

She held her breath, willing him to get on with it.

His grip on her fingers tightened as he searched her face. "Would you be my wife?"

The butterflies left and her heart stopped for a moment. This was exactly what she'd hoped he'd say. Was there ever a woman as lucky as she? "Yes." She drew a breath. "Yes, I would love to be your wife."

He bent his head, lightly touching his lips to hers, and drew her into his arms. "You've made me the happiest of men, my love."

"Do you love me?" She hoped it was not just a term he used for all women.

Andrew smiled. "Above all things. You are everything I've been searching for."

"I am?" She searched his face. Small lines crinkled at the corners of his eyes and his smile broadened.

"Yes. I knew from the moment we began going over the accounts together that you were intelligent and had a quick, practical mind." Andrew kissed first one hand then the other. "That you are a joy to look at commended you to me as well."

Cicely lowered her lashes. "It is good that you were impressed first by my mind. Beauty fades."

Andrew placed a finger under her chin, raising it. "To me, you will always be lovely."

Bubbles of happiness like those in champagne flowed through her. Cicely felt so light, she could be floating through the air. This was what it meant when people said their happiness was complete. "That's good, because I love you as well."

Andrew's lips met hers, sending sparks shooting through her, like the fireworks on Christmas.

Was that what Eugénie had experienced with Mr. Munford? Good Lord, she must speak with Andrew about his friend. Maybe he'd have some influence with the man, but first . . . She slid her arms around Andrew's neck and returned his kiss. *This* had definitely been worth waiting for.

"Open your lips." Though she didn't understand what he intended to do, she did as he asked. His tongue slipped into her mouth. The sensation was strange but pleasurable, as if they were becoming one person. When his tongue stroked hers, she returned his caresses. *Oh my, yes.* This was very good. Frissons of pleasure made her whole body tingle.

He lifted his head. "I've wanted to do that since the night we met."

She glanced at him, shy for the first time. "I thought you did. If I'd known how nice it would be, I would have as well."

His soft chuckle filled the air. "May *I* say, I'm very pleased you didn't know?"

Cicely grinned. "Yes, you may. I'm glad you are the first man to kiss me."

He took her lips again, this time with more urgency. She opened to him, reveling in the heat. His hand moved slowly down her back, causing her breasts to press against his hard, muscular chest. She could stay here, with him, forever.

He groaned, then lifted his head. "We should tell your parents. They'll be wondering what your answer was."

"That is why you were so long in arriving in the drawing room!"

"Yes." A sheepish grin appeared on his face. "I am only surprised your father agreed to entertain my suit so soon."

"I told him how I felt." Cicely touched her lips to his. "As for wondering, I think they already know." She paused for a moment, considering how to approach the problem of his friend. "Andrew, before we go in, I need to discuss something with you."

A wrinkle appeared on his forehead. "What is it?"

"Eugénie."

His brows shot up. *"Eugénie?"*

What could have caused that reaction? "The friend who was at the warehouse with me."

"Oh, Good Lord. Are you going to tell me she is Mrs. Wivenly's daughter?"

Cicely nodded. "Yes, but how did you know?"

He rubbed a hand over his face. "I knew this was going to catch him out."

"What is it?" How had Andrew known who Eugénie was before now?

"I think we should sit." He took out his handkerchief and cleared the flower petals from the bench, then waited until she sat before taking his place next to her. "Now then. Tell me about the lady."

"Eugénie Villaret de Joyeuse is, as you know, Mrs. Wivenly's daughter from her first marriage. She and her stepfather were very close. Eugénie called him her *beau-papa*, not so much because it's the word for step-father in French, but because he was so good to her. She never believed the manager, Mr. Howden, when he said the company was losing money, but her mother forbade her from interfering." Cicely glanced at Andrew but could tell nothing from his expression. It was as if a mask had settled over his face. "So Eugénie and I decided to look at the books. We hadn't been there long when you and Mr. Munford came in."

A tick formed in Andrew's jaw, and a deep frown appeared on his countenance. "Go on."

Cicely prayed he wasn't angry with her or Eugénie. "When we got to my bedchamber, she looked so strange that I asked her what had happened. She told me Mr. Munford had kissed her, and I think more besides. She was very affected. You see, she'd never been kissed before and kept touching her lips. I promised I'd help keep her away from him." Cicely paused. "I know he's your friend, but I don't think he's a very nice man."

"He has many good qualities, but"—Andrew's lips formed a thin line—"there are times when he fails to consider the consequences." He rubbed his temples as if he was getting a headache. "His name is not Munford. It is William, Viscount Wively."

"Wively!" This changed everything, and Cicely didn't know if it was for the better or not. "I don't understand. Why did he lie about who he was?"

"He wanted to learn what was going on here before he announced his presence. Now that he has, he's dismissed Howden and will find a new manager who can be trusted. Other problems have cropped up as well."

"What will Lord Wively do about Eugénie?"

Andrew raised her hands to his lips. "Don't worry." Andrew's voice was a low rumble. "You can leave your friend's problems to me. It is past time Viscount Wively was taught a lesson."

Cicely breathed a sigh of relief. "I knew I could count on you."

"You may always depend upon me." Andrew stood, drawing her with him, wrapping his arms around her. "For the present, we have a wedding to plan. I do not wish to wait long before making you Mrs. Grayson."

Mrs. Grayson. That sounded perfect. Cicely smiled. This was all going so well.

Chapter 8

Hervé, Vicomte de Villaret de Joyeuse, pushed back from the dining table of the house he'd borrowed in the Queen's Quarter of Charlotte Amalie. He turned his attention to the servant cleaning the table. "When Mr. Shipley arrives, send him to the library."

"Oui, Monsieur le Vicomte."

Several moments later, the servant left. Hervé hated this place. The heat was far worse than the Languedoc region of France, where his family's estate was located. He would not have been required to come here at all if his former sister-in-law, Sidonie Wivenly, had not refused to consider the excellent marriage he proposed for Eugénie. Yet she had, and the only option he could think of was to convince Mr. Nathan Wivenly to his side.

Hervé had only wanted to speak with the man before Wivenly reached St. Thomas. Then the pirate he'd hired made a mess of things, killing the crew and abducting Nathan Wivenly. Hervé was certain that the man would have come around to the marriage—after all, he was a man of the world—but he was still on death's door when Hervé had to leave Martinique and travel to St. Thomas. Now time was running short, and Wivenly would probably not be disposed to help Hervé. The only choice was to keep the man where he was until Eugénie was wed.

Imbéciles et incompétents. Now Hervé was forced to use Shipley. Who'd already attempted to forcibly abduct Eugénie and failed.

What should have been a simple matter of making a good marriage for his niece and the house of Villaret de Joyeuse had turned into a farce. Sidonie had no business refusing him. Eugénie owed something to her father's family. That was the purpose of a woman, to wed in furtherance of her family's well-being. Sidonie owed him as well. After all, Hervé had allowed her to keep the child. He sighed. No good deed goes unpunished. He should have insisted the child be brought to France years ago after her father died. Still, perhaps it was better Eugénie had remained in the West Indies. With the situation being so unsettled for years in Southern France, anything could have happened to her. When the door opened, he glanced up.

"Monsieur." Shipley held his hat in his hands and bowed. "I've been told a few more days is all it will take for the widow to agree to anything."

Hervé slammed his fist down on the table, making the standish and Shipley jump. "*Non.* I will not wait any longer. You shall go today."

"But monsieur, the final report of the company's demise has not yet been delivered to Mrs. Wivenly."

Why was he surrounded by stupid people? "You will do as I have told you. Make the offer to buy the company with an additional one thousand pounds to be settled on Mademoiselle Villaret. Raise the amount if you have to. I want that girl."

Shipley, *le grossier*, backed out of the room bowing. "I'll do it this afternoon, monsieur."

* * *

It was going on four o'clock when Will dismissed the clerk for the day. He'd eaten luncheon at his desk while he juggled the various books and contracts. At least he had begun to understand the shipping business a little. He'd have to get someone in to manage it before he left, but it was important to be conversant with the workings of the company. His aunt and uncle's son, Benet, was still at Eton, and much too young to take over. There was also the problem of what to do with the rest of the family. He didn't like the idea of leaving without a man to watch over them. Will poured another glass of rum.

Footsteps pounded on the stairs, and a moment later Andrew appeared at the door, grinning like a loon. "Given up already, or did you sack the clerk as well?"

Leaning back in the large wooden chair, Will replied, "His name is Smithwick." He lifted the bottle. "Rum?"

"I believe I will, but you shouldn't have any more." Andrew sank down into one of the two chairs on the other side of the large desk. "Now that your name is out, you need to introduce yourself to your aunt. It wouldn't do for her to discover you are in St. Thomas at the party tomorrow evening."

"My aunt is in mourning. I doubt she'll be present, but you're right, some busybody is bound to tell her between now and then."

Andrew checked his watch for the second time in as many minutes. "Her eldest daughter will attend."

"Without her mother to chaperone?" Will had forgotten he had the step-daughter to deal with as well. And with everything else going on, he'd had no opportunity to search for his mysterious lady.

"Yes," Andrew continued, "it appears the Whitecliffs are good friends with the Wivenlys." He glared at Will. "Their daughters were raised together."

What the devil was wrong with that? "Very well. I'll go now."

"Good," his friend said curtly.

Will grabbed his hat and cane. "How did your luncheon go?"

"Quite well. I'll accompany you to Main Street."

As soon as they'd attained the street, Andrew walked off in the opposite direction. That was strange. Will hoped there wasn't something amiss at his aunt's house. Unlikely. If there was, surely Andrew would have said something. Good thing Will had made a point of discovering the location of Wively House earlier.

When he arrived, Will knocked on the front door. It wasn't large by English standards, but from what he'd seen in the West Indies, it was substantial.

An older black man dressed as a butler opened the door. "Yes, sir. How may I help you?"

Will handed the man his card. At least he knew his uncle didn't keep slaves. He paid all his servants and employees fair wages, which was the reason, up until Howden, there had been no problems.

"Lord Wively." The butler's face was as impassive as any he'd seen in England. In fact, the man reminded him of his father's butler, albeit much darker. "Mrs. Wively will be very glad you have arrived."

Will inclined his head slightly.

The man took his hat, gloves, and cane. "If you will come with me, my lord?"

He followed the butler down a short corridor to a large room whose oversized windows and doors gave views onto the harbor.

"Lord Wively has come, ma'am."

A slender, dark-haired woman garbed in black rose to greet him. "I knew the earl would send help. My husband always spoke so warmly of his nephew."

Mrs. Wivenly's English was perfect; only the slightest hint of her French accent remained. She reminded Will of someone, but for the life of him, he couldn't think whom. Will took the offered hand and raised it to his lips. "My father remembered him fondly."

"Please have a seat. My butler, Bates, will bring tea."

"Thank you." Leave it to the English to insist on hot tea in the afternoon, even in these climes. "I've missed a good cup of tea."

Her lips made an attempt to curve up and failed. "I'm afraid we are in quite a fix, and I do not understand how it came about. Yet Mr. Howden assures me we are indeed desperate." She glanced down at her trembling hands and quickly clasped them together before looking up again. "I know nothing of the business." Her eyes pleaded with him. "I haven't known what to do."

Mrs. Wivenly collapsed back onto the sofa, as if she didn't have the strength to remain standing. He definitely couldn't leave the family here, essentially alone without a man to look after them. Will took the chair opposite her. His aunt's face was drawn into tired lines. Damn Howden. If this were England, Will would have the scheming piece of scum put on the next ship to the West Indies and hope he died along the way. As it was, he'd just have to kill him. Will leaned forward, taking one frail hand in his. "Please don't worry. You did the best you could do by writing my father. You may leave all your problems to me."

The strain in her countenance leached away, and her light brown eyes seemed less worried. She tucked a lock of dark brown hair behind her ear. Who the devil did she remind him—?

"Maman, Bates said Lord Wivenly had arrived."

That voice. Will shot to his feet and stared at the doorway, which provided a perfect frame for Mrs. . . . *God no, Miss* Villaret, as she moved from the sunlight into the darker interior of the room. He barely kept his jaw from dropping.

She was even more striking than the last time he'd seen her. Though she still wore a gray gown, at least this one was fashionably cut. She should wear a color better suited to her, but of course, she was in mourning as well.

"Yes, my dear." His aunt finally smiled. "We have been saved. Lord Wivenly shall take care of everything. Eugénie, this is William, Viscount Wivenly. My lord, my daughter, Miss Eugénie Villaret de Joyeuse."

Keeping his eyes on her, Will bowed. *How in the name of God could he have been so mistaken?* The fat was in the fire now. He'd have to propose and quickly, before his aunt and subsequently his father and mother heard what he'd done.

His gaze caught *Miss* Villaret's and her eyes widened, reminding him strongly of a deer about to bolt.

She backed steadily away from him, back from whence she'd come. "Maman, I forgot"—she glanced around— ". . . something. I'll return immediately."

One more step and she was out of the room, closing the door firmly behind her.

Mrs. Wivenly drew her brows together. "I fear I must apologize for Eugénie. I do not know what's got into her."

He did.

Damn. Andrew had been right. Will had managed to spring a better trap for himself than all the Miss Stavelys in England could have done. There was no way in hell he was going to explain to his aunt he'd been trying to ravish her daughter. More important was stopping Eugénie from getting away before he could secure her promise to wed him. Surely that would settle any thoughts she might have of telling her mother what he'd done. After all, he thought bitterly, marriage to a future earl would overcome much. He'd be leg-shackled, but at least he desired the woman. He'd enjoy every minute of bedding her.

Will wracked his brain for a reason to go after her. "Mrs. Wivenly."

She smiled at him as if he was her savior. If only she knew the whole she wouldn't be so sanguine.

"Please call me Aunt Sidonie. We are family, after all."

That was better, he hoped. "Aunt Sidonie. There was one more thing I wanted to say."

She nodded encouragingly. "Yes?"

"I met your daughter at the Whitecliffs the other evening." Better to allow her to think that than tell the truth, and pray Eugénie spent enough time over there that his aunt wouldn't become suspicious. "I want to ask for her hand in marriage."

Aunt Sidonie shook her head as if trying to clear it. "My lord?"

"Will, if you please, Aunt. As you said, we are related."

"Very well, then, Will. This is very sudden."

If only she knew. "Yes." If he was going to be struck down by the gods, it would be now. "It was love at first sight for me."

She clasped her hands as if her whole world had righted itself. "If Eugénie wishes to marry you as well, who am I to object? This is exactly the sort of match I have always wanted for my daughter."

Now all he had to do was convince Eugénie, but that would not be difficult. "If you'll excuse me, I'll ask her now." He bowed, started to walk out of the parlor, and stopped. "Do you happen to know where she is?"

"I just saw her go toward the wash-house. Down the stairs to the right. The servants will direct you."

"Thank you."

He strode toward the side of the room. Jerking open the door, he was surprised to find steps going in both directions on the outside of the house. He'd never seen anything like this. He hurried down to a lower landing, passing what smelled like the kitchen. There the stairway connected to a terrace on one side and continued lower. A maid directed him to a terraced garden below, where he found even more steps, then a path leading to four small buildings set close together. When he'd gone almost to the end of the stairs, he caught Eugénie's gaze as she glanced up. He locked eyes with her for a moment before she turned and ran.

Drat the woman! He didn't care if he had to chase her to Main Street and everyone in St. Thomas knew he was after her. There was no way he'd let her get away now. Whether she wanted to be or not, she was his.

Eugénie caught a glimpse of Lord Wively moving rapidly down the stairs to the work yard. His stern face showed no emotion, but anger emanated from every pore, spurred every step. She couldn't speak to him now, not when he was so furious. What would she say, and how would she react? Not to mention he'd lied to her about who he was, and Maman could never know what he'd done. She must have time to gather her thoughts before confronting him and making sure he did not betray her.

She glanced at the wall. If she was fast, she might make the gate before he reached her. Picking up her skirts, Eugénie darted toward safety. Once away from him, she could decide what should be done. Perhaps he'd leave for England or another island, or even America.

As she reached out her hand to lift the latch, fingers as strong as steel wrapped around her arm and the next thing she knew, he was dragging her toward the empty wash building.

His voice was a low growl. "We need to talk."

She dug the heels of her half-boots into the dirt, raised her chin, and said in her haughtiest manner, "I have nothing to say to you, *my lord*."

"Well, I have plenty to say to you, *Miss* Villaret de Joyeuse."

He picked her up and carried her into the laundry, then set her down and grasped her arm again. *The beast.* She was sure to have bruises.

"Such as," he continued, "why didn't you tell me who you were that night at the warehouse?"

Just like an arrogant man to try to place the blame on her. "*Incroyable.* I am not the one who lied about my name or who I was."

Lord Wively clenched his teeth so hard, his jaw was sure to crack. "I told you I was from the earl. You should have trusted me."

"Trust you?" She would scratch his eyes out. "Why should I, when you chased me around and kissed me like I was a *putain*?"

He raked his hand through his hair. "I thought you were a widow."

"We have plenty of widows here, my lord." Eugénie curled her lip in her best sneer. He would not touch her again. She would never allow it. "Most of them are too busy grieving for their husbands to play games with you." She jerked her arm free. "But by all means, see how many of them want you." Eugénie whirled on her heel to leave when he caught her by the waist, pulling her against him. "*Cochon!* Pig!"

"I know what a *cochon* is." A hint of humor entered his voice as she struggled to free herself. "But thank you for the translation."

"Let. Me. Go." Where were all the servants? Surely someone could hear them and come to her rescue.

He lowered his tone to a caress. "I've not finished with you yet."

Her heart crashed against her chest as the tip of his tongue lightly touched her ear, then one hand cupped her breast. She stifled her gasp. How dare he treat her like this? Cicely was right. He didn't care who he harmed. Eugénie brought her foot down on the arch of his boot, turned, and slammed her knee into his groin.

Lord Wively doubled over, gasping in pain. "What the devil did you do that for?"

"You treat me like a whore. I treat you like a *canaille*." She straightened her shoulders and started to walk away, then stopped. "You may let yourself out through the back gate. Only gentlemen are allowed in the house."

Lord Wivenly's roar reached her a moment before he did. She should have hit him harder.

"You little termagant."

He really was stronger than he looked. Pain contorted his features as he captured her, forcing her back against a wall. His hands held hers over her head, and he trapped her legs with his body. Wivenly would not touch her again. She would not allow it! If only she could move her legs or had her dagger, she would hurt him so badly he could not get up. "What are you going to do, ravish me in my own house?"

"Don't think the idea hasn't occurred to me." He leaned back a bit, and his gaze raked her body as if he could see through her clothing. Almost as if he was inspecting his goods. "Though even *I* would be a bit pushed to do that at the moment."

Eugénie fought to pull her hands free. Oooh, she'd punch him if she got the chance. "If you don't let me go, I'll scream."

"It won't do you a bit of good." His voice was as soft as a caress.

A shiver ran through her. He brought his head down and claimed her mouth. Eugénie pressed her lips together. *Non!* She would not respond. She did not want him.

Yet as he fluttered his lips over hers, they opened, wanting him. Her traitorous body responded to his touch as a thirsty man craves water. His tongue danced with hers as his hands possessively roamed her body, lighting sparks where his fingers touched. She was clay being molded by him.

"There now," he whispered, as if trying to gentle some frightened animal, "that's better."

Tears pricked the back of her eyes as his tongue traced her jaw. *Mon Dieu*, what had he done to her? Why was she acting like this with him? "You cannot do this. You'll ruin me."

"I've already ruined you. Now, I'm going to marry you. As soon as possible."

Marry her? "You cannot."

"I can and I shall."

"*Non.* You *cannot!*"

What the hell was she saying? Will leaned back and pierced her with a gaze meant to intimidate. He didn't understand her at all. Most women would give their eye teeth to marry him, and Miss Villaret was refusing? No, she said he couldn't, but what reason could she possibly have? "Why not?"

Her breasts heaving under the modestly cut gown was the only sign that she was still upset. "You need the consent of both my guardians."

He shrugged lightly. "You'll be twenty-one in the next week or so." He tilted her face up, bringing his lips down on hers. "I can wait that long."

"It is my youngest sister that has a birthday. I am already twenty-one." Eugénie raised her chin and smiled sweetly. "That is not the age of majority here."

Will jerked his head back, feeling as if he'd been slapped. *"What?"* She had to be wrong. "What do you mean?"

A smugness that made him want to shake Eugénie crept into her voice as she said, "It is five and twenty."

"*Twenty-five?* What the deuce are the Danes thinking?"

Apparently it was her turn to shrug, and she did. "That one-and-twenty is too young."

He glared down at her. "Who are your guardians?"

"Maman."

"That's easy enough." He smirked, and watched as her eyes spit fire. "I already have her consent."

"You arrogant, perfidious brute." She began struggling against him again. "I cannot believe you spoke with my mother before saying anything to me."

"It is the way this type of thing is usually done." He held her fast as she bucked against him, trying to escape. Damn, she'd be a challenge. Not like any of the English girls his mother would likely pick for him. "Who is the other one?"

"Your father," she spat.

Will didn't believe her. "How is that possible? He's your trustee."

Her lips curved into a tight smile. "The court here approved Papa's will. He left it like that."

"Damn." The curse was out before Will could stop it. "I'm sorry. I should not have said that with you present."

"On the docks, I have heard much worse." Her chin went up a notch. "Besides, we have already established you are not a gentleman. I am not sure I want to marry you. I wish for a husband who will treat me with kindness. Not like a blood—"

"That's enough," he barked. Good God. What was it about her that had him acting like a barbarian? "Hasn't anyone ever told you, ladies don't use certain words?"

Neither did gentlemen for that matter, but he might make an exception in her case.

One well-shaped brow lifted. "I have no need to use them with anyone else."

He was going to kill her. Eugénie had to be the most difficult, temperamental woman he'd ever met. "Well, they don't."

God, he sounded like a prig.

"I am perfectly ladylike when I'm treated as such." Her eyes flashed. "Which you do not."

Even if it only lasted a few weeks, this was going to be a long betrothal. He wanted her in his bed now, before he could murder her. "We should go up immediately and tell your mother you've agreed to marry me."

She shook her head. *"Non."*

What the hell was she up to? "What do you mean, no?"

"You ask a great many unnecessary questions, my lord. I already told you I wish to marry someone who treats me properly." She glanced up at her hands.

Will hoped he wasn't making a mistake by letting them go. Still, he couldn't very well keep her pinned against the wall until the wedding. He released her wrists. "Very well."

She rubbed her reddened flesh. He had no doubt she'd make him pay for each bruise.

"I shall have marks, then everyone will know you abuse me."

If he strangled her now, he'd be doing them both a favor. "I let you go, what more do you want?"

"A proper proposal." She raised her chin again. At this rate, she'd be staring at the ceiling. "The kind a gentleman would make."

Maybe he'd just slit *his* wrists, and let someone else deal with her. "I suppose you want me to go down on one knee."

"As a matter of fact"—a small smile tilted her lips—"yes, that would do nicely."

Will stifled a groan, glad none of his friends were around to see this. Kneeling before her, he reached for one of her hands, but she whipped them behind her. "Miss Villaret de Joyeuse, Eugénie—"

"A gentleman would not use my name until I'd given him permission."

He bit the inside of his lip. An English miss might have been a better choice; at least they respected his rank. "Miss Villaret de Joyeuse, would you do me the honor of being my wife?"

She pulled her full lower lip between her teeth. "I must think about it."

Murder was too good for her. "You let me make a fool of myself, only to reject me?"

"Just because I did not throw myself on you does not mean I refused you." She scowled. "I said I would think about it. I will give you an answer later. After all, this is very sudden."

He curled his hands into fists; otherwise they'd wrap

themselves around her beautiful neck. "There is nothing hasty about this."

Eugénie opened her eyes wide. "Oh, but there is. Before, you only wanted me as your mistress."

"How the dev . . . Why would you think that?"

"We women know these things."

Eugénie stepped away from him and walked quickly away. This time he let her go. If he caught her again, only God knew what he'd do, and he needed to figure out how the devil they were to marry. He'd be damned if he'd wait for a letter from his father. He sank back down to the floor, his groin still throbbing painfully. It was probably too much to hope the hotel had ice.

Chapter 9

In the event Lord Wivenly decided to watch her depart, Eugénie held her head high and shoulders straight as she marched up the stairs. Conceited, insufferable pig. If he thought she would fall at his feet, he would soon learn she was made of sterner stuff. He was stupid besides. If she hadn't been a gently born virgin, he would have been happy to make her his mistress. How much clearer could he have been? Rushing down to propose once he discovered her identity. Rot, as Papa would have said. Had no one ever denied the man anything?

If her mother only knew what Lord Wivenly had done . . . But no, Maman would expect her to be betrothed, and she'd wonder where Lord Wivenly was. Drat the man.

Eugénie stopped. She was almost at the main level of the house, where her mother was. Yet if she went back down the stairs to her rooms, Wivenly might see her. Perhaps she could go through the front and flee to Cicely's house. Eugénie stepped softly through the door into the hall, trying to make as little noise as possible. Everything would be fine if she could escape detection until she had a plausible story. Unfortunately, she was a very bad liar.

"Eugénie, my love."

God was punishing her for going against her mother's wishes. "Yes, Maman."

"Where is Will?"

"Who?" Had another man been here?

"Lord Wivenly, of course."

The brute hadn't even told her his name. "He had to return to his hotel."

Her mother had a confused look on her face. "I thought he would take his leave of me. That *is* how things are done."

Now what to say? That he would have trouble walking? She didn't truly know he'd left. He could enter at any moment. "He asked me to offer his apologies. There was an emergency."

"Strange," her mother said, smoothing her skirts. "He did not mention it to me, but"—she smiled—"he was so determined to see you and propose."

Not knowing what falsehoods the scoundrel had told her mother, Eugénie asked, "What did he say, exactly?"

Maman's eyes grew misty. "Only that he'd fallen in love with you at first sight when he saw you at the Whitecliffs'." Her brows drew together. "My dear, why didn't you tell me he was here?"

Oooh, he was going to pay for putting her in this position. Though Eugénie had to admit it was a very good lie. His lordship had probably had a great deal of practice. "He wanted to tell you himself." Clasping her hands demurely in front of her, Eugénie gave her mother the most innocent expression she possessed. "I could not dishonor his wishes."

"It makes me so happy you are betrothed and your future is resolved."

Eugénie turned her choke into a cough. She really was

going to make Lord Wively more miserable than he'd ever been in his misspent life.

Bates knocked on the open door. "A Mr. Shipley here to see you, ma'am."

Maman drew her brows together and gave a slight shake of her head. "I don't know anyone by that name. Why should he come here?"

"Shall I tell him to leave?" Bates asked.

"No, show him in. Eugénie, please remain with me."

"Certainly." She was just as bemused as her mother. "Who could he be?"

A large man with a pot-belly and florid face came into the parlor ahead of Bates. "Mrs. Wively?" Her mother inclined her head, and he turned to Eugénie. "Ah, this must be Miss Villaret. A pleasure to meet you both." He paused for a moment, but when Maman didn't offer him a seat, continued. "I've spoken with Mr. Howden about your circumstance. It is my greatest desire to relieve you of your concerns. I am prepared to offer you a fair price for Wively Imports and settle one thousand pounds on Miss Villaret if she will agree to marry me."

The room spun, and Eugénie grabbed the back of the chair next to her to steady herself. Was the man mad? He acted as if she and the company were for sale to the highest bidder.

"Mr. Shipley," Maman said in a cool tone, "we have no plans to sell the company, and if we did, the proper person to apply to is the Earl of Watford. He is the trustee until my son is of age." Her lips curled into a tight smile. "As for my daughter, she is betrothed to Viscount Wively, my late husband's great-nephew."

All the color leached from the man's face and for a moment Eugénie expected him to fall over dead. After a few moments when he appeared to struggle with himself, he bowed.

"Well then, it seems I was misinformed." He placed his

hat on his head. "Thank you for your time, Mrs. Wivenly. Miss Villaret, I wish you happy."

Once she heard the front door shut, Eugénie turned to her mother. "I wonder what that was about? How strange to receive an offer of marriage in such a manner." Not to mention two in one day. Maman dropped her head into her hands. Eugénie couldn't stand her mother being so miserable all the time. "I'll have Bates bring you a sherry. Our lives will be better now, you'll see."

When her mother raised her head, tears sparkled in her eyes. "Thank God, Will got here first. Papa would be pleased to see you so well settled. I hope Will will be as good to you as your papa was to me. Love in a marriage is important."

Her mother never discussed her marriage to Eugénie's father, but she knew it had been an arranged match. She blinked back the hot tears that threatened. Once the sherry came, she called for her ten-year-old sister, Valérie, and convinced her mother to rest on the chaise.

When Maman was settled, Eugénie said to her sister, "Read to Maman. I will return shortly."

"What is wrong?"

"I'll explain later, *ma petite*. I have some correspondence I must attend to, after which I will return."

When Eugénie entered her parlor, which was on a level that she shared with her brother, two floors beneath the main part of the house, a note with Cicely's seal was propped up on her desk. Eugénie opened it and sat with a plop. Her friend's betrothal would be announced tomorrow at the soirée. Cicely was so lucky to have found the man she wished to marry. Mr. Grayson would make her a fine husband. At least one of them would wed for love. Eugénie would marry because she'd been stupid enough to allow the devil to kiss her. The thought made her stomach tighten, and she felt ill.

Tears flooded her eyes, but she refused to allow them to

fall. What kind of life would she have with a rogue who didn't truly care for her? He would go on with his life, bedding women and then leaving them. Well, what was sauce for the gander was sauce for the goose. If he was unfaithful to her, Eugénie had no reason not to do the same. She would find love. She deserved that much, even if it was not with Lord Wivenly. She pulled out a piece of paper from her secretaire and sat down, considering the wording carefully as she wrote to her betrothed. It would be a *mariage de raison*. A point she would make clear to him.

Will made his way gingerly along the streets to the hotel and his chamber. He poured a glass of brandy—rum wasn't quite up to this. "Tidwell, a small bag of ice if you can manage it, please. I'll bathe later."

"Yes, my lord."

By the time Will changed into the light linen dressing gown and repaired to the parlor, his valet had returned. "Where shall I put it, my lord?"

He held out his hand. "I'll take care of it. I need some time alone."

"Yes, my lord." Tidwell bowed. "Mr. Grayson said I should wish you happy."

Of course. He'd known who Eugénie was before he'd sent Will to her house. That's the reason his friend had been so angry. Andrew should have warned him. Maybe then Will would have taken a different tack. "The lady has not accepted yet."

Tidwell stepped out of the room then returned, handing Will a folded paper with a seal. His name was written in a neat feminine hand. "This came while you were out."

He must have stayed in the wash house longer than he'd thought. "Thank you."

Once Tidwell left, Will placed the cloth bag of ice on his

nether parts—they might never be the same again—and opened the letter.

Lord Wivenly,
I shall accept your offer of marriage as long as it is
on equal terms.
Eugénie Villaret de Joyeuse

On equal terms? What the devil did the little vixen mean by that? Will tossed back the fine French cognac, closing his eyes as he enjoyed the burn of the liquid traveling down his throat. He'd figure it out later. This had to have been one of the most trying days of his life, and right now he wanted a nap. Perhaps he should have given in and married one of the scheming young ladies in England. At least now he wouldn't be sitting here almost emasculated.

The ice and brandy were doing the trick, when a loud laugh interrupted his state of lethargy.

Andrew. His so-called friend sauntered into the parlor, grinning as he took in the bag of ice. The cur. "I am pleased I can be a source of amusement for you."

Andrew poured brandy in a glass and sat in the chair on the other side of the small table. "What did you do to cause the lady to damage your bawbels?"

Will tried to move and winced. This was taking longer than he'd expected. Who knew such a small female, in skirts no less, could deliver such a wallop. He hoped he'd be able to attend the entertainment tomorrow evening. "I asked her to marry me."

Andrew took a sip of his drink. "Did she hit you before or after the proposal?"

"It's all a bit fuzzy now"—especially after the brandy—"though I believe it was before."

"Ergo"—his friend lounged back in the chair—"my question. What did you do?"

"I may have been a bit angry"—this was not, after all, completely his fault—"but she's a shrew. She called me a pig and a blackguard, and accused me of deceiving her." He picked up the missive and tossed it to Andrew. "Then she sent me that."

Andrew perused the note and started to laugh so hard he had to wipe his eyes.

"I fail to see what is so funny." Will glowered. His friend wouldn't think it humorous if it had happened to him. "I can't even figure out what the deuce she means by it. Equal marriage indeed. All that French thinking about liberty, equality, and fraternity must have gone to her head."

Andrew stared at Will for several moments before saying, "What terms did you think of when you decided to marry her?"

That was easy. This wasn't a love match, after all. "She'd remain in the country most of the year. I'd trot her out during the Season, unless she was breeding, and I'd, in general, go on with my life."

"Your injuries must have damaged your brain as well," his friend said in a wintry tone. "From what my betrothed, Miss Whitecliff, told me, Miss Villaret is an innocent, or she was until you got your hands on her, but she is not at all stupid. Do you think she doesn't know what you have in mind?"

Visions of Eugénie's pliable body pressed against another man raced through his brain. If she thought he'd stand by while he became a cuckold, she could think again. She was his and would remain so. His jaw clenched. "I won't allow it."

"I suspect you've met your match." Andrew put his glass down and stood. "Have a good time feeling sorry for yourself. I trust you'll be better tomorrow for the party. Remember, we've been invited to dinner as well."

Will poured another glass of brandy. He would not allow Eugénie to lead him a dance. Love was all very well, and he would have enjoyed it except for the fact that every man who fell in love was a slave to his wife. Living under the cat's paw would never happen to him. He'd calmly explain to her how their married life would work. She really had no choice in the matter.

He thought of the way Eugénie had kissed him. Not as innocent as her friend and Andrew thought. Will would make her tell him who taught her how to kiss, then find and beat the man to a bloody pulp. He rose, pleased his groin was no long as painful. Fate was with him again.

Will spent the next day at the office and warehouse of Wively Imports, ensconced once more with Smithwick. Around the middle of the morning Andrew finally appeared, though other than explaining a few matters concerning the business to Will, he may as well not have been there. Andrew's mind was clearly on Miss Whitecliff and their marriage settlements. Will thought he should probably discuss that issue with Eugénie and her mother. He groaned. *Not the ladies. Damn.* His father was trustee. What a devil of a mess this was.

"My lord?" Griff said, interrupting Will.

The devil, now he'd have to re-add the whole column again. "What?"

His groom rubbed his eyes and blinked. It was much dimmer in here than outside. "You're lookin' a mite peaked."

"If I want a medical opinion," Will growled, "I'll go to the doctor. What did you find out about Shipley?"

"Did a runner."

Howden must have alerted the man. "When?"

"Early this morning on a ship to America. Took everything he owned which, from what the landlady said, weren't that much."

Will pulled out the papers Andrew had left earlier concerning his research into Shipley's business, and swiftly read the information. The man was a fraud. No money, no property, as far as Andrew could tell. Shipley even left an unpaid bill at the tailor's. He put that page down and looked at the next one. A number of deposits from an unknown source had been put in Shipley's bank account. *Bloody hell*, he was a straw man. The question was, for whom and why involve Eugénie?

He flipped open Howden's journal to the last entry.

Shipley suddenly pressuring me concerning Miss Villaret.

It was always possible that Shipley had seen her from afar and fallen in love with her, but considering the rest of the information it seemed highly unlikely. Which begged the question: Who was really after Eugénie, why did they want her, and what was the best way to protect her?

He ran a hand over his face. Of one thing he was certain. No man, other than him, would ever touch her.

Hervé Villaret de Joyeuse sat in the shade of a room open to the breeze, a wet cloth clinging to the back of his neck. Soon he'd be able to transport his niece onto the ship waiting for him in the port and depart for Martinique. The captain was already nervous of the weather and wanted to leave immediately.

"Milord?" His valet entered carrying the same letter he'd departed with.

"What happened?"

"Monsieur Shipley has left the island."

The *bâtard* had better not have taken Eugénie. "Alone or with the girl?"

"Alone. At least no one I spoke with saw Mademoiselle."

"*Merde!* Now what will I do, *hein*?" Even though it was too hot to pace, Hervé could not think while sitting. Kidnapping her would cause an uproar, but it might be his only choice. He'd waited patiently, yet the weather would close in soon, and he'd not be able to leave for months. He needed to get her to a French territory where his guardianship of her and his trusteeship over her property would be recognized, and he could easily find a priest who would do as he was told. It was the only way to recover his family's fortune that had been lost during the rebellion.

"Get Monsieur Yves. *Maintenant.*"

"I am right here, Brother."

Yves sauntered into the parlor, half-drunk already. Well, he would sober soon enough when told they were close to losing everything. "It is time for you to make yourself useful."

Yves took a drink of wine. "And what task would you have me perform?"

Hervé smiled without humor. "You will abduct Eugénie."

The glass in Yves's hand fell, shattering on the tiled floor. "Are you mad?"

"Shipley has run."

"Contact that man, Howden. He is for sale."

"Non." Hervé shook his head. "It is too dangerous. If Sidonie knew we were here, she'd find help to hide our niece. This is the only way."

"Merde," his brother swore. "You are taking too big a risk."

"Yves, she is our last chance. I must have her." Hervé wiped a cloth over his face. "And soon."

"This will not be easy." His brother grabbed a new glass, filling it with the chilled white wine on the sideboard. "How much time do I have?"

"A week, perhaps two. No more." He paused to allow the seriousness of the matter to sink into his brother's head. Hervé would never have thought it of his mother, but she must have played their father false to have given birth to such an imbecile. "The captain says it will soon be too hazardous to sail."

"Bon." Yves bowed, turning back toward the door. "We must do what is necessary. Do not be alarmed if you do not see me for a few days."

Hervé couldn't believe what he was hearing. Never in Yves's worthless life had his youngest brother taken the initiative. "What if I need to give you instructions?"

"I am truly not as simple as you would like to believe." Yves grinned and strode from the room.

Soon their lives would be as they had been before the revolution. Perhaps Maman had been faithful to Papa after all.

Chapter 10

Eugénie leaned back in the large metal bathing-tub, inhaling the scent of coconut oil and bay leaves. It was time to dress for the dinner and small soirée at the Whitecliffs' home. She had still heard nothing from Lord Wivenly. He had not even bothered to respond to her letter accepting his proposal. If he thought to make her suffer by not answering, he would soon discover she did not cow so easily. The man thought only of what he wanted, and nothing about what she might like. Lord Wivenly was far too used to having his own way.

"Marisole."

"Yes, miss?"

"I shall wear my coral silk gown with the low neckline this evening." Since her *beau-papa*'s death, Eugénie had insisted on wearing subdued colors. Although Papa was not a blood relation, she had mourned him as if he had been, yet now . . . now she was at war with Viscount Wivenly, and would use every weapon in her small arsenal.

Marisole held up a piece of lace. "Do you want the fichu, miss?"

"Not this evening." Tonight his lordship would see what he could never fully have unless he was a good husband. "Help me rinse my hair, please, Marisole."

"Yes, miss. Will you wear braids again?"

The prim braids that should have protected her from a man like Lord Wivenly. "No, let it curl."

"Très bien." Marisole clapped her hands. "I will fix the knot with the pearl combs. You shall be even more beautiful."

Eugénie rose, and her maid handed her a towel.

A half-hour later, her hair had dried, Marisole allowed long tendrils to frame her mistress's face, then twisted the rest of it into a knot high on her head. Eugénie donned a pair of earrings from her jewel box.

When Marisole was done, she stepped back. "His lordship will not be able to take his eyes off you. Oh, *pardon*. I forgot to wish you well on your betrothal. You will be very happy with such a handsome man."

How was it the servants seemed to always know what was going on without being told? Eugénie hid her frown. No matter. Handsome is as handsome does, and thus far, Lord Wivenly had not shown himself to be very good-looking at all. Yet no one must know how much she regretted this match. She forced a smile on her face. "Thank you. I'm sure I will be."

She went to Maman's room and found her seated before her dressing table, her maid styling her hair. Perhaps Eugénie's pending nuptials would make her mother happier. Giving silent thanks to the Creator her mother would attend the soirée, she smiled and entered the chamber. "Maman, will you be at the Whitecliffs'?"

Her mother took out a handkerchief and dabbed her eyes. "Mrs. Whitecliff has promised it will be a small gathering of our particular friends, and assured me it is perfectly proper for me to attend."

"If she says it is then it must be. You know how correct Mrs. Whitecliff is on all matters."

Maman met Eugénie's gaze in the mirror. "You are lovely, Eugénie. I am glad to see you wearing that color. Papa would be pleased."

Once more, tears filled her mother's eyes. If only Papa hadn't died. Eugénie would do anything to make her mother happy again and ensure her family was taken care of—even wed the devil.

She rushed forward and hugged Maman. "No no, you must not cry. This evening we will be gay." Eugénie took her mother's handkerchief, pressing it gently to the corner of one eye. "Promise me no more weeping. Papa would not have liked it."

Maman gave a watery chuckle. "I give you my word to have fun this evening."

Dropping a kiss on her mother's cheek, Eugénie smiled. "That is all I can ask."

She turned to leave.

"Wait a moment, my dear. Dorat, I want Eugénie to wear the long pearl necklace I've been saving for her. You know the one?"

"Yes, ma'am."

Eugénie watched in the mirror as her mother's maid twisted the matched pearls twice around her neck and affixed a larger pearl pendant surrounded by diamonds to both strands. She was almost afraid to touch it. "Maman, when did you get this?"

"Papa brought it home for you to wear on your come out, but I think this occasion will do just as well." Maman blinked rapidly. "If only he could see you."

"Yes." Tears threatened to flood Eugénie's eyes as well. They had both turned into watering pots. "If only he could."

She left her mother's chamber, making her way to the wooden door set in the solid masonry wall bordering their property along the step street. She climbed up two steps, which put her at the gate to Cicely's house, arriving a full hour before dinner, as requested. Though resigned, if not overjoyed, by her own betrothal, Eugénie was determined not to ruin her friend's good mood. It wouldn't be fair and wouldn't make her situation any better. At least Maman was happy. That had to mean something. So little had gladdened her since Papa's death.

Eugénie pasted a smile on her face, pushing aside the fine muslin covering the door to her friend's parlor, then walked into the bedchamber.

Cicely stood as her maid laced up a turquoise gown the exact color of her eyes. Eugénie caught her friend's gaze in the mirror. Her friend had never looked happier. "You are beautiful. I can see how well your betrothal suits you."

"It does. Andrew—that is Mr. Grayson's first name—is everything I thought he would be when I first saw him. We both agree fate brought us together." She held out her hand to Eugénie. "But you are lovely as well. That coral is your very best color. I remember when we picked it out."

Eugénie's smile faltered. She could no longer keep up the happy façade. "This was Papa's favorite shade on me."

Cicely nodded to her maid, and the woman left. "You miss him very much."

"Yes. I can't help but think that if he were here, none of my family's problems would have occurred." Then again, her friend would not have met Mr. Grayson. Papa always said good frequently comes out of bad; still, she'd rather have her father. Eugénie's throat tightened. She would not weep any longer over her problem with Lord Wively. He wasn't worth it. She was determined this evening would be a happy occasion for at least Cicely and her Mr. Grayson. "I'm delighted for you."

Cicely placed her arm around Eugénie's shoulders and led her to a small sofa. "I heard from Andrew, that you and Lord Wively shall wed as well."

Eugénie didn't want to discuss his lordship, yet there was no way out of it. She and Cicely had been friends for far too long for one to fool the other. "Yes, but ours is not a love match." If only Eugénie could bring herself to tell her friend what happened earlier; yet some things were not meant to be shared. "We will have a marriage of convenience, nothing more."

"Are you sure?" Cicely's brows knit. "I remember what you told me about the kiss, and now that I've experienced the same thing"—she worried her bottom lip—"are you not even a little in love with him?"

Eugénie had been so angry and hurt, she hadn't even thought about what feelings she might have for Wively. Still, what difference would it make? "It doesn't matter. He thinks with his man parts and only wants me in his bed."

Cicely gasped. "He never said that to you, did he?"

"No, but that is what he had planned all along." A spark of fury came over her. "He thought I was a widow."

Cicely stared at Eugénie with wide-eyed shock. "You may have to marry him, but you do not have to put up with such boorish behavior. It's time you make him work for your affection."

Staring at a pretty painting of an island hanging on the wall, her stomach clenched as she contemplated her life. "It will not work. He does not at all care about me."

Several moments later, Cicely said firmly, "I don't agree with you."

"*Vraiment.* Wively thinks of nothing but . . ."

"Of course he thinks of that, all men do." She pulled a face. "What I mean is, that is not *all*. When I think back to that first night, he was attracted to you like a moth to a flame." Nodding her head in a decisive manner, she continued. "I think he may love you as well, but doesn't know it, or doesn't want to admit it."

Eugénie shook her head so hard her hair loosened. "I do not love him. How could I, after the way he's treated me?"

But . . . could her friend be right? Each time Eugénie and Wively came together, it was as if lightning struck them. A small kernel of hope bloomed in Eugénie's heart and the cannon ball in her stomach shrunk a bit. "Besides, how would I know?"

"I agree he has not given you much reason to. Yet somehow I still believe there is a chance for the two of you." A dreamy look appeared on Cicely's countenance. "I shall ask Andrew. He will be able to advise us."

Oh, *non, non, non.* Eugénie's eyes widened in spite of herself. "You cannot. Mr. Grayson is Wively's friend!"

"True, but Andrew is not particularly pleased with Lord Wively right now." Cicely rose, went to her desk, took out a piece of paper, wrote a note, sealed it, then rang for her maid. A moment later the door opened. "Please have Josh take this to Mr. Grayson and wait for an answer."

The woman shook her head as she took the missive. "That poor young man. The way you've had him running back and forth all over town, Cook's going to have to feed Josh extra portions at dinner."

Cicely's cheeks turned a pretty shade of pink, and Eugénie grinned. "How many messages have you sent?"

"Well, it doesn't seem like that many, but"—her friend's face grew redder—"we've been having a conversation." The tightness in Eugénie's stomach went away as mirth poured forth inside her, and she laughed for the first time in what seemed like days. "If your written conversations are anything at all the same as your regular ones, you'd better have Josh fed triple portions."

Cicely's eyes sparkled. "*That* is the expression you need to show Lord Wively this evening."

Eugénie caught a glimpse of herself in the mirror. Her eyes shone and her countenance was nicely flushed. This was exactly the face she should have on when her betrothed arrived. She prayed her friend was right and Wively really was in love with her. Still, after all he'd done to her, he would need to court her properly. He must behave toward her with respect and conduct himself as a gentleman should when he cares for a lady. The same as Papa treated Maman.

Other women might run to him when he snapped his fingers; Eugénie would not.

A knock sounded on the parlor door of their hotel chambers, and the Whitecliffs' footman, Josh, entered with yet another missive in his hand. Will couldn't imagine running a servant back and forth with messages as Andrew and Miss Whitecliff had done for most of the day. What was so important it would not wait another quarter hour?

Andrew read the note and grinned before scribbling an answer. That infernal smiling had been going on all day as well. At least one of them had something to be happy about.

Will frowned. He hadn't sent a reply to Eugénie's letter. What he had to tell her would be better said in person, and he wasn't looking forward to his conversation with his betrothed. Nevertheless, he had to make clear to her how their marriage would work. He had no intention of being ruled by a slip of a woman. Neither his father nor any of his recently married friends could make a move without their wives' permission. That would not happen to him. "What can we expect this evening?"

The breeze had died and the air was thick with humidity. So much for his collar and cravat.

"From what I understand, it will be something along the lines of a soirée."

No dancing, that was good. The pain in his testicles had dimmed to a dull ache, but he didn't want to engage in a lot of movement. Thank God Eugénie had been hampered by her skirts and her diminutive size, and at least she hadn't had another weapon.

A piece of advice Marcus had given Will before he left England nagged at him. Ah yes. His friend had said that women in this part of the world were proficient with knives. A trickle of sweat ran down his back. Surely Eugénie didn't know how to use a dagger. Despite her French accent and temper, she'd been raised as a well-bred Englishwoman. Yet so had Lady Marsh, and according to her husband, she was more than proficient. Perhaps some rethinking of how to approach Eugénie might be in order, or he'd never sleep well again.

"If you're done grimacing to yourself," Andrew said, "we should be going."

Will stood slowly, taking inventory of his parts. All good. "I'm ready."

They departed the hotel, then climbed back up the Ninety-Nine Steps. Though why it was called that when there were one hundred and three of them, Will didn't know. They'd soon wear a path so deep the bricks would need replacing.

He hated hills. Why was it that all his tutors thought hiking up and down mountains was the only way to exercise a boy? A good ride would have done just as well and have been far less painful. When he thought of all the boots he'd worn out, his father had probably paid the local cobbler enough to retire early in style.

It didn't matter how lovely they looked at a distance, or the grandness of the view, he'd be happy if he never saw one again. Once his family had moved down from the Lake District to Watford, he promised himself he'd never climb another hill. Now here he was on an island with nothing but mountainous terrain.

Once Will was married and returned to England, his father would expect him to take up residence at the heir's estate outside of Keswick, in Cumberland, in a house surrounded by hills. That had been another reason to put off marrying for as long as possible. If ever a man required a brandy, it was him, now.

When they reached the top of the steps, Andrew turned in the opposite direction from Wively House. It was then Will realized that Whitecliff House was separated only by the stair street from where his betrothed lived. Andrew and Will were admitted to an elegant salon with windows open to the sea breeze. As Will surveyed the room, he almost didn't recognize the elegant young lady whose glossy chestnut curls shone beneath the glow of the candles as his affianced wife.

Her lips tilted enchantingly as she gazed up at a giant of a man who appeared several years older than Will and had the squarest jaw he'd ever seen.

When the gentleman returned her smile, anger of a type Will hadn't known before surged through him and he wanted to knock the other man's white teeth down his throat.

"Wively?"

He tore his eyes away from Eugénie and the other gentleman and attended Andrew, who stood next to an older couple.

"Mrs. Whitecliff, allow me to introduce my friend, Lord Wively. Wively, my future in-laws, Mr. and Mrs. Whitecliff."

Will bowed over the lady's hand, then shook her husband's. Will's gaze strayed again to Eugénie.

"My lord?"

He jerked his attention back to the couple. He'd apparently missed a question from Mrs. Whitecliff. What the deuce was wrong with him? "Excuse me."

"No need to explain, my lord." Mr. Whitecliff gave a bark of laughter. "Eugénie's quite in her looks this evening."

"Yes, sir." There was no denying that.

Will had been staring at her like a besotted fool. If she'd been lovely before, she was dazzling in the silk gown that brought a sparkle to her skin and revealed every curve of her lush form. A single pearl hung suspended below each exquisite ear on a thin gold wire, calling attention to her graceful neck. Every movement of a pearl made him want to catch it between his teeth, then slowly run his tongue over her shell-shaped ear. He could still taste her warm skin.

Soon. Somehow he'd have to discover a way to marry her without delay.

As he stood with Andrew and the Whitecliffs, Eugénie still hadn't even acknowledged Will's presence. Although, by the way she seemed to notice everyone but him, she knew he was there. Did she really think he'd allow her to ignore him? She smiled at the man again. *The minx.* If that kept up, he might drag her out of the room.

"You are a lucky man," Mr. Whitecliff said, once more interrupting Will's thoughts. "Not as lucky as Andrew here, but I'll have to admit to being partial."

Before Will could think of a response, Miss Whitecliff came to join them. She tucked her small hand in Andrew's arm, unlike Will's betrothed, who was too engrossed with another man to greet him. Cicely's face glowed as she looked up at Grayson. That rankled, and Will had had enough of Eugénie's Turkish treatment. It was time she knew to whom she belonged.

He inclined his head to Miss Whitecliff, who gave him a tight smile, before he strode over to stand behind Eugénie, so close her skirts brushed his breeches, and he had a view of the soft swell of her creamy bosom. Though she still ignored him, her shoulders straightened. He lifted his hand and twisted one of the wispy curls on her neck around his finger. The rise and fall of her breasts quickened.

Now he had her attention. "My dear, please introduce me to your friend."

She stilled for only a moment. "My lord, may I present Mr. Bendt Henriksen, a friend of my family's. Mr. Henriksen, my *fiancé*, Lord Wivenly."

Will drew her possessively against his body. It may not have been proper, but he wasn't in London, and a compulsion to lay his claim on Eugénie overrode any other consideration. He started to incline his head, then remembered the custom here was to shake hands. He held out his hand to greet Mr. Henriksen. "My pleasure. I'm glad to meet any friend of my uncle's."

The man clasped Will's hand and grinned. "Good to meet you as well. I wondered who would finally catch our little Eugénie. Congratulations, my lord."

He gave a polite smile. "I count myself fortunate to win such a prize."

Eugénie sucked in a sharp breath. His smile broadened. As long as they were in company, she had no recourse but to take what he dished out. This was much more entertaining than trying to make her submit to his dictates. He slid his hand from her waist over her lush bottom and pinched just hard enough to get her attention.

She gave a satisfying little jump. "Oh!"

"Is anything wrong, my love?" Will asked with all the solicitude he could muster.

Eugénie's face was a polite mask as she turned toward him, but her eyes flashed, promising vengeance. "No, not at all. I remembered something I forgot to tell Miss Whitecliff." Eugénie curtseyed to him and Henriksen. "Please excuse me."

Will wrapped his fingers around her arm. "If Mr. Henriksen will forgive me?"

"Not at all," the Dane said. "I should pay my respects to Mrs. Wively."

"I shall accompany you, my dear."

"What," Eugénie hissed, "do you think you are doing?"

"Merely remaining close to you." Will lowered his voice so only she could hear. "I have no intention of allowing you to flirt with other men."

Even if they had apparently known her all her life.

"Indeed, my lord?" Her tone was pure challenge.

"Do not push me," he said, using clipped consonants.

She raised one haughty brow but said nothing more as they approached Andrew and his betrothed.

Miss Whitecliff slid a concerned glance at Eugénie. "Are you all right?"

Will moved his hand to her waist, and her breath hitched. "I am fine. The air is perhaps a little stifling at times."

"If you'd like," Will said, bending his head toward her, allowing his breath to lightly caress her neck, "I can take you outside."

Her body stiffened slightly, and she swallowed. "No, thank you, my lord. I shall manage here quite well."

Andrew opened his mouth as if to make a comment just as the butler called the party to dinner.

Will escorted Eugénie to the dining room and was disappointed to find himself seated at the opposite end of the table from her, on Mrs. Whitecliff's right. He'd not considered that the table arrangement would be so formal here in the West Indies.

Once the meal was completed, he sat through what seemed to be an interminable round of toasts to both him and Andrew until the other guests began to arrive. If Will hadn't known better he'd have thought it was all designed to keep him from being alone with Eugénie.

As they left the dining room, he was held up by an introduction to an older lady, allowing his affianced wife to leave the room on the arm of yet another gentleman. By the time he entered the drawing room, Eugénie, *the vixen*, was already surrounded by her court. The dolts hung on her every word. He strolled over to her, but just as he was within an arm's length of her, she moved away. At first he followed, but it didn't take him long to catch the humorous smiles and looks on the other guests' faces. Damnation. They were laughing at him. He grabbed a glass of champagne.

Half-way through the evening, Will leaned against the side of a window, his blood coming to a boiling point as Eugénie seemed to drink in every compliment the other men gave her. Each time he'd tried to bring her back under his control, she'd danced skillfully away, keeping just out of his reach as yet another person congratulated him. How many of the men had she kissed?

He'd briefly considered flirting with some of the other ladies, but, as Andrew reminded him, this was a small community, and Will was the newcomer. Nevertheless, his temper frayed more with each smile she bestowed on another gentleman.

Across the drawing room, Miss Whitecliff spoke in Eugénie's ear and the ladies left the room.

Another glass of champagne was pressed into his hand.

"If you'll take a bit of advice from one who has known her since she was a small bit of a girl," Henriksen said and waited until Will nodded. "A spirited woman is like a fast ship. She needs a light hand on the tiller. Too much and she'll have you turning in circles."

She was certainly doing that. She'd bested him at every turn. In fact, she was like no other woman he'd ever met. "Thank you."

The man took a sip of his wine. "I think your friend Mr. Grayson wants you to join him."

Will pushed himself away from the wall. Andrew stood next to the door where the ladies had made their exit. "Have a good evening, Mr. Henriksen."

"You too, my lord."

Once in the corridor, Will tried to keep the frustration from his voice, but his words still came out in a low rumble. "Where is she?"

"The ladies are waiting for us." Andrew rubbed his jaw. "You may see Miss Villaret only if you promise to behave."

Behave hell. Will's jaw tightened. "I've conducted myself perfectly well."

Andrew's brows shot up. "You've acted like a perfect jackanapes, and if you weren't so caught up in what *Viscount Wivenly* wants, you'd realize it. I'll take that as a no."

Damnation, would they all conspire to keep him from her? "I'll be fine."

"You won't say or do anything to offend her?"

Will ran a hand over his face. "I'll be the perfect gentleman."

"See that you are." Andrew frowned.

Women. They changed everything. Look at what Marcus and Rutherford had done to Beaumont by helping Serena, now Lady Beaumont flee to Paris, and now Andrew had turned on Will. Why was it the moment a man fell in love, he abandoned his friends? It damned sure wasn't going to happen to him.

Chapter 11

Eugénie waited with Cicely on the torch-lit terrace at the top of the garden. She'd seen the lines of Wivenly's face become rigid. During the evening, his eyes had grown colder as he'd glared at her, becoming more and more upset with her as the night went on. She prayed it was due to jealousy, but perhaps he thought of her merely as an object to possess. If only she hadn't been so naïve and stupid as to allow him to kiss her, none of this would be happening.

The sound of long, quick strides ringing on stone reached her just before Mr. Grayson and Wivenly arrived. His friend whispered something in Wivenly's ear, and he nodded. Yet his lips were set in a straight line. He glanced at her and smiled. If only she knew if the expression was real, but in this light, she couldn't make out what was in his eyes.

Wivenly took her hand and bowed, kissing the tips of her fingers. "Eugénie, my dear, I think we have started badly."

Well, that was the first thing he had said she agreed with, but what to do about it? "I believe you are correct, my lord."

"Let us stroll."

When she inclined her head, he held out his hand. She'd expected him to place her fingers on his arm, yet he wrapped his arm around her waist as they walked to the end of the veranda.

He leaned against the stone balustrade, turning her to face him. "The moon and stars are beautiful tonight."

Polite conversation was a good way to begin. "Yes. I have frequently admired the view."

"You are beautiful as well." The back of his hand caressed her cheek and continued down her neck.

"Thank you. It is the first time I have worn colors since Papa died." Tingling followed his fingers and she shuddered. How could she respond to him so easily when she wasn't even sure she liked him that much?

Slowly, oh so slowly, he drew her to him. Her breath came in small pants as he traced the low neckline of her bodice with one finger.

She shouldn't allow this, not if she wanted to make him realize she was serious about being treated well. Yet when she would have protested, her body responded to him, to his heat, and the memories of the other night.

Wively tilted her head up and his lips touched hers. Once again, she followed his movements, touching her tongue to his, slanting her head when he did. His hand cupped her breast and she moaned. She was in heaven.

"Who taught you how to kiss?" His voice was a low growl.

Eugénie didn't understand. He ran his tongue over the outside of her ear. She must not have heard what she thought.

"Who else has touched you?" This time his voice was rough. "As your betrothed, I have a right to know."

That, she could not mistake, but why would he think . . . ? "No one."

"Someone showed you how to kiss," he growled.

How dare he insinuate she was a not pure? She jerked

back out of his arms. "*Imbécile. Stupide! You taught me.* No one else has ever touched me."

Eugénie punched him on his shoulder as hard as she could before wrenching herself out of his arms. Glancing around, she saw Cicely at the other end of the terrace. Eugénie lifted her skirts and ran toward her friend. Tears blurred her eyes, and now she knew. He may lust after her, but he would never trust her, and without that there could be no love. What kind of life would she have with a man who would never care for her?

Will stared after Eugénie, her slippers barely making a sound as she left. *He* taught her? Impossible. She'd known what she was doing the first time he had kissed her. She'd tell him the truth one way or the other. Will let out a low roar as he started after her. Out of nowhere a fist slammed into his face, almost knocking him down. Where the devil had that come from? He whirled around, ready to fight back, when a blow to his jaw threw him off-balance.

Andrew?

Will stumbled and fought to regain his footing. "What the hell was that for?"

"You'll get another one if you don't watch your language." Andrew stood ready to go at Will again. "I thought you were going to behave. What did you do to upset Miss Villaret so much that *my betrothed* had to go after her?"

Will rubbed his chin. He'd need more ice. "I asked her who she'd been with before me."

Andrew stared at him as if Will had lost his mind. "I never knew you could be such an addle-brained idiot."

"It was clear she'd had experience." Will wasn't giving up yet. He had to be correct. "Since I'm marrying her, I have a right to know."

"If we hadn't been friends for so long," Andrew said almost conversationally, "I'd pummel you to within an inch of your life."

"I don't know why you're blaming me."

Andrew started toward Will as if he'd strike him again, then stopped. "You dunderheaded clodpole. Miss Villaret had *never* been kissed, *never* been touched before you."

"How would you know?" He didn't believe it. The way she responded to him was too passionate to have been her first time.

"Miss Whitecliff confided in me because she was concerned you were a threat to her friend."

"She must be . . ."

Andrew's body tensed, and suddenly Will rejected the fleeting thought that Miss Whitecliff had lied to Andrew. As if a hot-air balloon had descended with a crash, his anger and self-righteous rage deserted him. He had enough sisters that he could imagine what their reactions would be if a man falsely accused them of dallying. All his breath left him as he finally admitted to himself, he'd wronged her this time in a way she might never forgive.

He raked his fingers through his hair. "Oh God, what have I done?"

"I don't even know if you can repair the damage you've caused." Andrew glanced back at a lit path for a moment before fixing Will with a glare. "What's got into you? It's not like you haven't known enough women. Every time you're around Miss Villaret, you"—he shook his head in disgust—"act like a buffle-headed clunch."

Will scrubbed his hands over his face. What *was* happening to him? It was as if she made him lose his mind. Did his mother forget to tell him that madness ran in the family? "I don't know. I've never met anyone like her. I can't keep my hands off her. I'm envious of any man she even looks at, but I can't seem to be at all civil to her. It's not like me."

"I can't tell you what's wrong either. I've never seen you lose your self-control where a woman was concerned." Andrew's mouth tightened. "You'll have to learn how to treat her, or you're going to have one hell of a marriage, if she'll agree to marry you at all."

Not marrying her was not a choice. If their families ever discovered what he'd done . . . Somehow Will had to make up with her, but his mind was completely blank. "I don't know what to do."

"How would you gain the good graces of another lady?"

Despite himself, Will smiled. "You mean a female I wanted to bed?"

His friend cast a glance toward the heavens. "If you have to think of it as bedding her, then yes. Provided, that is, you want to marry Eugénie."

Oh, Will definitely *wanted* her in his bed, but he'd never thought in terms of *wanting* to marry. After he discovered her identity, he'd decided he *was required* to marry her. Yet even when he'd thought she'd been a bit free with her favors, he still *intended* to wed her. Getting in her good graces would be hard, considering he'd never been there in the first place.

He'd do what he always did when a lady was miffed. "I'll start by sending her flowers."

"Then do it. Lots of them."

The only problem was, Eugénie was different. Will wasn't quite sure how that was, but he sensed she would not respond like most women. "Do you think it will work with her? Perhaps I should talk—"

"No," Andrew said in a tone that sounded suspiciously like an order. "You are not to go near her until she allows it."

Will's cravat tightened as sweat beaded his brow. That could be a long, long time. What if his aunt started asking questions? If only he could marry the vixen immediately and be done with it. Of course, even if he'd had the means to do that, he'd probably find a knife stuck in him. Something told him if Eugénie didn't already carry a dagger, she would very soon, and she damned sure wouldn't hesitate to use it on him.

* * *

The morning following the disaster with his betrothed, Will sent his groom to the flower market. As he was tying his neckcloth, Griff returned empty-handed.

This was not good. "Where are the flowers?"

Griff fiddled with his hat. "Ain't got a market hereabouts."

Will almost rolled his eyes. His groom wasn't usually so dense. "Why didn't you go to the florist?"

"Ain't got one of them either."

They must have something. Will ran a hand through his hair. What the deuce was going on? He'd seen a flower arrangement at the Whitecliffs'. "I need to find a bouquet."

"Sorry, my lord. I looked all over town and didn't see any at all."

Damn and blast. "Get your breakfast and meet me down at the warehouse. I'll ask around."

"Yes, my lord." Griff bowed and left the bedchamber.

Will finished his cravat before strolling into the parlor, where he found Andrew already digesting a good portion of fruit. Will strolled to the sideboard and inspected the offerings. "There is apparently no flower market in town."

Andrew glanced up with a smug expression. "That is what I was given to understand."

Will paused in the process of selecting a baked egg. "Then where am I to find flowers for Miss Villaret?"

A grin split Andrew's face. "You have to go to someone's house and ask to be allowed to pick a bouquet from their garden."

The egg slipped off the serving spoon Will held. "Ask a private person for flowers? I've never heard of such a thing."

Andrew nodded. "There is a woman in the Queen's Quarter who raises roses and lilies, among other plants. I have her direction. You may go immediately after breakfast. I was told it is better to pick the blooms in the morning."

Will retrieved the egg and took a piece of Dum bread stuffed with cheese. "I'll send Griff."

"You'll go yourself," Andrew said, "or you won't have them at all. The woman is particular about who she sells them to."

"Give me the directions." Will heaved an exasperated sigh. Was nothing easy when it came to Eugénie? He finished his breakfast as Andrew explained how to find the residence. An hour later, after tromping up a hill, losing himself in the jumble of streets, and having to ask directions from an old man who gave Will a knowing look. Half-way up the hill called Queen's Quarter he finally knocked on the door of a house quite a bit smaller than his aunt's but not as tiny as others he'd seen. It appeared to have only one floor as opposed to the multiple levels of the Wivenly and Whitecliff houses. Eugénie had better forgive him after making him go through all of this.

An older woman answered the door and Will handed her his card. "Good morning, ma'am. I am Lord Wivenly. I was advised you might be willing to sell me a bouquet of flowers."

"I might." She rubbed her finger over the raised letters on the card. "What do you need them for?"

He resisted the urge to run a finger under his collar. "My betrothed and I had a slight disagreement, and I thought to sweeten her."

The lady held the door open. "I'm Mrs. Rordan. What is the name of your betrothed?"

"Miss Villaret de Joyeuse."

"Eugénie? I didn't know she'd got engaged." The old woman squinted her eyes and stared at Will. "You must be related to her step-father, but I don't see much of a resemblance."

"Um, no. My great-uncle took after his mother's side of the family."

Mrs. Rordan nodded. "Well, if you managed to get Eugénie's back up, you'll need something nice."

Managed to distress her? When was she not upset?

The lady turned and started shuffling down a corridor. "Don't just stand there, young fellow. Follow me."

Will stepped in and closed the front door. "Yes, ma'am."

She led him out the back door to a sloped garden filled with flowers.

"I don't know what you did to get yourself into trouble. Seems like most young men are worthless fribbles when it comes to women, but I'll try to help you out." Mrs. Rordan grabbed what looked like curved scissors from a basket. "I've known Eugénie since she was a child, and if anyone deserves to be happy, she does."

Will nodded and followed the older woman around the garden. By the end of an hour, she had cut several flowers and a vine with small white blooms, and he had learned more about the island, such as where he could find the best fans and handkerchiefs and that the reason for the tension between the Danish and English populations was England's law prohibiting the slave trade.

He also discovered more about his betrothed. He'd not known, for example, how much time she spent with the missionaries, teaching the slave children to read and do their figures. Unfortunately, none of what he learned would help him out of the hole he'd dug for himself.

Mrs. Rordan pointed to the lily. "This will tell her you're sorry." She wrapped string around the stems and trimmed the ends. "Here you go. I don't want to see you back here until you need flowers for the wedding."

He held out a purse to Mrs. Rordan, which she refused. "Use your money to buy a ring."

That's what he'd forgotten. "Thank you." He held his arm out and escorted her back into the house. "I shall give your regards to my Miss Villaret."

"You'll give her my love and tell her I look forward to seeing her on Sunday."

"I'll do that." He bowed. "A pleasure to meet you, Mrs. Rordan."

"Harrumph. Go now before they wilt."

As Will turned, the door closed behind him. It occurred to him that other than the small pieces of information Mrs. Rordan let drop, and the fact that Eugénie was an innocent who kissed like a wanton, and had a temper, which seemed to be reserved solely for him, he really didn't know much about his betrothed at all. Though she was becoming more and more intriguing. Who was this woman he planned to marry?

Will walked back down the hill toward town, then cut over to a street leading to the area where Eugénie lived. Finally he reached the front of Wively House. The door swung open before he knocked. The butler stood before him. "Bates, I am here to see Miss Villaret."

"I'm sorry to say," the butler said in a tone that was polite but firm, "she is not home to you, my lord."

Will should have expected this. He swallowed his retort and gave the bouquet to Bates. "Please give her these and tell her they bear a message."

The butler bowed. "I will do that, my lord."

The door closed. Will heaved a sigh. Apparently she really wasn't going to make this easy for him. Then again, neither would his sisters have. No matter what, he would not be reduced to groveling.

Chapter 12

Marisole scratched lightly on Eugénie's door. "Miss, Lord Wively brought these for you."

Eugénie glanced up from her book at the bunch of flowers, already in a vase. One pale yellow rose nestled beneath a lily; the rest of the arrangement was made up of pink roses in full bloom. Old Blush unless she missed her guess. A few closed buds and a jasmine vine added white flowers and greenery. Purity, forgiveness, new love, and amiability, but did he know what the flowers stood for? "Did he say anything?"

"Yes, miss. Mr. Bates said his lordship said there was a message in the flowers."

Her heart lightened as she brushed her nose against the blossoms, taking in their spicy scents. He must have gone to Mrs. Rordan and told her they were engaged and that they'd had an argument. She was the only one who had flowers like these. No man had ever given Eugénie flowers before, and he'd had a long walk to Mrs. Rordan's house to get them. Perhaps he truly was sorry he'd treated her badly and wanted to make up with her.

Eugénie smiled and wondered what her old friend would have said to Wivenly. At least he was trying to make amends. Perhaps she should forgive him. Cicely said Andrew had a talk with her betrothed last night after he'd hit Wivenly.

"The next time Lord Wivenly comes, I will receive him."

Marisole's forehead wrinkled. "Are you sure, miss?"

"Yes, positive." Eugénie didn't think he'd visit again today, but surely tomorrow he'd come to apologize.

The next day, Marisole brought a package. Eugénie opened it to find a prettily painted fan of chicken skin on delicately wrought ivory. She searched for a note and found none. "Did his lordship not ask to remain?"

"It was sent from the modiste directly, miss."

Perhaps Wivenly was afraid of being rejected again. She vowed to give him another day, but the morning brought a package of bonbons, the day after a shawl of Norwich silk, and the following day, lace-edged linen handkerchiefs. Still no notes or anything from him, and he'd had them all delivered by the shops.

Eugénie paced the parlor where she'd waited all week for him to come. He wasn't a weak man who was afraid of her. Did he think he could buy her with these—these gifts? Clearly he didn't care enough about her to bring them in person, and if he didn't care, she would not either. In fact, she would not marry him. No one but Cicely and Wivenly knew that he had kissed her. He could say his father forbade the match. She gathered his presents into a bundle. If he didn't visit tomorrow, she'd send them to him at the Queen, even the flowers, as he'd not meant what he'd said at all.

Will strode down the length of the parlor and back again for at least the thirtieth time. He had waited all week to be summoned by Eugénie, but had not even received a note to either thank him or refuse his gifts. Why hadn't he heard from her? One would have thought that after six days of peace offerings she'd relent and invite him to visit, at least for tea. This wasn't going at all as he'd expected.

He fingered the ring in his pocket. It wasn't the family heirloom he'd intended for his bride, but it would suit her beautifully, if he ever got the chance to see her again.

There was also the continuing problem of how to wed her. He'd consulted a Danish lawyer. Eugénie was correct. They needed permission from both guardians for her to marry. The solicitor also told Will he would not be allowed to use the power of attorney from his father to give himself permission to marry Eugénie. Secondly, she wasn't being at all cooperative. Not that it mattered until he'd heard from his father. He closed his eyes, repressing a shudder. Papa would laugh himself silly when he received Will's request to wed Eugénie. At least he wasn't going to be humiliated in person.

He turned at the end of the parlor. Why the devil hadn't she sent for him? Eugénie had to be the most contrary woman he'd ever had the misfortune to meet.

"Stop pacing," Andrew ordered in an amused tone. "You are going to wear a hole in the carpet."

Will stared at his so-called friend. "It's been six days, and I haven't heard from Miss Villaret at all."

"When was the last time you went to the house, hmm?" Andrew raised a brow.

If he didn't watch it, Will would wipe the smug expression from Andrew's face. "Six days ago," Will muttered, "when I tried to give her the flowers."

Now that he'd said it out loud, it sounded a bit ridiculous, but he'd never had to bring a woman round before.

"Six days?" Andrew had his I-can't-believe-you're-so-daft look on his face. "Did it not occur to you that after your behavior at the soirée, she might expect a little in-person groveling from you?"

No, he'd thought she didn't want to see him. "After I was turned away at the door, I had the presents sent to her." Will ran his hand through his hair. Maybe there was something to be said for being chased. "I've been waiting for some sign she's over being angry with me, and I've run out of things to buy."

"Sent? By the shop?"

Will nodded.

"You have turned into a dullard." Andrew shook his head slightly in disgust. "You were supposed to have presented yourself to her to have a peal rung over your head."

Why did no one tell Will these things? "I've never had to do that before. Baubles always worked in the past."

"Yes, with widows and high-flyers. Not a woman you mean to marry."

Will wanted to kick something or put his hand through a wall. "Why didn't *you* say anything?"

"In case you haven't noticed"—Andrew closed his eyes briefly—"I've been planning my own wedding, which will take place on Tuesday, if the vicar shows." His voice softened a bit. "Truthfully, I didn't realize you and Eugénie hadn't made up until Cicely mentioned it earlier."

"Oh God." Will collapsed on the chair. "What a mull I've made of it all."

Andrew pressed a glass of brandy in Will's hand. "I'd say that about sums it up."

He'd go to his betrothed first thing tomorrow.

"There is one other thing you should know. Eugénie is deuced upset that you haven't been by."

Damn. He'd have to go get more flowers. Mrs. Rordan wouldn't be happy. Now he'd have to grovel to two women. He took a slug of the brandy as his friend for once said nothing. "Congratulations on your wedding. I'll stand up with you, of course."

Andrew smiled. "I wouldn't have anyone else. By the by, I'll be moving to Whitecliff's house after the ceremony. Cicely and I will live there until we go back to England."

Will nodded. "I understand."

They were quiet for several minutes, then Andrew said, "What exactly does your father's power of attorney say about the Wively children?"

"The children?" Will didn't understand.

"You are aware that Eugénie has sisters still here?"

"Yes, of course." He rubbed a hand over his face. "What of them?"

"It occurs to me that you might not want to leave everyone in St. Thomas when you sail back home."

He hadn't had time to think about the rest of the family, yet he should. In fact, if he hadn't been wallowing in self-pity, he'd have gone to Wively House to discuss the situation with his aunt. "I have the power to make the arrangements, but the widow must agree." He set his tumbler down, splashing brandy over his hand. "I'll talk to Aunt Sidonie."

Though first he'd have to deal with the bane of his existence, Eugénie Villaret de Joyeuse.

The next morning, which happened to be the seventh day since he'd seen her—Will was sure there was something biblical about that—he marched up the hill to Eugénie's house. Knocked on the door and was admitted by the butler. Bates's countenance barely registered any emotion but managed to portray his doubt about the advisability of Will even being here.

Will rolled his shoulders. Even the servants seemed to know he was on probation. "I'm here to see Miss Villaret."

The butler bowed. "I shall inquire as to whether Miss is at home."

How was he going to climb out of this cavernous hole he'd dug for himself? After a while, he opened his pocket watch. Quarter past ten. He'd been left to wait for over twenty minutes. Summoning up all the information he had about women, he'd be lucky if she saw him at all.

"My lord," Bates announced, "Miss Villaret will see you in the blue parlor."

A few moments later he entered a small room painted the

same color as the ocean, to find her staring out one of the many windows. On a chaise were all the presents he'd sent during the past week, including the wilted flowers. A heavy weight lodged in his stomach. She was going to try to jilt him.

"Lord Wivenly, miss," Bates announced before backing himself out of the room. "I shall be in the corridor if you require assistance."

When the door closed, Eugénie turned. The tip of her nose was red and her eyes puffy. If she was this distraught, Will might still have a chance. He opened his mouth and shut it again. That part of his body had already got him into enough trouble with her.

"My lord." She clasped her hands before meeting his gaze. "I have given our situation much thought, and I believe it would be better if we did not marry."

The urge to drag her into his arms flooded him, but he forced himself to remain where he was. After a few moments, his voice sounded rusty as he asked, "Better for whom?"

"Both of us." Her sad, brandy-colored gaze focused on a place over his left shoulder. "It is clear we do not get along."

They'd be getting along a lot better if she'd been the widow he'd first thought her to be. Her chin became mulish as he stared at her and tried not to do or say anything stupid. "We . . . I have had some misunderstandings with regard to you. Given time, I'm sure we can work them out."

She stared at him as if he was daft. "From the beginning you have had a bad opinion of me." Eugénie glanced away for a moment. Her voice trembled. "Though you have sent many lovely things in the past week, you have said nothing of changing your belief."

Bad opinion was not exactly true, but she wouldn't look at it that way. If God was supposed to protect fools, he'd better start now. "I acted hastily in forming my estimation." Will swallowed. "I'm sorry."

"Please"—she shook her head slowly—"I cannot keep your gifts. Take them and go."

The knuckles on Eugénie's fingers were white. He couldn't be wrong. She must care for him at least a little to be so troubled.

Another tack was needed. "We must marry." When she didn't respond, he played his trump card. "Or have you forgotten I ruined you?"

All the color drained from her face, but her stance was still defiant. "A few kisses . . . No one knows."

Will beat down the primitive warrior begging him to take her in his arms. Still, he couldn't stop himself from stepping closer. "Even one kiss would have been enough, but you know as well as I, it was more than that."

She shook her head again. "The fact remains, I am still a virgin, and no one need ever know about the night we met."

Every nerve and sinew in him braced to do battle. He still wasn't sure why it mattered so much that she belong to him. He just knew it did. The same way he knew he'd do everything it took to make her understand she was his. If Eugénie thought she was getting out of this betrothal without a fight, she could think again. He raised a brow. "Grayson knows, your friend Miss Whitecliff knows, and your mother will know."

That did it.

Her jaw clenched and the fire leaped into her eyes as they snapped back to him. "You would threaten me with exposure?"

Will stepped closer. "No, but believe me when I tell you, mothers always know." She opened her lovely, rose-colored lips, and he held up his hand. "Don't ask me how they do it. I've never figured it out." His next pace brought him within arm's reach of her. "Perhaps when you are a mother"—*of our children*, he added silently—"you will tell me."

"Do you not understand?" Tears filled her beautiful

brown eyes. "I cannot marry a man who thinks I am a loose woman to be easily had."

He rubbed his forehead. Well, he hadn't expected she was going to make this easy for him. "I realized days ago that you are not. Grayson told me the truth, and I've been trying to make it up to you ever since. That"—he waved his hand at the items on the chaise—"is what those were about."

"*Stupid!* Don't you see?" She brushed angrily at a tear trickling down her cheek. "You should not have had to ask your friend. You should have believed *me*."

Good, better her yelling at him than weeping, though she seemed to be accomplishing both at once. "I *do* believe you."

"What about the next time?" She strode around the parlor, her skirts whirling agitatedly around her slim ankles. "Mr. Grayson won't always be around to assure you I am telling the truth. I cannot go through my whole life under a cloud. Always being suspected by you of doing something I did not do." She stopped. "You made up your mind about me when we met."

Will opened his mouth to deny her accusation, but the words froze on his tongue. She was right. He'd sized her up and had decided what role she would play in his life. Then, when he'd discovered he was wrong, she'd turned his world on end. Yet his treatment of her hadn't changed. The real question was why he'd so stubbornly clung to his first impressions. He'd have to figure that out later, but now he needed to stop her from backing out of their engagement.

"I have an idea." He glanced at the gifts, and lied. "We will spend time learning about each other, then if you still find you cannot bring yourself to marry me, I will release you."

Eugénie eyed him suspiciously. "How long?"

"Until my father answers my request for your hand."

"That could be months!" She began pacing again.

He could understand her concern if she would miss a Season waiting for him to convince her, but—"Did you have other plans?" Another man? He damn well couldn't say that. "An urgent . . ."

She turned and glared.

"I mean—" Will tugged at his cravat, which had unaccountably tightened. Tidwell was going to murder him. "This seems to be a fairly quiet place."

"Very well. Have it your way." Eugénie picked up the bundle. "You may still have these back."

A kernel of an idea began to form, and he gave her his most charming smile. "Would you walk out with me tomorrow?"

She pulled her lower lip between her small white teeth. "For what purpose?"

"So that I can begin getting to know you, and you may learn about me."

It was several moments before she answered. "Nine in the morning, before it becomes too hot."

Will bowed, plucking the collection of presents from her as he rose. He'd be damned if he'd wait until the morrow. "I shall see you later."

True to his word, Bates stood right outside the parlor. He escorted Will to the front door. "Good luck, my lord."

"Thank you, Bates." Will donned his hat. He was going to need all the good fortune he could get to change her mind. "I shall return in a couple of hours."

After he visited the flower lady again, and found some pretty paper to wrap her presents in, that was.

Nathan Wively stared at the mulattress and the huge black man. He had too many questions. Who were they, how could they help him escape, and what the devil was he supposed to do for them? "You have the advantage of me."

The woman grinned softly. "I apologize, sir. I am Miss

Elizabeth Marshall, and this"—she gestured to the man—"is my betrothed, Mr. Joseph Conrad. You naturally wish to know more about us."

Nathan nodded and pulled out a chair from the table so Miss Marshall could have a seat. Conrad stood behind her, as if guarding the lady from any harm. Nathan shook his head. If only they knew how weak he really was.

Miss Marshall folded her hands calmly in her lap and glanced up at her affianced husband for a moment before turning back to Nathan. "I am from Tortola and have been a free woman all my life. My father ensured that I had funds to do what I wished." She grinned. "Within reason, of course. I have a small but profitable millinery business. Because my mother was a slave, I have devoted my life to helping others become free."

Nathan glanced at Conrad. His countenance remained impassive.

"Mr. Conrad and I met when I was on a mission to St. Croix." A soft smile dawned on her face as the man placed a large hand on her shoulder, and she patted it with her much smaller one. "He pretended not to be able to read and write so the missionaries would bring him to the church. I soon discovered his deception."

Conrad shook his head sadly. "She was too intelligent. I thought she would tell them."

"You did not!" she exclaimed, insulted.

A large smile cracked his face. "I was at your mercy."

Nathan had never seen a darker-skinned person blush before. In fact, it might only be the chagrined look on her face. "Go on, please, Miss Marshall."

"We started a correspondence, and after several months, Mr. Conrad informed me he'd earned enough from side jobs to buy his freedom. He is very stubborn and would not allow me to contribute."

The good humor left Conrad's mien. "I may be a slave, but I have my honor."

"Yes, my love. It was not a criticism but merely an explanation. As I was saying, his owner had agreed to allow Mr. Conrad his freedom for a sum certain. Unfortunately, the contract was not in writing, and when the old man died, the son refused to allow Mr. Conrad to purchase his freedom. Instead he was sold to the owner of this plantation, Monsieur Leyritz." She glanced at her betrothed again. "I approached Monsieur about purchasing Mr. Conrad, but the man set the price ridiculously high, unless I agreed to—" She paused for a moment, and Nathan could swear she was blushing again. "I'm sorry, my dear."

"There is no need," Conrad said, his Dutch accent more pronounced than it had been before. "You are correct that the man asks too much." He took her hand, holding it as if it were a fragile piece of glass. "It was to force you into a type of slavery."

Miss Marshall cleared her throat. "We have decided our only recourse is for Mr. Conrad to escape to Tortola, where he will be allowed to live as a free man and we can marry."

Nathan glanced from one to the other. "I take it that is where I come in?"

"Yes." Miss Marshall nodded. "We need your assistance in hiring a ship to take us to one of the British islands. I do not need your money."

Nathan felt his lips curl up. "That's a good thing, Miss Marshall, for I haven't any. Nor any of my possessions other than these clothes. In fact, how did you know I was here?"

"Pirate attacks are not as common as they once were, and the news that it was your ship spread quickly." She slid a look at Conrad before continuing. "When Mr. Conrad discovered a white man was being held here, he smuggled a letter out to me." Miss Marshall gave Nathan a rueful smile. "I saw you once at the Moravian mission on St. Thomas with your eldest daughter. I came right away, hoping to find you alive."

Nathan's throat tightened. Good Lord, how he missed his wife and children. If his captors hurt them, he'd kill the blackguards. "My family, do you know if they are all right?"

Miss Marshall's lips formed a thin line. "It is only talk, and I cannot confirm any of it, but it is said that your manager is stealing from the business and trying to get your wife to sell."

His hands curled into fists. He'd kill Howden! "I need to return immediately. How soon can we leave?"

"I understand you were quite badly injured."

He hadn't been that close to death. At least he didn't think he had. "Just a broken head and leg. Nothing out of the ordinary."

Conrad barked a laugh, but the woman just smiled softly. She was the most restful person he'd ever seen, particularly under these circumstances.

"We must assess your ability to travel." Her voice was low and vaguely comforting. "It will not serve any of us if you were to sicken."

"I quite agree." Nathan grinned. "Shall I stand and skip around the chamber?"

"Can you?"

She had him there. "Probably not, but I can walk the length of the room several times before I tire."

"We were going to take you to a small harbor, but you'd have to cross over the mountain." She shook her head thoughtfully. "It will not work."

Conrad moved next to the door. "Someone is coming. We need to go before anyone sees us, but will return later today or tomorrow." He furrowed his brows. "Hopefully with a better plan."

The couple left as quietly and quickly as they'd entered, and he got into bed.

Not three minutes later, the woman Nathan had decided was the housekeeper, entered with a dirty-looking white man. She placed a tray down on the table. "Tell Willy here if you need help getting up."

"I think I can manage, but thank you." He rose, steadying himself against the bed for a moment, more for effect than need. "Do you know when I'll be released?"

"Can't tell you. The monsieur's guest"—she pronounced it mon-sure-e—"didn't tell me. You're in no state to go anywhere any way."

Nathan smiled to himself. "Yes, you're probably correct." He walked with deliberately hesitant steps to the table and sat heavily. "Thank you for taking care of me."

"After the first scare, you weren't a bit of bother." She left the room, taking the man with her.

Nathan removed the lid, inhaling the fragrant stew. Wherever he was being held, the cook was definitely French. That, unfortunately, didn't tell him a damn blasted thing, and he'd forgotten to ask Miss Marshall. He dug into the food. Regaining his strength would be the key to his escape.

Once he'd finished eating, he strode the length of the large room and back again until the shuffling of feet could be heard in the corridor. By the time the door opened, he was in bed pretending to doze.

"There now," the housekeeper said, "what did I tell you? He's in no shape to try to leave us. You just go on back to taking care of the field slaves and let me do my work."

"Just as well," Willy replied. "I got to take a load over to Le Marin in the morning. I'll be gone a couple of days."

"That's clear across the island!"

"Don't I know it," he answered in a rueful voice. "That's why I needed to make sure Mr. Wively ain't got no fight in him."

"What are you goin' to do about the big Negro?"

"I got someone to put a powder in his food. He'll be down for at least a day or so."

Le Marin, Nathan formed a plan of the island in his mind. He must be on the north end of Martinique. Only a day or two sail from St. Thomas, if the winds were right. He closed his eyes, intending to sleep, but rest wouldn't come as he tried to pin his location more accurately. The only small harbors were on the west. Which placed him due north of Saint-Pierre, the island's major port, where a gentleman owed him a favor. Provided his escape was successful, he'd be home in less than a week.

Chapter 13

Eugénie stared after Wivenly as he strode from the parlor with a jaunty step. Her meeting with him hadn't gone at all as she had planned. When Wivenly stood close to her, his scent, very male mixed with something spicy, overwhelmed her common sense, and all she wanted to do was breathe him in. Perhaps if she didn't allow him so close to her, he would not be able to make her do things she didn't want to, such as kissing him. Though when he was not acting like a beast, she liked him very well.

She sank onto the window seat. Why, why, why had she agreed to his plan for them to get to know each other better?

Because you want to be near him.

The voice in her head seemed almost as if another person had spoken.

He was right about one thing. She had nothing else to occupy her time. Her younger sisters were engaged with their governess, her brother was in England, Cicely had time for nothing but her wedding, after which she'd spend most of her days and nights with Andrew, and there were currently no children to rescue.

Why couldn't Eugénie's path with Wively be as easy as her friend's?

Possibly it would be better if she learned about Wively as well. After all, it appeared she'd be stuck with him. Or perhaps she'd find he was in some way unsuitable, and she could make him leave. She refused to think about her mother discovering what he'd done with her.

A few minutes later the door opened. Thinking it was Wively returning to confuse her even more, she didn't look up.

"What," Cicely asked, "are you in such a brown study about?"

"You remember I told you I would break off my engagement to Wively." Eugénie raised her gaze to her friend and frowned. "Somehow he talked me out of it."

Cicely cocked her head to the side, appearing to be as confused as Eugénie felt. "But he took back his gifts?"

"Yes. I do not understand him at all." At this point, she didn't understand herself either.

Her friend sat next to her. "He is definitely not as easy to comprehend as Andrew. I wish I knew how to advise you."

Eugénie's lips drooped. She probably looked like the wilted flowers that had sat on the table. "He is coming tomorrow morning."

"Is he? Being gloomy won't help. I think you should tell me exactly what occurred." Cicely smiled brightly and took Eugénie's hands, squeezing them. "Yet first, what will you wear for Jeanne's birthday dinner? It must be something pretty."

"I haven't given it much thought." Eugénie didn't really want to celebrate anything this year, but Maman looked forward to it, as did the children. "I'll find something."

"Then you shall wear your yellow and cream gown, and I'll give you one of your birthday presents early." Cicely rose gracefully.

Eugénie sighed. Everything about her friend was charming and bubbly.

"Come with me," Cicely said. "We'll have luncheon on the terrace at my house."

"Wouldn't you rather dine with Andrew?"

"I love spending time with him, but at present, I'd rather be with you." She grabbed Eugénie's hand and tugged. "We still have two weddings to plan."

"It will take months for mine to come about." She raised one shoulder in a shrug. "He must receive permission from the earl to marry me."

Cicely stopped and slowly raised one blond brow. "Eugénie Marie Louise Villaret de Joyeuse, you haven't told him you can marry on Tortola, have you?"

"Non." She lifted her chin. "And unless he can tell me why he is so determined to marry me, I shall not. He would carry me off just so he could have his way."

Her friend raised her eyes to the ceiling for a moment. "He'll be angry when he finds out."

"To me it matters not one whit." Eugénie snapped her fingers. "He wasn't even interested in spending more time with me today."

Did he know nothing about women? How were they going to learn about each other if he kept leaving?

"Well, in that case," Cicely said, linking her arm with Eugénie's, "you have my permission to make him suffer."

"Merci beaucoup." Her heart lightened. "You are very good to me. We will make a wonderful campaign against Viscount Wively."

Will had a quick meal at the Parrot before his meeting with the solicitor who'd promised to take a look at Uncle Nathan's will. With any luck at all, there would be a way to marry Eugénie without having to wait for his father's permission. He paid his shot, then made his way to Wimmel-skasts Gade, which the English called Back Street, and the office of Mr. Olesen, *Advokat*. Will left a quarter hour later with a recommendation that Eugénie file a suit in the court to allow her to become emancipated. Waiting on his father would take less time, assuming the letters were not delayed or lost.

He arrived at Mrs. Rordan's house and knocked on the door.

"Lord Wivenly." She narrowed her eyes. "What brings you back so soon?"

His hands started to sweat. There was nothing like being taken to task by an old woman one barely knew to make one feel six again. He cleared his suddenly phlegmy throat. "Apparently I did not follow through as I should have."

She stood back, allowing him to enter the house. "Sounds like what my nephew did when he courted his young woman."

Breathing a sigh of relief, he followed her through the house, then opened the garden door for her. At least he wasn't the only one who had problems with women. "I trust you have many great-nieces and -nephews now."

"No, not at all." Mrs. Rordan picked up the basket and handed it to Will. "She rejected him. He was so heartbroken he went off to sea." Pausing, she tugged on a pair of leather gloves. "That was over twenty years ago. I haven't seen him since."

"I'm sorry." Will tugged on his neckcloth. He must speak with Tidwell about the amount of starch in the damned thing.

Mrs. Rordan waved her hand. "He's probably better off. She married for position and has since turned to fat." She clipped a pink rose, placing it in the basket. "There aren't enough bonbons in the West Indies to make up for an empty bed."

"Did her husband die?"

"No, he'd rather sleep elsewhere." She cut a few more flowers. "And the whole island knows it."

Will found himself feeling bad for the woman whose husband cheated on her. Yet, hadn't he planned to do the same to Eugénie? Though now he knew he would not, could not be unfaithful to her. When had that changed? "It cannot be a comfortable position for her."

Turning, Mrs. Rordan regarded him with a steady gaze. "Not for any woman."

Will held out his arm to escort her back to the house. "I quite agree."

A saucy smile appeared on the old lady's face, and Will could see vestiges of the beauty she'd been. "Eugénie is a lucky young woman."

"As I am a fortunate man." He was surprised to find he meant it. If only his affianced wife would concur.

Instead of going back toward town, Will skirted Denmark Hill to another step street—the place seemed full of them— ending up near Wively House. He was about to knock on the door when a movement caught his eye. Eugénie and Miss Whitecliff stood by the lower gate. Eugénie kissed her friend on the cheek, then turned to cross the step street to her own house. As soon as the Whitecliff gate closed, a man Will had never seen before darted out of his hiding place behind the bushes lining the street, grabbing Eugénie. *What the hell?* He dropped the flowers and ran.

An arm as strong as iron caught Eugénie around the middle, knocking all the breath out of her. She struggled to get air back into her lungs again, making ready to scream, when a gloved hand covered her mouth. *Mon Dieu.* Biting down on the gloves, she kicked her legs back, but her skirts hampered the movement. Then she threw back her head, hitting his chest, but it was more like wood. Perhaps if she made enough trouble, he'd drop her. She squirmed and struggled as best she could, but he just laughed.

"There is no one around here this time of day to come to your rescue, and I'm being paid far too much gold to deliver you."

Gold? Who would pay . . . ? *Slavers*. Had someone decided to stop her from saving the children by abducting her?

She elbowed him in what felt like a rib, yet he didn't loosen his hold at all.

She could not disappear. It would kill her mother.

Suddenly the blackguard's hold slackened, and Eugénie slipped enough for her feet to touch the stone steps. She screamed as loudly as she could. When the sickening sound of crunching bone reached her, she glanced over her shoulder. Wivenly stood a few steps up, making him even with the giant. He ducked, but droplets of blood sprayed out, landing on the stairs and bushes. Oh God, she prayed it wasn't Wivenly's.

Eugénie had to do something. He'd never win against that *canaille*! But what? If only she had her dagger, she'd stab the scoundrel who tried to kidnap her. She must begin carrying it everywhere, even to Cicely's house. The only thing she had was a hat pin.

A very long, strong hat pin.

It might not help much, but anything was better than nothing. Pulling it out, she moved behind and to the side of the giant.

"Eugénie, no."

She heard Wivenly bellow as she pierced the man's armpit with the pin.

The blackguard roared and reached out for her, but other hands pulled her away. People started filling the street and the thug fled, pushing men out of his way.

Her heart thudded as if it would escape the confines of her chest, and the roaring in her ears deafened her. A wave of nausea gripped her, and she started to topple, but strong arms held her up and the familiar scent of an unknown spice calmed her fear.

Wivenly.

"I've got you." His voice was gentle and calm. "You'll be all right."

She nodded against his strong chest, wanting to burrow into his warmth, wanting to feel safe again.

"You're much too quiet." He picked her up. "That can't be good."

She glanced up. His cravat had blood on it. "You're hurt."

"Not much," Wivenly replied smugly. "He got my eye, but I broke his nose."

Eugénie threw her arm around his neck, hoisting herself up a little to see the damage. If she could concentrate on him, perhaps she wouldn't have to think about what had happened. "That is going to need a beefsteak."

He grinned down at her. "Probably."

They'd reached the Whitecliffs' gate. "Take me to Cicely. I do not want Maman worrying."

"Very well." Wivenly furrowed his brow, then winced. "But we must tell her about this at some point."

Eugénie didn't want to tell Maman at all. It would worry her too much. Yet she was not so stupid as to believe that the man, or another, would not try again. And the neighbors would certainly say something to Maman or the servants. "We may discuss it after your eye is taken care of."

"Will, what the—" Andrew, stood on the stairs, glancing from her to Wivenly before opening the garden door. "You're going to have a nice bullace."

She wondered what Andrew was not saying. "Yes, but he broke the brute's nose."

"That doesn't surprise me in the least." He laughed. "Will's extremely handy with his fives."

"Oh no." Cicely's hand went to her lips. "Look at you. What happened? Was that you I heard screaming?"

Really, Wivenly's eye wasn't that bad. "He will be fine. We just need a beefsteak."

"No, it's you!"

For the first time, Eugénie glanced down. Her skirt had blood on it. Warm air hit her arm where her sleeve hung half off. "I am well. I felt a little faint, so Wivenly carried me."

Andrew put his arm around his betrothed. "Come, my love. Let's get them inside." He slid Wivenly a stern look. "Then they'll tell us what happened."

"Wait a moment." Cicely pointed to some shrubs beside the stairs. "What is this doing here?"

A large bouquet of pink roses lay in the top of a bush.

Wivenly shifted her in his arms and picked up the flowers, handing them to Eugénie. "These are for you. I'd just come from Mrs. Rordan's house when I saw you being abducted."

They were a little battered, but not much. She buried her nose in them, taking in the sweet scent. "Thank you. They are lovely."

What would have happened if he'd waited until morning to visit her again didn't bear thinking of. If only he could be like this all the time.

Hervé swirled the fine cognac in the glass as he stared out over the peninsula that made up one side of the harbor. He was bored and tired of waiting for Yves to bring him Eugénie. Yet it was not easy kidnapping a young woman who didn't seem to go anywhere but to the house across the step street and was never left alone when she did. Even watching her movements and those of her neighbors was not easy. There was no place to conceal oneself for any length of time, and lately there was the added irritant of a young gentleman who appeared to be courting her. Hervé took a sip, savoring the burn of the wine as it slid down his throat.

Yves strode swiftly into the room, came to a halt, and

shook his head. "We would have had her but for that young man who saw Adao snatch her."

"Where is this Adao now?"

"Where the authorities will never find him." Yves poured a glass of white wine. "Why do you not simply tell her we have her step-father, and if she wants to see him alive again, she will come with us? We can make marrying the *comte* a condition of Mr. Wively's release. Now that we have lost Shipley, one of us will act as the proxy for the *comte*."

Running a hand over his face, Hervé glared at his brother. "Not only is that crude, but how do you propose I convince her he is alive?"

His brother took another swig of wine. "Show her something that belongs to him. We are family. There is no reason for us to do away with her step-father. Naturally she will come with us."

No longer able to remain sitting, Hervé stood and walked to the windows. "I have nothing. When the pirate captain brought him to me, Wively had only the clothing on his back."

"Ah, *mon frère*." Yves smiled slowly. "You may not have a memento, but I do."

Hervé turned sharply, piercing his brother with a glare. "What?"

"His dagger. It is an original. It has his initials and his family's coat of arms on it."

That might work. "Keep watching her. For this she does not need to be completely alone, yet we must choose our moment carefully. Neither her admirer nor Sidonie can be anywhere around."

Chapter 14

An hour after the attack on Eugénie, the constable had departed with hers and Will's statements. Will reclined on a chaise in the main parlor of the lower level of the Whitecliff home with a piece of raw beefsteak over his eye and a glass of rum shrub in his hand. His betrothed sat perched on the edge of a chair next to the chaise, looking particularly fetching in a soft green gown, and ready to fly away at any moment.

Andrew and Cicely, as Will was now allowed to address her, shared the small sofa across from him.

Earlier, Josh had been sent to the hotel for a change of clothing for Will, which arrived with Tidwell. Not that Will really expected his valet to remain put. Over the years, Tidwell had developed a proprietary interest in Will's wardrobe.

Cicely had sent her lady's maid to Wivenly House on the same errand, and Eugénie's garments had arrived with a servant as well.

This was the first time Will had been in a room other than

the main ones on the upper floor, and the arrangement fascinated him. "Are all the larger houses built like this?"

"Most of them," Eugénie replied. "You have the same type of thing in England, do you not?"

"After a fashion," Will replied. "Though the nursery level is usually above the parents' chambers and there is no terrace."

"That's what it is." Andrew gave a bark of laughter. "If one wishes to escape the nursery it's much more difficult. Will is mourning lost possibilities."

"Indeed." He grinned. "Yet it would have been so easy to sneak out, it'd hardly be worth the effort. After all, the chance of being caught was half the fun."

"Cicely," Eugénie pronounced, ending all discussion of Will's childhood possibilities, "has so much space because she is a single child. I share with my three sisters and our brother."

At home, his brothers and sisters were always underfoot, but he had never seen Eugénie's sisters. Now he knew the reason. There was no need for them to pass through the main floor to do anything, not even filch from the kitchen, as it was outside. Somehow he knew he'd miss the noise and confusion.

Andrew lightly squeezed his betrothed's hand. "This is where Cicely and I shall live until we travel to England."

For the first time, Will realized there was a problem concerning where he and Eugénie would reside. He could not see them living on the children's level of Wively House. Of course, it might be time to depart for England before he married her. That thought brought him back to his immediate problem, convincing Eugénie she wanted to wed him.

She lifted the beefsteak, appearing a bit fuzzy as she peered at his eye. "It is no use. I know nothing of black eyes." She allowed the meat to flop back down. "Andrew, perhaps you'd better have a look."

"I shall in a while. Tell us what happened."

Eugénie shrugged in her elegant Gallic way. "I do not know. I stepped onto the step leading to my gate, and suddenly the *cochon* grabbed me. I struggled, I bit him, but he was too large, and he wore gloves."

She paused for a moment as a shiver ran through her.

Will wished he'd insisted she sit next to him on the chaise. At least then he'd be able to touch her. Though whether it would provide the comfort he'd intend, he didn't know.

"Then"—she gave herself a small shake—"the scoundrel said he was being paid much gold to take me. The only thing I could think of was slavery."

Slavery! Will's fists clenched as rage and fear for Eugénie coursed through him. He wished he'd been able to kill the villain. If they could safely sail for England, he'd have them all on a ship tomorrow. Unfortunately the hurricane season was well underway. Then he caught the strange way Cicely was looking at Eugénie, and her answering shrug. What the devil was going on? Was there more to the attack?

Maneuvering himself around, he reached over and took her cold hand in his. "You must never be without protection. If there is money involved, the blackguard will try again."

She was quiet for several moments before saying, "We have only two footmen, one is older and the other still a boy. Yet even Josh could not have stopped that man."

"I'll send my groom, Griff."

She glanced at him in surprise.

In addition to keeping her protected, perhaps this would help encourage her to start feeling differently about him. "He has nothing better to do, and he knows how to fight and handle a pistol."

"I shall carry my dagger as well." She gave a firm nod. "Somehow we need to keep this from Maman."

That answered his question about whether or not she could use a knife. It didn't surprise him.

Cicely's brows rose, wrinkling her forehead. "I don't

know that you'll be able to. The whole street answered your screams."

"She's right." Will squeezed her hand. "Shall we tell her together? I can explain about Griff."

"Very well," Eugénie said in a barely audible tone.

He'd never seen her so still, so stoic. "What are you thinking?"

"That if my mother lost another person"—her voice hitched—"she would not be able to go on."

This was the time to take her in his arms; instead Will had a slab of beef on his face and their closest friends were present. Not to mention, no dark shadows he could tug her into, though that hadn't gone very well. "I promise you, she'll not have to." He eased himself up on the chaise and brought her hand closer, kissing it. "I'll keep you safe."

She turned to him, her eyes wide as if she almost didn't believe what he'd said. Then the corners of her generous mouth lifted. "Thank you."

He couldn't put a name to the surge of emotions coursing through him. It was almost the same as when he'd been given his first ice cream, or when he'd cleared his first fence, but infinitely stronger. Pride mingled with self-satisfaction and something else. It was that *something else* he knew he'd have to examine more closely when he was alone and could think, but right now, this was enough.

The remains of Nathan's dinner had been cleared not a quarter hour before. It was still light, but barely. Once the sun sank, darkness would fall quickly. None of the lingering sunsets of his youth in England here in the West Indies.

He stared up at the ceiling, waiting. Miss Marshall and Mr. Conrad said they'd return this evening. Though perhaps he'd already been drugged. A light scratching came at one of the windows before the shutter opened. Conrad lifted Miss Marshall through the opening. She sat on the sill before grace-fully swinging her legs inside.

"Mr. Wively." She smiled as softly as she had earlier. "Good evening. We don't have long."

"I must tell you," Nathan said, "they plan to treat Con-rad's food so that he'll sleep." Nathan related the rest of what he'd overheard.

The smile left her face. "Thank you for warning us. We suspected as much. Fortunately, one of the cooks for the slaves is also from St. Croix. She will make sure his food is not adulterated. At least if they think Joseph is drugged"—her hand flew to her chest and she breathed deeply, calming herself just as any well-born Englishwoman would do—"he will not be chained. I have arranged transport away from here. Not long after the overseer, Williams, departs, we should as well."

"Am I correct that we are not far from Saint-Pierre?" Nathan asked.

She glanced quickly at Conrad. "You are, sir. How did you know?"

"This is not the first time I've been on Martinique." Nathan grinned. "If we can get to the town, I have a friend who will assist us."

A scenario played through Nathan's head. "Will he be missed at breakfast?"

A look of revulsion appeared on Miss Marshall's face; she opened her mouth to speak when Conrad said, "No. I will not be missed until the evening meal."

Nathan would hear the rest of their story, but not now. "We should be safely out of their grasp by then."

Miss Marshall nodded tightly. "We'll come through this window to fetch you. Good night."

The couple left as quietly as they'd entered. He wondered about the unlikely pair. They appeared to take the travesty that had occurred to them when Conrad was sold in stride, but how much had they suffered at the hands of greedy, cruel men? All in the name of profit. Well, Nathan was proof that one did not need to make money on the backs of slaves.

His hand went to his breeches, then he remembered: The miniatures of Sidonie and Eugénie were no longer there. He'd have new ones made when he returned. This time of all the children.

Closing his eyes, he tried to force himself to sleep, yet could not. It was not Conrad who would be missed. It was Nathan. Damn. He should have thought of that earlier. How far could they travel before *his* breakfast was served?

Finally, he dozed fitfully, waiting for the soft scratching on the window, but it never came. Once it was light he rose, changing from his clothing to the nightshirt he'd been provided and returned to bed. The fear Conrad had been caught played with Nathan's mind, but no alarms had been raised. Waiting, not knowing what had happened, that was the worst part. No wonder so many wives chose to go to sea with their husbands. This was far more terrible than battle.

Exhausted, he must have finally slept as the sound of a tray being placed on the table woke him.

"Sorry, sir." A young woman with café au lait–colored skin glanced at him in fear. "I was tryin' to be quiet."

Why did all the servants and slaves here have either English or Dutch accents? Then it came to him. How utterly simple. Because they couldn't speak French or the native patois, it would be almost impossible for them to escape a French island.

"I was already awake," he lied.

"Is there anything else ye'd be wanting?"

Nathan rubbed a hand over his bristly chin. "Please have some warm water brought. I'd like to shave."

The woman glanced away. "Is that all?"

What the devil was she getting at? *Holy Jesus*. Someone sent her to see if he wanted to bed her?

"Yes," Nathan said in a firm tone, hoping not to have the offer repeated.

She backed out of the bedchamber, nodding as she went. "I'll tell the housekeeper."

Nathan removed the lids from the dishes. At least today's meal was more substantial. Meat, eggs, and bread. They weren't trying to starve him. He'd eaten half of it when a young man carrying a large pitcher of water arrived. After filling the washbasin, he reached out eagerly to take the tray, then stopped.

Didn't their master even feed them enough? Though God knew, growing boys needed a lot of food. "Go ahead. I've had enough. You may eat it here if you wish."

"It's all right." The lad shook his head. "I'll do the rest on the way back to the kitchen." He gathered up the plates. "Thank you."

"For what?"

"Not takin' Sukey when you could have."

"I would never—" Nathan closed his eyes for a moment. "You're welcome."

Despair, rage, and sadness warred for supremacy. He hated slavery in all its forms and fashions. He'd once known a man who'd been a slave himself in Egypt, had been freed, and now owned slaves on St. Thomas. Nathan didn't understand it at all and didn't want to.

He was drying his face when a bit of white on the floor caught his eye. A many-times-folded piece of paper. He listened for any sounds outside in the corridor before stepping quietly over to the note, picking it up, then opening it.

After dinner.

Nathan breathed a sigh of relief. Soon he'd be free.

Chapter 15

Eugénie caught her breath as Wivenly's warm lips brushed across her knuckles. His touch was different this time, soothing, not ravenous as if he had to possess her. Since the attack, her stomach had been a tight ball. It loosened now. She took a sip of the chilled white wine Cicely had handed her. Would she ever feel safe going out alone again? "I wonder if they will find the thug."

"If he is still on the island"—Cicely's hand made a tight fist—"they will find him. Our police are very good."

Andrew wrapped his fingers around Cicely's. "Anyone that large and Portuguese will be hard to miss."

Eugénie raised her brow. She had recognized his accent, but had not realized anyone else had.

Cicely opened her hand, twining it with Andrew's. "I heard him speak."

They always seemed to take comfort in each other that way, much as Eugénie's parents had done. If only she had not got herself into a mess where she must marry a man who did not love her, and for whom she had little regard. Though today, Wivenly had come to her rescue and brought her flowers, and now he held her hand. An awareness pricked the side of her neck, and she glanced at Wively. He was staring at her with his good eye.

"You've had quite a scare." His blue gaze was warm with concern. "How are you?"

Terrified. For herself, and her family, that the Portuguese might try again and this time would either succeed or harm someone who was trying to defend her. "I am fine."

Wively raised a skeptical brow.

"I worry about how my mother will take the news." She could not trust him with her fear, or her heart. "Since my *beau-papa*'s death, she has not been strong."

"As I told you, we will inform her together. She'll have no need to worry about you or anyone else."

Mayhap having a male Wively around would help, yet, other than his eyes, he did not look at all like her papa, and he certainly did not act like Papa. "It is my fervent wish that it be so."

"Andrew"—Wively removed the beef from his face—"take a look at my eye, will you? We need to go see my aunt before some well-meaning neighbor says something."

Rising, Andrew took the few steps to Wively and studied his face. "It will be black and blue for a few days. Can you see out of it?"

"It hurts." Will gently prodded the area around his eye. "But my vision is fine."

His valet appeared, seemingly out of nowhere, took the meat, and vanished just as quickly. A cooling breeze wafted through the doors. Will made ready to stand when she did, but Eugénie was frozen in the chair.

Her stomach tightened again. How could she add to her mother's worries? It seemed so selfish. "We should plan what to say." Even to Eugénie that sounded weak. "There must be a way to put the incident in a better light."

"Better light?" Wively uttered as if he couldn't believe what she'd said. "We tell your mother exactly what oc-

curred." He softened his tone. "Bad news doesn't get better with time."

Her spine bowed as she shrunk back into the chair. "I think—"

"Eugénie!"

Mon Dieu! They'd waited too long. "Here, Maman."

She appeared at the door followed by the Whitecliffs. "What is this I've been told about a man trying to take you, and why did I have to hear it from our neighbors?"

Wively unfolded his long frame in one fluid motion. "We were just about to come to you."

Eugénie took a gulp of her wine and waited.

Her mother stepped forward then covered her mouth with her hand as a gasp escaped. "Will, your eye."

"It will be fine."

Cicely poured wine for her parents and Eugénie's mother.

Wively signaled to Eugénie to join him on the chaise, and Andrew brought over two chairs. Once they were settled, she explained how the events unfolded.

At the end of the story, Maman's frown deepened. "You said he was being paid a great deal for you?"

"Yes. I immediately thought of slavers."

"Then why not take Cicely as well?" Mr. Whitecliff asked.

A low growl emanated from Andrew, and Cicely grinned.

"That," Wively said thoughtfully, "is a very good question." He glanced at Eugénie. "Perhaps it was not slavers. Who would want to abduct you?"

She shook her head and shrugged. "No one."

At least not anyone she would tell him about.

"Your uncle."

All their gazes swiveled toward her mother.

"What reason," Wively asked, drawing his brows together, "would either my father or any of the uncles have to kidnap Eugénie?"

Maman took a sip of wine, then fiddled with the glass.

"Not your family." She turned to Eugénie. "Your father's brother, Vicomte Villaret de Joyeuse."

"The Vicomte?" Andrew and Wively said at the same time.

The hairs on the back of Eugénie's neck prickled. She hadn't heard from her father's family in years. "What is it?"

"Dam . . . drat." Wively's hand tightened on hers. "He was the man behind the scheme to convince you the company was failing."

"Do you know a Mr. Shipley?" Andrew asked.

"Not precisely." Eugénie glanced from Wively to Andrew. "He came to my home after you left that first day." Warmth infused her cheeks. "He offered to marry me and buy the company." Had Wively known about that? What else was he hiding from her? "Why did you not tell me about Shipley and this Vicomte?"

"We"—Wively motioned toward Andrew—"thought it was over. Shipley left in a hurry as did the manager, Howden. We'd heard the sobriquet 'The Vicomte,' but were never able to find him." Wively scrubbed his face with his hand. "I didn't want to worry you."

It appeared there was a great deal of misplaced desire not to fret others going on. She swung her gaze back to her mother. "Maman, why do you think my uncle has something to do with this?"

That might explain today's attack and the strange men who'd chased her a couple of months ago.

"He . . ." Maman wrung her hands. "He wrote to me after your Papa left for England with a proposal for you to marry a French *comte*. The match would repair the war's depredations of the Villaret de Joyeuse family fortune. I responded, telling him your step-father would not countenance the match."

Without mentioning the proposal to me? "Maman, for what reason?"

"The *comte* is getting on in years and desperate for a son.

The ceremony was to be by proxy." She closed her eyes for a moment. "I could not allow you to wed in that manner. Eugénie, you deserve to be loved."

Yes, she did deserve to be loved, and if that was what her mother wanted for her . . . For the first time since she'd agreed to Wively's proposal, she knew she could not go through with any marriage unless she loved him and her regard was returned in full.

Eugénie's mood had shifted, but for the life of him, Will couldn't figure out what it meant. All he knew was it was more important than ever that she agree to marry him, and he didn't have long. "We are still missing information. Such as, if Shipley was employed by your uncle, how did his marrying you further the cause to wed you to the *comte*?"

"Mr. Shipley," Aunt Sidonie continued, "appeared to believe I was Eugénie's sole guardian. Perhaps your uncle thought to use Shipley as the proxy for the *comte*."

"Or," Eugénie said, "my uncle might have come forward with the offer again." She paused for a moment. "You must admit, even an elderly *comte* is better than a Shipley."

Will bit down hard on his inner cheek; a slight tang of blood soured his mouth. He drained his glass of rum shrub, and waited for someone to respond to her.

"Well, my dear," Mr. Whitecliff said, "you'll not need to worry about that with Lord Wively here."

The tension in his aunt's face eased, but not enough to satisfy him. "As I said earlier, I'll send Griff to keep watch when I cannot be with Eugénie."

"Thank you." Aunt Sidonie slid a glance to her daughter. "I will feel safer."

Eugénie remained silent, and he got the feeling he was somehow in competition with the unknown *comte*. "Allow me to escort you home."

The rest of their coterie walked with them to the front door of Wively House. At least his betrothed remembered to bring the flowers he'd brought her.

Will bowed to Eugénie. "You are handling this extraordinarily well. Please, do not hesitate to send a message if you need me. I shall see you in the morning." He raised her hand to his lips, placing a kiss on her palm. Her breath hitched as he closed her fingers around it. "Adieu."

She regarded him steadily, the spark of challenge back in her eyes. "Until then, my lord."

No woman had ever tested him the way Eugénie did. He was certain she desired him every bit as much as he craved her, yet she fought him every step of the way, and held herself back from committing to him. He'd have to discover what she needed him to give her before she'd allow herself to capitulate. Well, he had wanted to have to chase the woman he would marry. What was it his mother always said? *Be careful what you wish for.*

He certainly wouldn't take his charm and desirability for granted again. He bowed once more before making his way back toward the hotel. There must be a way to court her here that didn't involve kissing her senseless. That obviously hadn't worked the first time, and nothing had changed.

"Will."

He stopped until Andrew reached him. "Coming back to the hotel with me?"

"No. Cicely has decided to help you with Eugénie."

This was a change, and Will wasn't sure he trusted it. "Why?"

His friend shrugged. "Mind you, I'm not sure I understand it myself, but she apparently saw something in you this afternoon, and thinks you'd be good for Eugénie."

At this point, any aid was better than nothing. "Very well. I accept."

"Good." Andrew opened a door in the wall. "Cicely is waiting."

A half hour later he was armed with a short list of activities Eugénie enjoyed that he could partake in as well.

Including her teaching, which took place at the Moravian church on Sundays. Still, unless he wanted to end up reading poetry to her, he'd have to work quickly. There were woefully few things to do on this island.

Cicely narrowed her eyes. "You must promise me something."

Suddenly he felt like a small child getting caught doing something he shouldn't. "Anything."

"You may not—" She paused for a moment as warmth rose in her cheeks. "You will not attempt to seduce Eugénie. If it turns out she does not want you, then she must be free to carry on with her life."

"My love—" Andrew began.

Cicely held up her hand. "I will have his word."

"I will not do anything she doesn't want me to." There, that didn't tie his hands as much. Though not marrying Eugénie was not an option Will would freely consider.

"That's the problem." Cicely frowned. "She has no resistance to you."

"Will." Andrew's tone expressed a wealth of warning.

Keeping his hands totally off his betrothed was not what Will had in mind. "You have my word."

She smiled with relief. "Thank you. Believe it or not, I think this will gain you her regard faster than anything else."

It damn well better. He hoped Cicely was right.

The next morning Will knocked on the door of Wively House, with a new fan he'd purchased for her wrapped in paper and tied with a ribbon.

Bates opened the door and bowed. "This way, my lord." He led him to a small couch located to the side of the large main room. "I shall inform Miss Eugénie you have arrived."

A maid brought Will a pot of tea and cakes. This was much better treatment than he'd expected, but he'd yet to discover how Eugénie would respond to him.

* * *

"The green muslin walking gown." Cicely nodded emphatically.

Eugénie sighed. Her friend had come over shortly after breakfast and begun taking gowns out of her wardrobe. "Does it really matter what I wear?"

They were only going shopping.

"Of course it does." Cicely placed her hands on her hips. "It will put you in a better temper."

"There is nothing wrong with my mood."

She grabbed Eugénie's shoulders and turned her so that she faced the mirror. "Indeed?"

The woman gazing back at Eugénie looked tired and worn. "Oh my. I suppose I do look a bit blue-deviled."

"Yes, you do."

Eugénie pulled a face. "You needn't agree with me so quickly.

"Marisole, can you do something different with my hair?"

"Of course, miss." Marisole glanced quickly at Cicely. "And I think the green is a good choice."

Something was going on, and Eugénie was being kept in the dark. "What are the two of you up to?"

Cicely opened her cornflower-blue eyes wide. "Why, nothing at all. We only want you to look your best. That way you will feel more the thing."

Eugénie didn't believe Cicely for a moment, but donned the gown, then sat still while her hair was dressed in a topknot. Her maid teased out strands of Eugénie's hair so that spirals framed her face. The lady that stared back at her no longer seemed so careworn.

The clock struck eight. She had at least two hours before Wively would disturb himself to arrive. Enough time to see to some household tasks and shop with her friend.

A light scratching sounded on the open door.

"Miss?" Bates bowed. "Lord Wively is waiting for you."

Already? "I'll be up in a few minutes." She would wager her pin money that her maid and Cicely knew he'd arrive early today. Marisole clasped a necklace of local pearls around Eugénie's neck and handed her the matching earrings. Once she fastened the wire in her ears, she stood. "Thank you both."

"Have a good time." Cicely hugged her, wiggled her fingers at Eugénie before leaving. "I'll see you this afternoon."

Her friend was down the stairs before she had time to consider Cicely's words. Were they to meet later? No one told her anything. She mounted the first step. Marisole followed armed with a broad-brimmed bonnet, parasol, and gloves.

She reached the front room to find Wively munching on a biscuit. "Good morning." She curtseyed. "I didn't expect you so early."

He glanced up and swallowed. As he rose, his lips tilted up at the ends in a slow smile.

In two steps, he was in front of her and had possessed her hands. "You look charmingly."

"Thank you." A blush rose in her cheeks. Wively was behaving differently. His whole bearing toward her had changed, and she didn't know what to make of it. Oh Lord. She should have donned her gloves before greeting him. The touch of his bare fingers on hers caused Eugénie to lean forward slightly. His scent wrapped around her. This was not good. Hopefully, he'd leave soon. "Would you like more tea?"

"I'd like to take you for a walk." He grinned. "If you don't mind. I've been told there is a stretch of beach past the fort that makes for a nice stroll."

"Thank you." She returned his smile. "I'd like that." The area was one of her favorite places to go. The water was so clear, unlike near the docks. Wively would have had to at least ask someone . . . *Cicely*. She should have known. That was the reason she had decided to help Eugénie this morning. She would discuss her friend's behavior when she and Wively returned.

Eugénie and Wively left the house and made their way in the direction of the harbor. "What made you think of it?"

He glanced down at her in surprise. "Think of what?"

"The beach."

"I . . . I'm used to walking." He paused for a moment as if trying to think of a reason she'd accept. "I discovered this was a popular path."

Eugénie had to stop herself from laughing. She'd never seen him so unsure of himself before. "In England, where would you walk?"

Will let out the breath he'd been holding. He'd got over that hurdle easily enough. He hadn't wanted Eugénie to think her friend was conspiring against her by giving him information about what his betrothed liked to do. "If we were in London, I'd take you for a stroll in Hyde Park during the fashionable hour. You could view the Serpentine and throw bread crumbs to the ducks." Something he'd avoided for years, but would do for her. "Or, better yet, ride in my curricle."

"I remember being in a carriage," she said in a wistful tone. "When I was small, before we moved here."

"I'll teach you how to drive a pair."

"Are you a good, what do you call it?" She paused. "Whip?"

He let out a bark of laughter. "I'm considered a very good whip." It wouldn't do any good to tell her he belonged to the Four Horse Club; she wouldn't know what it was. "And a good instructor. I taught my two oldest sisters."

"*Bon.* In the event I am in England, I am glad you have experience."

Apparently he hadn't cleared the hurdle yet.

They'd reached the bottom of the steps and turned east, skirting around the back of Fort Christian. The air was already warmer, heavier. Will's shirt stuck to his damp skin, and he didn't need a mirror to know his shirt points had wilted.

Around them, the wind rustled through the tall palm trees, creating a sound almost like a light rain. They reached the other side of the fortress, and Will gave thanks for the breeze coming off the water.

She sighed. "There is no need for a carriage here. The only horses are at the plantations on the north side of the island. Everyone else uses donkeys to cart supplies or whatever."

"Much to my groom's disgust," Will responded wryly. "We discovered that after we arrived."

Eugénie's wide hat hid her face, and he couldn't discern from her light conversational tone what her feelings were. Yet now was not the time to press the issue. "Do you know how to ride?"

She nodded. "Yes. Papa"—her voice tightened when she mentioned his uncle—"borrowed a horse and taught me and the other children. He said it was a skill we must have."

They'd reached a path running along a narrow strip of beach. Pale turquoise water lapped the shore. Farther out, the color deepened. "Is this it?"

"It is." She raised her face to his. "We used to bring the children here so they could chase the waves."

Suddenly it was important to know everything about her. "Did you run on the sand as well?"

Eugénie smiled, but her eyes held a trace of sadness. "When I was young. Now it is not *comme il faut*."

He wanted to see her happy, skipping back from the sea, riding a horse and, by God, once she was his wife, she'd do whatever she damn well pleased.

"We could bring the children here, and I'd promise to turn my back and keep your sisters busy while you ran in the water."

She glanced up at him in surprise. "You would play with them?"

"Of course I would." He smiled. "I enjoy children."

They'd reached a small point jutting into the bay. There were no convenient benches around, but he found a large rock and spread his handkerchief over it for her to sit for a moment. The wind had picked up, blowing the dark chestnut tendrils around Eugénie's face as she stared out at the ships. Her light muslin gown molded to her body, giving him a view of all he wanted to touch. Damn, she was beautiful. At the Whitecliffs' party, she'd shone like a jewel, but today, dressed in green with small violet flowers embroidered on her gown, she reminded him of spring. Would Eugénie even like England? Emma Marsh, his friend Harry's wife, was from Jamaica and had adjusted well, but she'd come for her first Season knowing she'd probably remain.

Had Eugénie ever thought of moving away from the Caribbean, and how would he convince her if she didn't want to leave?

Chapter 16

Eugénie glanced at Wivenly. It had startled but pleased her that he liked children. That was definitely a point in his favor. Perhaps this getting to know him was a good idea.

She lifted her nose to the breeze. The wind was gaining strength and the scent of rain filled the air. No clouds, but she couldn't see to the east from here. She hopped down off the rock. "We'd better start back."

Wivenly held his arm out to her as he had on their way down from the house. She placed her fingers on it, and he tucked her hand into the crook of his arm. Unlike before, when he overpowered her senses and made her want what she shouldn't have until after marriage, being with him was comfortable. Her heart still beat faster when she was with Wivenly, but it didn't thud painfully, making it hard to draw a breath, as it had before. Perhaps she was becoming immune to him and soon he wouldn't bother her at all. Did that mean she would not love him? Maman and Papa always seemed affected by each other.

She stole a look at his lean profile. Though his linen drooped a bit, which was not surprising in this weather, he was still beautifully dressed. What would it be like to stroll or ride with him in London?

Under his hat, his neatly coifed brown hair was streaked with gold, and his lips—it wouldn't do to think about them and how they caused fire to course through her body. Oh dear, perhaps she was not impervious to him after all.

She sighed softly, and he glanced down. "Are you tired?"

"No, not at all." Eugénie didn't dare say how attractive she found him. God only knew what Wivenly would do with that knowledge. "It's such a lovely day. I'll be sad to see it ruined by rain, even though we always welcome it for our plants and cisterns."

"Rain?" He looked up, studying the sky. "I don't see any clouds."

"No, you won't until they are directly over us. It's in the air. We need it, yet I wish we had more time." Eugénie shut her mouth. If she didn't stop talking, she was bound to say something she shouldn't. Such as that she wanted to spend more time with him.

They were almost at the bottom gate to her house when a black cloud moved over them. "Quickly, come this way." She turned the key in the lock. "We shall have to take a chance of interrupting my sisters' lessons."

Wivenly held the gate, then closed and latched it behind her. He was on her heels as she made the porch leading to the children's level. The sky opened up as she touched the fine muslin hanging in the doorway.

He whipped his hat off. "You were right. It is as if someone ripped a hole in the cloud and all the water is pouring out. There were not even any warning drops."

What an apt description. Eugénie grinned. "Is it not like this in England?"

"No. The rain usually gives a man a fighting chance to get under cover."

Two of her sisters sat at a long table, the third was curled up with a book in a large leather chair that had seen better days. All their eyes were turned toward Eugénie and Wivenly.

She untied her bonnet and removed it as she addressed the governess, Miss Penny. "I'm sorry to disturb you. We would not have reached the top floor without a good soaking."

The girls' blue gazes stared up at Wivenly.

"Allow me to present—"

"Oh, we know who he is." Valérie, aged ten, waved her hand to include the other two sisters and their governess, Miss Penny. "Who could not?"

Eugénie set her lips in a firm line. "Nevertheless, ladies must wait to be introduced. This is Lord Wivenly. My lord, my sisters, Miss Valérie Wivenly, Miss Adelaide Wivenly, and Miss Jeanne Wivenly."

He smiled and bowed as if he'd been in a ballroom. "It is my pleasure to finally meet you."

"How do you know us?" Jeanne asked, as if he had witch's powers.

Adelaide rolled her eyes. "Eugénie probably told him." Then apparently couldn't resist adding, "Goose."

"I am not a goose," Jeanne retorted.

"Adelaide," Valérie said. "You are not to tease."

"You certainly are not." Miss Penny gave Adelaide a reproving look. "That will be quite enough."

She slumped back, pouting. "Well, she did."

"As a matter of fact," Will said, sliding Eugénie a mischievous glance, "your sister has said very little about you, but as if by magic, I will tell you your ages."

Jeanne's mouth dropped open until Penny gently tapped the child's chin, and the girl closed it.

Adelaide sat up, and Valérie raised a brow.

"You," he said, pointing at Valérie, "are ten." In an undertone he added, "Going on twenty."

Eugénie resisted the urge to grin.

He turned to Adelaide. "You are eight." The two older

girls were round eyed in surprise. "And you," he said, grinning at Jeanne, "are six."

Jeanne jumped up from the table, running around it to hug him. "You are very smart. Do you know Miss Penny's age?"

Wively picked Eugénie's youngest sister up, as if holding a child came naturally to him. He was really very good with them. He would make a wonderful father.

"I cannot tell you," he said to Jeanne. "It is impolite to discuss a lady's age once she is out."

"We'll never be out." Valérie groaned. "We are never even allowed upstairs except for dinner when it is only the family."

"Do you"— Adelaide glanced quickly at Miss Penny— "keep children locked away from all the adults?"

He glanced out at the garden for a moment, then looked back at the girls. "We keep them in the attic until they are able to be around Polite Society or until they outgrow the beds."

Eugénie wanted to giggle, but the children would be offended. Wively had told her about the schoolroom at his home and how his brothers and sisters made use of the large cherry tree next to one of the windows. "There, you see, it is not so bad here."

Her sisters nodded their heads solemnly.

"If you are all very good," he went on, "you'll be allowed to travel to England for your come outs."

Eugénie turned her back to the children and lowered her voice. "Are you mad? Who would sponsor them?"

"It will be eight years before Valérie is ready." His lips curved into an enigmatic smile that told her nothing. "I'm sure something can be arranged."

Once the rain stopped, Will escorted Eugénie to the main floor. Her sisters reminded him of his own. Valérie, in particular, promised to be a handful. They, like all young Wivenlys, needed outside distraction, and since their father was no longer around to provide it, the duty fell to Will. He grinned to himself. If he'd known all the work to be done here and that he would trick himself into marriage, would he have even made the trip? He glanced down at Eugénie's smiling face and hoped the answer would have been yes.

The fan was still wrapped and lying where he'd left it earlier. She picked it up. "What is this?"

"I brought it for you." He'd almost brought back the one he'd sent last week, but thought better of it. He'd return that fan to her later. She untied the ribbon, drawing it neatly out from the gold paper. He held his breath. "Do you like it?"

With a flick of her wrist, she opened it. It had spokes of pierced ivory, with delicately painted medallions on gold-tinted chicken skin. "It's lovely." Her smile broadened. "Even nicer than the one you gave me last week." A light blush colored her cheeks. "Thank you."

Will inclined his head. He was tempted for a moment to add a bit of flattery, but changed his mind. "You're welcome."

With the look of joy still on her face, she placed it back in the paper. "I shall bring it the next time we have an evening entertainment."

"I'd be honored." He bowed and a low rumbling sound came from his stomach.

Eugénie placed the tips of her fingers over her lips and giggled.

"Perhaps I'd better remove myself to the hotel and partake of luncheon."

"Or," she said, lowering her lashes, "you could join my mother and me here."

This was progress indeed. Will hadn't expected that she'd voluntarily spend more time with him. Perhaps she was softening toward him. A clatter of china and silver from the dining room on the other side of the large drawing room caught his attention. He'd certainly eat sooner if he stayed, and he'd be able to spend more time with Eugénie. "I'd be delighted. Thank you."

Waving her hand, she caught a servant's attention. "Add another place, please. His lordship shall join us."

A few minutes later, Bates brought a tray with what Will now thought of as the obligatory drink, chilled white wine. "Miss Eugénie, the mistress said she'll be here shortly."

He poured two glasses and left.

Will took a drink as Eugénie sank gracefully into a chair before taking her goblet.

After smoothing her skirts, she glanced up. "Do you sail, my lord?"

Her volunteering an activity gave him hope she actually enjoyed being with him. "Yes, I learned on the voyage here." A slight exaggeration, but she'd never find out. "Unfortunately, I don't have a ship."

"I do." She took a sip of wine. "Well, not a ship, but a sailing boat. It is more than large enough for two."

That hadn't worked. He sent up a prayer that he'd remembered enough not to make a fool of himself. "I'd be delighted to accompany you."

The mention of a boat brought him back to his duties to the whole family. He'd need to discover all their assets. It wouldn't do not to have plans for everything when it came time to leave.

Aunt Sidonie entered the room. "You plan on sailing tomorrow?"

Will poured his aunt a glass of wine. "Yes, I look forward to it."

A worried look appeared on her face. "You must first check with Porter, Eugénie."

Who or what was Porter?

"Yes, Maman." Eugénie caught her lower lip between her teeth as if to stop herself from saying more.

Raising his brows, Will asked, "Porter?"

A quick smile appeared for a moment on Eugénie's lovely face. "He is our gardener now, but if anyone can foretell the weather, he can. My mother is always concerned about storms this time of year."

"For good reason." The wine sloshed in Aunt Sidonie's hands. "Sailing can be dangerous at any season, but more so now."

"We will not leave the harbor." Eugénie leaned across the short distance to the sofa her mother sat on and gave the older woman a hug. "Will that put your mind more at ease?"

"Thank you, my dear." Aunt Sidonie's tone was even, yet when she took a large drink her hands shook nervously.

He didn't know what she was more frightened of: the water, weather, or the boat. After all, her husband had died at sea. Then again, perhaps she feared another attack on her daughter. Eugénie caught Will's eye and gave an imperceptible shake of her head. Was it something else altogether?

Nathan forced himself to relax and at least doze for a bit while he waited to hear from Miss Marshall and Conrad. He'd learned early on in his life to sleep and eat when he could. He awoke to the sound of a shutter opening. Through the upper windows, the sky was deep blue, but not yet fully dark.

"We need to go now," Miss Marshall said in a hushed voice. "While the housekeeper is eating."

He swung his legs over the bed and stood. "I'm ready."

"Come this way and Joseph will help you out."

This was silly. Surely the drop couldn't be that bad. Yet he was given no chance to try himself. Conrad lifted him as carefully as if Nathan were a baby, hefting him over the sill, then setting him on the ground. He tried to infuse more gratitude into his words than he felt for being treated like an invalid. "Thank you."

"We didn't want you to hurt your leg again," Conrad said before leading the way around the back of the house.

Though the large man and Miss Marshall were not walking quickly, Nathan struggled to keep up the pace. Perhaps he wasn't as fit as he'd thought. "I won't be sad to see the last of this place."

Conrad's teeth shone white in the dark. "Neither will I."

A quarter hour later, by Nathan's reckoning, his lungs and the one leg screamed for relief. He'd never been this feeble before, and he wondered for the first time how close to death he'd actually been.

"Mr. Wively." Conrad's hand touched Nathan's arm. "Are you all right? Would you like me to carry you?"

"No." His heart pushed into his throat as he tried to draw a deep breath, but he'd not be treated like an infant. "I'll be fine. How much farther until we reach the conveyance?"

"Just around the curve. That was as close as we thought safe to leave the cart."

The drive down which they walked was so dark he couldn't see the direction of the road. "I'll make it. Let's go."

Conrad kept his massive hand on Nathan's arm, which was probably just as well. By the time they reached an old cart harnessed to a mule, he couldn't have gone another step. Dark figures emerged from one side of the road. *Damn!* Caught before they'd even left the property. Yet, neither Miss Marshal nor Conrad seemed concerned, and no one made a move to stop them. *What the devil?*

"I'm sorry we didn't tell you before." Miss Marshall's quiet voice broke the silence. "I could not in good conscience leave behind those who helped us. The retribution would have been unthinkable."

Nathan knew the type of punishment meted out to slaves who'd helped others escape. He didn't have the strength to do more than incline his head before Conrad lifted him onto the wagon's seat. Miss Marshall slid in next to him on the

bench, took the reins, and started the mule. The rest—
Nathan counted three men and two women—walked alongside the cart with Conrad. At this pace, it would take them
most of the night to get to Saint-Pierre.

He hoped his friend, Vincent Beaufort, had retired early
this evening, for he'd be wakened before dawn tomorrow.

At what Yves thought was an early enough hour that no
fashionable person would be abroad, he tied his cravat in a
neat but unremarkable fashion. After donning a dark blue
jacket, tasteful waistcoat, pantaloons, boots, and high-crowned
hat, he set out for King's Quarter, where Wivenly House was
situated.

Yves climbed slowly up the Ninety-Nine Steps, as if taking in the sights. Each house seemed to have its corresponding gate built into the wall. That was what his Portuguese
tool had failed to take into account. One scream in this area
would bring out the rest of the inhabitants. Which was exactly what had occurred.

He was brought out of his reverie by the sounds of a man
and woman on the steps above him. Eugénie and a gentleman chatted as they descended the step street. Though the
girl had probably never seen a picture of his brother, her father, whom he resembled greatly, Yves paused as if to examine a hibiscus, tilting his head so that he'd not be recognized.

He waited, but no maid or footman followed. So lax,
these people on the island. In France an unmarried young
woman would never be allowed alone with a gentleman.
Unless, that was, they were betrothed.

What was the gentleman to her? Yves shrugged. It mattered not. Eugénie was spoken for. His brother had already
signed the documents.

He turned, trailing after the couple, making sure not to
come close enough for them to notice him. Soon they came
to a small group of piers where pleasure boats and yachts

were docked alongside. His niece led the way to a small sail-boat. After tossing a coin to the boy who held the rope to the boat, the man followed. Soon the lines were cast off and Eugénie set the sails while the gentleman rowed them into the harbor. So, his niece enjoyed boating. He'd have to keep an eye on how often she went out.

Yves could already feel the freedom her property at home would give him. Unbeknownst to Hervé, Yves had bribed a judge in France to make him trustee of her property. Not that that would do him much good here on St. Thomas, but he'd convinced Hervé to allow Yves to take the contract to the *comte*. He'd rewritten part of the contract so that the only property the *comte* was aware of was the monies his dead brother had settled on Eugénie.

Hervé didn't know that the house in Paris and estate in the Loire would remain with the family. In other words, with Yves. The property should have come to him and not Eugénie, in any event. It wasn't fair that he had received nothing.

He scowled, causing a young woman to shy away. With some effort he assumed an expression of ennui. Finally there would be no more begging for money from his brother. All he had to do was deliver Eugénie to the *comte*; and he'd do so soon.

Chapter 17

Eugénie led Wively to her small sailing dory docked at the warehouse's pier.

He caught her hand as she was about to descend the wooden ladder attached to the dock. "If you allow me to go first, then you can hand me the basket, and I can help you into the boat."

His offer took her by surprise. Even when she was young, she'd never been assisted into her boat. Papa had always insisted she learn to do everything herself. Yet she had the feeling that even her *beau-papa* would have expected her to accept Wively's offer. "Thank you, my lord."

He grinned as if she'd given him a gift, and she smiled back.

Once the picnic basket was stowed in the bow and Eugénie had settled herself next to the mast, she began unfurling the sail as Wively rowed them away from the dock. He needn't have done it. She was perfectly capable of maneuvering her way into the harbor under sail alone, and a brisk breeze already filled the linen sails.

Yet he *was* trying to be helpful, and having assistance was pleasant. Not to mention the way his broad chest looked as he pulled on the oars. If only he weren't wearing a jacket she'd be able to see his muscles working as he rowed. Where had that thought come from? This was not the time to allow herself to be distracted by his body. It was too difficult to think when that occurred. "We are far enough out. You may put the oars up now."

She was surprised when he did as she directed, without questioning her. She had not thought he would take orders from a lady. "Would you like to steer, or shall I?"

He gave a self-deprecating smile. "I may have overstated my abilities a bit. None of my family's properties are near the sea, therefore my experience is limited."

Eugénie stared at him for a moment. All men boasted, but not many would admit it to a woman. Would Wivenly allow her to teach him? Little by little she trimmed the sail until there was no luff. "There now." Keeping the boom steady, she moved to the stern and took hold of the tiller. "If you can mind the sheets, I'll steer."

He smiled with a bit more confidence this time. "I'm sure I can manage that."

Sitting on the middle bench, he turned to face her. "How long have you been sailing?"

"Since I was about ten." It was the one time that she and Papa could spend time alone together. The boat was too small to take the rest of the children. He'd been good picking something each child enjoyed and taking the time to give them his undivided attention for at least a little while.

Eugénie ran her fingers over the starboard side rail, blinking back the tears threatening to fall. "Papa built this boat for me for my twelfth birthday."

Wivenly checked the canvas. "Who usually accompanies you?"

"My maid."

He jerked his head around to her. "She rows?"

So much for keeping the truth from him. He would either take it badly and feel like a fool or not. "No."

"If she doesn't"—he paused as if trying to understand—"do you row?"

Eugénie gave a little shake of her head. "I can, but I do not unless the wind is in the wrong quarter."

His eyes widened, and his brows drew together slightly. "Then you didn't require me to . . . ?"

Oh dear. What did Maman say? Always let a man think you need him? "No, but I was very appreciative of your efforts."

"I'll be dam . . . darned." A boyish grin appeared on his face. "That takes a great deal of skill."

Eugénie had the sudden urge to kiss him. She certainly was not going to tell him that any competent sailor could do the same. "Thank you. Papa was a very good teacher." She glanced around, calculating the distance from the nearest ship. "We need to tack."

"Umm, yes, right." He took up a line. "Tell me what to do."

A burble of laughter escaped her. "You said you knew how to handle the sails."

He grinned ruefully. "Only on large ships."

"Well, it is not much different. We want the wind to fill the sail from the other side. I'll turn the boat into the wind. When the sail luffs, slacken the line, and we'll switch sides, then you trim the sail again."

Wively's lips pressed together as he concentrated on the task. When he had finished, he swallowed, causing the muscles in his tanned neck to move as if he'd just taken a drink. "I have it."

She'd never seen him not completely in charge before. Dragging her gaze from his face, she minded the boat as the linen slackened, then the wind caught again. Wively moved with sure, quick motions until the sail was full on the new tack. "Well done indeed."

When he looked at her, his eyes danced with joy. "Thank you."

Heat rose up her neck to her face. If only he was like this all the time. This was a man she could fall in love with. She cleared her throat. "We'll need to tack several more times before we reach the beach."

Wively glanced at the basket. "Ah yes. Food."

Unbidden, her lips curved in a smile. "Are men always hungry?"

He leaned closer to her. His voice was low. "Always. At least I am."

He straightened, leaving her oddly bereft. Was he afraid to kiss her while she operated the tiller? Then it occurred to her he had not attempted to touch her last evening either. Had he lost interest in her? Eugénie glanced at Wively, catching him as he stared at her with a heated gaze. Clearly he was still attracted, but he seemed to have changed tactics.

"Ship to starboard," Wively said sharply.

Drat. This was not a good time to let her mind wander. "Tacking."

It was early afternoon before she made the final push toward the beach where they'd rest and eat luncheon. He pulled his boots and socks off before climbing out of the craft into the water. Eugénie made to follow.

"No, you stay here." He took the dock line, pulling the craft onto the shore. "There's no reason for us both to get wet."

The water. Will had longed to get in the sea since he'd arrived. It was so clear and warm. Nothing at all like the rivers and lakes back home. He caught a grimace on Eugénie's face, which she quickly changed to a polite smile. Had she wanted to feel the water as well? He cast his mind back to their conversation yesterday. *Damn*. Of course she did. He'd find a way to give her the treat she wanted.

After all, other than about twenty ships in the harbor, they were alone. Surely no one would mind if she took off her shoes and stockings. Oh Lord. *Her stockings*. What he wouldn't give to roll them down inch by slow inch. Did her garters tie so that he could undo them with his teeth, or did she have the fastening? In this climate, they must tie. The metal on the others would rust. His groin twitched.

Keeping his face averted from Eugénie, he snarled to himself. *Haven't you got us into enough trouble? Mind your manners or we'll never get what we want.*

The blasted thing had a mind of its own. This courting without touching her would be the death of him.

"Are you all right?" Eugénie stood as if to climb out of the dory.

He grasped her by the waist and lifted. "I'm fine." His fingers burned as they came close to circling her small waist through the thin layers of muslin. It was all he could do to release her. Once she was on the ground Will grabbed the basket. "My stomach is complaining."

"Ah, I see." She reached in the boat, taking out a large cloth, then flicked it open.

Will helped her lay it on the ground.

She pointed to a corner. "Put the food here. We'll have to anchor the other corners with our shoes."

He hadn't noticed before, but the wind pushed at the cloth. He put his boots in place and watched as she removed her sandals. Will could have held her whole foot in his hand. It arched as she wiggled her bare toes in the sand. Just as well she hadn't worn stockings. The image of her removing them caused his chest to tighten, and he never would have been able to keep his promise to Andrew and Cicely.

Soon she had the dishes and plates arranged and was sitting cross-legged on the cloth. "There now. We may eat."

Will stretched out on his side next to her. He'd expected cold chicken, cheeses and fruit. There was fruit, but instead of chicken what greeted him were bits of fried dough that resembled a circle folded in half. "What are they?"

"Pattés. They are filled with whatever Cook has." She bit her lush lower lip as her brows lifted just enough to mar her brow. "I hope you like them."

He'd eat anything if it would smooth out her wrinkled forehead. "I'm sure I'll love them." He took the one she handed him and bit into it. The crust was still firm. Exotic flavors he didn't recognize burst both sweet and savory into his mouth. He swallowed and took another bite. It tasted like nothing he'd ever had before, but it was wonderful. "It's very good."

The worried expression left her countenance and her lips curved up.

"What is in them?"

Eugénie sniffed the piece he'd handed her before taking a taste. "Sweet potato, garlic, hot pepper, and conch. There are some other spices as well, such as curry."

Will finished and picked up another one. "Chicken, I think."

"Probably." She chewed and swallowed. "I take it you are used to something quite different. What were you expecting?"

"Cold chicken, ham, fruit, cheeses and bread, perhaps a bottle or two of wine." He told her of the picnics he'd had in England. "But the weather is much cooler."

She picked up one of the small jugs and took a sip. "Ginger beer. Have you had it yet?"

"Beer?"

"It is not the same as a small beer. It has no alcohol." Her face scrunched up, and he almost laughed.

"I take it you don't like regular beer?"

"Non." Eugénie held out a jug. "Try it."

He'd had gingerbread, but the taste of the drink was much stronger. "Not bad."

"I like it." She took a drink of hers. "Then again, I've had it most of my life."

Suddenly the breeze kicked up, and her hat, which she'd untied, flew off her head. Eugénie lunged to the side trying to catch it, but landed sprawled on top of him. Before he knew it, his arms were around her.

"Oh!" She gazed down at him, her sherry-colored eyes widening.

Her heart pounded against his chest, causing his breath to quicken. It would be so easy to close the few short inches and brush his lips across hers. His muscles tightened, wanting to taste and caress. *Lord.* This was torture of the worst kind. He had to get her off him before he made the worst mistake of his life.

"My bonnet," she said in a low, breathy tone.

"I'll get it." He practically barked the words.

Eugénie scrambled off him as he jumped up.

Spotting the hat near a rock a few feet away, Will dashed after it. A puff of wind picked the bonnet up again, causing it to skip along the sand. Eugénie laughed, clapping her hands as he dived to rescue the thing just before it landed in the water. "I have it!"

"I see that you do. Thank you. It is my favorite bonnet."

Well, at least the plain, wide-brimmed hat served a purpose rather than being solely decorative. Yet he wondered what she'd look like in one of the confections so popular in England. Better than most ladies, he'd wager.

His jacket and pantaloons were covered in sand, and he suspected he had it under his shirt as well. "Not that I minded going after it, but perhaps you'd better tie it this time . . ."

She gazed up at him, her eyes full of mirth. "You were very brave to ruin your clothes for my hat."

Will plopped down next to her, dropping the bonnet on the cloth. "I haven't ruined a suit in ages. My valet is probably beside himself longing for something to occur."

She took the hat, placed it on her head, and tied the ribbon off to the side. "My maid always complains I destroy my gowns. Yet she enjoys the new ones I buy."

"Ah, I think our servants would get along well." At least Will hoped they'd have an opportunity to find out.

The air cooled and Eugénie glanced off to the east. "We must start back."

"Rain?"

"I think so."

They quickly gathered up the remains of their luncheon, stowing them in the boat. Without stopping, she hiked up her skirts and started to push the craft into the water. The sight of her strong, well-shaped calves almost undid him again. What would he have to do to get her to agree to marry him? "You get in, I'll do that."

Eugénie nodded and hopped into the boat as nimbly as any seaman Will had ever seen. They might get wet before arriving back at the dock, but he'd count the day as a success. This was the most relaxed she'd ever been with him.

The air was warm, and although he kept track of the sail, he neglected to watch for obstructions as wind from the mouth of the harbor sped them on their way.

Suddenly, Eugénie barked an order. "Ready to jibe."

He scrambled to remember what she'd told him that meant when the boat turned away from the wind.

"Ware the boom."

He ducked but not soon enough to avoid the solid wooden pole. "Damn, that hurt."

"Are you all right?"

As they passed one of the ships at anchor, a sailor shouted out, "Better get yerself a real seaman, sweetheart."

"Aye," another called. "I'll be happy to oblige ye."

Will seethed, but Eugénie appeared to ignore the ribald comments coming from the ship.

"Stay still." Her fingers moved through his hair over the tender spot at the back of his head. "Not too bad, but you'll have a lump."

She leaned into him, her soft breasts pressing against his arm. His nose filled with the scent of lemons and warm woman. He stifled a groan. She'd probably think it was from pain and worry even more. God, he liked her touch.

Moving to his front, she tilted his head and gazed into his eyes. "Does it hurt much?"

Not as much as the jeers from the sailors. He could so easily reach out and kiss her. "No. Let's be on our way."

"I don't know what you were thinking." She released the tiller handle, moving it with one hand while the other tightened the sail. "But when you're crewing a vessel, there is no time for wool-gathering."

Soon they were moving swiftly through the water again. How the devil had she done that by herself? He wasn't going to sit there like an invalid while she did all the work. His pride had taken enough of a beating for one day. "I'll take it now."

She frowned a bit, but nodded and handed him the mainsheet.

Even with the accident, in less than half the time it had taken to arrive at the small inlet, they were back at the dock in Charlotte Amalie. His groom sat on a piling waiting for them.

"What is it?"

The older man's expression showed nothing as he took the picnic basket, bowing to Eugénie. "Jest thought you'd need a hand carrying everything back."

Once they'd returned to Wively House, Will raised Eugénie's fingers to his lips. "Tomorrow?"

She studied him for a few moments before responding, "Yes, be here no later than eight o'clock. I have somewhere I'd like to take you."

He waited until she'd entered the house before striding out of the small courtyard.

Once they were on the step street, Griff opened his budget. "Saw a swell lookin' at you and the miss this morning. He followed ye down to the pier."

Will waited as his groom paused for effect. "And?"

"I followed him." Griff's leathered face split into a smile. "Done found our Vicomte."

"Well done." Will slapped the older man on his back. "I always knew I could count on you."

"I telled ye I'd be better than that Tidwell."

Will would be old and gray before that war ended. "Yes, you did. Thank you."

"Weren't nothin'." Griff rubbed a hand over his grizzled jaw. "I've takin' a likin' to this Wivenly family. Wouldn't do to see them hurt."

"No. No, that wouldn't do at all, and I will not allow it." A feeling of satisfaction that his servant was also devoted to his cousins warmed Will. He hoped Andrew was at the hotel to discuss this latest news. Until then, Eugénie and her family must be kept safe. They'd reached the bottom of the step street. "Go back to Wivenly House and keep watch."

Griff tipped his hat and peeled off from Will. "I'll report if anything else happens."

Will nodded as he continued on to the hotel. He'd put an end to this Vicomte, whether he was Eugénie's uncle or not.

Tomorrow was Sunday, and he wondered if she would take him to the Moravian mission. She probably thought her teaching the slaves to read would shock him. Eugénie couldn't know, but after some of his mother's charitable starts, nothing could astonish him. In the meantime, he needed to have someone watch her uncle, and he was one man short.

"Can you see them?"

Cicely stood on the tip of her toes with a hand on Andrew's shoulder, trying to peer out the peephole in the gate leading to the step street.

"Would you like me to lift you up?"

"No no. I'm fine."

She pursed her lips in thought, and he couldn't resist brushing a quick kiss across her mouth.

"What are they doing?"

Andrew gave his attention to the scene on the step street. "Will and Eugénie were both grinning. She as if she had a joke to play on him, and he as if she could do anything she wished."

A breath caressed his ear as she sighed with relief. "That's good. Don't you think?"

Andrew actually thought that would remain to be seen. "He's touching the back of his head and wincing."

A curl bounced against his cheek. "They went sailing. He might have got hit by the boom."

Ah yes. He remembered sailors scuttling out of the way of the large wooden things on the ship, but that was a damned silly name for a massive piece of wood. "You wouldn't happen to know why it's called a boom, would you?"

A light lit in his betrothed's eyes. "Papa says it's because it goes boom as it hits a person on the head."

Andrew gave a bark of laughter. He'd come to appreciate his future father-in-law's wry sense of humor. "Very understandable."

He went back to looking through the hole. "Eugénie has gone inside, and Will's groom is with him now. Something is wrong."

"How can you tell?"

"They are both frowning."

Andrew glanced over his shoulder as Cicely drew her brows together. "Oh dear. I hope it's not to do with Eugénie."

"Most likely it is." He was concerned as well. Cicely was so often with her friend that any potential danger to one was a threat to both of the ladies. "Griff has left, and Will is grinning again."

"Perhaps he's thinking about being with Eugénie."

"That I don't doubt." But in what sense? The rogue had better keep his word to Cicely, or Andrew would pummel him. "Shall I catch up with Will and find out what is going on?"

She removed her hand and stepped back. "Yes, it is the only reasonable course of action." Her gaze focused on Andrew's lips. "Kiss me before you go."

"With pleasure, my love." He pressed light kisses along her lips, then ran his tongue over them, and she opened her mouth.

God, Cicely was so soft. She tasted of the finest honey. Her tongue tangled with his, and he drew her closer. Not being able to make her his was killing him. "I hate having to put off the wedding."

"We can't very well marry without a rector." Her arms around his neck tightened. "We could still . . ."

They'd received a letter from the clergyman on Tortola that he'd not be able to make the trip for another two weeks. "As much as I'd like to, you know we cannot."

He nibbled her jaw. Not only were there no special licenses here, there was a dearth of English vicars as well—none, in fact. The Danes made the process of getting married much easier than the English. Unfortunately, Mrs. Whitecliff wouldn't hear of a ceremony that was not performed by a Church of England clergyman. "What if something should happen to me?"

"I know. Yet at this rate, it will be months." A heavy sigh escaped her and she kissed him firmly. "You'd better go."

Andrew reached around for the latch. She was right. If he didn't leave now, his resolve might desert him. "I'll see you before dinner."

Their fingers touched until the last possible moment. Damn. Did nothing move swiftly on this island?

* * *

"Wivenly."

Will turned as Andrew caught up to him. "What have you been up to today?"

"Having my wedding delayed."

Will raised a brow.

"Rector can't come over for two more weeks," his friend said in an exasperated tone. "How did the sailing go?"

"Other than being hit in the head by the boom, very well." Better than that, actually. "Eugénie is an amazing sailor. She can handle the boat alone if she has to."

He wondered what other talents she had. If things went his way, he'd have a lifetime to discover them.

"Did she invite you to accompany her in the morning?"

"She did. My thanks to you and Cicely for telling me about her project." He glanced up. Dark clouds gathered overhead. If they were lucky, they'd reach the hotel before the rain started. "Andrew, my groom thinks the Vicomte is still interested in Eugénie."

"And?"

"I must keep Griff with her as protection."

"I agree."

Will and Andrew reached the next street and lengthened their strides. "That means I'll need another man. Unfortunately I don't know where to find one I can trust."

"I'd offer Josh"—Andrew's lips pressed into a straight line—"but I want him to remain with Cicely. He might know someone though, or the butler might."

The butler! Of course. Why hadn't Will thought of it before? Bates would want to help, and according to Eugénie, he knew everyone on the island. Will smiled. "You've just given me an idea."

They ran the last few yards to the hotel, reaching the stairs just as the sky opened up. Once on the porch, Will shook himself. "At least the rain here is warm."

Andrew laughed as a footman handed them pieces of linen to dry their hands and faces with. "There is that."

After he'd changed, Will found a card on the parlor desk inviting him to dine at Wively House that evening. Either his aunt knew of her daughter's reluctance to marry him and was on his side, or she'd forgotten to ask Eugénie if she minded his presence. Whatever the reason, right now he'd take all the help he could get. "Tidwell, order a bath."

"Already done, my lord." His valet bowed. "I gathered you would dine out this evening."

That didn't answer the question of how he knew when Will would return.

"If you will refresh yourself with a glass of chilled wine, my lord, I shall call you when it's time to bathe."

Will also didn't understand how his valet had the wine waiting as well. Then again, Tidwell had always been one step ahead of Will when it came to this sort of thing. "Thank you." Will joined Andrew in their parlor. "Sorry about your marriage plans."

Andrew took a healthy drink of what looked to be a rum shrub. "I'm about ready to go fetch the fellow myself."

Will found the wine and poured a glass. "Which island is he on?"

"Therein lies the problem." He tossed off his drink and poured another. "If you can believe it, other than St. George's in Road Town on Tortola, there are few actual churches in this part of the British West Indies. A grave oversight that ought to be addressed. I cannot believe no one had the forethought to establish one here while we had possession of St. Thomas. The vicar from St. George's goes to the other islands to perform services and other ceremonies."

"I suppose you could run him to ground in Tortola?" Will took a sip of wine. "I looked at a map when we were on the ship. It doesn't appear that the sailing between the islands is that long."

"That is a thought." Andrew's jaw clenched. "All I have to do is convince my future mother-in-law that a wedding breakfast can be held as easily a few days after the event."

"My lord, your bath is prepared."

"Thank you, Tidwell."

Andrew stared at Will. "How does he do that?"

He shrugged. "I have no idea, but I'm glad he does."

"I'll see you later."

Will lifted a brow.

Andrew grinned. "We're invited to Wively House as well."

Will left the room. Why was he always the last to know anything? Then again, Eugénie hadn't known either. At least he wasn't alone in his ignorance, and he looked forward to seeing her this evening. His body tightened in anticipation.

Simply to spend time with her. Nothing else.

Wasn't it enough he was skirmishing with Eugénie? Did he have to fight with himself as well? He'd never had to court a woman, never had to keep his hands off one before. She had dealt a blow to his confidence when she'd tried to reject him, but he would come about. Somehow, Eugénie Villaret de Joyeuse would soon be his wife.

Chapter 18

Yves stood on the deck of the sailing ship *Unconquerable*, growing bored with the captain's endless litany concerning how they must return to France soon.

"Monsieur," the man pleaded, "it will soon be too dangerous in these islands."

He toyed with Nathan Wivenly's pocket watch. "How long have you been a captain?"

The man drew himself up. "Over ten years. Which is how I know the threat this place holds. Countless ships and crew have been lost during this time of year."

Yves brought a handkerchief scented with lavender to his lips as he yawned. "Then we shall remain on Martinique until it is safe to sail again." He lowered his gaze to the captain. "You *are* capable of sailing there, are you not?"

A shadow of fear passed over the man's face. "Indeed, monsieur."

"Splendid." Yves smiled in a way that always made others wary of him. He would make the captain think again about arguing with him. "Be ready to leave on a moment's notice. I know not when I shall need you."

The captain bowed. *"Oui, monsieur."*

He'd come on board to search through Wivenly's trunks for an additional object with which to convince his niece Eugénie if it became necessary. But the captain had engaged him in another discussion of the area's dangers. Little did the man know that Yves, his brother, and niece would all be on their way to France as soon as Eugénie was on the ship. Of course, Hervé would send word to release Wivenly, but Yves had no desire to find out if Sidonie's husband was as stupid as she when it came to his plans to marry Eugénie to the *comte*. They'd find a priest on St. Martin and leave for France as soon as the ceremony was completed. Long before Nathan Wivenly could stop them.

Eugénie was already dressed for the evening when Cicely knocked on the parlor door. Her friend entered, followed by Josh carrying a tray with champagne and two glasses. Were they celebrating something? Perhaps there was good news about the wedding.

Josh poured two glasses and left.

Eugénie took the flute her friend handed her before Cicely collapsed onto the sofa.

"It's been put off again."

"The wedding?"

"What else?"

"Oh no." Eugénie set the flute down and hugged her friend. "I'm so sorry."

Cicely sniffed. "There is nothing better than champagne for disappointments, but I didn't wish to drink alone." She picked up the glass Josh left on the table. "Besides, I thought one of us may have something to celebrate."

Eugénie took a sip, then shook her head. "No. Although it is progressing nicely." Maybe even better than that. He had not lost his temper when the boom hit his head, and he appeared to actually like that she could sail well. "Wively acted today as if he was courting me."

"Did he indeed? Well that *is* good news." Cicely held up her glass. "We shall drink to continued good luck on that front." A moment later, Cicely gave a heavy sigh. "The worst part is Andrew won't touch me past kissing until we are wed."

Eugénie, in the middle of swallowing, choked and grabbed for a cloth as the wine spurted from her nose and mouth. "*What!* I cannot believe I heard you correctly. You want him to . . . ?"

Her friend downed her glass and poured another. "Yes." A pout formed on her lips. "But he won't."

Oh dear. When Cicely was determined to have something, she was a force to be reckoned with. Andrew probably hadn't yet seen that side of her. "Don't drink too quickly, or you'll be fuddled before dinner."

She stared at her champagne. "Perhaps if he had a bit too much to imbibe. No. It wouldn't work. He'd probably just fall asleep."

Eugénie tapped her finger on the glass. There must be something she could say to talk Cicely out of doing something she'd regret later. "Are you sure your mother won't agree to a Lutheran or Methodist pastor performing the service?"

"Mama won't even entertain the idea."

"Miss Eugénie." One of the footmen, Billy, stood at the door to the stairs. "The mistress wants you to come up."

"We shall be there directly." She held her hand out to Cicely. "Let us go. We're bound to come up with some plan."

"I hope so." Cicely placed her glass down and rose. "I don't want to wait to marry Andrew."

"Of course you do not." Eugénie linked her arm with her friend's. "Still, this is no reason to take drastic action."

They mounted the stairs to the upper level. Wively was already with Maman, and a few moments later, there was a knock on the door heralding the Whitecliffs and Andrew. Bates served wine and rum shrubs before announcing dinner. Maman insisted Wively sit at the head of the table.

No one had used that chair since Papa had died. Eugénie's throat tightened even as she realized how proper it was that Wively, as the only male of the family, take his place there. Due to the numbers being uneven, and the fact that Cicely wished to sit next to Andrew, Eugénie took the chair to Wively's left.

He reached over, placing his large, warm hand over hers. "You still miss your father terribly, don't you?"

She nodded, blinking back tears forming in her eyes. "I'll be fine."

"Take it one step at a time." His low voice washed over her like a calming wave. "For the moment, we'll just get through dinner."

She glanced down the table as his hand squeezed hers in reassurance. Everyone else, busy discussing the perfidy of the traveling vicar, paid no attention to her and Wively. "Thank you."

He kept hold of her fingers until Bates served the soup. Wively really could be very kind, when he wanted to be.

He looked at his soup. "Tell me what this is."

She took a breath, inhaling the spicy scent of ginger, garlic, and onion mixed with greens. This was one of her favorites. "Callaloo. It's a specialty of Cook's. She mixes spices, greens, crab, and I don't know what else together."

"If it's half as good as the pattés"—he grinned—"I'll love it."

Wively gazed at Eugénie as she dipped her spoon into the soup. Under his regard, her heart sped up. She had to stop reacting to him in this way. Perhaps she was just tired from today. It had been a long time since she'd gone sailing.

Once the bowls were removed, she glanced around the table to see if there was anything else that would require describing, but nothing stood out except for the fried plantains. Surely Wivenly would have eaten those by now.

Billy and Bates began serving, and Wivenly asked what she liked and made selections for her as if they were in a strange place and he had to assist her. It was so sweet, but also ridiculous at the same time. No man had ever treated her in this way. To Eugénie's surprise, she giggled.

"What is this, Miss Villaret de Joyeuse?" His brows came together, yet his eyes danced with mirth. "Will you share your joke? Have I amused you?"

She met his gaze, and his eyes captured hers. In that moment, something shifted, yet she couldn't say what. "You know you have, and I thank you."

He flicked a look at the others, still engaged with wedding talk. "I only want you to be happy."

Her chest contracted almost painfully as she tried to think of a response. Yet what could she say to that? He'd never been *this* nice before. Not even while they'd been sailing.

Fortunately, Mrs. Whitecliff took that moment to glance over at them. "We've all neglected the two of you dreadfully. Please forgive us."

"It is no matter at all." Why did her voice sound so breathless? "I know how disappointed Cicely and Andrew are."

Mrs. Whitecliff smiled. "Still, that was no excuse to ignore you and Lord Wivenly."

Wivenly gave Cicely's mother a smile she'd never seen before, polite but a bit distant. "I assure you, we understand."

The older woman's eyes widened for a brief moment. "Ah, I believe I comprehend you, my lord."

There appeared to be a hidden meaning behind what

she'd said, but Eugénie had no idea what it was. All she knew was that Wivenly could not alienate the mother of her closest friend. "He didn't mean . . ."

Mrs. Whitecliff patted Eugénie's arm. "It's perfectly all right, my dear. There is nothing for you to concern yourself about."

Then the woman turned back to the other conversation.

"I do not understand what happened between the two of you."

He shrugged and handed her a piece of the Vienna cake Bates had placed on the table. "Try this."

Before long, Maman signaled for the ladies to remove to the other room, while the gentlemen stayed to enjoy their port. Still confused over the exchange between Mrs. Whitecliff and Wivenly, Eugénie walked next to the older woman. "Please tell me Lord Wivenly did not offend you."

Mrs. Whitecliff's lips tilted up. "Not at all."

This was too much. Must she ask directly what had occurred? Eugénie placed her hand on Mrs. Whitecliff's arm. "I do not understand."

The woman paused. "Part of the problem with keeping you and Cicely here rather than sending you to London for a Season is that you have never learned the more subtle forms of communication."

That explanation didn't clarify anything. An apprehension crept into Eugénie, making her stomach uneasy. If she did not know these other ways of talking, and she married Wivenly, how would she go on in England? Everyone would think her provincial at the very least, or perhaps even stupid.

Mrs. Whitecliff was still speaking of the advantages of acquiring "Town bronze," while Eugénie grappled with her new fear of not being sophisticated enough for Wivenly. If Andrew was in shipping, he probably did not travel in the same circles, therefore it would not be a problem for Cicely. Even if he did, she was the epitome of how an English lady should appear. Yet Eugénie had the darker hair and complexion of southern France and looked French or Spanish. And there was her accent. Because Papa had always called her his little French girl, she had studiously avoided learning to speak and act like an Englishwoman. How would Wivenly's family take to her? The British in Jamaica did not like the French. That was the reason Papa had chosen to remove to St. Thomas and its more cosmopolitan atmosphere.

Even if Wivenly thought he loved her, how long could it last when she was so ignorant of the world?

"Eugénie?" Her name was a soft caress on Wivenly's tongue. "What is bothering you?"

"Oh, my lord, I didn't see you enter." Mrs. Whitecliff fluttered her fan. "I was just explaining to Eugénie that you did not give offense when you indicated to me you were enjoying your tête-à-tête with her. Very appropriate in our little gathering, but not, of course, among strangers."

Wivenly bowed slightly. "As you say, ma'am. Thank you."

"Don't think of it." Mrs. Whitecliff smiled. "Now, I must go ensure my family is not planning to have a Lutheran or Methodist minister perform the wedding ceremony."

She glided away, making a direct line for her husband, Cicely, and Andrew.

Wivenly took Eugénie's arm, strolling with her to the other side of the large room. "What was there in that to upset you?"

She lifted her gaze to his, and his eyes searched hers. It was only fair that she tell him of her fears, even if he did think her unsophisticated.

Will waited for Eugénie to speak, but the fringe of her shawl seemed to suddenly be in need of attention. He couldn't imagine what the other woman had said to Eugénie to have her so hesitant. One of the things he loved about her was that he always knew where he stood. He may not always like it, but he was never in doubt.

He placed one finger under her chin, raising it. "Whatever it is, I want to know."

She sighed. "I asked Mrs. Whitecliff what your exchange with her meant, which led to a discussion of how Cicely and I are not as polished as ladies who have had a Season. Then I began to think that, if we marry, I might be an embarrassment to you. Or your family may not like me because I'm French."

He caught her hands as they waved around. "I came here to escape the young ladies of the *ton*. Some might think their conversation interesting, but to me it was banal." He raised one hand then the other to his lips. A slow blush rose in her cheeks. "Very few of them care about the sufferings of those around them. We've only touched on certain subjects, but you have a passion I find refreshing."

Her eyes widened. "I do?"

"Yes, and if there is anything you need to know and I'm not around, either my mother or my friends' wives will be happy to help you."

"And the fact that I am French?"

Will couldn't help but chuckle. "My family will think you exotic."

"That is good." Her countenance brightened. "Then the only thing we have to decide is if we suit."

He glanced around the large room and cursed the lack of parlors and other chambers. If they were in England, he'd walk with her in the garden, or spirit her off into a morning room, and show her how well they suited. As it was, their friends and family left them alone, but they were still in complete view of everyone.

Mr. Whitecliff and Andrew bowed to Aunt Sidonie. It appeared the evening was at an end. "I shall see you in the morning."

"Do not forget to be here at eight o'clock."

Wively was still holding her hands. He turned them, placing kisses in her palms. "I could never forget."

He walked out with the others, and after bidding the White-cliffs a good evening, strolled to the hotel with Andrew. "That was quite a discussion you had with Mr. Whitecliff. Did you resolve anything?"

"No. Though I have learned my betrothed is not one to give up. I think we may have talked her father around, for all the good it does us. Whitecliff is not stupid enough to go directly against his lady."

Will heaved a sigh. "At least you know you'll wed. Eugénie is still unsure."

"You've never had to work for a woman's affections before." Andrew's voice was laced with humor. "It's good for you to have your will thwarted. Eugénie won't allow you to run roughshod over her."

"I'm starting to know what Marcus, Beaumont, and Rutherford went through in courting their wives."

Andrew gave a shout of laughter. "I heard about Beaumont's problems securing his bride. I didn't know about the others."

Will smiled wryly. "According to them, it took all their determination and skill to bring their ladies up to scratch."

"Are they happy?"

He waited a moment before replying. "Yes. Happier than they've ever been."

"There you are, then," Andrew said. "Marriage can't be all bad."

No. Living with a leg-shackle wouldn't be bad at all. If he could only get Eugénie to agree to wed him, he'd gladly live under the cat's paw. Will climbed the stairs to the first floor. Despite the fact that Eugénie was leading him a pretty dance, he wouldn't have her be other than what she was. Whether she recognized it or not, he had made progress this evening. She wouldn't have been concerned over how his family would react if she wasn't already half-way ready to marry him.

As Nathan's small group of fugitives reached the outskirts of Saint-Pierre, the night sky deepened to a dark sapphire. It would begin to lighten soon. He tried to convince himself they'd succeed in their escape. Throughout their journey he'd listened for any sound that would indicate they were being followed, but there had been nothing. Until just a few moments ago, there was not even a farmer bringing his goods to market. Still, it wouldn't be long before someone at the plantation discovered they were missing. He prayed that he and the others would be safely ensconced in his friend's apartment by then.

All night he'd half expected to hear the beat of horses' hooves bearing down on them. Though, as dark as it was and with the horrible condition of the road, a rider would be risking not only his life but the animal's as well, traveling that fast. Still, the poor mule was so old, it had taken more than twice the time as a good horse to arrive at Saint-Pierre, and he didn't want their party to be caught now.

Aside from Miss Marshall and Conrad, they'd been joined by the young man who'd left the message for him about the escape; Sukey; Ben, who was the slaves' cook's helper; Mary; and her husband, John. Mary had a small bump showing beneath her gown and Nathan figured her to be about four or five months with child. If their luck held, the baby would be born free.

Under cover of a large tree, Conrad brought the wagon to a halt. He climbed in the back, and Miss Marshall covered him with empty sacks, saying, "He is too large to go unnoticed. When they begin to search, they'll ask about him first."

Nathan nodded. "You're right." He was still tired from lack of sleep, but getting them to safety was all that was important. He wondered if the donkey could handle the load. "I can walk if need be."

"No," Miss Marshall responded quickly, "it would not do, especially going into town. Are you well enough to handle the reins?"

He must be more fatigued than he'd thought. Of course he couldn't be seen to walk while a colored woman rode. Thank God for Miss Marshall's quick wits. "I'll be fine. Give them over to me."

After he'd threaded the ribbons through his fingers, she climbed down. "It's only another mile into Saint-Pierre, and the roads will be better soon."

The closer they got to his friend's house, the more Nathan's tension eased. They were so close to freedom.

Despite it still being dark, people were on the streets as they drove into town. A few glared, others studiously looked away, as if the vegetation on the side of the road was more important. Gradually the traffic became heavier as they came closer to the town, and the sky lightened. As with sunset, dawn came quickly, adding to the danger of discovery.

He steered the wagon toward the docks, turning in the alley behind the main shopping street where his friend had his apartment. A bachelor, Vincent lived alone above his business. "Come with me."

Except for Miss Marshall, who took Nathan's place in the cart, he herded the others into the small entryway to a staircase hidden from the outside.

"Remain here. I'll be right back." He climbed the stairs to the large apartment above, then pounded on the door until the shuffling of feet could be heard on the other side.

"Who is there?" Vincent asked in French.

"It's Nathan Wivenly."

There was the sound of locks being drawn back, and a

moment later the door flew open. "*Nathan!* Good God, man. I'd heard you were dead."

He grinned as his friend drew him into a hug, a thing he'd only allow a Frenchman to do. "I'm extremely hard to kill. I've been held captive for the past several months."

Vincent stepped aside, motioning with his hand. "Come in. Come in. You must tell me everything."

Nathan hesitated. "Vincent, I brought some people with me."

"Of course you have." Vincent gazed steadily at Nathan, but the corners of Vincent's lips kicked up. "How else would you have escaped? Bring them up. All of you must be bone tired to arrive at this time of day."

Nathan breathed a sigh of relief. "Thank you."

"There is no need. I will rouse Gus, and he can get coffee and breakfast prepared. Then we'll make places for your friends and you to sleep."

Nathan summoned his small coterie to the apartment. Conrad led the group and one by one they entered, glancing around, their eyes wide with fear.

Vincent smiled and bowed. "You are safe here, my friends. You were very brave and will be rewarded. Come let us break our fast, then we shall discuss what you will require in the way of assistance."

"Conrad," Nathan asked, "where is Miss Marshall?"

"She said there is a livery close by. She'll return the mule and cart, then come here."

He didn't like the idea of her alone at this time of day "I'll go—"

"No." Vincent took Nathan by the arm. "If someone is looking for you, you will do Miss Marshall no good. Tell me what she was wearing, and I'll go to the stables."

Vincent left, and for the next quarter hour, Nathan and Conrad paced, until the door opened revealing Miss Marshall and his friend.

"What took you so long?" Nathan asked as Conrad wrapped his arms around her.

"The gentleman she'd borrowed the mule from was still asleep. We chose to wake the groom instead."

Nathan nodded. Fatigue dragged him down. It had been a long night, but finally they were all safe, or as safe as they could be.

Vincent clasped Nathan's shoulder. "Eat. Then sleep. We have much to arrange."

Yes, such as ensuring they had a way off the island before his captors figured out where he and the others had gone.

Chapter 19

The sky was rapidly becoming lighter as the sun quickly rose. A gentle breeze stirred the muslin draped over Eugenie's bed to keep the mosquitoes at bay. A deep purr rumbled against her side, and she slowly stroked her Chartreux cat. "What am I to do, Penelope?"

The cat's raspy tongue licked Eugénie's fingers. "I greatly fear I am falling in love with Wivenly, and I have no idea how he feels about me."

Penelope moved so that she was half lying on Eugénie's chest. Large yellow eyes blinked as if now ready to listen. "I know that is not what I thought would *ever* happen, but you see, lately, he had been very kind. While we were sailing yesterday, he was so much fun to be with. He even chased my bonnet." The warmth of seeing Wivenly covered with sand, laughing at himself, flooded her. "And when I landed on top of him, his eyes got that look that he has when he wants to kiss me, yet he did not. Last evening during dinner and afterward he *was* a little high-handed, but so solicitous. I had the impression he just wanted to spend more time alone with me."

Eugénie sighed.

The cat moved her head, encouraging Eugénie to scratch her jowls. "Do you think he truly cares about me, or is he only attempting to convince me to marry him?"

Penelope dipped her head so that Eugénie's fingers were now on the cat's head. "You think I should just ask?"

The purring grew louder. "First let me see how he does today at the church. If that goes well, I will say something."

The cat made a small chirping sound and rearranged herself on her back. Eugénie stroked Penelope's stomach until the noise of her maid preparing the wash water roused her. "Let us go. One way or the other, this will be an eventful day."

An hour later, she entered the empty drawing room expecting to find Wivenly waiting. In fact, she had been looking forward to seeing him. So much for his behavior last evening. She had told him it was important to leave at eight. The children were not allowed to remain away from the plantation for very long. She swallowed past the lump in her throat. Very well. She'd leave without him.

"Tidwell?" Will struggled with the foot-wide length of linen, which at the moment had the stiffness of a wooden board. He could not be late for his appointment with Eugénie. He wouldn't put it past her to leave without him. If nothing else, she'd be upset if he was tardy.

His valet stood with several of the neck-cloths at the ready. Normally they draped over Tidwell's arm. Now they almost stuck straight out.

"Yes, my lord."

"Is it the salt air, or have you been adding more starch to the laundry?"

"More starch, my lord."

Drat it all. Tidwell knew Will didn't like starch. "I suppose you have a good explanation."

"Of course, my lord." Tidwell's tone managed to convey surprise that Will would ask, and just the tiniest bit of disdain that he couldn't figure it out for himself. "Your cravats have an unfortunate tendency to droop in this weather."

"We *are* in the tropics," Will retorted in his driest voice. The one that had stopped matchmaking mamas and pretentious toadeaters flat yet appeared to have no effect on his valet.

"That may be the case, my lord." Tidwell hadn't moved a muscle. "However, one must at least maintain the *appearance* of a gentleman even in rustic living conditions."

Will finally managed to get the cloth wrapped around his neck and in position so that all he had to do was carefully drop his chin down a few times to make the correct arrangement. He would have glowered, but it would ruin his neckcloth. He settled for a lofty tone. "I *am* a gentleman."

"So you say, my lord."

Blast the man. Will remained still while Tidwell began the process of maneuvering the sleeves of Will's coat over his shoulders. "Tidwell, how long have you been with me?"

The valet ran his hand over the jacket, smoothing out any wrinkles. "Since you were at Oxford, my lord."

Will frowned. "That long? Tell me again why I hired you?"

"You did not, my lord. His lordship, your father, hired me. Something to do with purple and yellow striped breeches which made his lordship bilious."

It all came back to him now. His father threatened to remove Will from Oxford unless he took a valet. Still, that was a damned long time ago. Will picked up his pocket watch, and Tidwell attached the object to his waistcoat. "Less starch in the future, Tidwell."

His valet stepped back, executed a bow, then said in a supercilious tone, "We shall see this evening how your cravat holds up."

As he joined Andrew in the parlor, Will wasn't sure if he'd won that argument or not. To take his mind off Tidwell and his starching madness, Will turned to his friend. "What are you and Cicely doing today?"

"I have not yet been advised of all our plans." Andrew rose and stretched. "But I believe the Wivenlys and the Whitecliffs shall dine together again."

Though he had made progress last night, Will wondered if Eugénie would invite him. If not, he'd have to wheedle an invitation from his aunt. He checked his watch, and it could all be undone if he didn't leave immediately.

Tidwell entered the parlor with Will's hat, cane, and gloves. He donned his modified topper, tilting his new wide-brimmed hat fashionably, pulling down the rim the slightest bit to shade his face a bit more. "I'm off." He glanced at his valet and narrowed his eyes. "Even if this cravat wilts, no more starch."

Tidwell bowed. "As you wish, my lord."

Will didn't believe the man for an instant. At this point, he was just happy they weren't arguing over hair powder and patches.

When he stepped outside, a stiff breeze blew in from the harbor, a welcome change from the oppressive heat of the past couple of days. The only time he'd been comfortable was on the boat and at the beach.

Griff sat at the top of the step street, whittling a piece of wood. "Morning to ye, my lord. Not much goin' on yet to-day, but it's still early."

"Have you seen anyone at all?" Will raised a brow and waited.

A grin split his groom's face. "A young'un no one seems to know is spendin' time around here."

Will couldn't share his groom's good humor. He had to assume that whoever wanted Eugénie hadn't given up.

"You worry about tying the lady up right and proper." Griff tapped his nose. "I'll take care of this end."

Will nodded. "Do what you must."

The door to the house opened before he knocked.

The butler bowed, and in a censorious tone said, "My lord. Miss Eugénie is in the parlor."

Damn, he was late. "Thank you, Bates. I'll not keep her waiting any longer."

He strode down the short corridor. Eugénie, dressed in pale yellow muslin, was donning a bonnet trimmed with turquoise and yellow ribbons. He'd never seen a lady's hat he'd liked better. "You look charmingly."

"Oh." She widened her eyes and her chin rose, taking on a mulish cast. "I was getting ready to leave. I thought you'd forgotten."

"Not at all." Her expression did not bode well for him. "My apologies, I was delayed."

Drawing on her gloves, she raised an imperious brow. "*That* is obvious."

What a little Tartar. Will almost laughed out loud, but if he did she might never forgive him. Instead he held an arm out. "Shall we depart?"

She placed her fingers lightly on his arm as if to limit their contact. That wasn't going to happen. He twined her arm in his. There, much better.

Fire flashed in her eyes. "Did you have to do that?" She glanced down at his hand covering hers. "Where I had my hand was perfectly proper."

Acceptable if she were his mother, aunt, or sister. He'd be damned if he'd put up with that sort of distance from his betrothed.

He waited until she looked at him again before answering. "Indeed." She gave a tug, but he held on. "I wouldn't want you to fall down the stairs or trip over rubble in the street."

Eugénie narrowed her eyes. "Oooh, you . . . you . . ."

"*Considerate man* is, I think, the term you are searching for."

Despite herself, her lips twitched. She shook her head. *"Eh bien. Allez."*

Wivenly was impossible. He shouldn't make her want to laugh when she wished to remain angry. Fortunately, they would still arrive at the church in good time. What would he think of her close involvement with the Moravian mission? If Wivenly was one of those men who thought it was better to support one's causes from a distance, she could not marry him.

Eugénie glanced at him, taking in the way his jacket appeared molded to his broad shoulders. He must have had help putting it on. His biscuit-colored pantaloons clung to his well-shaped, muscular legs, and his boots reflected her own image. She hoped his footwear was up for the walk. It was only about three miles, but much of it was uphill. She led him behind the fort, then over to the road leading to the north side of the island.

Half-way up the hill, he stopped. Sweat rolled down his face, and he mopped it with his handkerchief. "Where are we going?"

"To the Moravian church. It is where I read to the younger slave children and teach the others how to read and do their numbers."

He sucked in a breath. "Very well, lead on."

Perhaps she should have warned him. Though from what Papa had said, she thought the English liked to walk. "Do you not have hills in England?"

"We do. When I was young, my family lived in the Lake District. It is nothing but hills." Wivenly grimaced. "However, I was dressed for the occasion, and it was not quite so hot."

He truly did appear to be miserable, and Eugénie was surprised he hadn't complained. As he stared straight ahead, she noticed a bit of red on his neck, just below his chin. Had he cut himself? She studied it more closely. Not a cut, a rash seemed to be developing where his cravat rubbed against his skin. "We have a nice breeze today, and there will be water at the church."

He nodded tersely. "I'm fine."

"The walk back will be downhill." Eugénie bit her lip. Could she have said anything more inane? "I'm sorry."

Wivenly started to turn his head and winced. "Normally it would not have been a problem, but my valet, Tidwell, is distressed by my cravats drooping and added so much starch I could barely tie this one."

No wonder Wivenly's neck was being chafed raw. That Tidwell was an *imbécile*. How could he do something so stupid! "He should care more for your person than your clothing."

Wivenly didn't look at her when he responded. "Ah, therein lies the rub. He believes by ensuring my dress reflects my status as a gentleman, he *is* caring for me."

Eugénie began to protest, but thought better of it. Wivenly must be a kind master indeed to give his valet so much latitude. Yet this was partly her fault as well. She'd withheld where they were going to see how he'd react.

"Is that it?"

She glanced up at the white building ahead of them. "Yes."

"The walk was not long." He grinned down at her. "Just vertical."

She felt like such a shrew. His poor neck would be bloody before they returned. "I am happy you are not too upset."

Wivenly held the door open, stepping aside for her to pass. "Not at all."

Some of the children were already seated at the long tables with books. When Brother Sparmeyer greeted them, she smiled. "My lord, may I introduce Mr. Sparmeyer? He is one of the two missionaries who run the church mission. Brother, this is Lord Wivenly, my step-father's great-nephew."

Wivenly held out his hand. "It is my pleasure to finally

meet you. I've heard a good deal about the work you do here."

Beaming at him, the missionary returned her betrothed's grip. "I'm glad to meet you as well. Your uncle gave us much support. If only my own countrymen were as liberal in their views as you English are. Since the islands were turned back over to the Danes, the situation with both the freemen and slaves has worsened." Brother Sparmeyer smiled sadly. "I could discuss this all day, but I know Miss Villaret is anxious to see her students."

She was, but she also needed time to think. Never had she thought Wively would behave in such a kind fashion toward the missionary, especially after she'd not warned him about the hill. He must be hot and in pain, yet he was as gracious as if he were in England. Perhaps if they had met under different circumstances, she would not have formed such a low opinion of him, or he of her.

The injustice she had done Wively today ate at her. She would find a way to make it up to him.

"If you'll excuse me." She bobbed a slight curtsey to Wively.

He inclined his head. "Of course, my dear."

It wasn't until several moments after she'd begun the lesson that the warmth of Wively's gaze on her back left her. An hour later when the children were called to leave, he was still in deep conversation with the pastor.

Suddenly he glanced up and grinned. *Mon Dieu*, Wively was a handsome devil. He could probably have any woman he wanted. He certainly made her think and feel things she did not wish to. His focus on her caused a tingling to course through her body, and she rose to go to him. This attraction she had to him was not at all helpful in her effort to make a rational decision whether or not to marry him.

He held his hand out. "Shall we go?"

When Eugénie moved past him out the door, he caught

her arm, twining it once more in his. She gazed up at him. His poor neck was even worse than when they'd arrived. "You should remove your cravat."

"First I shall escort you home." His tone was low but firm.

The silly man. If it had not required going to the hotel without a chaperone, she would have spoken to his valet herself.

Eugénie gave herself an inner shake. How was it he alternately fascinated and irritated her? This courting was very nice, much better than when he kissed her. *Non.* If she was honest, she liked his kisses too much. What she didn't like was the feeling of being out of control, consumed by him. "What did you and the brother speak of?"

"Ways in which I could aid the mission."

Her heart gave a leap as she stared up at him. "You would do that?"

"Your father is not the only member of my family to support the freedom of others, as well as different causes." Wively gazed back at her. His lips curled slowly into a smile. "My father was responsible for helping to pass the bill ending the slave trade." The look in his eyes turned wry. "Unfortunately he was not as successful in freeing them."

She thought of the babies and small children she'd saved and tears pricked the back of her eyes. She blinked them away. "Papa said it will be years yet."

"I'm afraid I have to agree."

Three quarters of an hour later, as they strolled past the hotel, she spied Cicely and her parents entering. It must be close to noon. Cicely had told Eugénie earlier she wanted Andrew to host them. Surely they would not mind company, and it would give her an opportunity to tell Tidwell what she thought of his methods. "I see Cicely and Andrew. Let us join them. It will also give me an opportunity to speak with your valet."

"Yes, let's."

He allowed Eugénie to lead him toward the front steps. Would she really beard Tidwell?

Eugénie and Will entered the parlor on the heels of Andrew, Cicely, and Cicely's parents.

Tidwell stood in the doorway leading to Will's bedchamber appearing a bit nonplussed. Nothing could have pleased Wively more. It was about damned time his valet had a surprise.

"My lord, I did not expect . . ."

Eugénie turned to Tidwell with a dazzling smile on her face. "Ah, you must be the estimable Tidwell I have heard about."

Tidwell glanced at Will, who couldn't keep from smiling, then back at her. "Yes, miss."

She reached up and gently tugged at his cravat. He winced as the rough cloth rubbed against his neck. It hurt much more than he'd expected.

"You see this redness?"

Tidwell cringed.

"This is what happens when you use too much starch." She raised one brow, her voice a gentle command. "I trust you will not do so again."

Tidwell glanced at Will for a moment before replying, "No, miss."

"Bon." Eugénie nodded sharply. "We understand one another. Please tend to his lordship immediately so we may eat luncheon."

For putting Tidwell in his place, something Will had never been able to do, he could have kissed her. Right there in front of everyone. As he followed a subdued Tidwell into his chamber, it occurred to Will that a wife could actually be a very useful thing to have around. No one had ever actually taken his side in domestic disputes before. In fact, all of his father's senior servants treated Will as if he were still barely breeched. But a wife would set them straight. Hadn't Beaumont said something of the sort about his wife? Who would have thought that a lady one was to protect could actually defend him?

Will removed his neckcloth, handing it to Tidwell. Then Will took the cool, wet cloth Tidwell passed to him, putting it around his neck. The dampness alone soothed his chaffed skin. Before Will donned a lightly starched cravat, his valet spread some sort of cream on the rash. In less than half an hour, he'd rejoined the others.

Eugénie handed him a cold glass of wine before turning to study his injured flesh. "Hmm."

He took a large drink. "Hmm, what?"

"You shall escort me home."

"I had planned to do so."

Andrew's valet entered, followed by some of the hotel's servants with luncheon. The conversation, because the Whitecliffs and Andrew could discuss nothing else, centered on Andrew and Cicely's nuptials, or lack thereof. An hour later, Will and Eugénie made their escape.

She stopped them in front of the bottom gate to Wively House, and pulled the key out of her reticule.

He said nothing, but watched as she opened the door. Where was she taking him?

"Come." She motioned for him to follow her, as if he would not. "We must talk and this is the only place we can be private. Keep your voice down."

They entered a large parlor, much like the main floor's but not as deep. The back must be dug into the hillside. Flanking the room on each side were two additional rooms.

Eugénie's maid walked into the parlor from one of the side rooms. She glanced at Eugénie, then at Will, and back to Eugénie again. It was clear from her confusion that no other man had been here before.

"Miss?"

"Marisole, take this, please." Eugénie removed her bonnet. "We'd like some refreshment. I also need some clean cloths, cold water, brandy, and salve. His lordship has a rash."

Once Marisole departed, Eugénie went to a white and blue porcelain contraption in the back corner of the parlor. "What is that?"

"A type of gargolette the Danes use to filter and cool the water." She poured two glasses, handing him one. "Why do you wish to marry me?"

"Why?" Will lowered his tumbler. Thankfully he'd not had any in his mouth or it would have gone all over him.

Hell and damnation. He thought he'd been doing so well courting her. Now he suddenly felt like the fox at a hunt. Why wasn't it enough that he wanted to make her his wife? He should have known it wasn't going to be as easy as he'd thought. He had a mother and younger sisters. Women always wanted to talk of their feelings.

She stuck her chin out in a belligerent manner. "Yes. I wish to know."

He didn't want to have this conversation. Mostly because he had only a vague idea himself, and he'd only recently come to the conclusion that a wife could be useful to have. Unfortunately, he had no glib answer to give her. Somehow he had to get her mind off this topic. A diversion was needed.

Kissing usually distracted her, and would put her lips to better use than trying to make him think and talk about things he'd rather not. He lowered his head, brushing his lips across her mouth. Will pulled Eugénie to him. Her supple body was warm against his. He wanted to bury his nose in her hair, kiss his way down her neck to her lush mouth. Run his palms over her . . .

"Non." She pressed her lips in a tight line and turned her head away. "Tell me."

God, he'd better come up with something, fast. Then he

remembered everything she'd done today, and what the brother had told him. "You are compassionate, fiercely loyal, and intelligent. My life will never be dull with you."

She sighed, and her body softened against his. He slid his palm down her back and cupped her bottom. "And your derrière fits perfectly in my hand."

Will tightened his grip as Eugénie sucked in a sharp breath and attempted to pull back. "*Oh! You* . . . you are not a . . ."

"Gentleman?" He grinned, finishing her sentence. "Sadly, I fear Tidwell agrees. Though I do have some redeeming qualities."

She slowly raised one finely shaped brow. "Name one."

How did he manage to always get on her bad side? Something told him if he didn't come about now, it would be bellows to mend with him. Why was he having such a problem? From the beginning, Will had wanted Eugénie to be his. The idea that another man would ever kiss her had his blood boiling. Every time another man glanced at her, he wanted to make sure the world knew she belonged to him. Good Lord, he'd even begged flowers for her twice and promised not to touch her until she agreed to marry him. He'd never even considered doing anything like that before.

Then this morning when Eugénie had taught the children, he'd had a vision of her with their children. He wanted to see her holding his babe. Not to mention that despite all the angst Will had caused her, she'd waged war on Tidwell and won. Will might as well admit it: If he wasn't in love, he deserved to be in Bedlam. And if he couldn't bring himself to tell her, he'd lose Eugénie for good. He took a breath, then blurted, "I'm desperately in love with you."

Her head jerked back. "I-I . . ."

The bane of his life seemed shocked into silence.

A trickle of sweat rolled down his back as he waited for her to continue. His lips hovered over hers. Perhaps if he kissed her . . . ? Will groaned. Probably not a good idea.

Eugénie's eyes searched his. "You are?"

"Absolutely."

"You don't merely want my . . . my body?"

If this went on much longer, she was going to be the death of him. "There is no *merely* about my desire for your exquisite form." He ran his palm down her back. "From the very first, you were a siren call to me." He placed a soft kiss on her temple, pulling her closer. "I love you from the tip of your head to your toes and everything in between."

Will touched his lips to hers. The taste was manna to his starved soul. He'd need to keep a tight rein on his desire, or at this rate, he'd scare her away again.

Her mouth softened beneath his. "I did not wish to, but I love you as well. When I saw the rash, and you didn't complain at all, then at the church . . . I had thought to test you."

Will grinned. "I had an idea that might be it."

"It was then I knew, but I needed to hear it from you."

As he ran his tongue along the seam of her lips, she opened. He caressed her tongue, and the warm cavern of her mouth. "I was a little daunted by trying to figure out how to make you even like me."

Her head lay against his chest. She nodded. "Sometimes you are not very likable."

"No?" A sense of satisfaction filled him as he ran his thumb over her nipple, and she shuddered.

"Non." Her tone was breathy. "At times you are illtempered and domineering."

Oh God, he wanted her. No other woman had ever felt right in his arms. "You'll have to take me to task when I get out of hand." Drawing back, he placed a finger under her chin, tilted her head up, then kissed her, deeply. "I want you to like me."

"I want the same." A sultry smile appeared on Eugénie's lips as her hands slid up over his shoulders, and she kissed him. "I believe it is time we wed, my lord."

A groan came from deep inside him. "If I could have figured out how to accomplish that feat, you'd already be Viscountess Wively."

"It is very simple." She patted his chest, with a smug look. "We sail to Tortola. It is not at all far. With a good wind, only a few hours."

"Tortola?" It was that simple? Of course, twenty-one was the age of majority in the British islands and, not being in England, they did not fall under the Marriage Act. They could be married immediately, as long as they could track down the vicar. He drew his brows together, spearing her with his gaze. "How long have you known this?"

"I don't know." She lifted one shoulder in an elegant shrug. "A few years. I have heard it said, that the British islands are our version of your Gretna Green."

"Which means Cicely and probably Andrew know as well." And didn't bother to share the information with Will. His scowl deepened. "I'll kill him."

Chapter 20

"You may not murder Andrew. He must stand up with you when we wed." She took his hand. It wouldn't do to allow Wivenly to become overwrought. He didn't behave well when he did.

Eugénie reached up and kissed him. "Come, let us tell everyone and make plans to leave as soon as possible. I'll send a note to the docks to ready the ship."

"That boat we were out on won't carry more than three people."

She glanced up at his handsome face and tried not to laugh. How could he possibly think they would take the dory to Tortola? "No, we'll take the *Sidonie*. It is the one we use when all the family comes."

He jerked her to a stop. "Why didn't I know about this boat before?"

Because he probably would have tried to force her to go with him somewhere. "You had no need to know. It is not part of the business."

"Eugénie." He spread out her name as he said it.

"Oh, very well. I wanted what we have right now. I didn't

want to marry you until I was sure of your affections." She took a breath. "If you had been aware . . ."

A wry smile twisted his lips. "I would have forced you to marry me."

She peeked up at him, surprised to see even a hint of contrition in his face. "Yes, and I could not allow that to happen."

Wivenly's arms closed around her. "I'm marrying you because of your wisdom as well."

"First, my lord, I must care for your neck. I do not like the job Tidwell did."

"Eugénie, I would like you to use my name."

She drew her brows together. "I already call you Wivenly."

"No. My friends call me Will."

She wanted her own special name for him. "Would you mind if I use William?"

"Not at all." He drew her to him. "I'd like it more than anything."

Marisole returned as he removed his cravat, and it was a good thing. His poor neck was so inflamed that he must be in excruciating pain. She quickly sniffed the salve, some sort of grease. *Imbécile!*

"Oh, William!" Eugénie picked up the sponge from the basin of cool water her maid had drawn. "I will kill Tidwell."

He flinched as she touched his neck with the sponge. When she unfastened the shirt buttons, her fingers shook with rage and something else she had trouble defining, a desire to touch him she was unfamiliar with, and a need to protect him. A V of curly, dark gold hair appeared. It was all she could do to stop herself from caressing it. She cleared her throat, and quickly cleaned the area with coconut soap. "Now the salve."

Oh dear. She almost didn't recognize her voice it was so breathy.

The corner of his lips quirked up into a crooked smile. "Having any problems, my love?"

Oooh, he was infuriating. Eugénie was that close to dashing the whole bowl of water in his lap, yet he wouldn't be able to go out if he was wet, and his shirt would stick against his hard chest. She stifled a sigh. Ever since Cicely had put the idea in Eugénie's head, she'd thought about what it would be like to make love with him. Now that they were to marry, and he loved her, there was no reason to wait. *Oh! This must be what Cicely has been feeling.* And unlike Andrew, William—Eugénie was sure—would agree they need not find the vicar first. Tomorrow she'd tell him they could make love. She could wait until then, perhaps.

Will's body tightened as, with shaky fingers, Eugénie applied the salve. If her maid hadn't been present, he'd have found a way to claim her now. As it was, he'd have to distract both of them. "Who lives on this floor?"

Her throat moved as she swallowed, and he wanted to run his tongue down its length. "My brother, Benet, and me."

"You led me to believe you lived with the other children."

"Non." She shook her head. "You chose to think that, and I did not correct you."

He willed his body to relax. "I would never have forced my attentions on you."

"I know, but you would have made it . . . difficult to refuse you."

"You're right." He cupped her cheek and kissed her lightly. "I did say I love you for your intelligence." He buttoned his shirt and sniffed. What had she put on him? "What was in the salve you used? It doesn't smell bad at all."

"Aloe, a plant we have here known for its healing properties, and a bit of lavender."

His neck was already starting to feel better. Will retied his cravat. "Let's find everyone. We have a great deal to do."

A line appeared in her forehead. "There is not *so* much. We shall take provisions from the house, and pack——"

He kissed her. "There is if we must find a place to hide Tidwell's body."

"Oh, that." She laughed. "I will throw him overboard for the sharks."

Will dragged Eugénie onto his lap, ignoring the shocked gasp from her maid. As far as he was concerned, the woman would have to get used to displays of affection or find another position. "You're a bloodthirsty wench."

Eugénie gave an exaggerated sigh. "It has always been my failing." Her lips brushed his neck. "I protect my own."

"As do I."

Another sigh was heard from across the room. Will glanced over. He couldn't believe it. The maid stood with her hands clasped, a wistful expression on her face, as if she were watching a Drury Lane play. At least there would be no trouble from that quarter.

"Perhaps you shouldn't kill Tidwell," Will whispered. "We could play matchmaker."

Eugénie slid a look at her maid, pursing her lips. "Hmm, we shall see how they get along."

"I was teasing."

She widened her lovely brown eyes. "I am not. I do not understand why they should not be happy as well."

The head of something that resembled a cat peeked into the parlor, then quickly ducked back. "What was that?"

Eugénie glanced at him as if he was mad. "What?"

"A gray thing."

She jumped off his lap. "Probably my cat, Penelope. She does not like strangers. Once she becomes used to you, she is very affectionate. Come, we should tell the others."

"Miss, come quickly!" Marisole, who'd left the room, ran back in, beckoning urgently.

Will followed Eugénie onto the terrace and to a long building which held the servants' quarters. Her maid opened the door to one of the rooms. Inside, a black girl who couldn't have been more than fourteen or so, paced, holding a small, fussy baby.

"When did she arrive?" Eugénie asked in a businesslike tone.

"Just a few minutes ago." Marisole led the girl to a chair, pressing a glass of water into her hand. "I've sent for food."

"Has anyone contacted the captain?"

The maid shook her head. "I do not know. This was quite sudden."

The girl must have noticed Will for the first time, because she gave a start. He gave her an encouraging smile. He'd known of his great-uncle's activities in helping free slaves, but not that Eugénie was involved. Though it shouldn't have surprised him. Still, he didn't like the danger it presented to her. "How can I help?"

His betrothed glanced up, her brows drawn together, chewing her bottom lip. "I must ensure the girl has a place to go, then a safe way to get to the harbor."

"If she can remain here overnight, she could come with us tomorrow."

Eugénie rubbed her forehead. "No, she must leave as soon as possible. One of our neighbors might hear the baby. Though you are correct, we can use our departure to cover taking her to the ship. Yet first I must speak with Cicely."

Now that was unexpected. "Are you telling me she is involved as well?"

Eugénie grinned. "Yes, her father has many connections in the British islands. Cicely finds people to help the newly freed slaves." She took his hand. "Come, let us inform Maman and the girls of our marriage."

They walked the short distance from the servants' quarters to the house, then to the level above Eugénie's, which was devoid of children.

One of the two maids cleaning said, "The children are with the mistress, miss."

Upon reaching the top floor, Bates informed them the family was out for the next few hours.

That was a disappointment. Now that the final decision had been made, Will wanted to tell someone, not to mention make arrangements for the girl and baby. He looked down at Eugénie. "Shall we visit Cicely and Andrew now?"

She twined her fingers in his. "A very good idea."

When they got to Whitecliff House, Cicely, her father, and Andrew were gathered in the large main room.

Cicely glanced from Will to Eugénie and squealed. "Oh." She quickly put her fingers over her mouth. "I should not have done that. Am I right, though? You have decided?"

Eugénie nodded and all Will saw was a flutter of muslin before Cicely threw her arms around his betrothed. "I'm so happy for you. Both of you."

Andrew and Whitecliff strode over and slapped Will on his back, then hugged Eugénie.

"This calls for champagne," Mr. Whitecliff said.

"Yes indeed." Cicely took Eugénie to the sofa. "When will you marry?"

"We'll sail to Tortola tomorrow or as soon as it can be arranged."

Eugénie glanced at Will. Her eyes swam in tears, but she'd never looked happier, and he wasn't going to let her down. "I'll go from island to island if need be to chase down the vicar."

The butler came in with the bottle of wine and flutes. Once they each had a glass, Andrew held his up. "A toast to never hiding in trees again."

Will gave a short laugh. He'd almost forgotten about the main reason he'd left England.

"You were hiding in trees?" Eugénie's eyes rounded. "Why would you do such a thing?"

He slipped his arm around her waist. "Believe it or not, I'm considered quite the catch in England."

Andrew grinned. "For the sole purpose of becoming his viscountess, young ladies used to plot to be found in compromising positions with his lordship."

Eugénie's jaw dropped for a brief moment. "Did so many fall in love with you?"

If she hadn't led him such a chase, he might have been a bit insulted by her astonishment. "Not me"—Will tightened his hold on her—"my title."

Her expression quickly turned to fury. "They will not do so again."

That was one of the things he loved about Eugénie. "See what a good viscountess you will make me?"

"I shall make you a good wife." She nibbled on her bottom lip. "I will request lessons from your maman for the other."

"Nonsense," Cicely said firmly. "You will be perfect." She glanced at Andrew. "If only we could be wed as soon."

Whitecliff set his glass down with a snap. "You shall be. Eugénie, my dear, if you don't mind, we'll take the *Song Bird* instead of the *Sidonie* and all travel together and hunt down the vicar."

Cicely clapped her hands. "Papa, this is famous. What a wonderful idea! We shall have a double wedding." She stopped and her face fell. "What will Mama say?"

Whitecliff's jaw firmed. "She will, for once, do as I ask her. Now, if you children will see to the packing, I shall send a message to the ship. Eugénie, I imagine your mother will wish to accompany us."

She squeezed Will's hand. "And the children."

He rose. "I'll tell Tidwell he'll have to launder my cravats."

"Yes," Eugénie said. "He must do that, or he will answer to me. Yet, I think he and I understand each other."

Will had no doubt his valet did not wish to be on the wrong side of her temper.

"What the deuce is this about your neckcloth?" Andrew studied Will as if seeing him for the first time today. "What happened to it?"

"Too much starch. What did you think?"

A wide grin split Andrew's face. "I thought perhaps Eugénie had tried to string you up."

Whitecliff groaned and both ladies giggled. Will did his best to frown. "It was a near thing, I can tell you."

"Yes, it was," Eugénie retorted. "Now come, we have much to accomplish."

"Meet back here for dinner," Whitecliff said. "There is strength in numbers."

"What time will we leave, Papa?" Cicely asked.

"We sail at first light. Which means we need to be on board before then. I'll send the baggage down this evening."

Cicely rose up on the tips of her toes and gave him a kiss on his cheek. "Thank you, Papa."

He patted her on the back. "Let's just hope we can bring your mother around, or she'll be in a taking for quite some time."

Will had never thought he'd look forward to being married so much. Now he knew how his friends felt and the reason all of them, even Beaumont, were happy to wed. Once they were in England, Will would introduce them to Eugénie. His friends' wives, Phoebe, Anna, Serena, and Emma would take his wife under their collective wing. He pressed his lips to her head, happy to finally have everything settled.

On the covered terrace of the house in which they were staying, Yves listened to the boy he'd had keeping a watch on Eugénie. The problem was the child's patois was so strong, he had trouble understanding what the child was saying.

"Dem old ladies, go wi' dem little ones. Nothin' else. Den that big one, he ask what I doin' an' I leave."

"You did not see either of the younger ladies."

The boy shook his head. Yves flipped him a coin. "Do the same tomorrow."

"Yah, mister." The child scampered off.

Yves was running out of time. Hervé was growing impatient, and it was time for Yves to show he was as much a Villaret de Joyeuse as his older brothers. He went to his chamber and found his valet. "How well have you got to know the staff?"

The man sniffed. "Quite well. Though I keep my distance."

"I require a man who can charm women."

"There is such a one. He is very popular with the fairer sex."

"Send him to me. I have a job for him."

"Oui, monsieur."

Yves poured a glass of the chilled white wine his valet always had on hand for him. What he wouldn't give for a red wine, but in this climate they went off too quickly, and one could not always imbibe brandy. Less than a quarter hour later, his valet knocked on the door and entered the chamber, followed by a mulatto. "Monsieur. This is Henri."

Yves studied Henri. Well-built, the young man appeared to be in his early twenties. His skin was the color of café with cream, and his eyes a startling green. Yves knew of any number of high-born ladies in Paris who would be unable to resist taking him to their beds. Yes, he would do very well. "I have need of someone who can seduce a servant for information."

Instead of bowing and agreeing immediately, Henri said, "For a price."

The man was insolent, but Yves needed him. "Naturally. Which currency do you prefer?"

"English pounds."

Of course he would, especially if this Henri thought of leaving St. Thomas. "I shall pay you thirty."

Henri's brows rose. It was a great deal of money. "Half now. Half when I bring you the information."

Bah! That was not what Yves had planned. "Very well." He snapped his fingers and his valet went to a chest, then brought back a small bag. "Here you are."

Henri nodded. "Whom do you wish me to seduce and what information shall I provide you?"

Yves described the house and location. "I want to know when my niece is usually alone in a place where she can be abducted. She cannot always be with other people. One of the maids should do. I would say my niece's dresser, but those women tend to be almost frigid. The position is too good to throw away."

Only then did Henri bow. "You will have your information, monsieur."

Frowning, Yves watched the servant leave. He was well-spoken for his position, almost too well-spoken for his situation. He glanced at his valet. "Find out more about him for me."

"Oui, monsieur."

It wouldn't do to have a traitor in their midst.

Henri made his way to his quarters. He wasn't expected on duty again for another hour, and this assignment would require some thought. He knew Wivenly House well. His uncle Bates was the butler there. Mr. Nathan Wivenly had helped Henri's family buy his freedom. He spat. Though how much that freedom was worth in any of the Danish islands was debatable. The government and Danish population treated freemen with more disdain than they treated slaves.

Whatever the Frenchman wanted with Miss Villaret could not be good, and Henri must find a way to interfere with the man's plot.

He had almost enough saved up to travel to Tortola and

set up his own business. The money the Frenchman offered would give Henri the rest of what he needed and then some, but he would not harm any of the Wively family in the process. By the time he visited his uncle tomorrow, Henri would have a plan that would best serve both his purposes, as well as protect the lady.

Nathan awoke to the sound of a chair being dragged over to him. He stretched and took inventory; a little sore, but he didn't seem the worse for wear. Shortly after he'd eaten that morning, he had fallen asleep. The most imperative thing for him to do now was to regain his strength. The aroma of strong coffee floated on the air, and he opened his eyes.

"Good morning, or afternoon as is the case." Vincent grinned. "After hearing what you've been through, I decided to let you sleep."

Perhaps now was the time to discover what *had* actually occurred. "You probably know more than I." Nathan propped himself against the pillows, then took the mug Vincent held out to him. "Thank you. What time is it?"

"Almost one." He waited until Nathan had taken a sip. "Do you really not know how you came to be on the plantation?"

"I had a broken leg and arm, as well as a cracked head. I suspect some of my ribs were fractured as well. I hadn't given it much thought until recently."

Vincent's expression was grim as he nodded. "Pirates attacked your ship. You were the only survivor."

Nathan had a vague memory of the attack, but nothing afterward. He clenched his jaw so tightly, it hurt. Damn them, killing his captain and crew. "What I do not know is the reason for all of this."

Vincent leaned back in the chair and folded his arms across his chest. "Your step-daughter."

"Eugénie?"

"Do you have another?"

Trust his friend to joke at a time like this. "Very funny. Tell me what you know."

"What I know, I pieced together from everyone's stories. Her uncle, the Vicomte Villaret de Joyeuse, wants to marry her to an older French *comte*. It appears the family is rather done up, and Eugénie is the only lady in the family of marriageable age to offer in wedlock."

Nathan sipped the strong black coffee as his friend related how Villaret was responsible for the death of Nathan's crew and the destruction of his ship. If he found the blackguard, he'd kill him. An English frigate had seen the fight and given chase, then returned to find the crew dead. It was, of course, assumed that Nathan had died as well. And now Eugénie's uncle was on St. Thomas. There was no way in hell he'd allow the rogue to get his hands on his daughter.

"I need to get home as soon as possible. Can you get me a description and the name of the ship?"

"Naturally." Vincent grinned as he handed Nathan a piece of paper. "I have been busy while you slept. It is already done, my friend."

"The *Unconquerable*. We'll see about that." He glanced back to his friend. "How soon can we depart?"

"I'm outfitting my ship now. We will go aboard before dark." Vincent took a sip of his coffee. "The only problem is your rather large friend."

That wasn't much of a surprise. Mr. Conrad would have made a good circus giant. A giggle from another room reached him. "I assume you have a plan?"

"You could say that." Vincent glanced at the door. "I have a friend who works in the theater. She is completely trustworthy and, I think, almost finished."

Nathan seriously doubted if anyone could disguise Conrad enough to get him aboard in broad daylight. Setting his cup down, Nathan made to rise, but Vincent stayed him. "I'll send my man to you. Once you are dressed and have eaten, join us."

The next hour was taken up with bathing, shaving, dressing, and eating. Fortunately, Vincent and Nathan were about the same size. Nathan had not known how hungry he was until he dug into the savory stew filled with beef and vegetables and had consumed a loaf of fresh bread. He hadn't been aware of it, but at the plantation he had been fed with the intent of not allowing him to regain his strength. He made his way to the drawing room. Unlike the houses in St. Thomas, the French replicated their native architecture in Martinique and the rest of the French-held islands.

Miss Marshall had her hands crossed over her stomach, laughing. Conrad sported an old-fashioned gray wig, and his skin color had been lightened to almost white. His lips were pink, and someone had fashioned a frock coat with wide cuffs and a great deal of gold. He was in the process of entertaining the others by walking around stooped over with a cane, spouting the occasional French curse. He resembled an old man who insisted on dressing in the fashion of the previous era.

"Do you think he'll do?" Vincent asked.

"I think he might." Nathan grinned. Hiding Conrad had been his most pressing concern. "We should load him on the boat while it is light enough for everyone to see."

"I agree." Vincent took Nathan by the arm, leading him to the far end of the room. "The plantation's overseer is looking for you and the others. Fortunately, the only descriptions they have given out are of Conrad and Miss Marshall."

This was bad news, but not unexpected. "I knew it wouldn't take long. Have you been able to arrange all our papers on such short notice?"

"They are being made up. We'll have them before we depart." Vincent glanced at the others. "Everyone, including you, will be in disguise. You must take care to speak French. The

slaves' owner"—Vincent's lips thinned with disapproval—
"did his best to ensure none of them could speak my language. It is our good fortune that he did not succeed. Even
Miss Marshall speaks very good French. She is an impres-
sive woman."

Nathan nodded. "She told me their story. I agree with
you. Not many women would do as she has done."

A boy burst into the drawing room and spoke in rapid patois to Vincent. He turned to the rest of their group. "We will
soon have visitors."

Vincent strode to one of the ornate wall panels, pressed a
leaf, and a moment later it opened, revealing a comfortable
room with chairs and a sofa. "Everyone but Mr. Conrad,
please. You must be silent."

When the group was settled, he closed it again and glanced
at Nathan. "Go to your room. The authorities are not searching for a white man, but I do not wish to give them reason to
tell the overseer about you."

Knocking sounded from the door below as Nathan returned to his chamber, praying none of them would be
caught.

Chapter 21

Before leaving Whitecliff House, Eugénie had told Cicely about her visitors. Fortunately Cicely knew a family in Virgin Gorda who would help them. William had insisted on escorting the girl and her baby to the ship, along with the trunks. After dark, mother and child would be moved to the boat that would take them to safety.

Once they were gone, Eugénie finally had time to reflect on everything that was happening. She hadn't known she could be this blissful and content. It was as if one of the fairy tales her mother used to tell her had come true. If only Papa were alive, her happiness would be complete. What a surprise Maman and the girls would have when they returned.

When they finally arrived home late in the afternoon, all the children looked as if they'd been through a mud puddle. Eugénie bussed her mother's cheek. "My goodness, what have you been up to?"

"We were invited to Mrs. Spivey's house." Maman removed her bonnet and grimaced at the children. "She has a fishpond and a Great Dane dog."

Nothing more needed to be said. Eugénie struggled not to

laugh. "I understand. It appears that they had a wonderful time."

"Indeed."

The governess shooed the children downstairs, and was about to follow them when Eugénie stayed her. "Miss Penny, please remain. Maman"—Eugénie took a breath—"I have news for you. Lord Wively and I have decided to sail to Tortola tomorrow to find the vicar and marry. I would like you and the children to accompany us. The packing is complete, and the trunks sent to Mr. Whitecliff's ship." Eugénie gave her mother a moment to take in what she'd said. "Cicely and Mr. Grayson are coming with us and will wed as well."

Eugénie waited as her mother stared at her as if in a trance. She resisted the urge to wave her fingers in front of Maman's face. "Are you going to say something?"

"Well—" Maman shook her head as if trying to clear it. "When you make a decision, you do not do it in half measures." She hugged Eugénie. "I knew you had reservations, my love. Though I am pleased you have finally made your choice."

She returned her mother's embrace. "I did, but I have none now. This has turned out very well. He is truly the man I love."

"I must wish you happy," Penny said, "and I'm sure you will be. If it is all the same to you, I'll not tell the children until they are awoken in the morning."

Remembering Mr. Whitecliff's orders, Eugénie said, "We will leave before dawn."

"They will be ready." Penny smiled. "It's been ages since we've all been sailing."

Penny left Eugénie with her mother. It was time to give her the rest of the news. "We are dining next door. Mrs. Whitecliff was out when the decisions were made. I'm counting on you to help convince her that Cicely and Andrew should marry as well."

Maman looked happy for the first time since Papa died. "You can depend on me. Now, I must bathe and change." She turned, then stopped. "Eugénie, my darling, I am so very delighted for you. Wively will make you a good husband."

"I know he will." Eugénie hugged her mother. "I shall see you in an hour."

When she arrived at her rooms, Marisole had the bathing tub ready. "Thank you. This is exactly what I need right now."

"Yes, miss. Until we return, there is no saying that you'll be able to bathe."

Once dressed for dinner, Eugénie rummaged through her dresser. "Where is the fan his lordship gave me?"

"Here it is, miss."

A light tapping on the door made her look up. William smiled, and she made her decision. "Marisole, you may take the rest of the evening off. I'll see you in the morning."

"If you're sure, miss?"

"I've never been more certain of anything in my life." The look in his deep blue eyes, love and desire mixed together, made her want to remain here and be with him now. She'd begun to think she'd never have these feelings of wanting to belong so completely to a man. "Go now, I'll be fine."

Marisole slipped past Wively, but not before giving him a warning look. His head jerked back in surprise, and his gaze followed Marisole as she left. "What did I do to her?"

Heat crept up Eugénie's neck and into her cheeks. Telling her maid not to attend her tonight was much easier than telling William she wanted him to stay. Perhaps she would not have to say anything. She flipped open her fan and applied it vigorously. "She has strange humors at times. I wouldn't worry about it."

There must have been something in her voice, because he turned and stared at her. "I'm glad to see you carrying the fan I gave you. Though it doesn't seem to be working very well."

If anything, her face grew hotter. "It's just very warm." She moved toward the door. "We should leave. We don't want to be late."

His large hand caught her around the waist, pulling her to him. "Eugénie"—his voice was a low, seductive purr— "what are you keeping from me?"

Suddenly she felt very young and inexperienced. Perhaps she should wait until their wedding night. He dipped his head, pressing light kisses over her jaw and down her neck. Shivers of sensation rushed through her, and she sighed.

"You like that, do you?"

Eugénie's words were as languid as she felt. "Umm, it's nice."

"Only nice?"

She tilted her head to give him better access. "*Very* nice."

"I can see that after we're wed, I'll have to work hard to merit superlatives from you."

"Afterward?"

His tongue moved down over her neck. "You did say you wished to wait."

Oh Lord. She was blushing again. This was so unfair. Couldn't he see she wanted him to stay with her? "Yes. No. I mean—" He'd moved to her chin. A smile hovered around his lips. "Drat you. You are going to make me say it."

His lips touched the corner of her mouth. "Say what?"

That was enough. He was making a game of her. She hauled one arm back and punched him on the shoulder, and all the brute did was laugh. She hid her face against his coat. "You could make this easier."

Wivenly's chest rumbled a bit as if he held back a chuckle. "Are you inviting me to spend the night? Is that the reason your maid gave me such a look? You told her not to wait up for you?"

She nodded, rubbing her cheek against the smooth fabric of his jacket. "Yes, that was it exactly."

"I'd be honored, my love, but we really must work on overcoming your hesitation in saying what you want." Will sent a prayer of thanks to the Deity.

That brought her head back up. Eugénie's luscious lips formed a perfect O. "You mean you want me to . . ."

"Trust me. It will make our lovemaking that much better."

For the third time, her face turned a lovely shade of rose. It was a pity they had dinner plans. He kissed each finger one by one. When Will got to the fourth finger of her right hand, he remembered why he'd come to her rooms. "Give me a moment." He pulled out the ring from a waistcoat pocket. "As I didn't know I'd be getting married, I neglected to bring a family ring. He slipped the one he'd bought over the finger of her right hand. "I hope you like it. I thought, because you like to wear knit gloves, a ring with no protruding stones would be better."

"It's beautiful." She held her hand, fluttering her fingers a bit. Gold, opals, and diamonds formed an alternating pattern. "And I'll be able to wear it while sailing." Eugénie raised her gaze to his. "I love it. Thank you."

A bell rang from somewhere above. "What is that?"

"The signal bell. It's more efficient than having servants running up and down the stairs. Each of us is assigned a number of chimes." She donned her gloves and tucked her hand in his. "Shall we, my lord?"

"What is yours?"

She tilted her head and grinned. "One, of course."

"From oldest to youngest?"

"Yes, my brother wanted to be number one as he is the boy"—her voice became wistful—"but Papa said no."

"You miss him a great deal."

"I do. I hope he is looking after all of us from above."

A chill raced down Will's back and he said in an under-voice, "Not too closely, I hope."

"What did you say?"

"I said I'm sure he is." He led her up the stairs on the side of the house, marveling once again how the walls surrounding the house and gardens hid a small world from prying eyes. They had nothing like this at home. "My love, I'd like to take your mother and sisters back to England with us. Yet before I mention it to Aunt Sidonie, I want your opinion."

"I think it is the best idea." She paused for a moment. "Where will they live?"

"With us, if you wish, or with your grandmother Wively. If neither of those choices pleases your mother, then I'm sure my father has a suitable property."

"I do not think it is possible for all of them to reside with Grandmamma." Eugénie's lips formed a *moue*. "She lives in a cottage. Which I do not understand, considering how well off Grandpapa was."

The only time he'd seen his mother do anything as vulgar as roll her eyes was when his great-great-aunt Wively referred to her house as a cottage. "Only if you can call a manor house with above thirty main rooms a cottage."

Eugénie's startled gaze met his. "Truly? That many rooms?"

"Indeed." He couldn't keep the dryness from his tone. "It is actually a house of grand proportions built to resemble a cottage. Much in the same way as Marie Antoinette's Hameau de la Reine. Your grandmother once visited Versailles and was so impressed by the idea of Hameau de la Reine, she had it replicated, though on a larger scale."

"Would she want Maman and the children?"

Will shrugged and shook his head. "I couldn't tell you. I know my mother and father would love to have them visit until all the details can be resolved."

"There you are, my dears." Aunt Sidonie didn't turn a

hair at seeing them together. "I am ready to do my part to convince Sally she must allow her daughter and Mr. Grayson to wed."

This was the most pleased he'd ever seen his aunt, and the first time he'd actually understood how devastated she'd been by his great-uncle's death. Will resolved to do everything he could to ensure she and the children were taken care of.

When they arrived at Whitecliff House, the battle lines had been drawn and the first engagement fought. As Mrs. Whitecliff was dabbing her eyes, it was obvious she had chosen tears as her weapon.

Aunt Sidonie flew to her side. "Oh, my dear. What has upset you so?" As she embraced her friend she motioned for the rest of them to go elsewhere. "There, there. We shall discuss the matter."

Almost silently, they repaired to Cicely's floor, followed by the butler and Josh, carrying a goodly amount of wine, rum, and brandy, as well as cheese and bread.

Will glanced at Andrew. "How long has that been going on?"

He ran his fingers through his hair. "Upwards of a half hour."

Eugénie drew her friend aside. "You should not have begun the conversation until Maman was here."

"There was no help for it." Cicely's chin firmed. "She saw the trunks being carried away." She slid an exasperated look to her father, who tossed back a glass of rum. "We might have been able to get away with telling her we were only accompanying you, until Papa said there was no reason Andrew and I couldn't marry as well."

Whitecliff stared into his empty glass, then filled it again. "Perhaps I should have led up to it, but how was I to know she would take it so badly?"

Pursing her lips, Cicely cast a look at the ceiling. One could almost see her biting back a retort.

Will handed his betrothed a rum shrub—she was going to need it—and leaned against the window.

"What," Eugénie asked, "is her main concern?"

"She wants a large wedding breakfast." Andrew's lips formed a thin line. "Mr. Whitecliff tried to explain that if we were already wed she could arrange one with more certainty than if we have to wait on the vicar."

Cicely took up the story. "But Mama had already worked herself into strong hysterics over the thought that I wouldn't have a proper ceremony."

Eugénie took a large swallow of the rum drink. "Leave it to Maman, she will smooth it over."

A half hour later, the butler returned. "Dinner is served."

Whitecliff, Andrew, and Will all raised their brows.

"The mistress has decided a wedding in Tortola will be the best course."

Will let out the breath he'd been holding. He'd dearly love to know how his aunt had talked Mrs. Whitecliff around so quickly. They piled out of the room and up the stairs. Aunt Sidonie sat with Cicely's mother, drinking champagne. If it wasn't for the children, he'd suggest she marry a gentleman in the Foreign Office. Clearly her diplomatic skills were being wasted here. Moreover, this was the first time he'd seen Sidonie not fretting over something. It made him wonder how different she had been before his uncle died.

Will leaned down and whispered, "I doubted you."

"Did you?" Eugénie took her bottom lip between her teeth but couldn't hide the smile shining in her eyes. "You should never do that, my lord."

"Obviously." He wondered how much of her mother's talent Eugénie had inherited.

Dinner conversation was dominated, once again, by marriage plans. Yet this time, he and Eugénie were involved as well. As it was not proper for his aunt to hold a large wedding breakfast, he and Eugénie would join with Andrew and

Cicely. That did not mean, however, Aunt Sidonie would be left out of the preparations.

Will, Eugénie, and her mother left shortly after dinner was finished. All through the meal, he'd tried to keep his thoughts off what would happen afterward when he had his betrothed to himself. Would she be shy or bold? Would she melt into him as she had earlier or demand a more active role? That he had no idea what to expect made him want her more than he had any other woman. What he did not wish to do was cause her the pain that was sure to come with her first mating. Suddenly all his anticipation of tonight changed to trepidation. It was entirely up to him to see she enjoyed herself.

He bid his aunt good night and was about to escort his betrothed to her apartment, when Aunt Sidonie smiled. "Will, I wish you a good night. We shall see you in the morning." She took her daughter's hand. "Eugénie, stay with me. I have some things I'd like to discuss with you. I've had Marisole bring your night clothes to my room."

Damnation! Fate had it out for him. Doing the only thing he could under the circumstance, he bowed. "Until morning."

Eugénie cast him a forlorn look. He took her hand and kissed it. "Dream of me."

She raised his fingers to her lips. "I shall."

His aunt's expression hadn't changed from polite indulgence. *Drat.* Somehow Aunt Sidonie had found them out. How much longer was he going to have to wait for Eugénie?

Chapter 22

Once more in his chamber, Nathan pulled a chair to the door, sitting heavily. If he heard footsteps coming his way, he'd bolt into the bed. The sounds of two pairs of booted feet pounded up the stairs. The main door opened, and Vincent greeted the new arrivals. He played a dangerous game keeping Conrad in the main salon for the visitors to see.

"Good afternoon, messieurs." Vincent's voice was a mix of haughtiness and welcome. "How may I assist you?"

"We are searching for a runaway slave." There was a pause. "He is hard to miss."

"Yes," said a second man. "We believe he was aided by a mulatta."

"I have not seen such a person. In fact, I have not left my house today, and the only gentleman I have seen is my old friend, Baron von Miskolc."

"May we speak with him?"

"You can, of course, try, but he speaks nothing but Hungarian. The only French he has been able to learn are curses." Silence reigned for a few moments, and finally one of the men said, "If he is very large, we would like to see him."

"*Naturellement*, but understand he is old and has been quite ill. His greatest wish was to visit our islands, but he fell sick a few days after he arrived. I have arranged passage for him back to Europe this afternoon. Please do not indicate by your expressions how poorly he looks."

Conrad erupted in gibberish. If the stakes hadn't been so high, Nathan might have laughed. As it was, he held his breath. If they passed this test, the rest would be easy. A few moments later, someone grunted as though he'd been hit.

"Excuse us, monsieur," one of the men said. "We will bother you no longer."

"I understand. Quite appalling, is it not?"

The upper door closed. Shortly afterwards the bottom door slammed shut as well. Nathan let out the breath he'd been holding.

He moved the chair back just before Vincent entered. "You heard?"

"Yes, what made them leave in such a hurry?"

Vincent's lips twitched. "Conrad hit one of the men in the stomach with his cane, and really the maquillage is such that he appears quite gruesome."

"Let's get the others out and ready."

Miss Marshall was fitted with a stylish wig in light brown, and gown to match, and the others in the street clothing of servants to a wealthy aristocrat.

"Nathan," Vincent said, "you will escort Miss Marshall along the promenade while Monsieur le Baron and his servants board the ship. Take the stairs on the north side. A dory will await you."

Nathan clasped his friend's hand. "I can't thank you enough for all you're doing."

"We are not done yet." Vincent grinned. "I shall accompany you on the voyage. I have a great desire to see your lovely wife and daughter again."

Nathan shook his head. "Eugénie?"

"Alas, no, my friend," Vincent said in a tragic tone as he placed his hand over his heart. "Jeanne has captured my heart. Eugénie is too savvy for an old man like me. She would try to change me."

Vincent was right. Eugénie was a force to be dealt with. Nathan hoped her uncle had not got to her yet. Instead of giving himself over to circumstances he had as yet no control over, he gave his friend a look of mock sternness. "Be careful you don't make my youngest promises you can't keep."

"Ah, *bah*," Vincent scoffed. "I will be dead before she comes out."

"Not unless you plan on dying in the next twelve years," Nathan retorted.

His friend's jaw dropped. "She is that old already? Time moves too quickly, my friend."

"It does indeed." Nathan clasped Vincent's shoulder. "When it is time for Jeanne to marry, she could do worse than a man like you."

Vincent grinned. "But much younger than I am, I hope."

"Yes." Nathan smiled. "Much younger."

Vincent's valet joined their small party. "The baggage has been sent to the docks, monsieur. I shall collect the papers on my way there."

"We'll come immediately," Vincent responded. "Do you have the carriage ready?"

"*Oui.*"

"Very well, Baron, we must depart."

Conrad leaned heavily on his cane, giving every impression he could barely walk.

Vincent grabbed Nathan and kissed him on both cheeks. "We shall see you soon. Be careful."

"You as well," Nathan said.

Miss Marshall watched, concern etched in her features, as the rest of their little group left. Getting to the ship was the most dangerous part.

"They will be all right," Nathan assured her.

She turned to him. "I can only trust in God."

A half hour later, the dresser fussed with Miss Marshall's gown and placed a wide-brimmed bonnet on her head before stepping back. "*Bon*. You will do."

Nathan held an arm out to her. "Are you ready to take the air, ma'am?"

"Yes indeed." She placed her hand on his arm. "Lead on."

When they reached the street, the hairs on Nathan's neck pricked, but he stared straight ahead. They were being watched, and it wouldn't do for anyone to see his concern.

Eugénie flopped back in her bed, then punched the pillow. Mama's talk consisted of the information that Eugénie probably wouldn't enjoy her first experience in the marriage bed as there would be some pain, but with a considerate husband, she would grow to enjoy it. Then one of the nursemaids brought Jeanne up to her mother. She'd had a bad dream and wouldn't settle, giving Eugénie the excuse to repair to her own chamber. Unfortunately, William was probably on his way back to the hotel.

This was so unfair. When she finally wanted William's attentions with her whole heart, and he wanted her, they were parted. If only she'd thought to give him the gate key. No, even that would not have worked. He thought she'd be spending the night with her mother.

She groaned and tried not to think about his caresses and kisses. Yet her breasts swelled with want and a strange throbbing started between her legs. She let out a low moan.

"I hope that was for me." Humor tinged William's voice.

Eugénie struggled to free the sheets entangling her legs. "How did you know I'd be here?"

"Andrew and I were on the steps talking, when I heard one of your sisters cry out." He found the overlap in the mosquito netting around her bed and sat. "Having younger brothers and sisters, I knew it was just a matter of time before you'd return to your chamber." William took her hand and kissed it. "I waited until I was sure your maid was gone."

"How clever of you." She took his palm, pressing it against her cheek. "Will you stay with me?"

"If you still want me." He lifted her onto his lap. "What did your mother tell you?"

Eugénie burrowed her head in his neck and breathed in. The scent of the salve was still present, but under it was his own very male musk. "That I would not enjoy marital relations the first time, but if you were a good husband, I'd come to like it." She raised her head and trailed her tongue along his jaw as he'd done to her. "I still want you."

"Let me see if I can make you enjoy our lovemaking the first time." She started to untie his cravat. "We need a light and a towel."

Eugénie stopped. She hated to ask, then again, he knew she had no knowledge of the act. "Why?"

"The towel because you might bleed a bit."

"Bleed?" Maman had not mentioned that part.

"When your maidenhead tears." William drew her closer. "I'm sorry, my love. Perhaps I shouldn't have mentioned it. From what I understand the pain is not much."

"No." Why did it have to hurt at all? "I would rather comprehend what will occur."

William's tone roughened as if he were in pain. "We can wait, if you wish."

Eugénie leaned back, trying to search his face in the dark. "Will that change anything?"

He shook his head. "No, but it might allow you to accustom yourself."

Or make a mountain out of a molehill. She took a breath. "I do not wish to wait." She made herself smile. "Now tell me why you want the light."

William kissed the corner of her lips, then nibbled his way down her neck. "Because I need to see you, my darling. God, Eugénie, it feels as if I've been waiting an eternity for you."

His hard, firm lips pressed on hers. She opened her mouth to him, reveling in his taste. He lifted his head, breaking the kiss.

"Flint in my bedside table."

Papa had built the netting on frames that stood out a few feet from the beds, so that one could move around at night and not set the fabric on fire or trip over it.

Eugénie closed her eyes against the light when it flared. When she opened them Wivenly's jacket and waistcoat were already on the foot of the bed. He untied his cravat. It was so intricate she would never have got it undone. The rash around his neck was already improved, but she renewed her vow never to allow his valet to do something like that again. What a thing to think of now, yet from this night on, she would be, in effect, his wife and responsible for him.

The cravat joined his other clothing. He toed off his evening pumps. Eugénie's mouth dried. The shirt was next. She'd felt his hard, broad chest enough that she was now anxious to see it. He pulled the linen over his head. Golden-brown hair curled over his muscles, tapering down to his breeches. She licked her lips.

A wicked grin appeared on his face before he turned his back to her.

No no. Eugénie wanted to see all of him. "What are you doing?"

"I do not want to scare you."

She didn't understand. "You are beautiful. How would seeing the rest of you frighten me? I have seen drawings of statues, you know."

Even as Wivenly's breeches dropped to the floor, his shoulders shook with laughter.

How dare he insult her at a time like this? She raised her chin. "I fail to see what is so funny."

"Oh, my poor love." Mirth caused his voice to tremble. "Not even a real statue. This is a bit different."

He turned and the little thing that graced most of the drawings was much larger and sticking out straight against his stomach. "Oh."

Before she could think of anything to add, he slipped into her bed. "As fetching as this nightgown is, I would much rather have you out of it."

That was what he'd meant earlier. She squeaked, "Me?"

A warm glow lurked in his eyes. "Um-hm. You've had a look at me. Now it's my turn."

Fire lit her cheeks. "I am sure I cannot be that interesting."

"For instance, I'd like to see how far down your lovely blush goes." His lips touched the base of her neck. "Is it only to the top of your breasts?" The top button of her gown sprung free. "Or does it go lower?" By the time he'd finished speaking, all the buttons were undone. He moved one side of the nightgown off her shoulder. "Lovely."

Her heart thudded so quickly she could barely speak. Maman hadn't said anything about this either. "It is?"

"Even more than I'd imagined."

Will could feel the tension in Eugénie. He kissed and licked his way down to her breasts, taking one already tightly budded nipple in his mouth. Coconut. He'd not known what it was before, but they'd had it at dinner this evening. "Relax, my love."

Soon she pressed up into him. That was better. If only her mother hadn't "prepared" Eugénie. He'd been told anticipating the pain was the worst part. Will moved to the other breast as he played with the first, rolling her nipple. Little mewing sounds escaped from her lips. "That's it. Feel, my love, just feel."

He kissed down over her slightly rounded stomach before moving between her legs. The moment he touched his tongue to the pearl hiding in her dark curls, her fingers gripped his head, and she moaned. It was a damned good thing they weren't aboard a ship where everyone could hear them. He kept his tone low and soothing. "That's right. Let me love you."

Eugénie's hips pushed up. Her musk swirled around him. She squirmed and tossed. When he entered her with his finger, her sheath clamped tightly around him, and she cried out. "Good. That's good, sweetheart."

When she was as wet and prepared as he could make her, Will moved over Eugénie, rubbing his member against her labia before slowly entering her. She gasped, and he took her mouth in a hard kiss, trying to stop her from thinking about the pain. Her maidenhead gave way easily, but she was so very tight, and he needed to ensure she had some pleasure from her first time. "Easy now, my darling."

God, he hated hurting her. It was as if someone had stabbed a sword into his gut and twisted. Stroking her hair, he wished he'd had the forethought to take it out of the braid. He pressed kisses over her lips and face. "Are you all right, my love?"

For a long moment, Eugénie lay so still beneath him he was concerned.

"I think so," she finally responded.

"Talk to me." He prayed she didn't hate what he'd done.

"It feels strange to have you inside me." Her beautiful eyes met his and she smiled. "I like it."

He let his breath out. "You'll like it more the next time. I promise."

"I suppose," she said dubiously, "that is the way of it. What do we do now?"

Will wanted to laugh with joy. "We're not done yet. You let me know when I can move again."

Eugénie tilted her hips toward William, and he responded by pressing in. It was like a dance in a way. One with very intimate steps. "I am ready."

"Put your legs around me."

He showed her how and they moved together again. He kissed her neck, and rubbed one breast with his palm. The throbbing need she'd felt earlier returned and intensified. Slowly he withdrew, then entered her more fully. She met him, needing him deeper. When he withdrew and entered her again, she welcomed his hard warmth. Soon hot waves spread through her and a quaking started, until it exploded. Their bodies were slick with sweat, and she clung to him as he pressed deeper, until he was hers and she was his. William called her name, then his mouth claimed hers, and he shuddered.

This was nothing like Maman had told her to expect.

"Eugénie, my precious love, are you all right?"

The flame from the candle flickered. His chest pounded against hers, and a peace she'd never felt before stole over her. This was how it was supposed to be. "William, I'm in heaven."

His head tilted toward her. "I'm there with you. Eugénie, I love you."

She reached up, touching her lips to his. "And I love you, but it is very hot."

"It is." He rolled off her, allowing a cooling breeze to caress their bodies before he wiped her nether parts with the towel.

When he took it away, there was blood. At least the whole house and her mother wouldn't know that she and William had anticipated their wedding vows. "You were right."

"Not from experience, I assure you."

"Non?" She hadn't wanted to think about the other women he'd been with, but . . .

"No. I've never"—he paused—"taken a virgin. That is the right of a husband."

The mattress dipped as he threw the cloth on the floor and blew out the light. When he lay back down, she rolled against him. Eugénie's heart lightened. "There are many who do not think as you do."

"Too many." His hand found hers. "My mother and the wives of several of my friends are involved in foundling homes."

They lay without even a sheet covering their nakedness, allowing their bodies to cool. She should probably be embarrassed, yet it was comfortable, and he really couldn't see her. "When I was very young, there was a maid who was with child. She let me feel the baby when it moved. The next day, she was gone."

William's voice was gruff. "My uncle?"

"Non. It was a long time before Maman married Papa. When my other father was alive."

"We should sleep." William wrapped his arm around her. "In England I would have tucked you into me and held you all night long."

Eugénie smiled. "Even to me it is warm. Good night . . . my love."

He leaned over, kissing her lightly. "Good night, my heart."

She didn't think she'd actually sleep. Yet, the next thing she knew, the bed dipping awakened her. Will sat on the side, putting on his clothes. "What time is it?"

"It's time I leave, or we'll be caught out."

The sky turned the deep blue it did before dawn. She groped and found her nightgown. "I'll see you in an hour or so."

William brushed his lips across hers. "Any more than that, and I wouldn't go. Eugénie, I'll chase that vicar to the ends of the earth to be your lawful husband."

She closed her eyes for a moment to hide the tears of joy. She'd never been happier. "I know you will."

Nothing would part them now.

Chapter 23

Will arrived back to his hotel in time to shave and change his clothing. Except for having to leave Eugénie, he was happier than he'd ever been. How had he ever thought loving a woman would stifle him?

She was the most caring, courageous woman he'd ever known. He now understood perfectly why his friends were so solicitous of their ladies, and he couldn't wait to introduce Eugénie to all of them. Will hoped she would stop worrying about going to England.

The previous day, he'd discovered that Road Town was only about three nautical miles from the Charlotte Amalie harbor. If they could sail at eight knots an hour, he and Eugénie would be wed by this evening, if not sooner.

Will reached for the cup of coffee Tidwell brought. "Christ."

"Is there something wrong with the coffee, my lord?"

"No, I forgot about the damn marriage settlements."

Tidwell remained silent.

How the devil was Will to do this? He couldn't use his

power of attorney to draw them up himself. He was, after all, eloping with his beloved. Perhaps Mr. Whitecliff would act in his father's stead. Could Will allow that? Better than nothing at all. Besides, if they waited until they reached Tortola, she'd be of age when she signed them, and it would all be proper.

According to his father, Eugénie had property in France and a goodly sum invested in the Change. Until he came in to the title, which he hoped would be years from now, Eugénie was probably wealthier than he. Not that his father would begrudge raising Will's allowance now that he'd have a family to support. He and Eugénie would have to take up residence in the hills of the Lake District, but even that was a small price to pay to be able to marry her. Perhaps they could buy a small property by the sea. She'd feel more at home there.

He went into the parlor where Andrew was gulping a cup of tea.

"Let's be on our way," he said, swallowing. "We're meeting the Whitecliffs at the pier."

Andrew might be content to meet Cicely there, but Will would accompany his betrothed to the ship. "You can go to the pier. I shall escort my affianced *wife*."

Andrew turned a tired gaze toward Will. Deep circles underscored Andrew's eyes. "Haven't you been getting any sleep?"

"No." He bit off the word.

Will grinned. Thwarted desire could make any man testy. "Then it's time you were married."

Andrew opened his mouth, then shook his head and mumbled, "I'll see you there."

Will arrived at the top of the Ninety-Nine Steps just as the Wively ladies emerged from their house. Cicely accompanied them. Poor Andrew.

Will went to Eugénie, raising her fingers to his lips. "Let's find a vicar, shall we?"

Her sisters giggled.

Eugénie blushed, a pink he now knew stretched to her breasts. "Of course, my lord."

After twining her arm in his, he offered his escort to his aunt as well. Sidonie shook her head and took Jeanne's hand. "I'll help Miss Penny. These girls are being particularly silly this morning. Please, go on."

When his small group reached the docks, Will was surprised to find the hull of the Whitecliffs' boat painted a bright cherry red, as were the three masts. And, although it vaguely resembled the schooner he'd come across on, it was much more elaborate, with a raised deck and several port-windows on the aft third of the vessel. He glanced at Eugénie. "Red?"

Her eyes lit with laughter. "It resembled another ship and had been stopped a couple of times by the English frigates. Since red is Mrs. Whitecliff's favorite color, that's what he decided to paint it. He hasn't had any problems since."

"I suppose not."

Andrew waved from the deck, smiling. He came down and helped get the children up the gangboard where their hosts awaited his coterie. Mrs. Whitecliff showed them to a large cabin which had been built on the main deck, but set flush against the upper deck. It was fashioned into a combination dining room and parlor. Cabinets lined the inner wall holding books and china. Windows filled the other three sides, allowing a breeze to enter. The room was protected from the elements by louvered shutters now open and secured to the walls.

A maid scurried in with tea. Josh followed with butter, jams, bread, meats, and cheeses.

"Please," Mrs. Whitecliff said, "we will not stand on ceremony. Help yourselves. My husband assures me we will be in Tortola before dark."

"Dark?" Will's jaw dropped. "But I was told it wasn't far."

"If we could sail in a straight line it would not be," Eugénie said, taking a cup of tea from Cicely. "The problem is that we cannot sail against the wind. We'll need to go around St. John and approach Tortola from the other side."

Andrew smirked as he handed a cup to Will, and said under his breath, "I hope *you* sleep well tonight."

He was stopped from retorting by Eugénie offering him a plate of food. "Would you like this one?"

"Thank you, my love, but I'll fix my own. I imagine you're hungry." He'd not planned to spend this night alone. Surely, even aboard the ship, there must be a way to keep Eugénie with him.

"Thank you, I am starving." She paused, and tilted her head. "You'd better hurry. The children are on their way."

Sure enough, her three sisters burst into the room a moment later.

"I'm hungry," Jeanne announced to no one in particular.

"You're always hungry." Valérie held the plate away from the younger girl.

Miss Penny's brows rose. "You may make your sister a plate, Valérie. Adelaide, wait your turn. Neither Miss Whitecliff nor Mr. Grayson has eaten yet."

"I do apologize, my lord." The governess pushed a strand of hair aside. "The girls actually have broken their fast, but there appears to be something about eating on a boat that intrigues them." She turned her attention back to the children, just as Valérie reached across the table and snatched a roll. "If you cannot behave up here, I have schoolwork you can do in the cabin below."

That did the trick. The three of them settled at a small table and ate quietly. William held out a piece of cheese to Eugénie. "Soon we'll have children."

"I hope ours are better behaved." She took the cheese and nibbled.

"I'm afraid there is no chance of that. All Wively children are heathens." He grinned. "Ours will be the worst of all. You can't tell me you didn't run rings around your governess and parents." He leaned toward Eugénie, capturing her gaze, lowering his voice. "They'll have your dark hair."

"And your blue eyes." She smiled at him. Her eyes danced with laughter as she glanced at her sisters. "We'll need more servants to keep track of them."

"At least two maids for each one."

Her small pink tongue peeped out as she licked some jam from her lips, and his body tightened with desire for her. There must be some way for them to be alone, if only for a quarter hour. After that, he'd give some thought to this evening. "Speaking of servants, where is your maid?"

"Probably in my stateroom hanging my gowns." Desire flickered in Eugénie's eyes. "Where is your Tidwell?"

"Most likely doing the same."

"You know"—her breathing quickened—"the way out of the harbor is very interesting for many people."

"Perhaps"—Will's member hardened in agreement with the conversation—"we should suggest that your maid and my valet would like to view our departure from the deck."

Sun peeked over the hills to the east, and the captain called for the dock lines to be cast off.

Eugénie set her plate on the side table. "I think, my love, that is one of your better ideas."

She didn't know exactly what William had planned, but she was sure she'd like it. After he'd left this morning, she'd missed the comfort of his body, and the way he caressed her as they talked, as if he couldn't get enough of her. That strange throbbing at her core began again. She stood. "Wait until you see my maid go on deck."

Eugénie rose, quietly making her way to the opening between the bookshelves, then along the gangway to her cabin near the back of the boat. The door was open, and her maid hummed as she worked. "Marisole?"

"Yes, miss?"

"We are casting off. Would you like to watch as we leave the harbor?"

"Ah *oui*. That is my favorite view." A bit of pink crept into Marisole's cheeks, and Eugénie wondered if her maid knew what she was up to. "Thank you, miss. I'm almost finished here any way."

The ship rocked, indicating they were free from the dock. "You'd better hurry."

A few moments after Marisole left, Will's footsteps echoed on the wood floor. His cabin was half-way down the gangway toward the bow. "Tidwell, leave off here and go watch the view from the deck."

"Yes, my lord."

Eugénie went into the gangway where Will caught her up in a hard kiss, pulling her into his cabin, then shutting the door. "God, I've missed you."

"It hasn't been that long," she teased.

"Any time away from you is an eternity."

She didn't know how it was possible, but she was falling more and more in love with him.

His lips claimed hers again. Cooler air wafted around her legs as he pulled up her skirts. His already hard length rose between them. Frissons of pleasure raced through her, and she flung her arms around his neck, pressing her body into his. "Yes."

He chuckled softly. "You don't know what I'm going to do."

The place between her legs ached in anticipation. Eugénie didn't know how much longer she could stand it. "I trust you."

"Hold on tight, and put your legs around me."

He nibbled his way down her neck, then licked the soft spot at the base. How had she never known that was so sensitive? She wanted more. "I wish we had more time."

"I wish you were naked," he said in a seductive voice. "But that would be hard to explain."

She choked on a giggle as his thumbs caressed her breasts. What she wouldn't give to feel his fingers on her bare skin. "I wish I was too."

She clung to him. Her back was pressed against the wall and with one hand he lifted her, then released his member. "Feel this."

It rubbed back and forth against her most tender parts. Heat and need roiled through her. Lord, how she wanted him. "Now. Please now."

"Soon."

Suddenly she felt wet, and he entered her with one strong thrust. There was a twinge of pain, and Eugénie gasped. Surely he hadn't been that deep inside her before.

"You're sore." His brows drew together. "I should have thought."

"No, it's nothing." Already her desire for him was more than she could stand. If he stopped now she'd murder him. "I'll be fine."

He almost withdrew, then filled her again. Eugénie moaned. This was even better than last night. Will took her mouth, claiming her completely. The sensation of waves crashing carried her away again. She trembled as she convulsed around him, and he spilled his seed.

"Eugénie?" Her mother called.

Will placed a finger over Eugénie's lips. He lowered her down until her feet once again touched the floor. They waited, hearts pounding together, his breathing as ragged as hers.

"Where could that girl have got to?"

As soon as Maman's steps retreated, Eugénie let out the breath she'd been holding. "What shall I do?"

"*We* will go out as we came in. First go to your cabin." Will opened the door and looked out. "Come. I'll stay here so that no one can see you."

"Very well."

He grabbed her around her waist. "I love you."

She put her palm against his freshly shaved cheek. "I love you as well."

After she'd straightened her gown, Eugénie went back on deck. Spying her mother with Mrs. Whitecliff, Eugénie wandered around for a few minutes before going to the rail on the other side of the ship. They'd left the harbor and were on a larboard tack heading toward the east end of St. Thomas.

"There you are, my dear."

Eugénie could feel her mother's gaze on her face, but she stared straight out at the sea. No doubt her cheeks were still flushed and her lips swollen from William's kisses. If Eugénie didn't want to be locked in her cabin until they found the vicar, she didn't dare meet her mother's gaze. "Were you looking for me?"

"Yes. Where is Will?"

Eugénie glanced around as if she'd only just noticed he wasn't there. "I don't know. I imagine he'll be here soon. Perhaps he wished to speak with the captain."

Moments later, a tall, strong presence radiating heat stood behind her. A smile tugged at her lips. "I thought you'd got lost."

"Never." William's voice was low and a shiver ran down her spine, wanting him. "Not unless I took you with me."

"Ah, good," Maman said. "I dislike not knowing where people are when we are aboard a ship."

As she left, Cicely and Andrew joined them at the rail. She squeezed Eugénie's hand. "It won't be long now."

Will groaned and Eugénie grinned. He still couldn't believe it would take several hours to arrive in Tortola.

"Are you feeling all right?" Cicely asked William. "You're not ill, are you?"

Leaning back against her betrothed, Eugénie replied, "Soon is a matter of opinion. William was under the impression the journey took only three hours."

"Ah." Cicely patted William's shoulder. "It will go quickly. Mama has planned games after we get into Pillsbury Sound. Until then you can read if you become bored with the sights."

Maman and Mrs. Whitecliff returned to the parlor, while Cicely directed Andrew and William to set out chairs on the deck. Even with the wind picking up as they sailed around Dog Island, this might be the longest trip she had ever been on. Reaching Road Town had never been so important before.

Will was at his wit's end. They'd eaten, played charades, then cards. Just when he thought they'd arrive in Tortola earlier, the wind shifted. Every time he'd tried to cut Eugénie out of the group, her mother or one or more of her sisters were there with them. It was as if his aunt knew what he planned to do with Eugénie if he ever got her alone again. For her part, Eugénie cast him occasional looks of longing while keeping a smile on her face for everyone else.

Finally, shortly after four o'clock that afternoon, they sailed into Road Town's protected harbor, and dropped anchor.

"Andrew, my lord," Mr. Whitecliff said—Will had so far not been able to get the man to call him by his first name—"Let's see if we can chase down that rascal of a vicar."

"I want to go as well," Eugénie said.

"Yes, and I," Cicely added.

Whitecliff rubbed his chin. "Well, I suppose there's no harm, as long as that is, you two do not convince the vicar to marry you in town this afternoon. Your mother would have my hide."

Cicely and Eugénie exchanged looks, and an unspoken communication seemed to take place between them. Finally, Cicely said, "We won't, Papa."

Will helped Eugénie down the ladder and into the boat. Once they were seated, he murmured, "What was that about?"

A small smile graced her lips. "If we find him, we'll bring him back to the ship."

He slipped his arm around her waist. "Let's hope he's there."

Once on shore, they made their way to St. George's church, a large wooden building painted white, surrounded by a low fence, not a half mile from the docks.

A pale, harried-looking young man with light red hair giving directions to a middle-aged negro woman stood at the entrance to the church.

After she left, Will said, "I am Viscount Wively. We're looking for Mr. Stewart. Would you happen to be he?"

If it was possible, the young man turned even whiter. "I'm sorry to disappoint you, my lord. The Mr. Stewart you are searching for is off island at present."

"Then who are you?" Whitecliff asked in his brusque fashion.

"I am Mr. Anketil Stewart. Mr. Stewart's nephew."

Andrew ran a hand over his face. "Are you in the holy orders?"

"Well . . . yes . . . yes, I am." Stewart appeared about ready to lose his luncheon. "After a fashion, that is."

Eugénie, who'd been next to Will, stepped forward.

"Mr. Stewart, his lordship and I would like to wed, as would Miss Whitecliff and Mr. Grayson. Can you perform the service?"

Stewart took a breath, then let it out. "No. I am still only a deacon. Though I am able to perform most services, I cannot marry anyone."

Will's jaw began to ache from being clenched. He had a feeling he wasn't going to like the answer to his next question. "When will your uncle return?"

A bead of sweat dripped down Stewart's face. "You see, my lord, that's just it. He was supposed to have been back a senight ago." The man ran a finger around his cravat. "You are not the only couples waiting."

Cicely turned to Eugénie, with tears in her eyes. "What shall we do now?"

"Mr. Stewart"—she lifted her chin—"is there another church or vicar on the island?"

Taking out his handkerchief, he mopped his face. "Uh, no, none at all. I'm terribly sorry, but I have members of the flock to attend to."

With that he dashed off.

Will swore fluently under his breath. "Now what do we do?"

"I cannot believe there is only one church on this island." Eugénie's lips formed a thin line. "Let's ask around. I think Mr. Stewart was hiding something."

Will and his group were almost to the end of the path when a woman stepped out of the building they were passing.

"Excuse me." The woman, the same one the deacon had been speaking to earlier, glanced over her shoulder toward the church, as if she was afraid of being seen.

Eugénie stopped. "Good afternoon, ma'am, can we help you?"

"Are you looking to be married?" the woman asked.

"We are."

"You didn't hear it from me, but there *is* another vicar on the island. He is a Mr. Petherick."

Will closed his eyes and gave his head a shake. "Why would Mr. Stewart lie?"

She looked around again, and said in a low voice, "He's at St. Michael's. On the north side near Great Carot Bay. It's up on the hill."

"That still," Will said with clenched teeth, "doesn't answer my question."

A door closed, and the woman moved away. "The older Mr. Stewart don't like Mr. Petherick. He's called the pirate priest. I must go."

She lifted her skirts and ran to the small building to the left of the church.

"The pirate priest?" Cicely and Eugénie said in unison.

"I don't know if this . . ." Whitecliff's voice petered out as his daughter glared at him.

Cicely put her hands on her hips. "Andrew and I are marrying, Papa. As long as he is legally able to perform the service, I don't care what he's called."

Andrew cleared his throat. "I must agree with Cicely, sir. To my mind, we've waited long enough."

"That is what I think as well," Eugénie chimed in.

Whitecliff glanced over at Will. "I'm with them, sir."

The older man nodded. "Very well then, but not a word to your mothers about his moniker. We'd never hear the end of it."

As one, they headed back to the docks.

"Can you imagine," Cicely said with a laugh, "the stories we'll have to tell our children?"

"My father," Will responded, "will dine off this for a month, and my mother will be the envy of all her romance-reading friends."

"Oh, if only Papa were here," Eugénie said wistfully.

Will tucked her arm more securely in his. "I'm sorry he's not here to see you marry, my love."

"As am I." She straightened her shoulders. "He would be happy for us."

Whitecliff patted her arm. "I'm certain he would be."

For several minutes silence reigned, then Cicely said, "Papa, can we leave this evening, or must we wait until morning?"

He glanced at the sky. "It will be dark in just over an hour. The safest course is to wait."

"But, Mr. Whitecliff," Eugénie said as they stepped onto the pier, "surely we can make it to Soper's Hole before dark."

"You know, Eugénie, I believe you're right. Let's get ready to cast off again."

Will groaned, and Mr. Whitecliff gave a bark of laughter. "Never fear, my lord. Anchoring in Soper's Hole will give us a good head start on tomorrow's sail. As long as our pirate priest isn't gone, you will be wed before the day is over."

One more night before Will would be able to make Eugénie his wife in truth.

As they rowed nearer to the ship, the savory scent of meat cooking made Will's stomach grumble. He'd been so busy worrying about the marriage, he'd forgotten about food. That had to be the first time he'd done that.

Eugénie leaned closer to him, and his senses filled with her musk and lemon fragrance. How was he going to manage to be with her tonight? He needed her so much, the thought of not having her next to him didn't bear thinking of.

She cupped her hand around his ear and whispered, "I shall come to you."

Will sent up a silent prayer of thanks as the rowboat

reached the ladder. As Eugénie reached toward the ladder, he tried to steady her. "Be careful."

She flashed him a quick smile and scrambled up the ladder like she'd been born to it. It occurred to him that she probably had. Now all he had to do was suffer through the rest of the evening until everyone had gone to bed. An image of Eugénie naked in his bed imprinted itself on his mind. This was going to be a very long evening.

Chapter 24

Nathan tightened his grip on Miss Marshall as they strolled down the main shopping area before making their way to the waterfront.

"What is it?" she asked.

"I think we're being followed. Try to act naturally."

He brought them to a halt in front of a shop window. Though he still couldn't see anyone, the prickling on his neck didn't change.

When they reached the harbor, there were still quite a few ships anchored out. Vincent's schooner was positioned toward the north end. A good place to sail out quickly.

Miss Marshall's hand tightened on his arm. "Which one is it?"

"I'm going to point to the center of the harbor. Vincent's ship is the one with three yellow masts just to the right."

She heaved a sigh, then laughed as if Nathan had told her a joke. "I see it."

"The dory should be on the beach, directly in front of the yacht."

They resumed walking, but slowed their pace as he and Miss Marshall approached the boat with the name *Belle Amie* painted in yellow. It was exactly where it should be. A number of people strolled and hurried around them. "Miss Marshall, do you see anyone who looks out of place?"

She smiled as if he'd once again said something witty. "No, do you?"

"Nothing." They might get through this with no one the wiser. Yet instinct told him someone was near, and watching them. "I will hand you into the boat before I push it off the beach."

"Won't that tax your strength?"

It would, but he'd pay for it later when they were safe. "If they are searching for me, they'll look for a man who is suffering from weakness."

Miss Marshall nodded and laughed, allowing him to assist her into the dory. "You're right, of course."

He pushed them off, scrambled in, then grabbed the oars.

A tall white man dressed as a sailor sauntered along the beach. "Are you going to Mr. Beaufort's ship?"

Nathan stiffened. "We are."

"He sent me to row you out."

Nathan raised a brow of inquiry, and the man continued, "He's already got all his other dories aboard and doesn't need this one." The man waded into the water, leaned in close and pressed a piece of paper into Nathan's hand. "You can trust me, Mr. Wivenly."

He opened it and recognized Vincent's familiar scrawl. "Thank you, Mr. . . . ."

The man gave an almost imperceptible shake of his head. "No names."

The hair on Nathan's neck stood up. Something was wrong, but he couldn't figure out what it was. Vincent would die before betraying them. Nathan exchanged glances with Miss Marshall, giving his head an imperceptible shake. She inclined her head slightly, and clutched her reticule with one hand and the bench with the other. He placed his hand surreptitiously half-way down one of the oars. He had a choice—attack now, when the man wasn't expecting it, knowing there was a chance he was wrong, or wait until they were in the harbor, where it would be more dangerous for Miss Marshall and possibly him as well.

As the sailor lifted his leg to climb in, Miss Marshall struck his head with her reticule. He staggered back, giving Nathan time to pull strong strokes, propelling them into the harbor.

"Bitch!" the man growled. "All of your kind should be in shackles."

Her spine stiffened, but the only thing she said was, "If you need me to row, I am able."

Nathan's intention to head in a straight line had been thwarted. He knew that during their flight from the thug he'd gotten off course. After a few moments, while they were approaching the boats at anchor, Nathan said, "Look for Vincent or Conrad. If you don't see them, we'll have to think of something else."

Soon they heard shouts of welcome directing them to his friend's sloop. "Thank God."

Miss Marshall's smile was genuine this time. "Mr. Beaufort is truly our savior."

When they arrived at the ship, Conrad reached down to help her up the rope ladder. "Did you have any trouble?"

"Just a bit." She wrapped her arms around him. "I'll let Mr. Wively tell you."

Nathan hooked the lines up to the small boat for it to be raised before following her to the deck.

"What happened?" Vincent asked as soon as Nathan was aboard.

He handed his friend the note and told them about the man.

Vincent scrubbed a hand over his face. "We've either been compromised, or I have a traitor. There is nothing I can do now. We must depart quickly before anyone else attempts to stop us."

The anchor and sails were being raised as he spoke. Soon they were maneuvering their way out of the crowded harbor into the Caribbean Sea.

Nathan would be home soon. He just hoped he was in time.

With the wind coming from the east, the *Song Bird* made a speedy trip to Soper's Hole on the southwest end of Tortola. Eugénie stood at the rail gazing out over the water, William's arms encircled her as the sun sank below the horizon, encased in streaks of red clouds. Their luck was in, as her papa would have said. "The weather will be good tomorrow."

"How do you know that?"

"Red sky at night, sailors' delight. Red sky in morning, sailors take warning."

His hand moved over the small of her back. "It is always correct?"

She shivered with pleasure as the tip of his tongue touched the outer shell of her ear. "Always."

"Then God and fate are with us."

"I didn't believe in fate before I met you."

William's chest rumbled with laughter. "I've never been able to escape it. Nor would I want to. It brought me to you."

Eugénie turned in his embrace. "And you to me. I never believed I could be so happy and content."

His lips touched hers, and for a moment she pretended they were all alone on the ship. Then the squeal of a young girl and a crash brought her back to reality. She touched her forehead to his broad chest. "Should we go see what happened?"

"Not yet. They have Miss Penny, your mother, and the Whitecliffs. Let's stay here and enjoy the evening for a while longer."

After they'd eaten and joined the rest of their friends and family for another game of charades, and tea, Eugénie rose, and made a show of yawning. The sooner she could be with William, the better. She couldn't wait until they did not have to sneak around. "I am for my bed. We have another early morning tomorrow."

Fortunately, all the adults agreed and the children were struggling to keep their eyes open.

As Eugénie neared her cabin, her mother said, "Eugénie, Marisole will sleep with you tonight. I had a cot set up."

"*Oui*, Maman," Eugénie bussed her mother's cheek. "I shall see you in the morning. Sleep well."

What Maman didn't know was that Marisole slept like the dead and would awaken promptly at five o'clock in the morning. As long as Eugénie was back in her bed by then, no one would know she'd spent the night with William.

A little over an hour later, she lay on her side, waiting until the deep breathing of her maid indicated Marisole was sleeping, before slipping out into the passageway to William's cabin. The moment Eugénie's hand touched the latch, the door opened, and he pulled her in.

William's naked body gave off heat as he swooped her up, carrying her the few steps to his bed. She wanted to run her hands over his chest, and rub her own bare body against his.

"I heard your mother and was afraid you wouldn't be able to come to me."

"Nothing can awaken Marisole until she is ready. Besides, she will not betray us. Still, I do not wish to put her in an awkward position."

Placing his hand under Eugénie's nightgown, he slowly dragged the palms of his hands over her as he moved up her body, lifting the garment. "After tomorrow, I shall be paying her wages."

Eugénie caressed his strong chest, twining her fingers through the short curls covering the skin and sinew. "Nevertheless."

William stroked her back and derrière. "I won't argue with you."

Heat pooled in the place between her legs as he palmed her breasts. Her breath came in short pants. "Never?"

He laughed softly. "And deny myself the sight of you in a temper?"

"You are no—" His fingers stroked her center. "Oooh. That feels *splendide*."

"I love it when you forget your English."

He inserted one finger into her sheath, and she was about to forget much more. *"Vraiment?"*

"Truly." His tongue circled one nipple, causing it to furl tightly. "God, you're beautiful. I've missed you. I'm besotted with you."

She'd missed him as well. Eugénie stroked his back, then his chest again. "I like that you are, but it's too dark for you to know how I look."

"I can feel it." He bent his head, and took the now aching nipple in his mouth. "You taste like an exotic creature from the sea."

Frissons of pleasure raced through her, and the apex of her thighs throbbed in earnest. Oh Lord. Eugénie arched into him. "William, I want—"

"Shhh, my love. Tonight, we take this slowly." He licked and nipped at her neck. "Let me show you how much I love you."

Suddenly, Eugénie was much too hot. She remembered

just in time to keep her voice to a whisper. "I want this off." She tugged at her nightdress. "Help me."

"In a few moments."

He moved over her as he raked his tongue over her breasts down to her navel, then stopped. Every nerve in her body was on edge with wanting. If he didn't enter her soon she was going to scream. "Now?"

"Not quite yet." He chuckled wickedly. "Have patience, my sweet."

Eugénie spread her legs and wrapped them around Will, tugging. "I don't want to wait."

All she'd succeeded in doing was to pull his head and shoulders down to her already wet mons. His lips nuzzled her, and she almost cried out loud. He licked the nub nestled in her curls.

What was he doing? She gripped his head with her knees as her body sizzled. If he kept this up she would burst like a star. "I don't think you're supposed to . . ."

Her protest sounded weak even to her. Eugénie bit her lip, but a low moan escaped despite her effort.

"Like that, do you?"

She nodded, then remembered Will couldn't see her. Eugénie grabbed on to the sheets as the spiraling tension in her core tightened, then clamped one hand over her mouth. Just as she reached her peak, William entered her. In two, maybe three strokes, they both tumbled over the edge together. She'd died and gone to heaven.

He chuckled. "That is why the French call it the little death."

"*La petite mort*. I've heard the term, but did not understand it." She sucked in a breath, thankful for the breeze through the small port window. "Now I do."

Will rolled off Eugénie as he sucked in huge gulps of air. The small cabin's one port-window allowed little in the way of a breeze. He stroked damp strands of hair away from her face. He wanted to cuddle her close, but it was too damned hot. What he wouldn't give right now for crisp autumn weather and a fire. He laid his hand over her gently rounded stomach. "Can you feel how much I love you."

"Yes." Eugénie closed her long slender fingers around his. "I love you as well." Her voice hitched. "I never thought to have this much joy."

He stroked her cheek with the pad of his thumb, kissing away the tears. The thought of her crying, even with delight, unnerved him. "I never believed I'd find a woman who'd love me more than my title. If I hadn't met you, I would have allowed my mother to pick my bride."

"Oh no, William, you would not have done such a thing?"

"It doesn't bear thinking of now. I can't imagine my life without you, my love, I adore you."

He traced her lips with a finger as she smiled. "But now, my lord, you will live under the cat's paw."

"So I've been told." Will bent his head to kiss her when he heard the splash of something falling in the water.

"I told you not to bring your doll!" a high voice shrieked.

"You did not!" Jeanne cried.

Then there was a louder splash.

Eugénie was out of bed and yanking the door open before he could move.

"I'll murder them," she muttered, and ran out into the passageway.

Thank God, he hadn't removed Eugénie's nightgown. Will groped around and found his pantaloons and a shirt. After donning them as quickly as he could, he followed her to the deck.

"Jeanne," Eugénie called, "do not attempt to swim, just tread water until I get there."

One of the sailors dashed out holding a lantern. "Don't worry, miss, I'll get her."

The sailor started toeing off his shoes, and Will jumped in. He broke the surface and looked around. Jeanne. Her long-sleeved nightgown floated around her. She held something in her left arm and her free arm splashed around as she struggled to keep her head above the water. Her nightclothes were probably weighing her down. In a few strokes, Will had her.

"Over here, William." Eugénie held a lantern while the ship's hand lowered the ladder.

By this time, it seemed as if everyone was at the rail, and more lanterns had been lit. With the child in one arm, he swam to the side of the ship. "Here, give me the doll."

After he had the toy in one hand, he boosted Jeanne up the ladder with the other.

The little girl's lip trembled. "You'll take care of Charity, won't you?"

"Yes," he assured her with more calm than he felt. Good God, she could have drowned. "Go on now."

By the time he'd climbed up, Aunt Sidonie was dragging away the two girls.

"Andrew has fresh water on the stern for you to rinse off," Eugénie said, pressing a towel into his hands. She pressed her lips together, blinking rapidly. "Thank you for saving Jeanne."

All he wanted to do was take Eugénie in his arms and comfort her. "Are you all right?"

She nodded several times before answering. "Yes, though I shall thrash my sisters."

Anger was good. "I'll help you. They won't be able to sit for a week."

It was the first time that night he'd been able to see her clearly. Eugénie's dark hair fell in waves over her shoulders to her waist. Her light-colored muslin nightgown had ruffles around the neck and cuffs. She looked slightly disheveled, and her lips were still swollen from his kisses. With everyone awake, including Marisole, she wouldn't be able to spend the rest of the night with him. Will raised her hand to his lips. "Until morning, my love."

She lifted her hand, then dropped it with a frustrated huff. "*Oui.* Good night, William."

Jeanne trying to keep herself afloat had scared him to death. All he wanted right now was the one thing he couldn't have, Eugénie. When they had children, he'd hire nursery maids that woke at the drop of a hat, and he wouldn't allow dolls or any toys on board any ship they owned. Better yet, he'd have harnesses specially made for their children.

The next morning, Will awoke with the sense something was in bed with him. He reached out, touching a hard, damp object that he suspected was Jeanne's doll. "Good morning, Charity."

"She said she feels safer with you." With serious, deep blue eyes, Jeanne regarded him from the side of his bed.

"I daresay it won't last long." He rubbed a hand over his face. "She had a bit of a scare last night."

Jeanne nodded solemnly. "She thought she was a better swimmer than she was."

"It's hard to swim with all those clothes on." The scent of cooking invaded his senses, and his stomach grumbled, but he couldn't rise with Jeanne in the cabin. "I think she'll be fine now."

"Are you sure?"

Although it was the last thing he wanted to do, Will smiled. "Yes. It was terrifying, but you and Charity will be fine. You must promise me though, never to go out on deck without an adult again."

Jeanne nodded her head slowly. "Mama already told me not to."

He reached out, tugging on one of Jeanne's dark braids. "Run along, and tell Eugénie I'll be up directly."

A broad smile dawned on Jeanne's face. She picked up

her doll, holding it tightly against her. "I shall, but I ought to warn you, Eugénie is not in a very good mood this morning. I don't think she slept well."

No doubt, yet if all went as it should today and they found their pirate priest, she wouldn't have that problem again. "Yes, well, she was worried about you."

Jeanne leaned over and kissed his cheek. "Thank you. I'm glad you and Eugénie are getting married."

"As am I." On the other hand, if that vicar wasn't around . . . Will clenched his fists. He'd chase them all over the islands until he found one or both of them. "Run along now. I'll see you in a few minutes."

Once Jeanne left, closing the door behind her, Will rose. That was when he noticed the ship was already underway. If fate remained with him, he'd be wed to Eugénie in a matter of a few short hours.

Henri sat at a table under a large tamarind tree at Wivenly House with a glass of ginger beer in his hand. His uncle Bates sat across from him, sipping tea. The previous evening Henri had met with the Frenchman and spent the next day and a half gathering information. He learned bits and pieces from conversations the other servants and slaves had overheard. He'd tracked down the landlady for the so-called merchant, Shipley, and haunted one of the taverns catering to sailors until he was able to talk with one of the hands on the Vicomte's ship. Finally, Henri had enough information to approach his formidable uncle with his plan.

"You didn't come here only to drink Cook's ginger beer," Uncle Bates said. "What is going on?"

Henri had considered how he'd begin this conversation, and had decided to start with the worst news. "I've been hired to assist in Miss Villaret's abduction."

His uncle's fingers tightening on the handle of the delicate teacup was the only sign that he was in any way distressed. "Indeed?"

"Yes." Henri kept his eyes on his uncle. "And Mr. Wivenly is being held captive on one of the French islands, probably Martinique."

Uncle Bates held Henri's gaze. "I shall assume, as you are sharing this information with me, you are not in league with the Vicomte Villaret de Joyeuse."

Henri tried not to show his surprise, but couldn't stop his eyes from widening. "How did you know?"

"I didn't," Uncle Bates said, smiling slightly, "until you added the pieces to the puzzle that were missing. We had a suspicion it was Miss Eugénie's French family, but not enough to confirm it."

Henri took a drink, then told his uncle about the plan to marry Miss Villaret to a French *comte*. "Where is the family now?"

Uncle Bates took another sip of tea. "They've gone with the Whitecliff family to Tortola for a few days."

That would buy him some time, but why Tortola? Monsieur Yves had mentioned a gentleman . . . Henri grinned. "She's getting married."

"She and Miss Cicely both. When Miss Eugénie returns, she will be the Viscountess Wivenly."

"Ha! That will put a spoke in the Frenchman's wheel."

"It will indeed." Uncle Bates rose. "I must attend to my duties. I shall assign a look-out for the ship, and as soon as they dock, I'll send a message warning them to keep a watch over Miss Eugénie."

When Henri returned to his house, a message from Monsieur Yves waited for him. Entering the parlor, he bowed.

"What have you discovered?"

"The Wivenly family has gone on a short pleasure cruise with their neighbors. They should return in a day or so. I'll have someone keep watch at the docks."

The man's countenance darkened, then his lips twisted in a smile. "This could work. We shall be ready for her when she returns, and remove her immediately to my ship."

Henri bowed, careful not to allow his satisfaction to show. That is exactly what he thought the Frenchman would do. All he had to do was stop Miss Villaret from being taken.

As the *Song Bird* rounded the west end of Tortola, Andrew found Cicely sunk on a bench built into a small cabin near the bow of the ship. Her parasol sat abandoned next to her on the deck and a wide-brimmed hat graced her head. He sat beside her, sliding his arm around her shoulders and drawing her against him. "What is it? I thought you'd be happy."

She snuggled in, but a tear leaked from the corner of her eye. "If we find the vicar, I'll be happy. I'm just so afraid he will be gone as well."

"If he is, we'll chase one or the other of them down." He lifted the bonnet, placing a kiss on her cheek, then put it back down. "Believe me when I tell you, once Viscount Wively has the bit between his teeth, nothing will stop him, and he desperately wants to marry Eugénie."

Cicely pushed the floppy straw brim back and tilted her head. "Why call him by his title?"

Andrew grinned. "Because, my love, when he gets like this, he ceases to be Will, and will use all his rank and status to get what he wants."

"As he did yesterday morning?"

"Exactly. We won't return to St. Thomas until we are all wed." Andrew eyed her hat with dissatisfaction. If the sun weren't so bright, and the wind so high, he'd remove it. "Are there any other dragons I can slay for you, milady?"

Cicely shook her head. "Only one, but you won't."

"Let's see what happens today, shall we?" He had no

doubt she'd seen Eugénie's state of dishabille last night and put two and two together very quickly. He wanted to be with Cicely every bit as much as Will wanted to be with his betrothed. In fact, Andrew was about at the end of his rope. He'd heard there was a Methodist minister on Tortola, and if need be, he'd move heaven and earth to convince Mrs. Whitecliff to allow that man to perform the ceremony.

Chapter 25

Will held Eugénie in his arms as they stood at the starboard rail.

"That"—she pointed to a piece of land sticking out into the sea—"is Gun Point. We're almost through Thatch Cut. It won't be long now."

Will pulled her back against his chest. "How long is 'not long'?"

"About an hour to an hour and a half."

"Too long." He dropped a kiss on her head. Her hat was stuffed under a thick line to keep it from blowing away. He grinned. The last thing her mother had said was to remember her bonnet. No wonder Eugénie was always tanned. How would she feel about moving to cold, damp England, where bonnets were mandatory? For him England was home, but for her . . . Will wished he knew how Eugénie would like it.

His friend's wife, Emma Marsh, had got used to England fairly easily, perhaps Eugénie would as well. She knew they would live there, yet he had the feeling she didn't truly understand what it all meant. "Do you mind if we go inside for a while? I'm hungry."

She turned to face him and smiled softly. "I think you want to ensure Jeanne is all right."

"And Charity." Will had told Eugénie what he'd woken up to this morning.

She laughed. "Of course. The doll would be *désolée*."

Taking her arm, he was about to lead her toward the salon when he remembered her hat. He rescued it from the rope. "We can't forget this."

"No," she said, taking it from him and plopping it on her head. "Maman would not be happy."

Despite her attempt to appear light-hearted, Eugénie was worried about something. Was it only the wedding? She leaned against him as if she needed his support. "Is everything all right?"

She flashed him a quick smile. "As long as we find this pirate priest, I shall be fine."

"We'll find him." If only he were as sure of that as he sounded.

The instant they entered the parlor, Jeanne, with Charity in her arms, attached herself to him. "Charity says she is much better."

After he sat, Will picked Jeanne up, putting her on his lap. "I'm glad to hear it. I take it you've impressed upon her she should be more careful in the future."

Jeanne nodded. "Yes."

Eugénie blinked as tears misted her eyes. She was so glad he loved children and related to them so well. She could see him with their brood, giving advice, meting out fair punishments as needed. Despite their shaky beginning, she was lucky to have found William.

An hour later, word came from the captain that they were approaching Great Carot Bay. By the time she, William, Cicely, Andrew, and Josh were ready, the dory was waiting for them.

"We can't stay anchored out here all day," the captain said.

Eugénie took in the exposed bay. "We'll be as quick as we can be."

She tried not to think of what she would do if Mr. Petherick wasn't there. It was only nine o'clock. Surely they would catch him before he left his house. Her little group walked around the village, searching for anything resembling a church and found nothing.

Beneath her hand, William's arm tightened, and he blew out a frustrated breath. "Where the devil is the place?"

"We shall find it." She'd have to ask someone. This wandering around was getting them nowhere, and irritating them all.

A woman walking toward them stopped. "Good morning. I am Mrs. Leonard. May I help you find something?"

"Good morning, ma'am. Yes, thank you," William answered. "We're searching for Mr. Petherick at St. Michael's church."

She pulled a notebook and pencil from her skirt pocket, then pointed north, talking as she wrote on the paper. "Stay on this road and it will go up that hill. Right at the top you'll see St. Michael's and the rectory. It's not far. I haven't seen Mr. Petherick yet this morning, so I assume he'll be either at home or at the church."

Mrs. Leonard handed the directions she'd drawn to Eugénie. She could have hugged the woman. "Thank you so much, Mrs. Leonard. We would never have found it on our own."

Cicely and Andrew turned and began walking north.

William and Eugénie followed. When they arrived at the end of the village the path rose.

"Another hill," he muttered.

Poor William. Eugénie looked at what appeared to be a series of zigzags created by goats. "This is what Mrs. Leonard drew."

Andrew slapped William on the back. "If you want to get

married, Wivenly, you'll climb it." He took Cicely's hand. "Come, my love."

"A moment, my dear." She glanced at William. "You really do hate walking up hills, don't you?" Without waiting for his answer, she said, "Perhaps we can convince him to marry us on board the ship. Then you won't have to walk up the hill twice. Josh, go back to the *Song Bird* and tell Mama, Papa, and the Wivenlys that if we haven't returned to the yacht in an hour, to join us at St. Michael's."

"My love," Andrew said, "don't you have a gown you wanted to wear for the service?"

"I'll wear it for the party Mama's planning. Right now, I just want to be your wife. She smiled. "Besides, he might agree to come to the *Song Bird*."

The four of them trudged up the path and, just as Mrs. Leonard's drawing depicted, at the top of the hill there stood the squat stone church that was St. Michael's. Despite the hot morning, when they entered the church was cool. Pews lined each side of the aisle. Tall, glassless windows with their shutters pushed open gave views over Cane Garden Bay. There was no sign of the vicar.

"He's not here," Cicely said in a shaky voice.

Eugénie squeezed her friend's hand. This vicar couldn't be gone as well. "Perhaps he's at the rectory."

"We're not giving up yet," William added.

He led them out through a side door to a small wooden house not far from the church. The scent of cooking spices made Eugénie's mouth water, reminding her she hadn't eaten since early this morning, and then not much.

An older white woman with a pleasant expression, dressed simply in a faded blue gown and pinafore, answered the door. "May I help you?"

William bowed. "I am Viscount Wivenly. My betrothed, Miss Villaret, and our friends, Miss Whitecliff and Mr. Grayson, are looking for Reverend Petherick." Will's glance included Eugénie and their friends. "We'd like to discuss our marriage ceremonies with him."

The woman nodded. "I am Mrs. Petherick. Please come in, my lord. My husband has gone along the ridge, but he should be down any time now." She smiled. "You've come at a good time. He never misses his breakfast. Please have some tea while you are waiting for him."

Eugénie and Cicely breathed sighs of relief.

"Thank you." Will ushered Eugénie through the door, and Mrs. Petherick led them to a parlor off the main hall.

Once they were settled, a servant entered with tea, cool water, and cakes.

"You are not the only couples to have visited us lately." Mrs. Petherick's lips formed a *moue*. "Not that we mind, but I do wish I knew what Mr. Stewart was doing."

A quarter hour later, after they finished the tea and Mrs. Petherick told them about the church, the sound of boots could be heard coming from the back. Her face lit as she announced, "Here is Mr. Petherick now."

A handsome, tall, raw-boned man with a ruddy complexion and steel-gray hair pulled back in a queue entered the room. He glanced at his wife with a heat almost unseemly in a man of the church. "Mrs. Petherick, I hear we have visitors."

They all stood. *My goodness*. With his dark breeches, turned-over boots, and frock coat, he looked like a pirate from the previous century.

"My dear"—his wife took his arm and smiled up at him—"these nice young people would like to marry."

After she made the introductions, his gaze focused on Will. "Any relation to Nathan Wively?"

"Yes, sir." Will's hand rested on Eugénie's waist. "He was my great-uncle. Miss Villaret is his step-daughter."

The man rubbed his chin. "I was sorry to hear of his death." He turned to her. "Are you one-and-twenty?"

It was a good thing she didn't have to lie. She wouldn't have been at all surprised if the man could immediately discern a falsehood. "Yes, sir. My mother and Miss Whitecliff's parents are here as well."

"Very well. When would you like to have the ceremonies?"

"Immediately," Cicely and Eugénie said at the same time. Cicely continued. "Would you consider coming to the ship for the service?"

"If you would, please," Eugénie added. "All my younger sisters are with us."

The vicar rubbed his chin as he studied them. "I don't see why not. I'll meet you there in two hours."

Will held out his hand, and Mr. Petherick shook it, adding, "Bring a donation. We are a poor parish."

Mrs. Petherick smiled. "If you've finished your tea, I'll send our maid of all work to show you out."

A few minutes later, their little party was on the path, walking down the hill.

"Well," Cicely said, "he's certainly the strangest vicar I've ever seen."

"I agree, my love," Andrew responded. "But he can be as strange as he likes as long as he marries us."

Eugénie stopped, causing the rest of them to do so as well. "I thought we had to marry before noon?"

Cicely shrugged. "I suppose if one is a pirate priest, one may do as one wishes."

"That was my understanding as well, Eugénie. What time is it?" Andrew asked.

Will pulled out his watch. "It's going on eleven, but it is no matter. The Marriage Act doesn't apply here."

Andrew furrowed his brow. "Are you positive? I would not want to have an irregular marriage."

"Yes. I am quite sure." Will grinned. "Luckily for us, the Act is not in effect outside of England proper."

Eugénie tightened her grip on Will's arm and laughed as

happiness burbled up inside her. "In less than two hours we will be husband and wife."

Once Will, Eugénie, Andrew, and Cicely returned and told their parents the news, pandemonium ensued. Even for his eldest sister's wedding, Will hadn't seen such a fuss. Eugénie was whisked away from him. He was shooed out of his cabin by Tidwell, who informed Will that his kit must be repacked and taken to Eugénie's stateroom, but to return in an hour to change for his wedding. As Will walked down the passageway to the salon, wisps of thin muslin caught his eye. Someone shrieked, and a hand placed on the small of his back propelled him on his way.

Andrew and Mr. Whitecliff, who handed Will a rum shrub, appeared to be suffering from the same fate. Will took a long drink. "What the devil is going on?"

"Deuce if I know." Andrew took a pull of his rum. "There is apparently 'a great deal to do and not sufficient time,' or that's what Mrs. Whitecliff said."

"Don't go to the stern," Whitecliff warned. "A bathing tub has been set up."

Will's eyes widened in horror at the thought of a naked Eugénie being seen by anyone. There weren't any other ships, but the boat was positioned so that someone from the beach could see her. "You'll never tell me my betrothed is bathing for everyone in the harbor to see? I'll put a stop to that!"

"No, no." Andrew gave a bark of laughter. "A screen is being set up. The ladies will use the door from Whitecliff's cabin to access the stern."

"Well, thank God for that!" It struck Will forcibly that unlike some, he'd never become sanguine about another man seeing his wife naked. In fact, there were a few places in London he'd no longer be patronizing, and hostesses whose entertainments to which he'd not accept invitations. In fact, he'd make damn sure all of his friends put out the word that Eugénie was out-of-bounds. There were too many blasted rakes and rogues in Town for his liking. Perhaps he'd keep her at home in the country for a while. London might be too dangerous for a woman as innocent as she.

"My lord"—Whitecliff's voice broke into Will's thoughts—"is there something wrong with your shrub? Is the juice sour?"

"No, of course not." Will glanced up to see the man staring at him in concern. "Why do you ask?"

"Because," Andrew said patiently, "you've been scowling at it for the last several minutes."

Will took a swig. "Are you going to attend the Season with Cicely?"

"Of course I am. She'd never forgive me if she wasn't able to experience a London Season." His friend's eyes gleamed with mischief. "Worried about something?"

"No." He tossed off the glass and poured a brandy. "Why should I be?"

"Not concerned that Eugénie will succumb to one of the many rakes hanging around Polite Society?"

Andrew didn't need to say "like you"; it was written on his expression. "Damn it, she's so innocent." Will raked his fingers through his hair. "She's got no idea of the kind of men who prey on women."

"I suppose," Andrew's lips curled into a smile, "you'll have to keep her close to your side. Very unfashionable, I know . . ."

A low roar emerged from Will. "What the devil do I care for fashion? No man had better even consider approaching her."

Andrew lifted his glass in a toast. "My, how the mighty have fallen."

This must be how Beaumont felt with his wife. Suddenly it all seemed comical, and Will grinned, returning his friend's salute. "Indeed they have."

Not long afterward, he and Andrew were called to wash and change. When they were appropriately dressed, they reconvened in the salon, which Will noticed was empty of women. "Where are our ladies?"

Just then Cicely emerged, and behind her Eugénie. She took his breath away. The deep coral of her bodice was cut modestly, but the swell of her breasts rose just enough to tempt him. A strand of pearls circled her slender neck, and his tongue itched to trace where the necklace lay. Her skirts were layers of an extremely thin silk, giving her the appearance of floating toward him. Before long she'd be his forever, and even though the responsibility of caring for her as she deserved weighed heavily on him, it couldn't be soon enough. He held his hand out to her as she approached. "Eugénie, my love, you enchant me."

She touched her fingers to his and smiled shyly. "No one has ever said anything half so nice to me."

"That is because you turned your nose up at all your other suitors," her mother commented dryly.

Eugénie blushed charmingly as he brought her fingers to his lips. "I'm happy to be the first."

And the last, if he had anything to say about it.

The bump of a boat against the *Song Bird* hailed Mr. Petherick's arrival. Mr. Whitecliff went out to greet the vicar.

Mrs. Whitecliff glanced around the room. "I think everything is prepared."

Andrew placed his betrothed's hand on his arm. "We are ready."

"That's an understatement," Cicely mumbled. "I've been ready."

A few moments later, the vicar entered with Mr. Whitecliff. Dressed in a neat gray jacket, with a pearl and white waistcoat, black breeches, low pumps, and a plainly tied cravat, Will was pleased to note that, except for Mr. Petherick's windblown appearance, he looked like any other man of the church.

"Will Mr. Whitecliff be giving away both of you ladies?"

"Yes. I will."

Petherick bowed to the others. "Shall we begin?"

Eugénie took her place next to Will in his dark jacket and breeches. She had never seen him dressed quite so fine. Yet there was something else; she couldn't put her finger on it, but he had never been more handsome. His warm gaze captured her eyes as he repeated his vows in a low, steady voice. Her heart thudded so hard, she thought he must have heard it. His hand held hers more securely as she promised to love, honor, and cherish him.

"Obey?" Will murmured to Mr. Petherick.

"I've found it doesn't do much good. As long as you worship her, you'll not have any problems." He gave the ring he'd blessed to Will, and continued. "With this ring . . ."

Will slid the ring over the third finger of her left hand as he repeated the words. When the vicar pronounced them man and wife, Eugénie, Will, Cicely, and Andrew signed the register, then Cicely and Andrew were wed.

"My lady." Mr. Whitecliff hugged her. "I wish you very happy on your wedding day and throughout your life." He grinned at Will. "To you as well, my lord." The older man eyed Will shrewdly. "But I don't believe I have any reason to be concerned on that account."

A few hours later, leaning against the ship's railing, Andrew was joined by Will. Josh had been sent to fetch Mrs. Petherick so that she could join her husband at the wedding breakfast of sorts that was held as they sailed to Cane Garden Bay, where the ship would spend the night at anchor. Unfortunately, it turned out that the nearby plantation owner was having a house party, and the Whitecliffs knew the hosts and a few of the couples who were in attendance. There was, naturally, nothing for it but that the house party had to be invited as well, at least according to Andrew's new mother-in-law.

An awning had been strung in front of the salon to provide a shaded area. Cicely was stuck doing the pretty with her mother's guests.

"I've discovered," Will said, "the bad part of having the wedding here."

"And that would be?" Andrew was having the same thoughts. There must be some way for him to escape with his wife.

"One cannot whisk one's new wife away."

"True." He rubbed the spot between his brows. "But at least we're married."

"Thank God for that!"

Eugénie cast Will such a look of longing before turning back and smiling at something Mrs. Whitecliff said, that he stood. "I think I'll rescue my viscountess for a while."

"I wish you more luck than I had."

Will raised a brow, and Andrew grimaced. "You'd think I'd planned to steal Cicely off forever instead of residing at her family's home until we leave for England."

"Have you ever watched a dog cut sheep from a herd?"

"No, why?"

Will grinned. "I'm about to help you reclaim your bride. Be prepared to move as soon as I've engaged her mother."

What the devil was he planning? Andrew followed and watched with appreciation as his friend insinuated his way into the conversation. As two of the ladies simpered over him, he took a step to one side, causing Cicely to step back.

Andrew grabbed her hand and swept them behind one of the masts. "Alone at last."

Cicely giggled, but turned her face up to him for a kiss. He brought his lips to hers, teasing them before sliding his tongue into her mouth. He'd wanted her so desperately, but up till now this was all he'd allowed them to do. Now he slid his hands over her lush bottom.

"Oooh, that's nice."

Andrew moved on to nibble her ear. "Just nice?"

Her breath quickened. "Well, perhaps a bit more."

"I think we should find our cabin."

She pulled back a bit, her eyes wide. "Mama wanted to have a talk with me before then."

Aha, that's why Cicely had been kept from him. "And I think, as your husband, it is my right and privilege to answer all your questions and teach you everything you need to know."

She swallowed. "You do?"

"Absolutely." He took her mouth again, bringing her body flush against his. "Shall we go?"

Cicely melted into him. "Yes."

They made their way to the aft of the ship, through her parents' cabin to the part where the staterooms were located. She opened the door to her room.

Andrew drew Cicely into a long kiss. "I can't believe we're finally alone."

"Nor can I." She reached up and began untying his cravat. "My love, I'm a bit nervous."

He quickly unlaced her gown so that it gaped open, giving him a perfect view of the beautiful creamy mounds. His shaft hardened with anticipation. "I won't lie to you. This may hurt some, but I'll be as gentle as possible, and it will never hurt again."

She threw his neckcloth down, applying herself to his waistcoat buttons. By the time she was done, her gown had slid down over her generous hips to the floor. He shrugged out of his waistcoat, then drew his shirt over his head.

Cicely gasped. "Oh, I didn't know how well you look." She placed her hand on his chest, spreading her fingers through his curls. "Umm, I like this."

Good Lord, she'd be the death of him. He quickly removed the rest of their clothing, except for her shift. That would be gone soon enough, and he didn't want to scare her.

Swooping her up, he placed her in the middle of the bed and lay down next to her.

Her arms came around his neck, pulling him closer. "I want you to know I trust you."

He claimed her lips, running his tongue over her teeth, exploring the soft, warm cavern of her mouth before kissing and licking his way to her already tight, pale pink nipples. He'd waited so long to taste her, and she was just as good as he'd thought she would be. Vanilla and coconut.

She moaned, arching into him. His member throbbed with need. God help him, he had to go slowly for her. Andrew attended to her other breast, burying his head in her softness as he moved a hand to her damp curls.

Cicely spread her legs as Andrew settled between them. Her breasts still ached with wanting him, yet now his lips had moved to her stomach and his fingers rubbed her most sensitive spot. Hot desire streaked through her like lightning, causing her to lift her hips to him. "I want . . ."

He chuckled. "You're hot and wet. Soon."

One finger entered her. "So strange."

"Are you all right?" Andrew asked, concerned.

"Yes, more than all right. It—it's wonderful."

He grunted as his body grew as hard as a rock. Cicely pushed against his hand. "There is more."

"Yes."

He shifted over her, nudging his shaft where his finger had been. "Cicely, my love, hold on to me."

She twined her arms around his neck as he thrust into her. She gave a small yelp as a sharp pain took her breath away, and he stopped.

"How are you?"

That was an interesting question. Her sheath throbbed a bit, but the pain was lessening. Soon all she would feel was him. In her and around her. This was what it meant to be one. "Full." She wrapped her legs around him as Andrew began thrusting forward again. Soon pleasure spiraled through her, and her sheath clenched around him. He covered her lips with his, swallowing her cry, then shuddered and groaned.

"Cicely, my love, my wife."

For the first time she truly felt married, part of a new family. "Andrew, I love you."

He kissed her tenderly. "As I love you, now and forever."

Chapter 26

Eugénie glanced at Will, sighed, and gave her head a slight shake as Mrs. Whitecliff's friends and their daughters fawned over him. At first Eugénie hadn't understood why he'd joined the ladies, then she saw Andrew and Cicely sneak away. Apparently it was now Will who needed rescuing. Goodness, if it was this bad here, how much worse would it be in England?

She slid her arm in his. "If you'll excuse us, ladies, I must borrow my husband."

"Oh, so sorry, my lady," a woman with improbable blond curls said.

"We didn't mean to take up so much of his time," another woman in a purple bonnet added.

One of the younger women tittered. Really, you'd think they would have some sense of pride. The women curtseyed, and Eugénie almost returned the gesture, then remembered to incline her head graciously as she gave a light tug on William's arm.

"Ladies, my wife calls." He slipped his arm around her as they headed to the salon. "Thank you," he said in a low, heartfelt tone. "When I couldn't use the excuses I normally do, I found myself stuck."

"Oh, so you do know how to extricate yourself." Eugénie hadn't meant to sound like a shrew, but . . .

She felt rather than saw him smile. Of course he'd think it was funny.

"Oho, my lady. I didn't know you had a jealous streak."

"I don't." Drat the man. "It is only that I . . . well . . ."

He swung her around, kissing her soundly. "I promise you'll never have cause to worry. Drag me away from as many women as you please."

Warmth crept into her face. "I did not *drag* you away."

"Non?" He raked the pads of his thumbs over her nipples. "I plan on dragging you to our cabin and showing you how attached I am to you."

Eugénie's blood raced, and her throat dried. Dear Lord, William was wicked. "Attached?"

"Joined, shall we say?" His tone gave her no doubt of his meaning.

"I think that's an excellent idea."

"Good." He swung her into his arms, turned sideways, and walked down the passageway to the cabins.

When they entered what had been her stateroom alone, William slid her down the length of his hard body, letting her feel his need. He shrugged out of his coat, untied his cravat, and toed off his shoes. It was still daylight and this was the first time she'd have a good look at him. Unable to help herself, Eugénie licked her lips.

The beast chuckled. "That is exactly the reaction I want from you. Would you like to help?"

Hands trembling, she reached up to unfasten his shirt. This was ridiculous. She'd lain with him three times already. Finally the button came undone. "I don't know what is wrong with me."

His eyes simmered as he gazed at her. "Desire combined

with inexperience. Don't let it worry you, my love. Take all the time you need."

Taking a breath, she went to work on the rest of the buttons on his shirt and waistcoat. When his garments were lying on the floor, Eugénie stared at her husband. The curls covering his chest were lighter than she'd thought. She ran her palms over his hard muscles, and William groaned. Encouraged, she allowed her fingers to travel down to his breeches, tracing the width of his taut stomach to the buttons on his fall. His breathing quickened as she undid first one then the others, exposing his already rigid shaft.

Before she could touch it, William pulled his breeches and his stockings down, kicking them aside.

He turned her around. "Now it's your turn."

The back of her neck tingled as he fluttered kisses down her spine to the laces her modiste insisted upon using rather than tapes. As her gown loosened, he kissed each newly exposed place. Her chemise fell with her gown and stays. If nothing else, William was efficient.

He lifted her out of the puddle of clothing on the floor, then draped her clothes over a chair. She reached up to unhook her necklace.

"Leave it."

Staring at him, she dropped her hands.

"I want to see you wearing nothing but the pearls."

Eugénie stood before him wide-eyed, and a little nervous. Well she should be. Though she'd been nude with him the first time, she'd been in bed, not standing exposed before him. Will sucked in a breath. She was even lovelier now than in candlelight.

With one finger he traced from her neck, over her generous breasts, the deep pink nipples now tightly budded, to her small waist, then over the gentle swell of her hips. God, he'd never seen a more beautiful woman. The pearls looped around her neck set off her golden skin. Eugénie's pink stockings drew his gaze to the dark curls hiding her mons. The stockings would go next, but he'd peel them down slowly. Today was the time to savor every inch of his wife.

Will lifted Eugénie, placing her on the bed. He untied the ribbons of her sandals, then poured them both a glass of the champagne he'd had Tidwell attend to earlier. "To you, my love."

She gazed into his eyes, and he was captured all over again. "To us, my husband."

A gull screeched, but other than that, all was quiet. Will found he could barely speak. "Eugénie."

She took one long drink before setting the glass down. "William."

Dear Lord, he wasn't going to last. Slow would have to come later. He tossed off his wine, as she held out her arms. The glass slipped from his fingers and he rolled onto the bed.

"Love me."

"I do, sweetheart, I do."

He touched between her legs, to find her already wet. Eugénie arched up to meet him as he slid into her. Eugénie's legs wrapped around him, holding him tight, and he knew she was his home.

When Will awakened, it was dark. He'd never get used to the rapidity with which the sun went down here. He lit the oil lamps and was gazing at a sleeping Eugénie when a knock sounded on the door.

"My lord?"

"Give me a moment, Tidwell." Will made sure Eugénie was covered and threw on his dressing gown before opening the door. Tidwell averted his gaze from the bed as he carried in a large tray that he placed on a table.

Marisole followed holding a large pitcher and a bottle of wine. "The water is for drinking, milord. I shall bring more for washing later."

She busied herself picking up Will's garments and shaking them out. Tidwell's face turned an interesting shade of pink, but before Will could comment, Marisole said, "Teedwell, there is no need for embarrassment, they are married, no?"

A giggle, which turned quickly into a coughing fit, came from the bed. Eugénie buried her face in a pillow.

The maid helped Tidwell set out the rest of the plates, then led him out of the cabin. Before closing the door, she turned. "Milady, it is for me an immense joy you are wed. I have always wanted to be maid to a great lady."

Eugénie waved her hand in front of her face, clearly in an attempt to stop laughing. "Thank you, Marisole. I am very glad as well."

"*Bon*. Milord, you must forgive Teedwell, he will accustom himself. " She curtseyed and left.

His wife gave herself over to the laughter. "My lord, I believe your valet is a Puritan."

"No, a Methodist. Almost as bad." Will started to chuckle. "Teedwell?"

"She *is* French."

As was his wife. "Come, my lady-wife. Let's eat." Will gave her his best lecherous look. "You'll need your strength."

"Ah, my lord, so will you."

The following morning, Eugénie awoke in William's arms. She glanced out the port window, where she saw a bit of spray shoot up. It was barely light. What were they doing under sail already?

Will stirred, pulling her closer to him. This was an aspect of marriage she already loved.

Marisole crept into the cabin with the wash water.

"Why have we left so early?"

"Weather." She shrugged. "The captain said he saw the first signs of a storm and wishes to return to St. Thomas immediately."

Eugénie nodded. They had been fortunate so far this season to only get heavy rains, which filled their cisterns. The gulls had not yet left, so whatever storm was bearing down on them should not be so bad on land. Still, one wouldn't want to be caught in it out on a ship. "Are we expected in the salon for breakfast?"

A smile dawned on her maid's face. "No one said anything about you, but Miss . . . Mrs. Grayson was told to be present."

"Oh dear, that doesn't sound good. I suppose we'd better be there in support."

Marisole placed a hand bell on the dressing table. "Ring if you need assistance dressing."

"I shall." Eugénie glanced down at William. Was he as good at tying laces as untying them?

He yawned. "What is it?"

Eugénie watched him for a moment, enjoying his tousled hair. His eyes seemed bluer in the morning. "We have a storm approaching, and the captain has already weighed anchor. Also, Mrs. Whitecliff has requested Cicely and Andrew join them in the salon for breakfast. I think we should be there as well."

William pulled her down to him. "You are such a splendid wife that I have a present for you."

She grinned as his shaft nudged her. "Do you indeed?"

"Mmm."

His lovemaking was slow and tender. A change from yesterday and last night when she thought they would burn to cinders. Eugénie had never felt so loved and cherished. She shuddered. To think that at one point she had actually considered a marriage of convenience.

An hour and three gowns later, she rang for Marisole. William, she had discovered, became much too easily distracted to actually dress her. The farthest he'd got was tying the laces half-way up before the temptation to unlace them overcame him. She'd washed for the fourth time when Marisole knocked, then entered.

"*Bonjour*, milady."

"I need to dress quickly so that his lordship can make himself ready as well."

In under a half hour, Eugénie was coiffed and wearing a pale yellow muslin day gown, embroidered with tiny coral-colored flowers. She smiled at Will, who'd watched with a small grin on his lips while she'd donned her gown. He was probably plotting how quickly he could remove it.

"Your turn, my love. I shall meet you in the salon." She whisked out of the cabin before he could protest.

He heaved a sigh as the door shut then opened again to admit "Teedwell." If his valet ever heard Will call him that, he'd probably resign. Throwing off the covers, Will stalked to the washbasin. "The buckskin breeches and light brown jacket for today. We'll be on the ship for hours."

Tidwell bowed, then set about laying out the rest of Will's garments as Will washed.

Will and his wife had discussed moving into her apartment, but perhaps he could talk her into staying at the hotel for at least a few weeks. A honeymoon of sorts. One that wouldn't include curious children and his aunt. Though he had to admit, once he and Eugénie had married, Sidonie had left them alone.

He strolled into the salon just in time to hear Cicely, who was in one corner of the room with her mother, say, "We *want* to spend our time together. We've been married less than a day. If we were in England, we'd be on our wedding trip."

He glanced at Eugénie, who'd started to go to Cicely's aid but was forestalled by her mother. The hotel looked better all the time. Andrew shook off Mr. Whitecliff's arm, then strode over to his wife as Mrs. Whitecliff's lips pressed in a thin line and she said, "Cicely, my dear, you cannot live in a gentleman's pocket."

"Ma'am." Andrew took Cicely's hand and drew her to him. "I believe I am the better judge of how my wife and I should go on."

Eugénie sidled up next to Will, turning her head so that no one but he could hear. "That has been going on since Andrew and Cicely finished breakfast."

"What does Mrs. Whitecliff think she's doing? They're married, for pity's sake."

She gave a slight shrug. "I think she was not ready to let go of Cicely yet." Linking her arm with his, she led him to the dishes that had been set out. "Break your fast. We'll be back in Charlotte Amalie before too long."

"How is that possible? It took us hours to get to Tortola."

"We left very early and the wind is with us sailing back to St. Thomas." She helped him pile his plate with food and did the same to hers.

They sat at one of the small tables, and Josh brought a pot of tea, with milk and sugar. Will took a sip. "What do you think of us living at the hotel for a few weeks?"

"I have no objection." Eugénie chewed thoughtfully. "When do you wish to return to England, and have you told Maman your plan to take her and the children with us?"

He grabbed a serviette to avoid spewing his tea over the table. "How did you know I'd do that?"

She glanced up and frowned. "I am positive you mentioned it. If not"—she raised one shoulder in one of her elegant and very French gestures—"it must be because that is what you *would* do. You must return, and it would not occur to you to leave Maman and the children behind."

Will glanced around. "Where are our sisters?"

"In Maman's cabin with Penny, doing their lessons." His wife poured more tea into his cup. "The wind is so strong today, we thought it best if they were not on deck."

"Thank God for that." He didn't relish trying to keep track of them on the journey home.

"I think being in England for Christmas would be the best."

He searched her face. A small line had formed between her brows. "You do realize it will be much colder than here?"

"Yes, of course. We can have some warm clothing made before we leave, and the rest when we arrive."

"Very well then." He still worried about the transition for her. "If we depart at the end of October, we'll arrive in good time and be spared the winter gales."

Eugénie smiled at him, and it was as if he'd been given the sun, moon, and all the stars.

"Thank you."

When he shrugged, she placed her small hand over his. "It is a large burden to take on."

It would take a fair amount to get his aunt and cousins settled, but he and Eugénie would have help. Before they sailed, he'd write his friends and mother. Will grinned to himself. He supposed he should tell his parents he eloped with his father's ward.

Henri sat at the table in the servants' parlor where he worked drinking a glass of water, when the boy he'd enlisted to assist him ran into the room. "The ship you want comes now."

He slipped the child a silver coin and whispered, "Go to my uncle and tell him."

The lad dashed off as quickly as he'd entered. Henri stood. It was time to tell Monsieur Villaret and the Vicomte, but by the time the Frenchmen were ready to leave for the harbor, Miss—or he should say, Viscountess—Wively would be home, and once her uncle discovered she was already married, it would be the end of their scheme. Henri would have the rest of the funds to open his business in Tortola. He made his way to the parlor the two men used, entered, and bowed. "Milord, monsieur, your niece is back in port." When he looked up, he saw he'd addressed an empty room. Henri grabbed the arm of a maid passing by. "Where are they?"

Her eyes went wide. "I—I don't know. Perhaps the docks. That captain was here earlier."

He dropped his hand. "Thank you."

Damn, damn, damn. All he could do now was hope Villaret didn't know which ship his niece was on and that his uncle Bates's message would get there in time. He strode toward the door. He would probably not receive the rest of the payment, but there might still be a chance for him to intervene.

Chapter 27

Eugénie fiddled with her parasol as she stood next to the gangway, ready to leave the yacht. "Drat. Marisole, can you get this open?"

"I shall try." The maid took the parasol. "Where is milord?"

"Speaking with Mr. Grayson about the hotel arrangements. They must be changed if he and Cicely are staying there as well." Eugénie started down the wooden boards. "I'll go home and order something light for nuncheon while you pack what I'll need for the next few days. The rest can be brought over later."

"There is something wrong with this catch."

In moments she was on the pier, headed toward the main dock area. It would be so nice to have William all to herself.

"Eugénie, *arrêtez*!"

Who would speak to her in French and use her given name?" She stopped and turned. A man of medium height stood facing her. The hairs on the back of her neck stood on end. The man looked familiar, but she'd never met him before. Could it be her uncle? She raised her chin and used a tone guaranteed to stop any more familiarities. "I am afraid you have me at a disadvantage, monsieur."

"Ah, excellent. You have not lost your French." The man smiled, showing too many teeth and not all of them in good condition. "But you do not know me." He bowed. "I am your uncle Yves Villaret de Joyeuse. Your father's younger brother."

She resisted the urge to run back to the *Song Bird*. Though if she tried, her uncle could catch her easily enough. Perhaps if she kept him talking long enough, someone from the ship would be here soon. She slid a glance to his right. Behind her uncle and off to his side, Marisole had finally got the parasol opened. "I do not understand why you waylay me here. What do you want?"

The smile remained on his face but did not touch his eyes. "I see you plan to be stubborn. We wish what we have always desired, a good alliance for you."

It was on the tip of her tongue to tell him she was already married, but some feeling that he might prove a danger to William stopped her. "Go on."

He glanced at the *Song Bird*, but didn't appear to notice Eugénie's maid. "We have arranged a match with a French *comte*. He is older and wants only an heir. After you have given him one, you may do as you wish."

"I am not interested in your match."

She turned to go, but his hand shot out, stopping her. "If you want to see your step-father, Nathan Wively, alive, you will come with me."

Marisole had moved so that she was directly behind Uncle Yves with the parasol raised, ready to strike him. It wouldn't do much, but it might give Eugénie and her maid an opportunity to get away.

"My father died months ago." The moment the words

were out of her mouth, she knew they were not true. "Show me proof, or be on your way."

Yves reached into his waistcoat pocket and pulled out a watch. *Papa's.* Before her uncle opened it, Eugénie knew she would see the miniatures of her and Maman that Papa had had painted. Her heart pounded so quickly it created a roar in her ears. She struggled to keep her voice even. "Where do you have him?"

"In a safe place." Yves clicked the watch closed. "Once you are wed, he will be freed."

"*Non.* You must think I am exceptionally *stupide.*" Eugénie curled her lips in a sneer. "I will have proof he is alive and safe before I marry your *comte.*"

"You are a true Villaret de Joyeuse. My brother will be pleased." His grip on her arm tightened. "Come, we depart now."

Eugénie dug her heels into the dirt. "I cannot just leave. My mother will worry, and I need to collect a few items."

Uncle Yves's face flushed with anger. "You will accompany me now, or I will personally see that Wively dies a painful death."

Behind Yves, Marisole glanced at the yacht and gave a short nod. Eugénie's maid would make sure her family, especially her husband, would know where to look for her.

"Very well." She made her tone as cold as the English winters William had told her about. "But if he is not well, I shall never wed your *comte.*"

"I expect nothing less."

She went with him, being half pulled to a pier two wharves down from the Whitecliffs', where a rowboat was tied up and an older man waited.

"I have her," Yves barked. "We must go immediately."

After she was in the boat, a sailor climbed in, cast off the line, then took the oars.

"My dear niece," the older man said. "I am your uncle Hervé. I am pleased you have joined us."

She bit her lip, reminding herself that neither man would hurt her, not if they wanted to marry her off and produce a child. Eugénie raised her chin. "I may be here, but it is not of my choosing."

He reached over and patted her right hand. "You say that now, yet we are ensuring you shall have a wonderful life. One in which you will want for nothing. Your future husband has the ear of the king."

She fisted her left hand, feeling William's ring. What would her uncles do when they discovered she was already married? With any luck, her husband would have rescued her by then. The most important thing was to find Papa and free him. William would understand why she had to go with her uncle. He had to. He loved his family as much as she did.

Eugénie's maid crashed into Will as he strolled out of the salon. He steadied her arm, stopping her from bouncing back. *"Milord, milord, they have taken milady!"*

His heart dropped to his feet, and he struggled to breathe. How? Why had this happened now? He raked his fingers through his hair. He never should have agreed to allow her to go back with only her maid to protect her. "Tell me what happened."

Tears coursed down Marisole's cheeks, and she shook like a blancmange. Andrew pressed his glass into her hand and she drank.

Will glanced at the docks, but couldn't see his wife at all. He wanted to wring it out of Marisole, but that would only upset her more. "Go slowly and tell us everything."

She started in rapid French then turned to English. "I hear it all. Mr. Wivenly is alive."

"You mean they have her already?" A young, light-skinned man cursed.

"We'll have none of that around the ladies." Henriksen followed the young man up the gangway.

"Henri, what are you doing here?" Aunt Sidonie asked.

Jeanne jumped around. "Didn't you hear, Mama? Marisole said Papa is still alive."

The color drained from Aunt Sidonie's face. "Is it true? Nathan is alive?"

Suddenly everyone was there and talking at once. Will bellowed, "Quiet! Whoever has my uncle also has Eugénie, and I need to get her back." The noise stopped and everyone stared at him. "You, Henri, who are you and what do you know?"

Henri succinctly told them about the plan to marry Eugénie to a Frenchman.

Sidonie held her hands clasped together so tightly her knuckles turned white. "My first husband always told me never to trust his family, but I should have taken better care."

None of that mattered now. "Which ship are they taking her to?"

"There is a galley," Henri responded, "anchored not far from the mouth of the harbor."

"I know the one." Henriksen took out a spyglass and put it to his eye. "I see her."

"My daughter?" Sidonie's voice was tense with fear.

"No, the ship. Wait a moment. Got Miss Eugénie. She's in a dory heading toward the galley." He snapped the glass shut. "My ship, *Swift Wind,* is ready to go, my lord. I came over here to bid everyone farewell."

Will sent up a prayer of thanks. Getting the *Song Bird* ready for another voyage would have taken time he didn't have. "How soon can we set sail?"

"Half an hour. Don't worry. We'll catch up to her in good

time. I've got one of the fastest ships around." Henriksen dashed back down the gangway.

Will glanced over his shoulder at Josh. "Tell Tidwell to pack a few of my things. Marisole, do the same for your mistress. You have a quarter hour."

"Wait a moment." Aunt Sidonie put her hand on Will's arm. "I'm going as well."

"Mama," Adelaide said, "we all want to go."

Everyone stared once more at him. "Mr. Whitecliff, can you and your wife help Miss Penny take the children back to Wively House?"

"Of course, my lord."

"Will, that's not fair!" Valérie cried.

"I want to see Papa!" Jeanne began to cry.

"Listen to me." Will squatted down. "We don't know exactly where your papa is. If we have to rescue him, it may be dangerous. Having the three of you with us would only distract everyone from putting all our efforts into rescuing your papa and Eugénie. Sometimes the best way to help is by doing what you're told." He placed his arms around the children, pulling them into his embrace. "Promise me you'll remain here and listen to Mr. and Mrs. Whitecliff."

Though the girls slowly nodded, they appeared none too pleased.

Jeanne asked, "You'll save Papa and Eugénie like you saved Charity?"

"Yes," Will vowed to them and to himself. "You can count on it."

Mr. Whitecliff herded the children back inside the salon.

"Will," Andrew said, "if you'd like, Cicely and I will stay at Wively House and watch the children."

"Thank you for offering, but I have something else I'd like you to do. Believe me, I hate to ask you this"—Will glanced at Cicely, hoping she'd understand—"but will you come with me? I can use someone handy with a weapon."

Cicely's chin firmed. "If Andrew is going then so am I. I can help as well."

Will should have expected that. He didn't have time to argue with her and, to be fair, it wasn't right to separate them. "Very well. Get whatever you're taking." He started to leave the yacht, then stopped. "Which ship belongs to Henriksen?"

"I'll take you there, my lord," Henri said. "I blame myself for not keeping a better eye on the scoundrels."

"Take the dory, my lord," the Whitecliffs' captain said. "The *Swift Wind* is already at anchor."

"I'll send Henri back with the boat to pick up the others."

Less than an hour later, his ever-growing party was ensconced on board the sleekest schooner Will had ever seen, and they were heading out of the harbor. The quarters were not what he'd got used to on Whitecliff's yacht, but it was well-appointed and had room enough for everyone. There being no on-deck salon, they all stood at the rail until Henriksen called Will up to the helm.

"I didn't want to mention it in front of the ladies, but I've got guns if we need them." Henriksen glanced out over the horizon. "You do know we have a storm coming in?"

"I've heard. How bad will it be?"

"I won't know that until morning. If God's with us, we'll have Eugénie by then. What are you going to do about getting Nathan Wively back?"

Will rubbed a hand over his face. "If my wife has found out where they're holding my uncle, we'll rescue him. If not, then I have no problem beating the information out of the blackguards."

Henriksen nodded. "My thoughts exactly. We'll get along well, my lord." He smiled. "You're a fortunate man to have married Eugénie."

"I am." More than fortunate. She was the best thing that had ever happened to him. "And I have no intention of losing her."

Will's hand formed a fist, one he'd like to shove into a Villaret face. After which Will would find out what the hell Eugénie was thinking to go off on her own like this. He thought she trusted him to take care of her and her family. Apparently, that wasn't true.

Eugénie kept an eye on the seas. It was clear neither of her uncles had any knowledge of the Caribbean waters or sailing. Yves had argued with the captain when he'd plotted the route over to St. John. In what could only be an attempt to humor her idiot uncle, the captain had changed course, but gradually turned them east again before heading to St. Martin. From there they would sail down the islands to Martinique.

It had not been difficult at all to convince Uncle Hervé to tell her where Papa was. Hervé honestly thought they were doing the proper thing by ensuring Eugénie and the Villaret family's financial well-being. Yves, on the other hand, was dangerous. She'd have to make sure she was not near him when William rescued her. She would not put it past her uncle to use her to threaten her husband or kill him.

Last evening, she had pled a headache and excused herself from dining with the captain and her uncles, asking that a tray be brought to her. Perhaps if she continued to pretend she was ill, they would leave her alone. Eugénie ran a hand down her skirt. The dagger she had donned yesterday morning might come in handy after all.

She called for breakfast to be brought to her along with water for washing. As the cabin boy laid out the food, she asked if either of her uncles were awake.

"No, mademoiselle. They were up very late last night." He tapped his head. "By the number of bottles of brandy, I do not expect to see them until much later."

This was exactly the news she had wanted. Perhaps they

had even contracted mal de mer, and would not be able to take part in the fight, if there was one.

After she'd broken her fast, Eugénie glanced in the passageway. Seeing no one, she went to the helm to ingratiate herself with the captain and find out what weapons were on board. "May I look through the telescope?"

The man smiled indulgently. "*Oui, mademoiselle*. Shall I show you how it works?"

She returned his smile. "There is no need. I have used one once before."

Opening it up, she searched the sea, wondering where William was. She had not wanted to ask for a glass around her uncles. The less they knew about her sailing or other skills, the better. Finally three tall masts came in to view. The ship was moving so quickly through the water, it could only be the *Swift Wind*. William must have asked Mr. Henriksen to help him. Eugénie's chest tightened with joy. Soon she'd be with her husband again, and he would find Papa.

The *Swift Wind* was so close, they must have held off during the night to approach in daylight. She smiled to herself, closed up the glass, and handed it back to the captain.

"Did you see anything interesting? A whale or a mermaid perhaps?" The captain gave her a patronizing smile.

She schooled her expression into one of complete innocence and sighed. "*Non, monsieur le capitaine*. I see nothing but water. Thank you for its use." She started to turn, then stopped. "Oh, *pardonnez moi*." Eugénie gave him her most winsome look. "It is not that I do not trust your crew, but is there a key to my cabin I may have?"

"*Oui, oui, mademoiselle*. Of course." He puffed his chest out. "There is no insult. *Naturellement* a young lady wishes to lock her door. If you look in my cabin, on the wall by the door, the keys are kept there."

She widened her eyes. "In *your* cabin, monsieur?"

"Ah, *oui*. I understand your hesitation, but I assure you no one will bother you."

"Merci beaucoup." Eugénie lowered her eyes. "Perhaps I shall feel well enough to dine with all of you this evening."

He bowed. "It would be my greatest pleasure, mademoiselle."

Once below deck, Eugénie listened carefully for any sound indicating one or more of her uncles were awake. All she heard was snoring. Making her way quietly, she reached the captain's cabin and opened the door. Just as he'd said, a row of keys hung from hooks on the wall, and they were all neatly labeled. The problem was, none of the doors carried corresponding numbers or names. She grabbed the cabin keys. First she tried the captain's door. They all fit, but only one would turn. After replacing that key, she tried her lock, found the right key, then dropped it into one of the pockets she'd insisted on having in her skirts. That left three more keys. Staying alert for any noises that would signify someone else was coming, she picked the next door over. A loud snore reassured her. When she found the correct key, she snicked the lock shut and listened for the next snore. Instead, a door down the passageway opened.

"Bonjour, Eugénie."

Drat! Yves.

"Bonjour, mon oncle." She gave him a small smile, as if her head still hurt, while slipping the remaining keys into her other pocket. "Did you sleep well?"

He grinned. "As well as could be expected on a ship. I will be glad to return home. Are you feeling better this morning?"

She let her lips droop. "Only a little. I thought to take some air and return to my room. If you will excuse me."

Yves gave a slight bow. "Of course. Do not tax your strength. You must remain in good health."

As long as the *canaille* believed she was still unmarried,

he would do everything he could to keep her safe. Eugénie repressed a shudder, but what would happen if he discovered her deception?

She strolled past him, returning to the deck, where she strode to the stern. Several moments later, *Swift Wind* came into view. If Mr. Henriksen stayed on his present course, she'd be able to signal them from the port window in her cabin.

Yes, that was a good plan. At least then William would know where to find her. Eugénie prayed he'd come soon.

Chapter 28

Dawn was breaking as the *Belle Amie* sailed out of Marigot harbor, St. Martin. Nathan stood at the bow; the others in his group were still asleep. Within an hour of departing Saint-Pierre, everyone but Conrad, Miss Marshall, and Vincent had come down with seasickness.

Two days later, in an effort to combat the effects of mal de mer, Vincent ordered the ship to put in at St. Martin to pick up more beef. Fortunately for Nathan, once on board and in the fresh air, he had rapidly begun regaining his strength. He grinned to himself. It would never do to return to Sidonie in a weakened state. During his captivity the thought that he'd never see his wife and children again overwhelmed him to the point where he'd had to lock them away deep in his heart and try not to think of them over much. But now, now he was within a few short days' sail of St. Thomas. If, that was, they could outrun the hurricane steadily pushing them north. With any luck it would be nothing more than high winds and rain. Still, they would need to find a hurricane hole in which to wait out the weather if it became necessary.

As he and Vincent had agreed to take the others to Tortola before heading for St. Thomas, Nathan hoped they'd make Gorda Sound on Virgin Gorda in time. He strolled to the stern, taking in the waves and still-white clouds, knowing they could change quickly and at any time.

Vincent came on deck just as they entered the Anguillita Spur. "Good morning. Did you sleep well?"

"Well enough." Nathan handed his friend the spyglass. "I'll be glad to get home."

"It is a shame the weather will probably hold you up a bit."

Nathan nodded absently. His mind was so full, he couldn't think. Though the first thing he'd like to do was kill Vicomte Villaret. Gazing out over the ocean, Nathan searched for any vessels that might cause trouble, and stopped. "Hand me the glass."

"What is it?" Vincent asked as he gave Nathan the telescope.

"I'll tell you in a moment." He focused on something that looked like two sets of masts. Several minutes later, they came clearly into view. "What the devil is Henriksen doing out here?" It was then Nathan brought the galley into focus. For some reason *Swift Wind* was bearing down on the other vessel. "We're about to see some action." He shut the glass with a snap and bounded to the helm, shoving the telescope into the captain's hand. Thank God, Vincent had had the good sense to hire an Englishman. "See the two ships out there?"

"Yes, sir."

"We're going to join them." Then he'd see what his friend Bendt was up to, and ask if he required any help. Damn, it felt good to be able to be of use again.

A grin split the younger man's face. "Aye, aye, sir."

In no time they'd changed headings and were traveling on a path toward the other two ships.

* * *

Will stood at the rail of *Swift Wind* with Henriksen as the man handed him the telescope. "You can see the galley off to the larboard side, my lord."

He lifted it to his eye. *Damnation!* Yet there was no way in hell he'd admit to never being able to see a thing through one of these things, other than water. He'd have to have Eugénie show him how to use the blasted instrument. If he ever saw her again. He ground his teeth. "How long will it take to reach her?"

"Under an hour and you'll have your Eugénie back."

Will returned the glass to Henriksen. "Good."

A completely irrelevant thought floated through Will's mind. *His sisters would enjoy hearing about this story for months.*

"I would have approached sooner," Henriksen said, "but I wanted to see who has decided to join us."

Will shook his head, not understanding.

Henriksen pointed to a dark spot on the horizon that Will could barely make out. "Safer to know if it's friend or foe."

"Yes." Damn. He'd slept like hell, alternately missing Eugénie, worrying about her, and wishing he could turn her over his knee and give her the spanking of her life for not trusting him to deal with the problem. His teeth hurt from grinding them, and his stomach was so sour he'd only been able to manage a cup of tea and a slice of bread. "I'll wake the others."

Andrew and Cicely were at the long table in the room next to the galley. She smiled. "Good morning."

Will tried to return it and couldn't. "We have company."

Andrew stopped gazing into his wife's eyes long enough to glance up. "Who?"

"Dev . . . I don't know." Will told them what Henriksen had seen.

"I'll be right up," Andrew said, as he and Cicely both rose.

Were they joined at the hip?

Will scrubbed his face with his hand. "Thank you."

"Don't worry, Will." Cicely smiled up at him. "We'll have her back to you before you know it."

A half hour later, he was gripping the rail so tightly his knuckles turned white. "How much longer until we know?"

Andrew lowered the glass. "The unidentified ship has raised some flags. It won't be long now."

"It's Vincent Beaufort!" Henriksen called from the helm. "He's got Nathan with him!"

"How can you tell that from the flags?" Will called.

Henriksen laughed. "Not from the flags, my lord. I can see him."

"Thank God he truly is alive!" Aunt Sidonie's fist went to her mouth, and tears shone in her eyes.

Will had been so focused on the ship he hadn't even noticed his aunt on the deck.

Andrew turned to Cicely. "Get the pistols."

She nodded and dashed off.

"Mrs. Wively," Henriksen said, "please go below. Nathan would never forgive me if anything were to happen to you."

For a moment she drew her brows together as if she'd balk, then she inclined her head sharply. "Don't forget to call me when I can return."

"I won't forget."

Not long after Will's aunt left, Cicely returned with three pistols. She handed one to Andrew and one to Will, keeping the third one for herself.

She gave Andrew a kiss. "If the ship is boarded, I'll be near the middle mast."

"You'll stay out of the fighting?"

She placed her hand on his cheek. "Of course. Stay safe. You, husband, are not allowed to die."

Henriksen called for the guns to be readied.

They were rapidly bearing down on one side of the galley. While the other ship approached on the opposite side, it wasn't going to arrive in time to help.

How Henriksen did it, Will would never know. The *Swift Wind* came along the left side of the galley as the other ship flanked the right. Henriksen ordered the ship with Eugénie on it to heave to. Which, surprisingly enough, they did. Of course it might have been due to the guns pointed at them.

The other ship's captain was distracted by a dark-haired man of medium-height, waving his arms around when the grappling hooks landed, securing the galley to the *Swift Wind*.

Will searched the deck for Eugénie, but didn't see her anywhere. Were they wrong? Had she been taken on another ship? Or was she hurt?

"There she is." Cicely pointed to a port window where Eugénie leaned out, waving and blowing kisses.

God, he'd just lost at least ten years of his life worrying about her. He sent up prayers of thanks she was alive and appeared to be in good health. "I'm going to kill her."

"Are you coming," Andrew asked in a drawl, "or do you just plan to stand there staring at her?"

"Yes. Right now."

When Will landed on the galley's deck, the dark-haired man raced to the hatch leading to the lower deck,

That was where Eugénie was.

Will darted after the blackguard. If the cur touched her, he was a dead man. He reached the ladder as the blackguard was pounding on a door, yelling something in French. Eugénie answered. Thank God she had the sense to lock herself in.

Suddenly there was the sound of a door crashing into a wall.

He jumped the last few feet. "Eugénie, where are you?"

"At the end of the passageway."

"*Salope!* Who is that? Your lover?"

No one called his wife a whore. Anger boiled up in Will

and for the first time in his life, a red haze passed before his eyes. He'd kill the blackguard just for that. In a few rapid strides he was at the splintered door of her cabin. The scoundrel held her trapped against him. Her dagger lay on the floor.

"Villaret, I presume."

"Yes, and who are you?" the man spat.

"I'm Viscount Wivenly, and if you know what's good for you, you'll unhand my wife."

The man's eyes widened in shock, then he snarled, "Was your wife. Now she will be a widow."

She tried to jerk away, but her uncle's grip tightened, and he pulled out a dagger. "Stop, niece, unless you wish to die as well. You are no good to me married."

Eugénie started to struggle again. "You murdered my papa, didn't you?"

"No. I told you he is safe. Remain still."

She brought her foot down on Villaret's instep.

"Damn you!" he roared and backhanded her, sending her sprawling onto the floor. Her head hit the bunk.

The boat lurched, causing both men to brace themselves. Before Will got his footing, a flash of silver flew toward him. He ducked, and shot. The dagger struck the side of the doorway, where his head had been.

Villaret crumpled to the floor, blood pouring out of the hole in his chest.

Will picked up Eugénie. An angry red mark marred her cheek. He'd shoot her uncle again for hurting her. "My love, are you all right?"

She buried her face in his coat and sobbed. "I was so afraid he had killed you."

He wasn't going to tell her how close it had been. "A knife is no match against a pistol." William crushed her to him, kissing her as if his hunger would never end. "I'm going to wring your neck."

"I'm so glad you are alive and this is over."

Eugénie slid down his length, pressing her body into his.

As her fear lessened, her desire for him rose, and he walked her backward toward the passageway. "I know, but what else could I do? Papa . . ."

One hand cupped her derrière, holding her against his desire. "He's on his way here."

She tightened her grip and tried to put her legs around him. "*Dieu merci!* William, I love you so much for doing this for me."

He chuckled as his fingers brushed her nipple. "As much as I'd like to take credit, I didn't bring him to you, my darling. He's coming to us on another ship."

"What is the meaning of this?" Papa's angry voice boomed into the room, causing her to plant her feet firmly on the floor. "And who the devil are you?"

Eugénie began to laugh. Not the ladylike one with small giggles, but deep, from her stomach. Was she having the vapors?

"It's all right, my love. I'll protect you."

"*Non*, *non*. You don't understand."

Will refused to lessen his grip on Eugénie. "I, sir, am her husband." Will barked over his shoulder, "Who the hell are *you*?"

"*Papa.*" The word shot from her lips as if she didn't have breath for another.

Well, that answered that question.

"*Husband?*" Uncle Nathan stared at him.

Eugénie clung to Will as if to protect him from her father. "We married two days ago."

"You still haven't told me who *he* is."

Tucking Eugénie next to him, Will faced a man who looked almost exactly like his father. "Your great-nephew. William, Viscount Wively."

Uncle Nathan stared at Will as if trying to place him. "You look like your maternal grandfather."

"So I've been told."

"How did you marry my daughter when she's still under-age?"

Eugénie let go of Will and flew into her step-father's arms. "We went to Tortola." Nathan started, and she smoothed his coat. "Now, don't be angry. Maman and the girls came as well."

He narrowed his eyes, and Will narrowed his in response. Great-uncle or no, Eugénie was his, and no one was going to take her away from him.

"Did they?" Nathan asked suspiciously.

Clearly the man was not going to give it up.

She smiled. "Yes, Papa, and I'm very happy." She glanced over her shoulder at Will. "Now I have my husband and my father. Papa, Maman is on Mr. Henriksen's ship waiting for you."

Eugénie moved from her father back to Will. "I know she'd like to see you."

"And I want to see her, but first, who got killed?"

She covered her lips with one hand and gasped. "Oh."

Will glanced down at Villaret. Blood covered the front of the man's jacket where Will's ball had entered. Before he thought to stop Eugénie, she was staring down at the body.

He expected shock or some sort of horrified response, but instead she said, "Oh, I suppose we should do something about him." She glanced at Will. "Is he dead?"

"If he's not now, he will be soon." He pulled her back against him.

"When you are ready," Uncle Nathan said in a dry tone, "I would like to know exactly who this"—he pointed at the body—"is."

A shiver ran through Eugénie, but her voice was steady. "He said he was my uncle Yves, and he threatened to torture you and kill William. I think it is a very good thing he is dead. I only wish I could have done it myself." After a moment she added, "I will not feel sorry for someone like him."

Will bent to kiss her on the head, when a pounding started on one of the cabin doors.

"What is happening? Let me out," a man shouted in French.

"That is my other uncle." Eugénie curled her lip into a sneer. "I was able to lock him in his cabin this morning so that he could not cause trouble when you arrived."

He truly had never met any woman like her. Will rubbed his forehead before addressing his uncle. "How do you wish to handle this, sir?"

"We need to depart soon. In case you didn't know, there's a storm coming and we must reach the hurricane hole on Virgin Gorda before it does. Take Eugénie—"

"Non." Her chin took on a familiar mulish cast. "I will not be kept out of this decision."

Uncle Nathan raised his brows. "Very well. We'll have the body moved up on deck, then talk to the captain of this ship. Before I make any decisions, I must discover how much he knew of the plot to kidnap you."

The pounding on the door grew louder. "What about Uncle Hervé?"

"He can stay where he is for the time being." Uncle Nathan frowned as the pounding continued. "I can't see that he'll be of much help if we let him loose."

"Lord Wivenly, Nathan, is everything all right down there?" Henriksen shouted.

"Yes," Will answered. "We need a couple of men to move a body."

Less than five minutes later, Uncle Nathan had ascertained that the captain had known only that the two Villaret men were here to pick up their niece. Will pulled Nathan aside. "Eugénie doesn't think her Uncle Hervé is a danger." He rubbed the side of his face. "I don't know if I want to take that chance."

"The plain fact of the matter is that we don't have time to deal with it in any satisfactory manner," Nathan responded.

"We must leave now. I've told the captain he can either follow us or try to make it to Simpson Bay in St. Martin."

"Nathan!" Aunt Sidonie stood at the rail of the *Swift Wind*.

"Oh God. Sidonie, my love." Nathan's voice hitched. "We're coming now."

"Go to her, Papa," Eugénie urged. "We'll be right after you."

Will pulled his wife to him, kissing her hard on her lips. "Promise me you will never do anything like this again."

"No, never."

"Let's get out of here."

Chapter 29

The sky opened up as the *Swift Wind's* grappling hooks were removed from the galley and the schooner sailed free of the other ship. Once Eugénie was below deck, to her great consternation, she began to cry.

William wrapped his arms around her. "Sweetheart, what is it?"

"I do not know. Suddenly it was all too much." She chuckled wetly against his jacket. "Yet now I have everyone I love back with me and safe."

Cicely and Andrew coaxed Will, Eugénie, and Maman and Papa into a dining room next to the galley. "I believe the cook has some tea brewing. Sit down and tell us everything."

Eugénie turned to Papa, sitting next to Maman with his arm around her. "How did you get away and how did you find us?"

He told them of his escape. "You remember Mr. Beaufort?"

She nodded.

"I was on his ship when we saw the *Swift Wind* chasing down the galley."

"But where is he now?"

Papa grinned. "After Vincent realized we had enough men to rescue you, he dropped me off and told me he'd see us at Gorda Sound. With sick people aboard, he didn't want to take any chances of being caught in the storm."

"I just hope *we* get there in time," William commented grimly.

"Don't worry, my boy, we will," Papa responded. "With this wind we'll be there in no time at all." He glanced at her, William, Cicely, and Andrew. "Now it's your turn. How did both these marriages come about?"

Eugénie took a breath. "If Cicely and Andrew agree, I will tell you the whole story, but you must promise not to repeat any of it to Mr. and Mrs. Whitecliff."

William's arm tightened around Eugénie. "Are you sure about this?"

"Yes. I do not like keeping secrets."

Andrew's brows came together. "Cicely, my love?"

"If Mr. Wively promises, then I think he deserves to know. After all, it is hard to explain the rest without telling him about that night."

Papa squinted his eyes at them. "You are all married, and I wouldn't want to upset your parents, Cicely. I promise."

"Bon." Eugénie began the story by telling him when she and Cicely first saw Andrew and William. Andrew, Cicely, and William joined in at times to explain parts Eugénie didn't know. All of them left out William's kissing her in the alley. Her mother could continue to believe it was love at first sight.

By the time they'd finished the story, they'd consumed the tea, Papa had poured rum for everyone, and the cook brought stew and bread.

"Remind me not to go away again," he said in a wry tone. "I miss all the fun."

"I agree." Maman's voice trembled. "You do not need to go away again at all. We missed you so very much, my love."

"And I missed you." He kissed her. "It appears I have a lot of catching up to do."

Eugénie blinked back her tears of joy. It was so wonderful to have her parents together again. William's arm tightened, drawing her even closer to him. "I have everything now."

"Yes." His answer was a soft whisper against her ear.

Suddenly the ship rolled and they all reached for their mugs of rum.

Papa grabbed his cup as it slid to the end of the table. "We're in for a long night."

Cicely yawned. "I'm for my bed."

"As am I." Andrew stood.

"Yes. I am tired as well." Eugénie slid a smile at William. Usually waiting out a hurricane involved many tedious hours of trying to stay busy, yet tonight she'd be with her husband. The storm would probably not last long enough.

In their small cabin, Will released the last of the small buttons of Eugénie's gown, drawing the garment down over her slender shoulders. "How long will it storm?"

She shrugged, causing the rumpled muslin to slip to her breasts. "It depends on how fast it is moving." She pulled her arms out, pushing the gown over her hips. It landed in a heap on the floor. "Sometimes they just blow through, and at other times they stall. That is when the most damage is caused."

Will braced himself to keep from falling as the ship rolled. Eugénie tossed her petticoats over the desk chair as though the boat hadn't moved at all. "How do you do that?"

"Do what?"

"Not allow the ship's movement to bother you?"

She grinned then presented her back to him so that he could unlace her stays. "It is balance. I always feel the way she shifts. In the same way you would on a horse."

Once free of the stays, she sat on the bed, then removed her shoes and stockings.

Normally Will would want to do that, but he wasn't sure he'd be able to concentrate on her and stand at the same time. Instead he focused on getting his clothing off as quickly as possible, and grumbled, "I thought a hurricane hole would keep the ship from being tossed around."

Eugénie laughed. "It will keep us safe from most of the winds and high seas, but the boat will still roll."

Finally out of his clothes, he lurched toward the bed and almost fell on top of her. His wife went into whoops. He lowered his tone to one that promised retribution. "Laughing at your husband, my lady?"

Still giggling, Eugénie scrambled away, but he caught her foot. She might know more about ships, but he knew more about this. Will ran his tongue from her ankle to the tender spot behind her knee, pausing to suckle the soft spot. Eugénie gave a moan. Lying down was much better. "Not laughing now?"

Her breath stuttered as he moved his mouth higher, flicking her pearl with his finger as he tasted her essence. *"Non."* Her breath quickened. "Oh, William."

His member throbbed as if he hadn't had her in days, but tonight she was going to beg. "Yes, my love?"

She wrapped one leg around him as he held the other wide. "I want you."

Dragging his tongue over her engorged nub, he dipped it into her belly button. "How much?"

Eugénie arched into him, crying out as he took one nipple into his mouth and sucked, while rubbing his shaft between her legs. "Talk to me, Eugénie."

She wiggled, attempting to get both legs around him. *"Extrêmement!"*

Her eyes opened wide, she gulped air as he switched to her other breast, idly caressing the abandoned one. A sheen covered her body. *God* he was going to burst.

"William, s'il te plaît!"

He positioned his member at the opening of her sheath and slid into her inch by slow inch, as she clenched tightly around him, bringing him to completion. This hadn't turned out at all as he'd planned. He'd meant to teach her a lesson, show her he was in charge, but now Will was more deeply in love with Eugénie than ever. She could spend her life laughing at him, and he wouldn't mind.

"Stay with me, love."

"William, I—I cannot. I need . . ."

This time, Eugénie really was going to die. Tremors rushed through her body, and William began to thrust again. She hooked her ankles together, encouraging him. Waves crashed against the hull as the storm inside her rose once more. Their bodies were slick, and she anchored herself to William as the contractions began, threatening to separate them.

Deep in her soul, Eugénie suddenly knew she would kill anyone who tried to keep them apart, and he must feel the same about her.

She arched into William as he thrust into her. He groaned and shuddered. His warm seed filled her, making her wish they had already conceived a child.

Eugénie took his head between her hands, possessing his lips as he had possessed hers. She broke the kiss. "I love you."

The corners of William's lips tilted up. "It's about time."

"Oh, you." He captured the fist she had planned to pummel him with. "I did love you before, I just love you more now."

William rolled off her, drawing her against him as he lay

on his back. "When you left yesterday, I was worried and furious, and hurt, because you didn't trust me to take care of you and your family."

"But he would have—"

He touched a finger to Eugénie's lips. "Hear me out. All I could think of was losing you, or someone hurting you. I couldn't have borne it. I must have your trust, Eugénie."

She turned and stared at him. It had not even occurred to her he would feel betrayed by her actions. "But I did trust you, my love. I *knew* you would come after me, and when I saw *Swift Wind*, I had no doubt you would be on her. I locked myself in my cabin so that Uncle Yves could not use me against you, and I stayed there." She chewed her bottom lip. She may as well tell him the rest. "I would rather have stuck my dagger in him, but I had a feeling you would wish to kill him."

Both of William's arms came around her and his chest rumbled as he laughed. "You were right, my bloodthirsty vixen. I was more than happy to shoot him."

And because her husband needed to hear it again, she said, "*Bon*, and from now on, I will always allow you to protect me."

William kissed her, a lingering, tender kiss. "That is all I ask."

Nathan lay next to Sidonie, happy that he'd regained enough strength to make love to her properly. Now they lay side by side, hands clasped together, allowing the cool breeze from the port-window to waft over them. "How are the girls doing?"

"Better since Will arrived. He saved us. Not only from Shipley and Howden, but from melancholy. He is very good with the children." She told him about Jeanne's doll going overboard. "But it is nothing compared to how happy they'll be to have you back, my darling."

"Do they know I'm alive?"

He felt Sidonie nod. "Yes, but Will would not allow them to come with us."

"Thank God for that." Nathan hadn't known quite what to think about Wivenly. He was reputed to be a little bit of an out-and-outer. "You seem happy with his and Eugénie's marriage."

"I am, but if I'd known how they met . . ."

"She does take matters into her own hands."

Sidonie's voice trembled. "To be honest, I was not much help. I do not know what I would have done if events hadn't turned out the way they did."

Nathan wrapped his arms around her. "Don't worry. Everything worked out for the best." He kissed the top of her head. "The galley followed us here. After the storm has passed, Will and I shall deal with the other uncle."

"I'm glad the two of you will take care of him."

He kissed her again. "Sleep now, sweetheart."

Her breathing soon evened out and deepened, but Nathan was unable to sink into Morpheus's arms just yet.

Earlier today, when the *Belle Amie* had reached the galley, Henriksen had shouted that he'd seen Eugénie in a cabin down below. Nathan had caught a glimpse of a man dashing for the stairs, and followed. Yet before he'd reached the hatch, Wivenly had coolly dodged to the side as a knife whizzed past him, and shot Yves Villaret dead center in the chest. Nathan's dagger, the one taken from him in the pirate attack, stuck out from the wood next to his son-in-law's head, still quivering. Despite that, Nathan hadn't expected to find Eugénie in the fellow's arms, trying to climb him like a tree.

Fatigue washed over him. If anyone could handle his daughter, Wivenly could. At least she'd not been forced into marrying the old French count.

*   *   *

Will woke in dim light to Eugénie's bottom nestled snuggly into his groin. A cool breeze ruffled the sheet they'd somehow managed to pull up over them. The ship had ceased the periodic violent rolling that had awakened him off and on during the night. Now it was almost like the gentle rocking of a cradle.

His shaft twitched as if to remind him of how one got a babe to put in a cradle. He stroked over Eugénie's breasts down to the dark curls at the apex of her thighs, then rubbed lightly. A soft moan escaped her, and he grinned. "Wife?"

"Husband?" Her voice was soft, warm, and still a bit sleepy.

Need for her rose in him. "I want you."

"Yes." She reached behind, taking hold of his hard member. "I want . . . Ahhh. William."

Keeping steady pressure on her nubbin, he slid into her. "That?"

She rocked back against him. "Yes."

God, he couldn't get enough of her. Will stroked slowly at first. When he was certain she was about to shatter, he thrust hard and deep, coming with Eugénie as she clenched around him. Allowing the movement of the ship to lull him, he succumbed to sleep.

The next time he opened his eyes, sun beamed through the port-window, and Eugénie was gone. He sat up. Where the devil could she be? "Eugénie?"

"I'm here. I had to use the chamber pot."

Will's heart thudded in his chest. He was fully alert now. She came back to the bunk. "I couldn't wait any longer."

Damn, he felt like a fool. "No. It's fine."

She stroked his forehead. "After what happened, I understand. I had to look and assure myself you were here as well." Eugénie climbed back in bed with him. "The storm has passed. The captain will spend the rest of the day repairing any damage before we go home." A smile graced her countenance. "Unless something occurs, we have the day to ourselves."

Will shifted over her. "That will be a pleasant change."

"Yes, it will."

A knock sounded at the door. "Milady?"

Eugénie groaned. "*Oui*, Marisole."

"Mr. Wivenly wishes to see you and his lordship."

"Very well."

Will flopped onto his back. All he wanted was days, weeks of her to himself. Thank heaven her maid was French. "Pull the sheet over me. As soon as you are dressed, I'll call Tidwell."

"You may enter, Marisole."

Less than a half hour later, Eugénie was washed and dressed in a charming turquoise muslin gown. Once she'd gone, his valet arrived.

They met in the dining room, where Eugénie prepared him a large mug of tea and a plate of baked eggs, toast, and marmalade. Uncle Nathan sat close to Aunt Sidonie, transformed overnight from a grieving widow to a wife in full bloom. When she smiled, he knew what Eugénie would look like in twenty years.

As he practically shoveled down his food, Nathan said, "The French galley followed us yesterday. We must put an end to any of the Villaret family's scheming as it concerns Eugénie."

Will stopped eating for a moment. "I agree."

"I'd also like to see the marriage settlements."

He'd expected that. "Mr. Whitecliff took them to Wivenly House. I was at a bit of a disadvantage when we drew them up as I did not know the full extent of Eugénie's holdings."

"I do not understand." Eugénie set down her cup of tea. "I have nothing but what Papa gives me."

Will slid his arm around her waist. "No, my love. You

also have funds from your French father and property in France."

She glanced from Uncle Nathan back to Will. "Why did no one tell me?"

Her mother shrugged. "You were never interested, and I was not sure I knew everything. Your Papa always handled the finances."

Will took another sip of tea. "I decided Eugénie should keep whatever she owns and Mr. Whitecliff and I drafted a trust of sorts. In addition, I have settled what I own outright on her and any children. As you know, sir, I could not commit my father."

Nathan rubbed a hand over his face. "I realize you did the best you could under the circumstances, and you were extremely generous. We'll speak with your father when we return to England."

"Return?" Sidonie, Eugénie, and Will blurted out at the same time.

Nathan nodded. "After I took Benet to my mother in England, I began to think about moving the rest of the family back. It is not that I don't love it here, but I had the girls to consider and, to be quite frank, tensions between the Danes and English have increased." He glanced at Aunt Sidonie. "If you don't mind, my dear, I'd like to start moving the company to England."

"Whatever you wish to do, my darling." She grinned at him. "With two of our children living there, I think it is a good idea."

"When you're finished eating, Will,"—Nathan eyed Will's plate as if he'd just noticed how much food had been on it—"we'll visit the Vicomte Villaret."

"That will not be necessary." A man with a strong French accent addressed them, glaring at Uncle Nathan and Will.

"Sorry, Wivenly," Henriksen said. "He got past my man."

"Could we have more tea?" Aunt Sidonie asked.

Villaret stood ramrod straight. "I do not care for tea. As soon as I have collected Eugénie, we shall leave. Also, I wish whoever murdered my brother to be arrested."

Will clenched his teeth. Like hell he'd be arrested for killing that blackguard, nor would he allow Eugénie to go anywhere without him.

Chapter 30

Maman's hands flew to her lips as she gasped. At the same time, Papa and William both shot to their feet, towering over Uncle Hervé.

Will's voice was low and dangerous. "*My wife* is not going anywhere with you."

One corner of Hervé's upper lip rose. "You cannot have married my niece. I am her guardian, and you would have required my permission."

"The devil you are!" Papa bellowed. "The courts on Martinique and St. Thomas granted me guardianship."

The older man stood as if neither William nor Papa mattered at all. "But the French court awarded me guardianship just six months ago. This so-called marriage is void." He glanced at Eugénie. "Come, my dear."

She stood, grabbing William's arm as he lunged at her uncle. "Stop, all of you. Papa, William, sit. I cannot see over you. Now, perhaps we can clear this up without further bloodshed." Eugénie fixed a basilisk gaze on Hervé. "Though Yves got exactly what he deserved. We shall discuss that later. First, tell me, what is the age of majority in France?"

"Twenty-one."

"*Bon*. That is exactly the age in England. I turned twenty-one in August of this year. Therefore, I have no guardian in either of those countries, but I do have a husband."

Her uncle vibrated with rage. "*Impossible!* You are lying. I have the letter we received from your father telling us of your birth."

"That missive," Maman said, grinning with relief, "was written when Eugénie was a year old and we knew she would survive. Many babies do not."

Hervé suddenly seemed to get smaller. "You are telling me she is truly twenty-one?"

Maman nodded.

He glanced back to Eugénie. "Then why did you agree to go with Yves?"

Thinking about her other uncle caused anger to rush up inside her. "He threatened to torture and kill Papa."

Papa pointed to William. "Your brother also attempted to kill Lord Wivenly."

Hervé collapsed into the chair near the door. "I knew I should not have trusted Yves. This is horrible. We will be paupers for years trying to build the estate back up again."

She'd had enough of their self-pity. "It is better than having nothing. If you had put the money and effort into your estates that you spent trying to make me marry an old *comte*, you'd be further along."

"Monsieur le Vicomte," the captain of the galley said from the door, "I insist we depart. I will not risk my ship again."

"*Oui, oui*. We shall leave now," Hervé responded in a tired voice. "The sooner I get home, the better." He rose, bowing to them. "*Au revoir*, Sidonie, Eugénie. Before I go I would like to know one thing. Who is this man you have married?"

William stood again, sketching a short bow. "Viscount Wivenly, heir to the Earl of Watford."

Hervé smiled wryly. "At least you still made a good match." And he sauntered out of the room.

"Well!" Cicely exclaimed. "I cannot believe he expected to just walk in here and take Eugénie away. And after finding out what a blackguard his brother was, he didn't even apologize."

Maman played with her cup, turning it around. "Before the revolution, they were an old and powerful family. Their presumptuousness knows no bounds. I am just happy Eugénie is of age."

"Except in the Danish West Indies," Will muttered, sitting once more.

Eugénie kissed his cheek. "Now that we are married, you do not have to worry about that."

A few minutes later, Monsieur Beaufort appeared with a very pretty lady and the largest man Eugénie had ever seen.

"Bonjour, mes amis." He grinned. "I see my countryman is not happy." He swept a courtly bow. "Eugénie, you are as beautiful as ever. If this very large gentleman will move"— he glanced at William, who scowled—"I shall kiss your hand."

"Pay no attention to him, my love." Eugénie flicked her fingers at the man. "This is Monsieur Beaufort. I have known him all my life, and he is a dreadful flirt. *Bonjour*, Vincent. Meet my husband, William, Viscount Wivenly."

Vincent held out his hand to William. "I am pleased to meet you. Well done, keeping Eugénie in the family."

As the men shook, William said, "A pleasure meeting you as well. Thank you for rescuing my uncle."

Papa leaned back in his chair. "What can we do for you, Vincent?"

"I merely came to inform you we will set sail shortly. Miss Marshall wishes to marry as soon as possible, and the others want to get settled into their new home on Tortola."

Eugénie caught Cicely's eyes, and laughed. "I advise you to go to St. Michael's near Great Carot Bay and have the vicar there perform the service. Mr. Stewart, the rector of St. George's in Road Town, is hard to find."

"Thank you. We shall do just that," the lady said in a soft voice.

Papa stood. "I'll walk out with you, Vincent."

William took Eugénie's hand and rose. "I'd like to be alone with my wife for a while, if you don't mind."

"Go ahead, my dears," Maman said. "We shall see you later."

Once back in their cabin, William wrapped his arms around Eugénie, kissing her tenderly. "I can't wait to have you all to myself."

She nibbled his bottom lip. "I feel the same. In the meantime . . ."

His lips tilted up. "In the meantime, I've been thinking about the best way to get you out of that perfectly lovely gown, my lady."

"Have you, my lord? And what have you decided?"

Her bodice started to sag. "That I'm getting very good at this."

Epilogue

February 1817, the Queen Hotel, St. Thomas

Although they had planned to spend Christmas in England, finding a trustworthy person to manage Papa's concerns here had not gone as smoothly as he had hoped. Finally, Andrew's grandfather had found a man, but he did not leave England until January.

Eugénie pulled out the letters she'd received from the wives of William's friends. They all expressed their desire to meet her as soon as may be, and she was looking forward to meeting them. William had described all but one of them to her. He had not yet met Lord Huntley's wife. Now just one thing marred her happiness. She glanced around at the trunks and portmanteaux stacked up against two walls of the parlor. "Are you sure you are not up to coming with us?"

Cicely shook her head. "Not with this morning sickness. I think the journey would make it worse." She smiled. "We plan to travel in March or April. After all, I do not wish to attend my first Season as big as a house."

"I shall miss you." Eugénie blinked back tears. "But summer is not that far off."

"I'll miss you as well." Her friend hugged her. "Don't forget to write and tell me about everything."

Several carters began moving the luggage. "I shall write every week."

"Eugénie, my love." William handed her his handkerchief. "It's time. Your father sent a note that we must come now. Captain Black is waiting for us."

"Oui, oui." She hugged Cicely. "I shall see you in a few months."

April 1817, Dunwood House, London

Eugénie and William were ushered down a corridor toward the family drawing room of their friends Marcus and Phoebe, Earl and Countess of Evesham, whom Eugénie had met on a shopping trip to Town. A few days later, Anna, Lady Rutherford, and Emma, Lady Marsh, appeared as well.

Eugénie had been corresponding with the other ladies and was now eager to put faces with their names.

A cacophony of shrill squeals, deep laughter, and female admonishments met her ears. It sounded so much like home, she grinned at William. Ahead of them Marcus's butler, Wilson, bowed and announced in sonorous tones, "The Viscount and Viscountess Wively."

The room seemed full of ladies in varying stages of pregnancy or holding babies. Gentlemen lounged on the floor, playing with the children crawling or toddling across the floor. She touched her own swelling stomach.

Phoebe came swiftly toward them, taking Eugénie's hands in her own. "Welcome. I am so glad you are here. We put this off so that Serena and Robert could be here."

Marcus stood behind Phoebe, grinning. "Now that you're here, tea will be served soon, but I've got some very good sherry if you'd like to give it a try."

William hesitated. "My love?"

Anna and Emma waved at Eugénie. "Go on." She smiled up at him. "I wish to meet the rest of the ladies."

"Eugénie," Phoebe said, as she led her to an auburn-haired woman holding a tiny baby. "I know you've been in contact with everyone. Allow me to help you sort them all out."

"But this must be Serena, is she not?"

The woman shifted the child onto her shoulder. "Indeed I am, and you are Eugénie. When are you expecting?"

"In August." Eugénie reached out, stroking the baby's head. "How old is she now?"

Serena smiled. "Three weeks. Elizabeth will give her father gray hair before his time."

Down the long room, one of the men gave a shout of laughter. "Yes, that little girl is fate's way of getting back at Beaumont."

A tall gentleman with blond curls gave a mock scowl, but his green eyes were alight with mirth. "That's right, Rutherford. You'd better watch your son around my daughter."

Next to Serena, a lady with light flaxen curls shook her head at the men before grinning at Eugénie. "It is so good to finally meet you. I'm Caro. You are due not long after I am. It will be nice having our children so close together."

A beautiful woman with golden-blond curls bustled up to Eugénie. "You must be Eugénie. I'm Grace. That little scamp on the tall man is Gideon." She stroked her stomach. "He'll have a brother or sister around November."

"Well, isn't this a sight." An elegantly dressed gentleman with wavy, light brown hair entered the room, surveying it through his quizzing glass. "I hope you don't mind, Phoebe, but I told Wilson there was no need to announce me."

"Eugénie, allow me to introduce Mr. Featherton. Kit, Eugénie, Viscountess Wively."

"My pleasure, Mr. Featherton." She smiled as he bowed over her hand. "Do I call you Kit or Featherton?"

"I answer to both." He grinned. "The ladies usually call me Kit and the gentlemen Featherton."

"Very well, Kit it is. Please call me Eugénie." She glanced around. "Where is your wife?"

He flushed. "Don't have one. I am the odd man out in this circle."

William came up behind her. "Didn't I hear something about your father telling you it was time to settle down?"

The man's face turned so red, Eugénie thought poor Kit would choke.

"I told him I'd take a gander this Season, but there is a matter come up at the manor house my great-aunt left me that I must see to. I just wanted to come by and welcome you and your lovely bride back home." He shook William's hand. "Must go now." He bowed to her. "Very happy to have met you."

She stared as he walked away as quickly as he'd entered. Eugénie frowned. "Is it me, or was he behaving strangely?"

"It's not you, my love," William said. "Featherton has had a very strange circumstance arise."

Phoebe joined them. "I do hope it's nothing too serious. You gentlemen needn't tease him. Kit will marry when he meets the right woman." She raised a brow at William. "Just as all of you did."

Visit our website at
KensingtonBooks.com
to sign up for our newsletters, read
more from your favorite authors, see
books by series, view reading group
guides, and more!

BOOK **|| | /||** CLUB
BETWEEN THE CHAPTERS

Become a Part of Our
Between the Chapters Book Club
Community and Join the Conversation

Betweenthechapters.net